Phillip Mann was born in  in 194_. He studied English and Drama at Man_____ California. He worked for_____ in Peking for two years, b_____ pally in New Zealand, wh_____ Artistic Director of Dow_____ and ___ Drama at Victoria University. He has had many plays and stories broadcast on Radio New Zealand. He is married, with two children.

By the same author

Master of Paxwax
The Eye of the Queen

PHILLIP MANN

The Fall of the Families

Book Two of the story of
Pawl Paxwax, the Gardener

GRAFTON BOOKS
A Division of the Collins Publishing Group

LONDON GLASGOW
TORONTO SYDNEY AUCKLAND

Grafton Books
A Division of the Collins Publishing Group
8 Grafton Street, London W1X 3LA

Published by Grafton Books 1988

First published in Great Britain by
Victor Gollancz Ltd 1987

Copyright © Phillip Mann 1987

ISBN 0-586-20191-2

Printed and bound in Great Britain by
Collins, Glasgow

Set in Times

To my son,
Owen Mann

THE ANTHEM OF THE ELEVEN GREAT FAMILIES

First are the Proctors, the greatest and the best
They keep the great wheel spinning from the centre
   where they rest.

Second are the Wong the warriors, saviours of our race,
They chased away the Hammer and put them in their
   place.

Third is the Conspiracy of the Bogdanovich and Shell
They fight for truth and justice and liberty as well.

The Xerxes de la Tour Souvent are fourth on our list
Where love is found and tenderness, they are never
   missed.

The Paxwax Fifth are generous to the meek and mild,
They give the food that keeps alive every little child.

The Lamprey Sixth love the light, their father was the
   sun,
Their children are the stars that shine upon us everyone.

The Freilander and Porterhouse hold the seventh place,
They stopped the alien in his tracks and kicked him in
   the face.

The Longstock and the Paragon,
The Sith and Felice too,
Help keep the goblins on their knees
And so I hope do you.

1

ON ODIN'S HOMEWORLD

High on a stony headland, above a grey and white and roaring sea, crouched a small creature. In appearance it was like a dome of red wax. Its name was Odin.

Chasms opened up between the waves as they raced in to the land and thumped against the headland and hurled rockets of spray upwards. The wind caught the spray and drove it inland. Cold water spattered the small creature and sluiced over it and dribbled away down the cliff face.

Odin felt relief. The slap of the salt spray and the cut of the wind dulled the ache he felt inside him.

For days he had stood there while the storm battered the hard stony shore. Now the tempest was weakening. Fitful rays of pale sunlight were slicing through the clouds. Soon the sea would calm to a heavy swell. But it would never become truly calm; that was not the way on Odin's world. Already a new storm was brewing among the tight-packed ice boulders of the southern sea and within days that storm would break across the land, bringing joy to the Gerbes who lived by the shore.

But Odin would not feel it.

Odin was saying goodbye to his world. While he had crouched under the storm he had sent his thoughts out over the surface of the sea. He had joined with others of his kind. He had drawn strength from the veins of bright silvery thought which rippled across the face of his Homeworld.

Now it was close to the time when Odin must leave.

He had felt the Inner Circle calling him back, gentle

but irresistible. He had felt a call like duty, a compulsion like guilt, and he had no choice but to obey.

So, while the sun brightened the backs of the surging waves, Odin flexed his trunk. His glossy skin roughened as veins and flukes began to appear. Stealthily he withdrew his tough roots from the crevices between rocks.

Finally, all that held him steady in the face of the buffeting wind was his great basal sucker. Carefully, tactfully, he loosened its grip. Fine yellow tendrils at the side of the sucker emerged and began to feel about for purchase on the land. They stiffened, lifting him, and began to creep like a thousand small legs. The sucker dilated and compressed and Odin began to glide down the headland and away from the sea.

There was no turning back. For several days Odin toiled over a plateau of bare rock. Patiently he worked his way along valleys and up streams. Nothing stopped him and he never paused.

As he moved, he thought. The time on his Homeworld had given Odin perspective. He remembered Pawl Paxwax, the human with the awkward legs and strange yellow eyes. Odin had helped to save him, had helped to keep his mind calm at a time of crisis. When Odin left Pawl's Homeworld it was as though he had left part of himself behind. Now that man would be riding high, Master of Paxwax. Odin wondered if Pawl ever thought about him, and knew at the same instant that he did. Pawl had a quirky, defensive mind, quick to anger, but he was first and foremost loyal.

Odin remembered the time of their first meeting. How nervous and skittish Pawl had been, encountering his first alien and feeling it push into his mind! He was clumsy and maladroit at mind control. That was the way with humans. But he had adapted quickly. Then how easily they had flowed together!

10

There was the time later, when Pawl was being too defensive and Odin had bitten into his mind suddenly and extracted a memory of Laurel Beltane. That had been dangerous. Pawl's anger and distress had proved almost too much for the small Gerbes to control . . . but the shock had been worth it, because out of it grew a deeper trust. Odin remembered clearly the time they sat together and Odin revealed his 'face'. Pawl sat staring at him, yellow-eyed, as though memorizing every detail, and then he reached forward and touched one of Odin's tendrils. An act of trust for both of them. Though they can share with their minds, creatures that are alien to one another find touching the hardest act of all. Odin knew that, despite the wishes of the Inner Circle, he had come to share with Pawl Paxwax. He had moved dangerously close in sympathy. And could it be otherwise? Gerbes were not tricksters. They thrived on the easy intimacy of minds sliding over minds.

Every inch that Odin travelled was bringing him closer to Pawl's Homeworld, no matter how indirect the route. And what then? What when he was there?

Odin was not clear about details but he knew that somehow he was to accomplish the downfall of the man. That hurt. That made the stone within him throb and wrinkle. For the sake of the Inner Circle, for the sake of the whole order of aliens which Odin served, Odin must become a traitor. It was a monstrous defection from his nature and it would inevitably, without question, kill him. Odin knew that when the final crisis came and he betrayed Pawl Paxwax, he would still love him and would serve him to the end. And his own inevitable death . . . ? Odin thought about that too. Somewhere lonely, he hoped. Somewhere where he could dissolve unobserved; in a place where he could deposit his stone under the feet of oxen and let it be trampled down.

11

Odin could not read the future, but he had some sense of its shape, and it held nothing good for him.

With these dark but quite realistic thoughts in his mind, Odin travelled over cold stony uplands. He had other worries too. Questions which would not go away. He did not understand himself. Why had he offered to go to Pawl's Homeworld in the first place? That was not in the nature of Gerbes. Gerbes were quiet solitary creatures, lovers of wind and sea. Apart from assisting as translators, they did not join with the strong militant minds of Sanctum. The fighting could be left to the Hammer and the Parasol and the Spiderets. They delighted in such things. It was more in the nature of a Gerbes to let itself be killed than to kill. *Perhaps I was chosen*, thought Odin, *because I am meek. But why? And was it a free choice?*

Such questions could not be left and Odin decided to find out the truth when he was back on Sanctum.

Now the summit of the hill was close. The wind had freshened, driving before it pellets of snow which lodged under boulders and did not melt. Odin felt his glands lard his body with oils as the temperature dropped. At the crest of the hill and looking incongruous on the wild world was an aerial made of copper and bright blue strands of bio-crystalline fibre. This aerial was the only manufactured object on the entire planet. It was the only evidence that the Gerbes maintained links with outer space.

Settling to the ground as Odin approached was the blunt box shape of a magnetic shuttle. This would carry Odin quickly up into the darkness of near space where the Way Gate platform turned. The front of the shuttle broke open and a ramp lowered. Odin only had to enter.

There, at the lip of the shuttle, he performed a brief ceremony. He sent his mind out for one last time and felt the response of thousands of Gerbes scattered round the distant shore. It was like a great silver sea that for a moment engulfed him and made him dizzy. They were wishing him well in their many different ways. They were saying farewell.

Odin shook. His tendrils lifted and felt about in the wind. One by one, small Gerbes worked their way out of his tufted fibre and flopped down on to the cold stony ground. They lost no time in squirming and sliding their way out of the wind and under the rocks. Soon they would begin their own long journey to the sea.

It was over. Odin's last visit to his Homeworld was over. He knew he would never return. Odin's next stop was Sanctum where he would receive his instructions from the Inner Circle.

Odin mounted the ramp and glided into the shuttle and its door lifted and closed. He was alone.

2

ON BENNET:
THE HOMEWORLD OF PAWL PAXWAX

Fortune favours the brave, as they say . . .

. . . but still it helps to have powerful friends and Pawl
Paxwax, now undisputed Master of the fifth most powerful family in the known galaxy, did not know just how
lucky he was. Certainly he had no idea how extensively
Odin and the order of the Inner Circle had helped in his
survival.

Now the brief but bloody war was over. A speedy
inventory of his domain to see what damage the Paxwax
had suffered told a sorry tale.

Pawl was the victor because he had survived. He had
survived because the great advance of the Xerxes and
Lamprey forces had been stymied. But it had been a close
thing. The war had reached deep into his empire, where
a terrible price of burnt worlds and plain murder had been
paid. One such world was Thalatta, the Homeworld of
Laurel Beltane. The war had broken the vast network of
Way Gates which connected the empires of the Eleven
Families and it would be years before this damage could
be repaired. Many worlds had been overrun and it was
widely believed that in some parts of his domain, now
inaccessible, battle still raged. Most of the damage was
the product of desperation in the last stages of the war,
when the word went out: 'Kill. Kill anything.'

But now at least Pawl's empire was secure. The Families which had attacked him, the Xerxes de la Tour
Souvent Fourth and the Lamprey Sixth, were in disgrace
and licking their wounds. The Lamprey would never
recover. The sisters who ruled the Xerxes were made of

sterner stuff. They accepted defeat with a bitter, angry pride.

Being the man he was, Pawl's first action after the war was to marry. He married Laurel Beltane and thereby asserted his independence. His decision to marry this lady had precipitated the war and now it marked its ending. In some quarters there were murmurs that Pawl was thumbing his nose at the great Code which governed all relations among the eleven ruling Families, for Laurel Beltane was an outsider: her family, being the 56th, was low in the pecking order. But the Masters of the Eleven Great Families, swept along no doubt by the euphoria of battle, were magnanimous. Pawl was young (they said). He had demonstrated courage. He had a certain glamour. He had shown ruthlessness (and this they admired). Let him have his girl. He would learn with age. Soon power would work its corrosion upon him, striking at his idealism. Inevitably he would fall into line.

Pawl did not delay. He announced his marriage within hours of his victory. He accepted the good wishes of the Proctor First and the Shell-Bogdanovich Conspiracy Third. (He acknowledged that the Shell-Bogdanovich had been his greatest allies and members of that Family were the only ones to witness his marriage.) Old Man Wong, who ruled the Wong Second, sent him valuable presents: icons saved from the Homeworld of Homeworlds, Earth itself. The Xerxes Fourth and the Lamprey Sixth no longer mattered. Nor did the Confederation of the Freilander and Porterhouse. This unhappy family was engaged in a civil war and even while Pawl was counting his lost worlds, the Proctor and Wong began to dissect its empire. Soon the leaders of the Freilander and Porterhouse would be little more than petty chieftains.

The Longstock Eighth were courteous and distant. They had hoped that Pawl would choose one of their daughters. But when his announcement was made they bowed to necessity.

The outer families, the Paragon, Sith and the Felice, all showed themselves keen to see stability return. They were all ambitious and saw advantage to themselves in being associated with the victor.

So Pawl's marriage was accepted, despite the Code, but he married a sad bride.

The loss of her Homeworld and the death of her father left Laurel Beltane feeling a vast emptiness inside her. She and her brother Paris were now all that remained of the Beltane family. They could not accept that. Paris, being young – only in his mid-teens – found comfort in the gymnasium and combat room on Pawl's world. He trained day and night, working his body into a tight bond of muscle, and each night dropped on to his bed exhausted after killing a simulated army of Spiderets and Sennet Bats.

Laurel's defences were more complicated. She pretended that her father was still alive and that her Homeworld still shone, blue and gold, somewhere out in space. She convinced herself that sometime her father would call to her, friendly and kind and wise, and that they would swim together again, hunting Dapplebacks, just as they had when she was a girl.

But sometimes this defence gave way before reality and she knew that her Homeworld was no more than a black cinder. Pawl did what he could to comfort her. He loved her and pressed her close to him and whispered to her, trying in any way he could to combat the darkness which was souring her spirit. At such times Laurel held to him desperately. They made love passionately, trying to obliterate the memories. But in the morning it all came back. In her heart Laurel blamed Pawl for the destruction of her family. At the same time she loved Pawl, for he was good and kind and gentle, and was all that she had.

Pawl was at a loss for what to do for the best. Only occasionally did flashes of his one-time roguish mistress appear . . . and these he nurtured like a man protecting a tiny flame in a dark forest.

Make no mistake, Pawl's love for Laurel made him desperate. Privately he cursed the Xerxes and the Lamprey and the whole order of the Families which had led to this destruction. But no amount of cursing could change what had happened.

He knew that Laurel loved swimming and so he arranged for pontoons to be placed across some of the most attractive bays on his island to hold back the bright red algae which crusted the sea. The island was artificial. It had been constructed generations earlier by one of Pawl's ancestors and had many ornamental bays. He discovered that Laurel felt most at her ease when she was far away from the towers and courtyards and bustling streets of the main living quarters. Whenever possible he arranged for them to slip away up into the wild lands which bordered the farm enclosures. They carried provisions on their backs. Wynn, the giant bio-crystalline brain, took charge of the day-to-day affairs of the Homeworld during their absence.

Just now they were at a place where the Mendel Hills, watched over by the picturesque cone of Frautus, rolled down to the sea. A shallow beach of pebbles joined with the clear water, which lapped in slow waves. A brig of rocks poked out into the sea, and Pawl, who could not swim, scrambled over rocks keeping pace with Laurel, who dived and swam. In this interrupted fashion they were discussing a proposed holiday.

'It won't be all business, Laurel, that I promise you,'

said Pawl. Laurel lay back in the water, her finely webbed hands fluttering gently, holding her place as the waves rose and fell. 'We'll have as much adventure as we can. We'll get away from all this. But I want people to see you, to see us, to get to know us. The Paxwax have been distant for too long. That has been part of our trouble. We have retreated behind contracts. Moved secretly. Mixed only with our own. I once told a friend' – Pawl was thinking of Neddelia Proctor, though he did not mention that lady by name – 'that when I became Master I would throw open the windows and let some fresh air in. That is what we all need.'

Laurel rolled over in the water and dived with an easy scoop of her hands. She touched the sandy bottom, sending up a cloud of silt, and then rose to the surface and blew out lustily. 'Sounds fun,' she said, but her words held no conviction.

The truth was that Pawl needed to visit the outer parts of his empire. He needed to reassert the strength of the Paxwax. In some places, one-time minor officials had set themselves up as petty Warlords and were planning to secede from the Paxwax. This had to be crushed in the bud. There were diplomatic fences to be mended and new treaties to be negotiated. Pawl knew that if he and his new wife made themselves known he could win back the loyalty that had deserted the Paxwax during his father's time in power.

At the same time he wanted to give Laurel a holiday. He hoped vaguely that visits to strange and exotic parts of his domain would lift her out of herself. He wanted to show her the vastness of the empire she had inherited.

'*Sounds* fun? It will be fun. We'll make it fun.' He reached down and cupped water in his hand and scattered it over Laurel. 'You see. I'll do everything in my power to make you happy, Laurel. That is what I want more than anything else.'

'I know.'

Laurel wished she could say more. She knew the words that Pawl wanted her to say. But something held her back. At times she almost wanted Pawl to lose his temper with her and tell her to get a hold of herself. But she knew that he wouldn't. He was looking at her sadly, with his head on one side, a bit like a dog.

'You know, Laurel, we have to fight circumstances a bit,' said Pawl. 'Happiness doesn't grow on trees, as they say. We'll have to put the bad things behind us. Everyone suffered in this silly war. But life goes on.'

'I know. I know I'm being selfish. But I can't help it. Bear with me. Give me time. All this – ' she gestured at the sea and the high cliffs fringed with trees – 'all this is making me feel better. Soon I'll be myself again. When can we set out on your grand tour?'

Pawl accepted the change of subject. 'Well, I've been thinking about that. The sooner the better. Wynn can easily handle the day-to-day business. And Helium Bogdanovich has said that he'll keep an eye on things.'

Laurel smiled at this. 'So, Master of Paxwax, your planning is well advanced. And here was I thinking you were just broaching the idea.'

'I am. I am. Nothing is decided yet. But we'll have time to be alone. And Paris will come. There will be so much to see.'

'Anyone else?'

'Well, I thought perhaps Peron. He will act as my secretary. And I know he wants to visit the places where battles took place during the Alien Wars. He can be our guide.'

'And?'

'And Odin.'

'Hmm. Quite a party.'

Laurel turned her face away and swam out from the rocks. She did not want Pawl to see her disappointment. Pawl had tried to talk to her several times about Odin and though she wanted to feel close to the strange creature for Pawl's sake, she found she could not. Instead she felt ill at ease. In her heart she hoped that Odin would never return to Pawl's island. 'Have you heard then, from Odin?' she called.

'No. Not a word. But I have let it be known that I want to see him. I want him by me. He is a wise counsellor.'

Laurel did not reply. She was not sure how she felt about Pawl's evident interest in things alien. It was a new side to him, one she had never seen before, and she blamed this creature called Odin. 'Well, perhaps he is busy,' she called. 'The Inner Circle has a lot to do at present. Perhaps he was only sent to help you during the war. You must be ready for disappointment.'

'I know.'

Pawl sat on the rocks with his knees up to his chin while Laurel swam in a circle and then dived and rose close to him. 'Will you start writing songs again?'

'I hope so. I don't know. Perhaps.'

'You must. They are part of you. Part of us.'

In the time before they were married, before the war, Pawl had written many songs to Laurel. But since he had become Master of Paxwax, that bright spontaneity had dried up. Laurel knew that she was part of the cause.

'I'll strike a bargain with you, Master of Paxwax. If you will write songs for me again, I'll come on your holiday with you, and happily.'

Pawl nodded. 'I'll try,' he said.

Laurel reached up for him as though inviting a kiss and when Pawl offered his hands she seized them and then kicked back. Pawl toppled for a moment and saw Laurel laughing, and then fell with a splash into the water.

She held him firmly while he blew out and then cradled him in her arms while she swam back into shallow water. 'Welcome to my world,' she whispered. 'Now, you're not going to tell me that writing a song is harder than learning to swim, are you?'

'No,' said Pawl, standing in the shallows. 'And if songs will make you happy, songs you shall have. Will you go with me? Shall we tour round my domain?'

'We will.'

3

ON BENNET

Pawl wondered about himself. He had sat down intending
to let a simple love lyric flow, for he was in the mood and
the words were bubbling. But it seemed that the time for
love lyrics was over.

> The dog sat at the master's gate,
> Famished for a bone,
> But though it waited all the day,
> The master came not home.
>
> The sun dipped down. The shadows grew.
> The dog gnawed at a stone,
> And though it howled when the moon peeped out,
> The Master came not home.
>
> At twelve o'clock the thunder cracked,
> The rain came with a roar,
> Pelting the dog where it lay quite still,
> Outside the Master's door.
>
> The Master never did come home.
> He'd sold the place for gain.
> And a spideret with an eye for such things
> Ate up the dog's remains.

'What does it mean?' asked Laurel. 'I didn't expect a
sad song.'

'I think it is about innocence,' said Pawl. 'The innocent
always suffer. Isn't that the truth of things?'

'Yes.'

22

4

ON SANCTUM

Odin had left his Homeworld alone.

How different his arrival on Sanctum!

This was the secret world of the Inner Circle. It looked like a dead world spinning round a dying sun, but it teemed with life below its surface.

As he passed from the Way Gate on to the shuttle platform Odin felt the psychosphere of Sanctum surround him. It stopped him in his tracks: the world bubbled and throbbed with life and purpose. He felt it like a shock. It was like a beating of wings inside him, as though a bird was trapped. He had been so long on his Homeworld that he had forgotten how charged the psychosphere of Sanctum could be, and how violent, for gathered here on this one small world were the representatives of all the main alien species. They were planning their future.

Deeper than all the rest, almost like the voice of the sea itself, was the murmur of the Tree. It was calling to him, friendly and familiar, bidding him welcome return. The Tree was the guiding intelligence of Sanctum, and Odin responded to it with a mixture of awe and dread.

As a telepathic creature Odin was adept at reading all the flavours of thought. But the Tree was magnificent beyond Odin's understanding. Its presence was everywhere: in the stone walls and bright tiled walkways, in the smell of the air and in the silences. Yet Odin knew almost nothing about it.

He hurried forward. Waiting for him were fellow Gerbes. They presented him with his black gown and mask, the robes of the Inner Circle. The gown settled about him and adapted to his contours and began to protect him from the dry air. The mask fitted up under his dark hood and slipped firmly into place, held by fine red tendrils. He looked dumpy as he squirmed inside the gown. At a distance he could have been mistaken for a dwarf human being.

The Gerbes were eager for news, eager for a scent of their Homeworld and, as they travelled down to the surface of Sanctum, Odin let them share his memories of the storms and the flung spray and the biting wind. He felt their pleasure and hope.

Hope. It seemed to him that that one word summed up the psychosphere of Sanctum.

The Tree was calling him urgently, drawing him along the wide tiled thoroughfare towards its chamber. As he glided along Odin noticed a change in the creatures that he met. They seemed friendlier, more deferential.

He met a Hammer, bounding along with its great sting raised so that it brushed the ceiling. Once the Hammer would have driven past the Gerbes forcing it to cower back. Now the Hammer stepped aside and let him pass under its jointed hairy legs. He met a clan of Spiderets, who surrounded him, climbing on one another's backs and touching him lightly with their speaking feelers. Odin found it difficult to understand the Spiderets. They thought quickly, in short jagged sentences. All he could pick up was that they were friendly. They seemed to be involved in some ceremony of greeting. The Spiderets were always involved in ceremony.

Somewhere Odin felt the presence of a Diphilus. It announced itself in images, as it too was telepathic. Odin saw in his mind a cascade of fire. Immediately he drew back, for that thought could damage; and just as quickly the image transformed into a shining fountain of cool water. The Diphilus was gentle but sometimes careless. Being a form of life that fed on raw energy it found it difficult to comprehend the sensibilities of creatures that were not as robust as itself.

Finally Odin approached a vast cavern. He was aware of the aura that marked the Tree's presence. Waiting just inside the cavern was a Hooded Parasol. It was waiting for him. This was the creature that Odin used most often for eyes. Odin had a liking for the visible spectrum. The Parasol hovered, fanning its petals, which blazed with colours: scarlet and black, green and indigo. Odin could pick up its thoughts. USE ME, it said. WELCOME BACK TO SANCTUM.

Odin slipped into the mind of the Parasol and immediately could see.

Facing him was the Tree. It was simple, symmetrical and huge.

It rose from the soft fibrous floor of the cavern and did not branch until it almost reached to the roof. There it spread into a white moist canopy. Pale lights, like the reflection of sunlight on water, swarmed in its high branches.

Odin worked his way down through the cavern until he was close to the trunk and could reach out with one of his tendrils and touch it. The tree was very much aware of him. It spoke in his mind. Odin felt that if the sea could have spoken, it would have had this voice. But he was not fooled. Manipulation could take many forms and was as subtle as thought itself.

YOUR REST ON YOUR HOMEWORLD HAS DONE YOU GOOD, ODIN. YOU ARE STRONGER. I CAN FEEL IT. THE LAST TIME YOU SAT BY ME YOU WERE PALE . . . YOU HAVE BEEN DOING A LOT OF THINKING.

25

I HAVE.

AND ARE YOU HAPPIER?

NOT HAPPIER. MORE SETTLED. I DON'T THINK HAPPINESS MATTERS, DO YOU? WE DO THE THINGS WE HAVE TO. I HAVE ACCEPTED THAT.

The Tree pondered. YOU SEEM TO HAVE ACCEPTED A LOT. HAVE YOU ALSO ACCEPTED THAT YOU WILL NOT SURVIVE THE COMING EVENTS?

YES.

There was something in the air like a sigh. Odin was aware of a drawing closer. He knew that no one outside themselves could receive their conversation. THEN I SHALL TELL YOU SOMETHING THAT NO ONE BUT US NEED KNOW. NOR SHALL I SURVIVE. DO NOT ASK ME FOR DETAILS, FOR IF I KNEW THEM I WOULD NOT TELL YOU. I CANNOT READ THE FUTURE ANY MORE CLEARLY THAN YOU, THOUGH I HAVE A SENSE OF WHAT ACTION IS RIGHT AND WHAT IS NOT. LET ME JUST SAY THAT IF YOU SURVIVE AND I SURVIVE, THEN WE SHALL HAVE FAILED AND THE TIME FOR THE OVERTHROW OF THE HUMANS WILL NOT BE NOW. YOU SEE, WE ARE LINKED, YOU AND I. YOU NEVER IMAGINED THAT, DID YOU, SITTING ON YOUR COLD WORLD WITH THE SALT SPRAY RUNNING DOWN YOU? WE ARE BOTH PART OF THE COST THAT MUST BE MET IF THE HUMAN ORDER IS TO BE OVERTHROWN. AND WE SHALL SIMPLY JOIN THE LONG LIST OF ENTITIES, STRETCHING BACK TO THE TIME OF THE GREAT PUSH, WHO DIED FIGHTING OR WERE ABAN-DONED. THE ONLY DIFFERENCE BETWEEN US AND THEM IS THAT WE KNOW MORE. MUCH, MUCH MORE. AND WE CAN PLAN. WE ARE SHAPING EVENTS. AND IN ANSWER TO YOUR QUESTION: YES, I THINK HAPPINESS IS IMPORTANT. IT COMES WITH A SENSE OF PURPOSE. NOW, ANY MORE QUESTIONS, OR SHALL WE START PLANNING THE FUTURE?

ONE QUESTION, said Odin, stirring beneath his black robes. ONE THING I WOULD LIKE TO KNOW. WHEN I OFFERED MYSELF TO TRAVEL TO THE HOMEWORLD OF PAWL PAXWAX

AND HELP TO SAVE HIM, WAS THAT AN ACT OF MY FREE WILL
OR DID YOU COMPEL ME?

Again the sighing and the feeling of closeness. It was as
though Odin were a mouse bedded in the fur of a lion.
AH, YOU WANT TO KNOW THE SECRETS OF THE TREE. WELL, I
WILL TEACH YOU MORE THAN YOU EXPECT. THE DECISION WAS
YOUR OWN, BUT I WAS PART OF YOUR DECISION. YOU ARE SO
SLOW, ODIN. SO TIMID. YOU HAVE A GREAT SPIRIT, BUT YOU
ARE AFRAID OF IT. I HELPED YOU, THAT IS ALL. I LIBERATED
WHAT WAS ALREADY IN YOU AND LABOURING TO GET OUT. IT
WAS RIGHT THAT YOU WERE IN THIS PLACE, AT THIS TIME. YOU
SEE, MANY THINGS MAY SEEM STRANGE, AN ACCIDENT EVEN,
BUT NOTHING IS ACCIDENTAL. DO YOU UNDERSTAND?

NO.

YOU WILL. BUT WHAT WOULD I HAVE DONE IF YOU HAD
NOT OFFERED YOURSELF? THERE: THAT IS A TEASING QUES-
TION, COMPLETELY HYPOTHETICAL, BUT MY ANSWER MAY HELP
YOU UNDERSTAND. I WOULD HAVE TAKEN YOU — YES, YOU,
ODIN, FOR YOUR FATE IS MARKED ON MANY MAPS — AND I
WOULD HAVE SUPPLANTED YOU. I WOULD HAVE ERASED PART
OF THE LOVING MIND OF A GERBES AND SET IN ITS PLACE MY
OWN WILL.

WOULD THAT NOT HAVE BEEN SIMPLER? KINDER EVEN
. . . ? YOU WOULD HAVE SPARED ME PAIN.

SIMPLER, YES. BUT NOT SO GOOD AND NOT SO KIND. YOU
SEE, A SLAVE IS ONE THING, BUT A COMRADE IS BETTER.

That amused Odin. For the first time since his return –
for the first time for many days – he felt the healthy
release of laughter. He had never thought of himself as a
'comrade' of the Tree . . . it was preposterous, absurd,
silly . . . the Tree was . . . well, the Tree was the Tree. It
was as old as Sanctum itself and sometime friend of the
Craint. The Tree was the guiding intelligence behind the
whole of the Inner Circle, the organizing will of the aliens.

It was vaster than he could imagine . . . and now he was its 'comrade'.

DO WE MARCH INTO BATTLE TOGETHER, COMRADE?

EXACTLY.

Odin's humour began to subside. AND DO YOU HAVE A HOMEWORLD YOU HAVE FORSAKEN, COMRADE?

I HAVE THIS WORLD AND ANOTHER THAT I HAVE NEVER VISITED.

Odin did not understand this. IS THERE A HOMEWORLD THEN, JUST FILLED WITH TREES LIKE YOURSELF?

YES.

WHERE IS IT?

FAR FROM HERE. HIDDEN NOW. DEEP IN WHAT THE HUMAN KIND CALL ELLIOTT'S POCKET. BUT SOON IT WILL EMERGE.

WILL YOU GO THERE?

NO. AS I SAID, I SHALL NOT SURVIVE THE PRESENT MOVE-MENT ANY MORE THAN YOU. BESIDES, I HAVE A FULL LIFE HERE. DO NOT TRY TO UNDERSTAND ME, ODIN. JUST BE CONTENT WITH THIS KNOWLEDGE; IT IS VERY SPECIAL. WE ARE ALL IN OUR DIFFERENT WAYS SERVANTS OF LIFE, AND LIFE IS INFINITE. REMEMBER THIS CONVERSATION. ONE DAY YOU MIGHT HAVE TO EXPLAIN ME TO PAWL PAXWAX.

Odin had to be content with this sparse knowledge. He felt a whispering about him as the Tree withdrew. Then came the murmuring as the psychosphere of Sanctum reached through to him again.

NOW EVENTS ARE MOVING QUICKLY, PAWL PAXWAX IS JOINED WITH HIS LOVED ONE. DID YOU KNOW THAT? The Tree's tone was brisk.

I AM GLAD.

HE HAS BEGUN MAKING ENQUIRIES ABOUT YOU. HE WANTS YOU WITH HIM. YOU HAVE DONE YOUR WORK WELL. HE TRUSTS YOU.

I KNOW.

WHILE YOU HAVE BEEN AWAY WE HAVE BEEN CONSIDERING

OUR NEXT MOVES. WE MUST BE CAREFUL. THE WRONG MOVES NOW COULD THROW EVERYTHING INTO CONFUSION. I SHALL ASK THE DIPHILUS TO EXPLAIN.

Odin sensed the Tree send out a call to the Diphilus and immediately a creature entered the vast chamber. It rolled towards him like molten glass, but it transmitted no heat. It spoke as it rolled.

TELL ME, ODIN: YOU ARE CLOSE TO PAWL PAXWAX, HAS HE EVER EXPRESSED CURIOSITY ABOUT US . . . ABOUT WHAT HE CALLS ALIENS?

HE WAS CURIOUS ABOUT ME. HE DISCOVERED SOMETHING ABOUT THE HISTORY OF THE GERBES. A HUMAN CALLED PERON HELPED HIM.

GOOD. GOOD.

BUT HE HAS NEVER ASKED ABOUT OTHER ALIENS. HE IS VERY IGNORANT.

WOULD YOU SAY HE HAS A CURIOUS CAST OF MIND?

WHEN HIS INTEREST IS ROUSED.

The Diphilus glittered. THEN YOU MUST AROUSE HIS INTEREST. WE THINK IT IS IMPORTANT THAT HE SHOULD BECOME CURIOUS ABOUT ALIENS. HE MUST THINK OF US AS POTENTIAL FRIENDS, AS ALLIES EVEN. CAN YOU DO THAT?

I CAN TRY.

BUT ACT WITH CAUTION. IF HE THINKS HE IS BEING LED HE WILL REBEL.

I KNOW.

OF COURSE YOU DO. YOU KNOW HIM BETTER THAN ANY OF US.

AND THEN?

THEN WHEN HE FEELS CLOSE TO US YOU MUST KILL HIS LADY.

Silence. The Diphilus shone undisturbed. The Tree was a mumble of thought in the background.

WHY MUST I KILL LAUREL? asked Odin quietly, finally.

WHY, SURELY THAT IS OBVIOUS. TO BREAK HIS SPIRIT. HIS

LOVE FOR THE LADY IS HIS GREATEST STRENGTH AND HIS GREATEST WEAKNESS, AS THE TREE TOLD US LONG AGO WHEN WE SET OUT ON THIS ADVENTURE. YOU WILL KILL HER. YOU WILL MAKE IT SEEM AS THOUGH ONE OF THE FAMILIES HAS HAD A HAND IN THE MURDER. PAWL PAXWAX WILL TURN ON THE FAMILIES AND WHEN HE REACHES FOR A SWORD, WE SHALL BE WAITING. WE SHALL DO THE REST. YOUR WORK WILL BE OVER.

Over. Odin turned the word in his mind. *Over*. Such things are never over. But to the Diphilus he said, I UNDERSTAND.

The matter was left there.

Odin retired to the private chamber where the Gerbes lived on Sanctum. It was a place of sluggish waves, where the water always seemed oily. To kill was almost unknown in a Gerbes; Odin wondered how he would face it.

But now the plan was out in the open. Odin knew the extent of the part he must play. He could not even feel bitterness. It was as though his life was no longer his own. He was just a piece, moved by others. And what was Pawl? And Laurel? And the Tree? They were victims like himself.

Later that day Odin travelled to the Way Gate above Sanctum. He would allow no creature to accompany him. He felt contaminated. He did not want any other Gerbes to know what he was about. They thought he had an honourable part to play in the overthrow of the human worlds . . . let them think so. The truth would become known soon enough.

YOUR DESTINATION? asked the Way Controller.

THE PAXWAX HOMEWORLD.

And a whisper of thought, a shred of silver wrapped him about briefly. BON VOYAGE, COMRADE.

5

ON BENNET

'Right then, it is decided. No more arguments. No one can say we Paxwax let the grass grow under our feet. Here is what we do.'

They were in the vivantery, the very room where Pawl Paxwax and Peron had discovered the history of Odin's race. Pawl was at the head of the table addressing a small meeting. Those facing him were flushed and excited, for there had been much friendly argument, each person wanting to satisfy their own interest. Vivante cubes were scattered and books were open. There was also evidence that a large quantity of Seppel juice had been drunk.

At the back of the room, in the darkness near the door, stooped Odin. He had arrived that day and was now slowly immersing himself in Pawl's Homeworld. Pawl was as friendly and receptive as Odin had hoped and the Gerbes took pleasure in his quick spirit. Peron, too, was glad to see him. Odin could tell that Peron's hope was that one day he would speak in his mind. But for the time being he was content to watch. Paris paid him no heed, and Laurel . . . this was strange . . . Laurel was afraid of him. It was not a rational fear, it was instinctive. Her mind was closed and blank to him.

'So here is what we do. Are we all listening? First Laurel and I make official calls. There are a lot of those. While we are flitting about, Paris goes to Phonir and hunts land whales. Peron, you will come with us, and I know you want to explore the Lamphusae Stones.'

'Correct,' said Peron. 'There is a theory . . .'

'Shhhh,' said everyone.

'Next we'll all get together and have a few days on Lotus-and-Arcadia and then move back to the Paxwax domain and visit a world I've heard about called Forge. Always wanted to go there.' As he spoke Pawl was aware of Odin resting in his mind, just below consciousness. That day he and Odin had conversed and Odin had laid the idea of visiting the Hammer before Pawl. He had emphasized the excitement of meeting the exotic creatures. 'Peron, I'll expect you to have all the information about Forge. That's the world where the Hammer used to live. Should be interesting. It's a mining camp now. Then after Forge . . . bang, straight to Elliott's Pocket, and we'll stay there until we have to come home. There, that sounds pretty good to me. Anyone got any objections?' Pawl sat down heavily.

Laurel raised her hand. 'I'm not sure about Elliott's Pocket. It sounds very dangerous.'

'Sounds great,' said Paris.

Pawl waved his hands. 'The Pocket. Elliott's Pocket. I've just worked it out. We'll be there for the festival when they celebrate the deeds of John Death Elliott. Now that alone is a reason for going. But anyway, I have friends there. Dear friends. And remember . . . the Pocket saw some savage fighting during our recent disagreement with the Xerxes ladies and the Lamprey. But more than that, the Pocket is beautiful. It is the most beautiful place I have ever been. None of you have ever seen it. So let me tell you, all right? Pour me another Seppel, Peron, and get one yourself. All right?'

'All right,' said everyone in unison, laughing, and Peron handed Pawl a full glass.

'Now imagine,' said Pawl. 'Close your eyes and imagine a great undulating, billowing mass of green gas. It stretches as far as the eye can see. It is like wraiths of mist over a lake, and the locals, those who live in the Pocket, call it Emerald Lake. Suns burn in the lake. At night it glows in the sky. That is the heart of the Pocket. Round Emerald Lake turn all manner of worlds. I have seen the very fabric of space there pressed and strained and tortured to a mottle of red and blue. I have seen as many as twenty black holes, each like a frozen whirlpool, or some black and bearded alien eye whirling round before disappearing into the darkness. I have seen great barging planets, dogged by moons swinging in from nowhere, following an orbit which is logical but irregular. In this place, comets chase their tails and asteroids growl, and space is alive with every conceivable vibration.'

'Sounds magnificent,' said Peron. 'The true mystery of space.'

'It is. It is. The whole of the Pocket is a whirlpool. Whatever disappears into the dark always comes back eventually, but changed. The night sky is never the same for two nights together.

'Have I told you about the Snake? No? Ah well. The Snake is one of the regular sights. It curls directly round Emerald Lake. The Snake is a coil of dust and asteroids. It has the shape of a snake, but with a head like a bellows.'

Pawl glanced around. He was pleased to see that Laurel's cheeks were flushed and her eyes seemed excited.

'Why can't we go there first?' she said.

'Business, then pleasure. I want you to meet my friends. I want you to be able to relax with them. I want you to enjoy the Pocket, and you won't enjoy it as much if you think that you have a round of boring receptions to follow. No. The Pocket is our reward after our duties. We will depart as soon as Wynn has worked out the timetable. So, I give you a toast, lady and gentlemen, to us. To excitement and the discovery of new worlds.'

'New worlds,' everyone echoed.

And that was the beginning.

6

ON FORGE

And so for a time Laurel and Pawl, accompanied by
Peron and Odin, shuttled back and forth through Pawl's
empire, making contacts, assessing damage and ordering
help for those systems which had been ravaged in the
recent war. They discovered, not surprisingly, that most
systems wanted an assurance of peace and security.

They met with the senior Proctor brothers on Central
and the patriarch of the Wong Family on An. They
attended receptions on the Homeworlds of the other
Great Families and it seemed to both of them that life
had become a round of Way Gates and banquets and
handshaking and smiling and intense private conferences.
Wherever they went they were attended by an honour
guard and privacy became a much prized commodity.
Occasionally they were able to slip away to some secluded
solar system and there view the ruins of past civilizations.
The alien wars during the Great Push had turned vast
tracts of space into a battle field, and despite the centuries
which had slipped past, the marks were still evident. It
was on one such visit, while they were looking down on
the remains of an alien city that had been fused to glass,
that Laurel felt the first stirrings of a child within her. She
kept this news to herself, treasuring the feeling, building
on it her hopes for the future. Pawl did not guess, but he
noticed a change in his wife, a lightness of step, a more
ready laughter, and he felt glad inside.

Finally the day came when they bade farewell to their
emissaries and donned simple travelling clothes and set

out for the lonely Way Gate of Forge, where Paris was already waiting for them.

Here are a few verses from the Song of Forge, which can still be heard occasionally in bars where miners gather to relive the days of their hardship and adventure.

> I'd rather burn in Hell boys,
> Or stand at Death's own doors,
> Than be working for the Paxwax
> In the mines on Forge.
>
> I'd rather lose my eyes boys,
> And sell them for two plums,
> Than see a Hammer lift its sting
> And start to beat its drums.
>
> I'd rather be a thistle boys,
> I'd rather be a snake,
> Than a miner down on Forge boys,
> When Hammer makes a break.
>
> I've seen a Hammer run boys,
> Like shadow over sand,
> I've seen a Hammer jump boys
> But never seen one land.
>
> I'd rather be in bed boys,
> Just me and Sara Brown
> Mingling love and liquor
> While the sun goes down.

Pawl Paxwax, now on his way to Forge, had never heard this song.

The Paxwax agent on Forge, one Milligan by name, sat back in his squeaky cane chair and fanned himself with his grimy, wide-brimmed hat. He was a chunky square man, solid with muscle and with a face that looked as if it had been hammered together from old machine parts. He was the kind of man who enjoyed, though he would never admit it, the grim bitter battle that a planet like Forge afforded. He was the kind of brave, foolish man who would without thinking try to hold a breaking hawser with his bare hands. He was the kind of man who would die poor after a lifetime of labour, his muscles run to fat and his small pension scarcely enough to get drunk on.

Milligan appraised Pawl with hooded, unsmiling eyes. He found it hard to keep his dislike and his distrust out of his voice. Pawl had just explained the reason for his visit to Forge. 'So you want to talk to the Hammer? I mean, you want to walk up to them and communicate face to face?'

'Exactly.'

Milligan stared at Pawl and his only movement was with his finger and thumb as he tried to smooth his spiky moustache. He saw a thin young man with soft hands . . . and who wielded power. A rich kid.

'Well, not wanting to be rude to you, sir, Master of Paxwax, but that's the silliest idea I've heard since old Ces tried to clean his teeth with a particle gun.' He paused to see if Pawl was going to offer any comment. Pawl didn't. 'See, you don't communicate with the Hammer. This is their planet and they know it. If you see one of the Hammer you just run away and hope it hasn't seen you first. I've been scared off this planet three times, and I don't scare that easy.' He cracked his big square hands for emphasis.

'I believe you,' said Pawl. 'And I didn't plan on just walking in there. I have taken some precautions.'

'A gun?' said Milligan, for the first time showing some real interest. 'A big gun?'

'Not a gun. The small creature with me is from the Inner Circle. He is a kind of ambassador.'

Milligan sniffed. If he'd the choice between an ambassador and a gun, he knew which he would have chosen. 'You are referring to that little fellow in the black clothes. I thought he was your pet or something.' Milligan muttered under his breath. He shifted in his cane chair. 'I take it the lady will be going along too?'

'No, she will be staying in the camp. The air and the dust don't agree with her.'

Milligan looked relieved. This at least accorded with his sense of right and wrong. 'She'll be safe with the boys in the camp and we can get her off planet quickly if the Hammer start causing trouble.'

'So,' continued Pawl, 'all I want you to do, Agent Milligan, is to provide us with the basic equipment for survival on this wretched world and point us in the right direction.'

'You mean you don't even want me along to help you?'
'No.'

Milligan sat forward abruptly and the front two feet of his chair banged on the floor. He stood up. 'Well. A fool and his life soon reach the crossroads.'

He reached across his desk, picked up a small box and tipped its contents into the palm of his hand. Four short, conical nose plugs fell out. He blew through them in turn and then handed a pair to Pawl. 'Here. They've been used once or twice but they'll do to get you over to the mess hut so we can get you kitted out. Get you some proper goggles too. No one can've told you what Forge was like. You sure came unprepared.'

Without waiting for any comment from Pawl, Milligan crossed to the main door and spun the wheel which unfastened the air-tight door. It cracked open slowly and a cloud of fine red dust filtered into the room. The door opened fully on its screw arms to reveal a dismal landscape of wind-smoothed rocks, billowing clouds of red

37

dust and low utility huts. In the distance, hardly visible, were steep hills and above them a purple sky.

'Walk sideways and put your face in your shoulder,' said Milligan. Pawl inserted the rough plugs into his nose. 'Breathe through your nose or you'll choke. It's not far.'

The mining camp occupied little more than a square mile of flattish ground. It was surrounded by a fence of charged particle screens which glowed eerily as they randomized the drifting grains of dust and sand. In the centre of the compound stood a gantry supporting a giant wheel which turned steadily, lifting ore from deep within the planet. Gathered round the gantry were the small prefabricated huts which constituted the only town on Forge. Here lived the crew that worked in the small mine. They were an outpost, for Forge was located at the limit of Pawl's empire. The closest neighbour came from the smaller families and beyond them was the Felice.

Though Pawl did not know it, the red star about which the hidden world of Sanctum turned was visible from Forge.

Halfway across the compound, Pawl opened his mouth to speak but the hot air dried his tongue and he closed his mouth quickly. Milligan trudged on, holding his breath, oblivious.

Inside the mess hut a modest meal had been prepared by the camp cook, who was also the quartermaster and doctor. Paris and Laurel were already seated. Peron was studying maps of the region. Away in one corner Odin squatted quietly, the cowl of his habit well forward, so that no glimmer of his pale mask was visible.

The cook, a bald-headed man with soft white hands, looked up from his dishes when Pawl and Milligan entered.

38

'Glad to see you, captain,' said the cook. His name was Sild. 'I was beginning to wonder. I am just about to serve.'

Milligan grunted. 'Huh. Well, while they are eating I want you to break out sets of masks, goggles and dust coats for the three gentlemen and – ' He gestured across towards Odin.

'The representative from the Inner Circle is already protected,' said Pawl.

'Going to look round the mine, eh?' said Sild, placing a heavy casserole in the middle of the table.

'Nope,' said Milligan. 'They plan on giving the Hammer a visit.'

Sild stared at them and then removed his white apron. As he did so his manner changed. 'As medical orderly . . .' he began and then caught Milligan's eye.

'I've already warned them off,' said Milligan. 'So you might as well save your breath.'

Sild retied his apron, but he looked very upset as he dished out the meal in silence.

Now that they were actually down on the surface of Forge, the prospect of meeting the Hammer had become suddenly daunting. What had seemed an exciting plan on Pawl's Homeworld looked distinctly frightening in the clotted light of Forge.

Odin's voice uncoiled in Pawl's mind. 'We shall be safe. I have the assurance of the Inner Circle. But we must do nothing that might upset the Hammer. So be of good cheer. You are about to see things which no man has ever seen before.'

And this was true. Since the battles of the Great Push and the defeat of the Hammer by the Wong there had been almost no contact between the two species. Peron had discovered what he could concerning the Hammer.

He had shared his knowledge with the others during the brief time they spent aboard the dirty Way Gate above Forge. They knew what the Hammer looked like, they knew that the Hammer had a language which consisted of drumming, they knew that the Hammer had once travelled between the stars; but how they had travelled, and how expansive their empire had once been, and what ideas shaped their culture, they did not know.

While waiting for the slow shuttle they had seen the ring of killer satellites that girdled the planet and stared down at its surface. These satellites would destroy Forge if ever the Hammer attempted to escape.

For all practical purposes the Hammer were a forgotten race.

Sild helped them dress and explained the survival apparatus. Other miners arrived, tired from the morning shift and with red dust round their eyes like goggles. The afternoon shift assembled, cleaned and refreshed and full of boisterous humour. They chipped in with advice about how to walk so that the gowns shed their dust and how to breathe smoothly through the filters. The dust coats were made of a light black plastic which hung down to their ankles like a smock. The air filters and goggles were incorporated into the same headpiece. It fitted snugly over the shoulders and could be adjusted with snag-straps. The headpiece made their voices sound distant and hollow.

'Now remember,' shouted Milligan when they were all kitted out, 'if a sandstorm blows up, just squat down. There's enough food supplies and oxygen stored in the lining of this smock to keep you going until we can dig you out. There's an automatic alarm also, so you don't have to worry about that.'

'Good hunting,' called Laurel. 'Make sure you take

some good vivantes. We want to know everything that happens.' They nodded and waved and made their muffled farewells.

Milligan opened the door and they trudged down the ramp which led to the rocky surface of Forge. In Indian file they plodded to the perimeter fence and there waited while Milligan killed the power and the fence faded. Then they walked through and began to follow a rough bulldozed track which climbed into the hills.

In the middle distance Pawl, Paris and Peron all looked like elder brothers of Odin as their black plastic smocks trailed in the dust. Odin was moving well. Once outside the camp he flowed with a strong, swaying peristaltic movement. 'Take care, little one,' said Pawl with his mind. 'This world is not kind to you.'

'It is a kinder world than it looks,' came back the reply, and Odin drove on.

At last they came to a place where the cut track ended and nothing but sand and boulder-strewn slopes faced them. Climbing became a matter of scrambling. Odin refused all help and steadily worked his way from one boulder to the next.

Unexpectedly they came to a narrow, smooth lane. It led them upwards to an outcrop of rock which roughly resembled the face of a human being, and there they rested.

They found themselves among low russet bushes. Peron wiped the dust from his goggles and pronounced that the air seemed clearer. He put his thumbs under the neck flap of his headpiece and lifted. Moments later, after a brief struggle, he stood panting and grimy-faced in the warm air. There was still dust, but the driving wind that had carried the dust clouds in the valley had gone. The air was thin, but he could breathe. Paris and Pawl looked at him like staring, blank-eyed owls, and then they too fumbled with their headgear and emerged sweaty and dust-stained. The fine dust of the valleys had penetrated everywhere, bedding into wrinkles so that they looked as if they were wearing war paint.

'That's better,' said Paris, and then he sneezed violently. They were aware of the echo of the sound as it rolled back to them.

They looked down and could see the tumbling dust storms which flowed through the valleys like silted rivers.

Peron picked a leaf from one of the low bushes. 'This is called pickel if I am not mistaken,' he said and slipped the leaf into his mouth and began to chew. Its juice was thick and malty. The aftertaste was close to aniseed. 'I have read that it is medicinal. It is certainly refreshing.'

Pawl and Paris selected leaves and began to chew. Paris spat his out quickly. 'Tastes like milk,' he said.

Pawl found the taste of the leaves invigorating but bitter, and was glad to spit the residue out over the edge of the outcrop where they rested.

Odin did not settle. He pointed one of his stunted arms up the path and then began to glide upwards. Even without telepathy it was obvious that he was telling them that he planned to take the lead.

'Follow slowly,' murmured Odin for Pawl's understanding. 'I have not yet made contact, but I can feel the Hammer watching. They know where we are. Be cautious. Move slowly.'

Odin began to climb up the smooth track. 'It can move quite quickly when it wants to,' observed Paris. 'Have you ever seen its feet?'

Pawl shrugged. 'You don't ask members of the Inner Circle to lift their skirts.' Paris and Peron laughed.

Odin reached the top of the track and disappeared into

a thicket after being outlined for a moment against the sky.

'Shouldn't we follow?' asked Peron.

'No hurry,' replied Pawl. 'Odin is our keeper. He is our ambassador. I think it is easier for him if we keep our distance. Remember the Hammer have no love of our species.'

The three men remained sitting, listening to the silence of the mountains.

Peron, with his eyes half-closed, looked down the long valley where they had climbed. His body had adjusted quickly and breathing was easier and the air more fulfilling. He looked at the swirling dust and the dismal rock falls and rock-strewn hills. Nowhere could he see the splash of green which he associated with life. 'It has its own beauty,' he said finally.

Paris looked at him. 'What are you talking about?'

'This place. Forge. This landscape. Look at it. It has none of the gentleness of home. Here I would die quickly even with food and water. And yet there are creatures that live here and call it home and are at home. They no doubt see it as beautiful. I'm trying to understand its beauty.'

The wind sighed in the valley. 'The dust's getting to you,' said Paris. 'Now if you wanted to see beauty, you should have seen my world. There was beauty and now it is gone.'

Above them something rattled. Dust and pebbles cascaded down on to them. They staggered to their feet and shook their headpieces and pulled them on. At first Pawl thought there was a landslide, but then he saw a vast creature moving above them. It was scrambling and sliding down the hillside, riding on the loose shingle. About twenty feet above them it came to a halt and Pawl

43

was aware of a writhing and a brief fierce drumming and then the creature churned the rocks and scampered away. It ran in a cloud of dust up the pathway taken by Odin.

Paris wrenched his headpiece off and spat and sneezed. He had received a mouthful of the fine dust. 'What the hell was that about?' he said finally. 'Were we being attacked?'

'Attacked? No, I don't think so,' said Pawl. 'Perhaps a warning.'

'I think we were being told to get a move on,' said Peron and that was all he would say. He blew dust from his headpiece and slung his pack on to his shoulders. Quickly the men gathered their possessions and set off on the trail of the Hammer.

'Did it see me?' asked Peron, working his shoulder into the dry earth and keeping his head well down under cover of the boulder.

'Hard to tell,' whispered Pawl without moving. He kept his eye pressed to the telescopic viewfinder of the vivante camera. 'If it did it didn't show it. It hasn't blinked for the last five minutes.'

'Shall I signal Paris?'

Pawl nodded. 'Odin should be up there by now.' There was an edge of worry in his voice. 'Best if we are all together.'

Peron squirmed round and nodded to a low outcrop of rock about ten yards from him. In response to his summons, Paris crept round the rock and began crawling like a lizard across the small clearing.

He arrived breathless, and crouched down and tugged his mask off. Underneath his black face was running with sweat and sores had opened round his neck where the headpiece had begun to chafe. He had fallen while they were climbing and the fall had damaged the mask so that dust could creep in. 'Any sign of Odin?' he breathed.

Peron shook his head.

They had seen Odin far above them, just reaching the place where they now hid. The small creature had evidently survived the passing of the giant Hammer. Then, just as Pawl was leading the way into the clearing, another Hammer had appeared, climbing on to a rock a mere two hundred yards in front of them. They had dived for cover. That was the situation they now found themselves in.

'Well, at least we can get a good look at one of them,' said Pawl.

Even at this distance, the presence of the Hammer was awesome. It sat on a long smooth rock, gripping the rock with its four rear pairs of legs. A front pair of legs lifted its torso almost upright. There was no mistaking how it gained its name. Its head was shaped like a hammer, but with a huge boss of wrinkled skin at the centre. Its black eyes located at the ends of its head were hooded and glazed against the omnipresent sand and dust.

Below the head and eyes was a long smooth neck of red scales which ended in a nest of feelers, one of which bore an uncanny resemblance to a human arm and hand. At the centre of the feelers was a dark opening which dilated as the creature breathed.

'Can I look?' said Paris, reaching up for the vivante camera.

Through the eyepiece the detail was clear and sharp. He saw the folds of metallic skin rise and contract along the spine like a bellows. He saw the high jointed legs and the great bunched muscles which marked the place where the legs joined the body. He saw rows upon rows of small white feelers which rippled up and down the length of the creature's body and which seemed to beat upon it. He saw the giant tail, twice as long as the

Hammer's body, which arched above it and ended in a sting, like a lantern, over the creature's head.

As Paris watched, it moved. Two of its front feelers reached forward and tore at something in front of it. Paris could not see clearly, but the motion was unmistakable. The dark orifice opened and revealed stumps of white bone which closed on a morsel of flesh and slowly masticated.

He handed the camera back to Peron, who passed it to Pawl. Pawl studied the mouth. He watched it ruminate, observing the delicate way the feelers picked up small pieces of flesh and flicked them aside. A stiff pointed tongue licked out for a second and disappeared. The lips closed to a tight button-like orifice and the creature became still again. Only the frill of feelers along its back and sides moved. Faintly Pawl could hear a drumming.

'What do you make of those things along its sides? I think they're making the noise.' He passed the camera back to Peron. Peron switched to the greatest possible magnification and studied the rippling feelers. 'They're drumming all right,' he said as he followed the pattern of beats. It was not a regular rhythm. As he listened and watched he could detect definite changes of emphasis and pitch. 'It seems to be striking its side . . . it can tighten its skin too.' He studied in silence for a few moments and then passed the camera to Paris. 'I could be wrong,' he said, 'and I know it sounds far-fetched, but it looks to me as though it is singing.'

Paris adjusted the magnification until he could look at the whole beast. 'It's got barbs on its legs and tufts of hair at the joints,' he said. 'It could rip you open just brushing against you . . . not to mention that tail.'

As he was focusing on the sting Odin's pale masked face appeared, bobbing across the viewfinder. They all watched as Odin's small figure, clumsy-looking in the heavy black gown, appeared round the side of the Hammer and mounted the rock where it sat.

Someone was with Odin. A tall humanoid, clothed in an identical black gown and mask, helped Odin and then perched on the rock between the legs of the Hammer.

'Ye Gods,' said Paris. 'Another of the Inner Circle. The place is crawling with them.'

The Hammer arched its neck gracefully and observed the two newcomers. One of its feelers snaked out and helped the tall humanoid to find its place. Suddenly the volume of noise rose and the sounding feelers along its side blurred with the speed of the drumming. Abruptly it stopped and the silence seemed strange.

The crouched humanoid turned towards where Pawl and the others were hiding and waved to them, beckoning. He placed his thin hands round his mouth and called. His voice was high and nasal and carried clearly. 'Trader say come. Move legs to us. No crushing. No killing. Trader will talk.' Above him the giant barb opened and closed.

'Well, at least that answers one question,' said Pawl. 'It knows we are here.' The three looked at one another. There seemed no alternative but to break cover and advance.

At the same moment that they stood up the Hammer reared. Holding itself with its two back pairs of legs, it raised the whole front section of its body and its neck arched as it stared at them. Its belly was pale and segmented. The muscles that had lifted the Hammer were clearly related to those that controlled its tail, for the tail rose stiff as an obelisk with the giant sting open.

They climbed through the bushes and boulders until they were under the rock where the Hammer stood. It watched them, almost cross-eyed, and then it backed jerkily off the smooth rock. The humanoid was held high with its head close to the Hammer's mouth. 'You are to follow. Talking will be in a better place,' said the alien and then the Hammer turned and ran speedily out of sight behind some tumbled boulders. All the while it kept up its loud irregular drumming. The last they saw of it was its high tail and mighty barb cruising above the rocks.

The rock where it had sat was completely smooth. Peron ran his hand over it. 'Must be a favourite lookout point. Must have been used for centuries.' The rock was blood-spattered and the carcase of a small lizard lifted its stiff claws to the sky.

Odin was waiting for them. He worked his way down and led them into the narrow defile where the Hammer had run. It was just wide enough to accommodate the body of one Hammer.

Odin moved with confidence but would not answer when Pawl called and this made Pawl feel uneasy. The training he had received on Terpsichore had been thorough: here he was walking straight into an ideal ambush. Everything was at stake. His only confidence came from a knowledge of how vulnerable they were. Why, he reasoned, would the Hammer bother with ambush when they could strike so easily? From the distance came oppressive drumming.

On either side of them rose the smooth red walls of the small canyon. Heads appeared above the walls, Hammer heads with bright black eyes. They watched the travellers, coiling and bobbing their long necks.

'What'll we do if they attack us?' asked Paris.

'Fight,' said Pawl, but he knew that particle guns would not save them. All his trust was in diplomacy.

The drumming was getting louder. They rounded a bend in the track and found themselves facing, only a few

48

hundred yards away, a steep hill. The roar that came from the hill was deafening and the three travellers clapped their hands over their ears. The hill was pock-marked with thousands of caves. Paths ran across its surface like veins. The hillside was alive with Hammer. They crawled over it and over one another and dipped into and out of the caves.

Odin turned away from the hill. He led them down into a shallow valley, under some russet-leaved trees and past a cavern where a river plunged into the earth. A river! None of them had ever thought to see clear running water in a dry land such as this.

Beyond the river they came to another narrow pathway which led sinuously up the hill. Waiting at the top was a solitary Hammer. It dipped its tail when it saw them looking up at it. The sound of the hill was now only a murmur like distant, undifferentiated thunder.

'Is that Trader?' asked Paris.

'I suppose,' replied Pawl. 'Hard to tell. They all look pretty much the same.'

They climbed and finally found themselves standing on a ledge facing a domed cave. On one side the hill fell away precipitously, so that they seemed suspended. They were at the height of the tops of the surrounding hills and could see for miles across the craggy upper plateau.

The Hammer was waiting. It was dripping with water. The water hung like balls of glass in the tough red hair that sprouted from the joints on its legs. Its scales gleamed. It looked like a giant ornament made of red tile and beaten copper.

The four creatures stood in an uncomfortable dirty group before it. It drummed softly and looked at them each in turn through its widespread eyes.

'Trader says you can water if you have a mind to. Not too long. Trader busy.' The humanoid alien was still close to the Hammer's nest of tentacles. Gently he was lowered to the ground.

'We would all feel better for a wash,' said Pawl, removing his cumbersome mask and goggles. 'The air here is sweet.'

'I lead. You follow,' said the alien, beckoning. He entered the cave opening, and as he entered a thousand small jets of water opened up, spraying him. His gown became hazy. Pawl followed and felt jets of ice-cold water against his face and in his hair. His body under the protective dust coat was pummelled. Then he was through. He looked back at the curtain of water. It seemed as though a rainbow closed the cave door.

Paris and Peron burst through and finally Odin. Odin paused in the doorway and let the water sluice over him. Pawl felt the waves of his contentment.

The inside walls of the cave were covered with a creamy ceramic substance which was both cold and hard. One wall had stiff bristles sticking out from it. They were sharp and unyielding. Peron guessed that it was here that the Hammer rubbed themselves after a soaking.

Three arches led away from the central chamber. 'Where do those lead?' asked Pawl. His voice boomed in the chamber.

'Sleeping rooms. Thinking rooms. Eating rooms. Children rooms. Working rooms. All rooms. All no go. Private rooms. Hammer only. Remove clothes and wash.'

'Will you join us?' asked Peron, peeling off his dust coat.

'I am Inner Circle.'

'Does that mean you don't wash?' said Paris and winked.

The humanoid alien did not reply but folded its arms across its chest. Its mask held the familiar, slightly sardonic smile.

Without ceremony the humans undressed in front of the alien. The fine red dust tumbled from their clothes and ran away in rivulets across the cream floor. Its resemblance to blood was unmistakable. They washed their clothes by holding them in the fine spray at the cave door and then wringing them out by hand.

'Do you have a name?' asked Pawl.

The tall alien bowed. 'My name is Lake. You may call me Lake.'

'We didn't expect to find another member of the Inner Circle on this planet. What is your place here?'

'I translate. I explain. I am useful. I am their parasite.'

'Translate, eh?' said Paris. 'Can you speak the language of the Hammer then?'

'Not speak. Only the Hammer can speak. They have many forms to their language. I know a bit. They drum simple for me.'

'But if you can't speak the Hammer's language, how can you translate? How do they understand you?'

The alien's body shook. It was laughing. 'The Hammer do not need me to understand. They need me to translate for you. The Hammer know many languages. Any language that has sound they can master. Trader knows your language. He could hear you as you climbed the path. Trader knows my language. We often talk, in the evenings. It is not a difficult thing really.'

That took some grasping. They looked at one another in surprise. 'I never thought that that thing out there, Trader, could understand a language,' said Paris.

'Where did Trader learn?' asked Pawl.

'I think the Hammer often listen to your people down on the valley floor.'

'Ha!' said Pawl. 'Well, that explains it.' He turned to Peron and Paris. 'You know, I wondered. I wondered when I first heard how ferocious the Hammer were, and how tough and how clever, why they would allow a puny little mine to stay on their planet. And that was the reason. They wanted to keep up with the language and they probably picked up bits of news too. Well, well.'

Paris stood in the doorway, letting the water pour over his hard-muscled body. Peron and Pawl joined him. They all had dust sores in their wrinkles and the cold water eased the irritation. When they were clean, they pulled their wet clothes back on and went outside. The hot dry air felt balmy.

The Hammer was waiting. In front of it was a low slate table on which were placed small chips of white and black stone. Pawl glanced at it casually and recognized with some surprise a Corfu board.

The Hammer drummed softly. 'Trader says be seated in front.'

They did as they were bidden and the great beast hunkered lower. They found themselves looking straight over the table and into its mouth orifice. The stench of its breath as it puffed out made their stomachs clench.

'I'm not sitting here,' said Paris. 'Apart from the smell, it's disgusting. I know it's its mouth, but it looks like its arse and its breath smells like a fart.'

A similar thought had occurred to Pawl but he had repressed it. Peron turned to Paris and said, 'Remember that Trader speaks our language.' His politeness was studied. He was about to say more but when he opened his mouth he gagged. He jumped up and ran to the edge of the platform and there gave vent to his nausea.

'We're sorry,' said Pawl as the three of them arranged themselves to the side of the Hammer and upwind of him. The Hammer drummed.

'Why sorry?' translated Lake. 'Your bodies smell like dead birds to me but I don't complain. All aliens smell. It is something you have to get used to if you want to expand your mind. Do you want I should hold my breath?'

'I think we will be all right if we sit here,' said Pawl. He had noted a certain lightness in the Hammer's words and this encouraged him. Peron smiled to himself and looked closely at the tall alien who was translating. He had observed that the alien spoke their language better when he was translating the Hammer's speech than when he was speaking for himself. It was an observation only and Peron did not know what to make of it.

Paris was glad to be out of the smell. He looked at the Hammer, trying to spot where it would be vulnerable. *Right in its mouth*, he thought.

Lake stepped between the Hammer's front two legs and squatted down. Two of the tentacles uncoiled from above him and rested themselves along his shoulders. Lake began to rock back and forth. He raised his masked face. 'I am trancing,' he said. 'Speaking easier when tranced.' His cowled head flopped forward and was supported by one of the tentacles.

Trader drummed. 'Shall we begin?' The voice came from Lake, but it was hard and deep and the nasality had almost disappeared. 'Trader is busy and does not have time to squander. You have business, I will trade. Talk for a game. Do I have a deal?'

'Game?' asked Pawl.

'This,' said Trader. A tentacle reached out and tapped like a finger on the table. 'I don't know what name you have for it but it is a passion with me. Talk for a game. Do I have a deal?'

'We call it Corfu,' said Pawl. 'I have played the game once or twice but I am not a master.'

'I believe you. I hope you will give me a stretch. Perhaps hold me to sixty-four moves.'

'I'll try. But no other conditions.' Pawl was cautious.

The game of Corfu, avidly played on Lotus-and-Arcadia, had a sinister reputation. It was a game of skill and cunning and estates had been lost, and lives too, on an outcome. It was always a game of face and if you did not wish to court dishonour you did not play. On Terpsichore Corfu was taught to stimulate mental discipline.

'No other conditions. A talk for a game.' The pointed tongue flicked from the mouth and a gobbet of saliva hit the ground in front of Pawl. Odin spoke in Pawl's mind. 'Return the gesture. It is a common way for those who have mouths to strike a bargain.'

Pawl spat.

The Hammer settled its huge body lower and drummed briefly. 'Begin.'

It was Peron who asked the first question. 'Can you write your language?'

For answer the giant tail extended over the Hammer's head and began to inscribe quickly in the sand in front of it. Lines, dots, squiggles, wedge shapes and curves appeared in quick succession. These were followed by a brisk line drawing of a bearded face which they judged to be a portrait of Pawl since he had allowed his stubble to grow. 'That is of course our technical language. There is no way to write our other language. It would take a lifetime to write a sentence and another lifetime to read it. So why bother? Do you have two lifetimes to waste? Do you have anything to say that is worth a lifetime?' The Hammer blew out gustily and erased the picture.

'How many languages do you have?' asked Pawl.

'Five.'

'And can you speak all of them?'

'No. I use four of them for flying kites and cooling stew.'

Pause.

'Could you say something to us in one of your other languages?'

'No. It would be a sterile exercise. Come on, quickly.'

'Do you live in the city we saw as we approached?'

'That is not a city. It is a school of sorts and I live far away from here.' The sting pointed vaguely in the direction of the distant hills. 'I came only to play.'

'This is a dry planet,' said Pawl. 'Where does all the water come from?'

'Underground and the mountains. In pipes.'

'Do you have a source of energy?'

'We live.'

'Technol – '

'Lateral gravity. Inertia sinks. Come. Come. Come. Come.' The tail straightened and then banged down on the ground behind the Hammer sending up a cloud of dust and grit. 'Your questions lack soul. They have no tease.'

'What makes you happy?' asked Peron suddenly.

The Hammer turned its head to him and then lowered until its throat wrinkled and its two eyes hung above him like black balls. Peron could have reached up and seized them.

The roar of the tattoo as the white sounding tentacles burst into action almost bowled them over. Words poured in a torrent from the entranced Lake. 'Making love in snow and forest. Turning in sand. Pulling down stars. Scratching where I itch. Playing. Cracking hard rocks together. Talking after mating. Jumping with all legs. Stinging.' It paused. 'There is a joy you will never know. The coil and flex of the sting. The release and the calm as the body resurrects.' The Hammer settled back. 'Next question.'

'Have you often stung?' asked Paris.

'Often.'

'And killed?'

'Always.'

'You fight . . .'

'We fight as we love as we breathe.'

Pawl was alarmed to see the large leg muscles at the rear of the creature begin to bunch. The Hammer's body was responding to the thought of battle. He changed the subject abruptly.

'The people on my Homeworld have heard of the Hammer but never seen any live ones. Can I make a vivante of you?' He held up the small camera.

'They will be terrified.'

'But they are curious too.'

The Hammer reached forward with one of its tentacles and lifted the camera from Pawl's hand as neatly as an elephant picks up an apple core. It looked at it, explored it, and then began to take images of Pawl and Paris and Peron. 'The expressions on your faces will certainly inspire curiosity.'

It tossed the machine back to Pawl who caught it.

'Record my sting for your children. Children like such things.'

Pawl did as he was bidden. 'Have you seen a vivante camera before?'

'Seen? The Hammer invented it long ago and handed it to your first comers. We are clever at inventing. It is a useful toy.' Pawl did not know whether to believe this but decided to say nothing. The Hammer was speaking again. 'Manipulation is not the start of intelligence but it helps. We have many hands – ' its tentacles writhed – 'and so many ways of perceiving the world. You have come a long way considering your limitations and your vulnerability.'

'What is the first step in intelligence?' asked Peron.

'Awareness of crisis.'

'And the second step?'

'Overcoming.'

The mood of the Hammer seemed to have changed, to have calmed, and yet at the same time there was an intensity, a scrutiny.

'What do we look like to you?' asked Peron.

'Look like?' The Hammer paused. 'Ah, eyes.' It began to sway its head back and forth as though weighing the question. 'We look with these – ' a tentacle flicked out and pointed to its eyes – 'but we also look with these.' A second tentacle snaked out and wrapped round Peron's arm and drew him in towards the giant mouth.

A warning voice in Pawl's mind told him not to move, not to reach for his particle gun. This was a moment he had anticipated, the time when the Hammer would test their courage and trust.

No such voice spoke to Paris. His hand dropped to his side, but before he could touch his gun, a tentacle writhed like a breaking rope and slapped him across the chest and sent him tumbling backwards. He sat up with his arms round his chest, fighting for breath.

'Put your gun on the floor,' said Pawl softly, filtering any anxiety from his voice. 'We have no advantage here.' Paris did as he was bid but his face showed the burning anger of humiliation.

The tentacle held Peron firmly while other feelers ran over his body with quick feathery movements. They explored his face and paid great attention to his hands. Then, with its examination complete, the Hammer let him go. Red weals showed on Peron's arm where the Hammer had held him. Peron staggered back and drew in gulps of air.

'Thank you,' he said to the Hammer. 'I thought you were going to kill me.'

The Hammer drummed loudly. 'I am laughing,' explained Lake in a monotone.

The drumming subsided to a murmur of conversation. 'Kill you? Why would I kill you? I want to learn too and what can you learn from something that you have killed? Now if I'd wanted to eat you . . .' The tongue licked out.

It is joking with us, thought Pawl.

'However, I can also see you with this.' The sting arched forward and opened and closed like a parrot's beak. 'I can smell you. When you were coming here like little lizards, I could smell you. I could smell your fear. Richest of all is your breath, because that comes from inside your belly and that tells me a great deal.' The Hammer's head turned and nodded to Peron. 'You are interesting because you are least afraid.'

'I'm very afraid,' said Peron.

'Not where it counts,' replied the Hammer. It turned to Pawl. 'You are interesting because I can learn least from you.' A tentacle licked out and touched Pawl lightly on the nose. 'You carry something inside you, some movement. There is more than you in you. A purpose.'

Odin's voice awoke in Pawl's mind. 'Do not be alarmed. The Hammer are great gamesters. It is guessing. Say nothing.' The tentacle drew back.

'What about me?' asked Paris. He had crept back to his former position. The Hammer glanced at him. 'Who are you?' it asked and raised its head. Paris did not reply.

Pawl was aware that in a subtle way roles had changed and that it was now the Hammer that was conducting the interview. Perhaps it had been this way from the very beginning.

'Ask the Hammer about the alien war,' prompted Odin.

Pawl looked at the Hammer. It looked such an unlikely candidate for space travel, so large and ungainly. And yet he had seen it run, watched its delicacy, and there were

58

hints a-plenty of advanced technology despite the barren appearance of the planet. The creature's intelligence was not in question.

'Have you ever travelled to the stars?'

'Ah, the stars. They are a memory in all of us. I have never left this rough planet but long ago we did. You know that. You keep us here. But one day we will return, whether in peace or war. Luck has favoured your soft bodies and we are very patient.'

'What do you mean, we keep you here?'

'Your satellites.' The sting pointed to the sky.

'Surely with your inventiveness you could overcome an obstacle like that?'

'We could. But what would be the use? We are few and though we fight well we would be swept back and perhaps the end would be worse than the beginning. Perhaps there would be no more Hammer. Perhaps you think that would be no bad thing.'

'Not at all,' said Pawl. 'I'm just surprised that you were left alive at all.'

'I think we were forgotten.'

'How were you defeated?'

'They came to us. One of your families. The Wong. We were to talk. We like talking. They sent men with bombs sewn inside them. Special bombs which contained disease. The disease spread. It turned our sinews to rubber and we could not walk. We became easy prey. But some survived. Now we are strong but still so few.'

'Would you like revenge?'

'Revenge would be sweet. But we are peaceful now. We have learned our lesson. We will not bother your kind again.'

Pawl thought, *It's lying. Given half a chance the Hammer'd come bursting out of here and there'd be no stopping them. They wouldn't make the same mistake twice.*

59

The Hammer drummed like the humming of bees. 'The meeting is coming to an end. You may ask one last question and then the game.'

'Would you travel to my Homeworld if I invited you?' asked Pawl.

'Is that an invitation?'

'Yes.'

The Hammer looked at him for many seconds until Pawl began to feel uncomfortable. Finally it drummed.

'Perhaps,' Lake translated. 'And now the game. You are familiar with the rules?'

Pawl nodded. He was the only one of them who had ever played Corfu. Though he had been a passably good player, his heart had never been in the game. Beyond skill, Corfu was a game of will and concentration in which victory invariably went to the uncompromising intellect. 'This may take quite a while,' he said to Paris and Peron. 'On Lotus-and-Arcadia I once watched a game that lasted for over a week. I suggest you rest.'

'You may move first,' drummed the Hammer. 'After which Trader says no more talking.' The Hammer released Lake, who slumped to the floor and shook his head. He toppled forward and lay still for a few moments, face down: then he crawled out from between the Hammer's legs. Odin glided to Lake and supported him as he tottered to his feet. Both creatures entered the cave. 'Play well, Master Pawl,' whispered Odin.

Pawl opened with a traditional gambit which the Hammer studied carefully. It countered with an aggressive move which, at this stage of the game, made it vulnerable.

Pawl pressed his advantage. He tried to build an attack but within five moves found himself neutralized.

Within ten moves it was obvious that he was facing a master and that the opening moves had been merely to test his psychology. The Hammer began to play more quickly. Pawl felt his advantage slip before its relentless power. The Hammer seemed to have five lines of attack to Pawl's two. The intervals between Pawl's moves grew longer and longer. The Hammer showed no impatience but it moved its own pieces with speed and assurance as though it had already foreseen the entire game. The pressure never let up.

After eighteen moves Pawl was facing defeat. His attack was in disarray and his pieces falling. On the twenty-second move it was all over.

The Hammer swept the pieces from the low table with a flick from one tentacle. Then it raised its bulk on its four rear legs. It stretched, towering above them, and then lowered back down. They had to dive away to avoid being crushed. It entered the cave hole without offering a single drum beat.

The water hissed down, sluicing over its jointed back and the high arch of its tail. Then it was gone.

Lake and Odin emerged hurriedly from the cave. Lake seemed to have recovered completely.

'What was wrong with it?' asked Pawl. 'Did I do something wrong?'

'I think Trader felt cheated,' said Lake. 'He had looked forward to the game so much.'

With the giant Hammer gone there seemed little reason to stay. The world seemed suddenly more ominous and lonely. From the distant hill came a steady grumble of drumming.

Slowly they made their way back, and this time not a single Hammer paid attention. It was as though they were too insignificant to inspire curiosity.

Pawl felt guilty, as though he had let the side down.

The meeting had offered so much . . . and there was obviously so much more to learn.

'I tried,' said Pawl to Peron as they passed the place where they had first met Trader eating the small lizard. 'And I never said I was an expert at the damned game.'

'You did your best,' said Peron, and trudged on. He was clearly disappointed.

Eventually they scrambled down the last slope and came in sight of the shimmering perimeter fence. Evening was falling and the sun of Forge was a blood-red disk low on the hills. The driven sand pattered against them and infiltratcd under their gowns.

The fence suddenly blanked out and there stood Milligan and beside him the smaller shape of Laurel. They ran to greet them, obviously relieved, and when the small party had crossed the perimeter the fence leapt up behind them.

'We were getting worried,' said Laurel. 'Mr Milligan was getting together a search party.'

'Well, we're all right. A bit sore. A bit bruised. Nothing a particle shower won't fix,' said Pawl.

'Did you see any Hammer?' asked Milligan. 'Did you get an eyeful?'

'We saw plenty.'

'And . . . ?'

'And I played Corfu with one of them.'

Milligan looked at Pawl. His eyes crinkled. He wasn't sure whether Pawl was joking or not. And then he started to laugh. He laughed all the way back to the mess hut.

Later that night, Laurel lay in Pawl's arms, enjoying the quiet before sleep. They were in one of the domed inflatable huts that were used to protect delicate machin-

62

ery and Milligan and his men had worked all day trying to get the place cleaned up for them.

'You still haven't told me what you felt out there, facing the Hammer. I know what you did, but not what you felt.'

Pawl didn't answer immediately but lay back, looking at the flickering lights which shone palely through the window and listening to the steady beat of the generator. The particle fence never slept. He was thinking how frail their defences were and wondering just how large the population of the Hammer really was and how extensive their technology.

'Humbled,' he said finally. 'I think that was what I felt. I hold no man my master but I have never in my life met anything, any human, any creature that so impressed me with its vitality. It made me feel like a shadow. You know, when it looked at me I wanted to crawl away and hide. And yet we talked to it. It understood us. And it beat me at Corfu. And it was funny too.'

'Funny?'

'Yes. It had a sense of humour.'

'I wish I'd come.'

'So do I. I think you'd have understood it better than me.'

Laurel shrugged and snuggled closer. 'I don't know. I'm not very good with aliens,' she whispered.

Pawl yawned. 'Well, there's a lot to admire about the Hammer, but not very much to like. They are cruel and overbearing and I can't imagine them ever working with another species. No, the Hammer are top or nothing. But I'd hate to be the Wongs if ever the Hammer got loose.'

Peron was quartered in a small office at the end of one of the long bunk rooms. He sat at an improvised desk and was reviewing parts of the vivante they had made while talking to Trader. Like Pawl, he was trying to sort out his reactions to the Hammer. In front of him was his journal. Peron did not write songs, like Pawl, but he was an inveterate note taker, and his journal never left him.

He wrote, 'The Hammer are gamblers. Hope Master Pawl did not reveal too much of his mind when he lost that game. That could be dangerous.' On the vivante was a close-up of the mouth of the Hammer. Peron remembered being dragged and the stench. He wrote. 'If their technology mirrors their nervous system then I think that in battle they will be invincible. They belong to a stronger order of life than our own . . . one more in tune, I suspect, with the harsh reality of creation.' He looked at that sentence and wondered exactly what he meant. 'We have ingenious brains but weak bodies. They have quick brains and are very strong.' He looked at the red weals where the Hammer's tentacle had wrapped round his arm. 'They respect courage. They seem to treat the Inner Circle as servants. That is interesting. I wonder what part little Odin plays in all of this. He seems to know a great deal. I am now reasonably certain that he communicates telepathically. No doubt he communicated with that creature called Lake and I am convinced that Odin cleared our way and kept us safe. I do not see how it could be otherwise. Which brings me to the final question, "Why?" I do not believe in simple philanthropy. Odin has his reasons. I shall watch him more closely than ever.'

Peron set his pencil down and stared at the vivante. The final images were of the hill where thousands of Hammer beat and crawled over one another. Then the image vanished and the vivante machine hummed to itself as it reset the program. He added one last sentence. 'I believe that we are being taught, that we are being edged along a certain path of understanding.' He could think of nothing more to say and so set his papers aside, stretched and crawled into his low camp bed. He was asleep within minutes.

Paris was nursing his side, touching a livid bruise where the Hammer had flicked him. He had not let the others know how badly he was hurt. No bones were broken but he would have to move with care for some days.

He was thinking about the Hammer. He was thinking about the giant sting. How he would like to have one as a trophy. He wanted to see them fight, to see that sting in action. He wanted to kill one. He imagined himself like the famous archer on Portal Reclusi, driving a bolt straight into that stinking hole it called a mouth.

Odin was recovering after the hard day. He had found a place under one of the huts and there sent his roots down to draw what nourishment he could from the dry stony soil.

He knew the Hammer of old. They were like a bonfire in the mind. They did not have thoughts that were easy to live with. They were just bundles of feelings that flowed like lava down terraces. They were bright as beacons, hard as shell, and always moved just ahead of comprehension. With the Hammer true communication was impossible. But the visit had been worthwhile. Pawl's eyes were becoming open. He was becoming interested in the aliens and that was just how it should be.

7

IN ELLIOTT'S POCKET

The departure from Forge was uneventful and the small party set out on the last long jump to Elliott's Pocket. Here they hoped to rest before returning to the Paxwax Homeworld and the busy, full life of managing the affairs of the Paxwax Empire. Much to his surprise Pawl found that he was looking forward to taking up the reins of the Paxwax. He was pleased also that Laurel seemed so much more cheerful. She had not yet told him about the baby inside her. She was waiting for the right moment.

The main Way Gate in Elliott's Pocket was above the planet called Lumb. Waiting here to greet them was the giant Pettet and his wife, the witch-woman, Raleigh.

Pettet, well over nine feet tall and with a mass of black curly hair and a tangled beard which reached down almost to his belt, took Pawl's hand when he emerged from the Way Gate and then threw his arm round his shoulders and squeezed him. In his affection Pettet was as clumsy as a bear. As a man he was frequently inarticulate and this led to a blunt, formal way of speaking, until he relaxed. Raleigh rescued Pawl and planted a kiss squarely on his forehead. She was a broad-shouldered woman with frizzy blonde hair, full sensuous lips and startling blue eyes. She stood a good three inches taller than Pawl.

Pawl made the introductions. He had tried to prepare Laurel for what to expect but could see she was perplexed when the giant bowed down low to her and took her small hand and kissed it. Ancient traditions still held sway in the Pocket. Laurel did not know what to say and was grateful when Raleigh took her other hand and led her through into the reception area.

The other introductions were straightforward. Pettet welcomed Peron and Paris and gave them gifts. But he didn't know what to do when Odin glided up to him. The small domed creature scarcely reached to his knees.

'I . . . er, knew you had a member of the Inner Circle with you but I didn't expect . . .'

'Allow me to introduce Odin,' said Pawl.

The giant bent down and peered inside Odin's cowl. He poked him gently with his finger. He was looking for some way to bid him welcome. Then he straightened up and whispered to Pawl, 'Is it human? I've not met many members of the Inner Circle. They don't have much business in the Pocket.'

'Not human,' whispered Pawl. 'Alien. A Gerbes.'

Pettet looked blank.

'Once called Quaam.'

That name registered with Pettet. 'Quaam. Surely that was a food, a delicacy served before the main meal. I've heard of that.'

Pawl threw his eyes to the ceiling. Only in the Pocket could quirky little fragments of knowledge such as that persist. Then he realized what thoughts might be passing through Pettet's mind. 'But we don't call Odin a Quaam. That name is dishonourable to them. And we don't eat them,' he whispered.

Pettet shrugged. There was a humorous glint in his eyes. 'Any friend of Pawl's is welcome here.' He turned to Pawl. 'We've got a couple of cows and a sheep down below you might like to meet . . .'

'Bah . . .' said Pawl, but then he saw the funny side and couldn't stop himself from laughing. At the same time he wondered how Odin was faring. He could not contact the small creature and wondered just what effect the giant's thought was having.

'Have no fear for me, Master Pawl,' came Odin's voice in his mind. 'Your friend does not savour me. It is you that he is laughing at. Besides, I have my defences.'

Pettet shook his head as though dismissing a thought. 'Shall I carry it?' he asked.

'No, Odin can manage on his own.'

'Can you speak with it?'

'Yes.'

'How?'

'With this.' Pawl tapped his head.

Pettet nodded gravely. 'Yes, such is not unknown. I shall be interested to know what Raleigh makes of it. Well, come on through. We live in strange times. Strange things are happening in the Pocket.'

The reception room of the Way Gate was decked out with festoons of scarlet and yellow cloth making it bright and cheerful.

'In my honour?' asked Pawl. 'You shouldn't; I told you no ceremony.'

Pettet grinned and his craggy face seemed suddenly younger. 'No, not for you. Though no doubt we would have done something. We are expecting many visitors.'

Beneath the bunting was a frieze of pictures painted by children. They showed the adventures of a big black space-ship with long tapering fins. It was called the *Fare-Thee-Well*. Staring down into the room was a portrait of a man with glaring eyes. Behind the portrait was the image of a blazing planet. 'John Death Elliott,' said Pettet, nodding up to the portrait. 'Today is the beginning of the Elliott Festival.'

'You said strange things were happening in the Pocket,' said Pawl. 'What did you mean?'

Pettet's face clouded over again and worry lines appeared. 'This,' he said, and led the way out of the reception room and into the shuttle chamber.

Windows rose from floor to ceiling. The other members of Pawl's party were standing there with their mouths open, staring out into space. They were drenched in vivid green light.

'Wow,' said Paris, 'is that Emerald Lake? It's bigger than ever I expected and brighter.'

'It is brighter than ever I can remember,' rumbled Pettet, 'and I have lived with it all my life. Something is happening in there. We don't know what. We think that perhaps there is a great sun rising. What effect it will have we cannot tell. We have many stories about things hiding in the Lake. You have come at an interesting time.'

'If that is a sun rising,' said Peron, his eyes glittering greenly, 'then you may find it scorches this world. Surely.'

Pettet nodded. 'Indeed, and we are ready to abandon this world at an hour's notice and steal away on the dark side. We are always ready.'

Laurel shivered. The blazing green sky seemed to oppress her. She glanced up into Pawl's face and was amazed to see that the green light had made his eyes glow a bright lime colour. It was as though the illumination came from inside him. She slipped her arm round him and felt his arm rest on her shoulders. 'Beautiful,' he whispered. 'Isn't it beautiful?'

'Don't stare for too long,' called Raleigh. 'You'll be mesmerized. We've all noticed it. Come round here and look at the other side of the Pocket.'

Reluctantly Pawl dragged his eyes away from the brightness of Emerald Lake and let himself be led to one of the other great windows.

'I recognize that,' said Laurel, pointing out to where a coil of asteroids lifted. 'That's the Snake. Right?'

'Right,' said Raleigh. 'And do you notice that bright sun in the centre of its forehead? That is the Eye of the Snake.'

'I thought it was supposed to be dangerous,' said Paris.

'It is. There is a vortex in the eye which ejects particles. It destroys anything it looks at. Many ships have been destroyed, many women and men too. There is even an old space creature that was caught before it could flee. They are all still out there. We have visited them. Well, Pettet has. They are like sculptures made of glass and copper. Nothing can live in the full light of the snake. Not unless it is buried deep.'

A dapper brown-skinned man with a face like the blade of an axe approached them. He wore a bright red scarf round his head and a gold earring.

'This is Haberjin,' said Raleigh. 'Now if you want to know anything about the Snake, ask him. He knows more about it than any man you'll ever meet.'

Haberjin laughed. 'That is because I am alive. I was once caught in the glare of the Snake for a few seconds. It made me boil. But I lived. I should be a glass man, but I am not.'

'Haberjin is the greatest pilot in the Pocket,' said Raleigh affectionately. 'But he takes risks. I only hope he lives long enough to tell his stories to his grandchildren.'

Haberjin shrugged. 'Life is a risk. If I die out there, at least I'll die discovering something. And there are so many ways of dying.' He laughed again, looking into the serious faces of the visitors. They were not used to hearing death talked about so freely and so frankly. 'Come on. Away, Pettet. Let's get these people down below. They'll begin to think we are morbid in the Pocket. The Snake's Eye is turning fast and the sooner we get below the longer we'll have for fun.' He winked roguishly at Laurel and that lady found herself starting to blush. The reason was

70

obvious. Haberjin wore his life openly and lightly and was terribly attractive.

Pettet nodded. 'We should move. We're expecting a lot of people through today. Come on. Let's go down.'

As they moved away Raleigh took Laurel's arm. 'Pay no attention to Haberjin. He can't help himself. He'd flirt with the mother of God given half the chance.' Laurel laughed at that.

Pettet led the way, ducking under the trusses which supported the roof of the Way Platform and down to the shuttle port.

Seated in the shuttle they looked down. Beneath them was a planet of fur. It looked like a cat rolled into a ball. Peron took out his journal and began taking notes. Leaning over his shoulder Pettet watched him draw. 'You know the entire planet is covered with one single shrub. It is the only form of life I know that actually feeds on the radiation from the Snake.'

'One shrub? How deep is it?'

'Miles. Each time we descend we have to cut a path. That is how quickly it grows.'

'And where do you live? In its roots?'

'No, we live deep under the rock. That is the only place that is safe from the Snake. You'll see.'

They descended slowly. Eventually they brushed through the upper fronds of the shrub. From time to time shuttle attendants wearing survival suits climbed out and cut branches back using sharp machetes.

'Surely you don't do this every time the shuttle goes up and down?' asked Peron.

'Not every time. It depends on the growth. Sometimes we just blast through, sometimes we fit saw blades under the shuttle. But you can't use particle fire on this stuff. It just drinks it up.'

71

Odin, squatting alone, followed this conversation and at the same time let his mind wander outside and flow through the close clinging shrub. He was not surprised to discover a crude sentience there. The shrub took pleasure in the passage of the shuttle and enjoyed the periodic pruning.

Midway down, the fibres became tightly packed. Creatures with narrow white carapaces grazed there. 'Those are Testudoes,' said Pettet. 'They never venture to the surface. They exude a kind of milk which we think is a delicacy. You may try some.'

'Yuk,' said Paris.

Gradually the fibres became thicker until they were the consistency of peat. 'Now watch,' said Pettet. 'We are close to the surface.'

Suddenly the fibres gave way to thick ropy roots which twisted round each other. The roots gripped the surface rock as though they had once been molten and flowed like wax and poured into every fissure and cranny. Then the walls became smooth stone. 'You see,' explained Pettet, 'what we call the planet of Lumb was once just a ball of rock spinning round close to the Snake. Then it broke away – probably pulled away by a monster like Mabel – and here we are. They say that the caverns you are now entering were first quarried by aliens and then opened up fully by John Death Elliott using his ship the *Fare-Thee-Well*. Who knows? But at least we are safe from the Snake here and we live a comfortable life.'

'Are there any other inhabited planets in Elliott's Pocket?' asked Peron.

'Oh many. Not all as secretive as this. We keep close contact. We are more like a family than you might think.'

'Ah,' said Peron, 'you have Way Gates and spaceships, like the rest of us?' To Peron, Elliott's Pocket was a totally new area of space. Like most outsiders, he had been brought up to believe that it was occupied by savages. This was a myth encouraged by the inhabitants of Elliott's Pocket.

'Yes,' said Haberjin with a wink at Pettet. 'We have Way Gates and spaceships and people like Raleigh.'

Peron looked blank. 'I don't . . .'

'What Haberjin means is that Raleigh is a psychic. Many women here are psychic. We trust them as much as you trust radio or vivante aerials. Elliott's Pocket is not like most of space. Different laws apply.'

Peron busied himself in his notebook.

The shuttle entered a cavern. Stone doors closed above them. Below were patterns of lights.

'Is that your city?' asked Paris.

'No,' answered Pettet. 'Those are our workshops. We don't have a city. When you come to know us better you will understand.'

'Life in the Pocket is precarious,' chimed in Raleigh. 'We have to be ready to move at a moment's notice. So the workshops are the most important parts of our civilization. We live in burrows. It is very comfortable.'

The shuttle landed on a stone ramp under the glare of arc lights and its doors swung open. There was no one to greet them. *How different,* thought Laurel, *from our other landings on the civilized worlds.*

Outside the air smelled surprisingly sweet. They seemed to have landed in a giant hangar. As they filed outside they found themselves amid a fleet of black spaceships of a design they had never seen. A man with braided blond hair sat astride a high antenna and waved to them. 'Welcome to Lumb,' he called. 'How are things up top?'

73

'Still quiet,' called Pettet, 'still bright.'

They climbed up the stone ramp and passed through a particle curtain and found themselves in a garden. Willow trees drooped above a lake. There were flowers and the path was fringed with pale blue moss. The lake shimmered. Lights from below revealed the clear water where pale fishes swam.

'Now,' said Raleigh, 'we are home. We are in the place where Pettet and I live. Rooms are assigned and you can rest or wander as you wish. Later we will gather for a feast to begin the festival.' As she spoke she gestured round the lake. There were holes, like caves, and in some of these lights were gleaming. Two youths and a young woman appeared at one of the cave openings and dived into the lake and swam across to them. They emerged, shaking the water from their hair.

'These are three of our children,' said Raleigh. 'I'll let them make their own introductions. They will help you. What would you like to do?'

Laurel glanced across at Paris and he nodded to her. 'I think that we would like to swim,' she said. 'Forge was a dry and dusty world.'

'Nothing easier,' said the woman. She had the same blonde hair as her mother. She opened her hands and showed they were webbed. She looked at Paris with a frank unambiguous interest. 'Race you,' she said, and ran down to the lake and dived.

Paris hesitated a moment and then stripped off his Way suit and followed her. Laurel glanced at Pawl and he smiled and spread his hands. 'We are in the Pocket now,' he said. 'Different worlds, different ways. Swim to your heart's content. Only find out where we are sleeping and I will join you later.'

'I don't think I will swim,' said Peron. 'I'm, er . . . not much given to that. But I'm too excited to rest . . .'

'Would you like to see some old star charts, ships' logs from the days of the Great Push?' asked Haberjin. Peron's eyes brightened. 'We have plenty. The Pocket is a museum. You'd be surprised what flotsam and jetsam ends up here.'

'Well, I'd be delighted,' said Peron. 'If it wouldn't be too much – '

'Trouble?' said Haberjin. 'Well, I was going to sharpen my teeth, but I suppose I can put that off for an hour or two. Okay with you, boss?' He glanced at Pettet.

The giant scratched his beard. 'Well . . . there's that old Wong ship we discovered a few years ago . . . the one that they'd used in the war against the Hammer. Might be a bit frightening . . .'

'No. No. No,' said Peron. He could hardly get the words out fast enough. Then he realized that he was being made fun of. 'I'd love to climb about in a Wong ship, if you have one. I'm an historian by profession.'

'We know,' said Pettet. 'Pawl told us. Find out what you can. We can't translate their old documents.'

'This way,' said Haberjin.

When they were gone Pawl turned to Pettet. 'We have a lot of talking to do, if you don't mind.'

'A pleasure,' rumbled Pettet.

'Don't mind me,' said Raleigh. 'I'll keep my eye on Odin.' She pointed down to the shore. Odin had worked his way down the path and found himself a moist place beneath one of the willows. 'Only one question, Pawl. Is your friend and counsellor telepathic?'

Pawl nodded.

'I thought so. Then I shall keep my thought neutral. I may even be able to prise him open a little. I have never shared with an alien before. Now, don't you two go getting drunk too soon. Tonight is when the festival begins. Bardol will be present. We'll expect you sober to hear him.'

Pawl and Pettet stretched out in Pettet's study and both lit up cigars. These were a present which Pawl had brought, since tobacco was almost unobtainable in the Pocket. They drank Seppel juice and slowly mingled snippets of news with old memories. They re-established their friendship, as old friends must after a long separation.

But gradually Pawl became aware of a reticence in Pettet. It was not coldness. It was not secrecy. It was embarrassment.

'Was the war hard here?' asked Pawl, probing.

'Hard enough. We lost many good men. But we would never have opened the Pocket to the Lamprey and Xerxes even if you'd asked us to. They never fitted here, and though the fighting was hard when we came to it, we always knew we would win. The women told us so. Raleigh warned us. She loves you, Pawl, as much as me.'

'I know. Can you tell how Raleigh reacts to Laurel?'

'She likes her. That I can tell. Laurel is the right woman for you, that much I know . . .'

'Yes. Go on.'

The giant stretched, and scratched and ran his fingers through his hair.

'Go on. You can say anything you like to me, Pettet. Get whatever is worrying you off your mind. What is the truth of it?'

'The truth is not easy. The truth is vague. Raleigh is a witch-woman, but she does not know everything.'

'Has she tried to read my future?'

'Yes.'

'And . . .'

'And there is a darkness. That is all she will say.'

'Does she see my death?'

'No, she has never mentioned that.'

'Laurel's death?'

'No, not that.'

'Then what?'

'Just a darkness.'

'That is very vague.'

'Yes.'

'Does Raleigh know you are telling me this?'

'Hell, no.' Pettet looked at Pawl in mock terror. 'She would skin me alive if she heard what I was saying. She asked me to say nothing.'

Pawl nodded. 'But yet you are worried. Thank you for your warning.' They smoked in silence for several minutes.

'So tell me,' said Pawl, 'what is happening up above, in Emerald Lake?'

Pettet hunched his shoulders and leant over his desk. 'It is my belief that that may be the cause of all our worries. None of our psychics know what is happening. Since the Lake started to brighten all our predictions have been nonsense. It is as though whatever is coming up from the Lake has muffled our psychic power. That may well explain why Raleigh cannot read your future. It is like a great damper and as the light grows brighter so our predictions grow worse. Everyone in the Pocket feels it. Not even the vivante cameras work properly now. I mean, they never worked particularly well in the Pocket, but now all we get are blurred images. We are used to physical danger and can cope with that. But now we don't know what to expect.'

'You have always said that the Pocket was unpredictable.'

'Yes. And now I feel like a man who stands in a deep mist and does not know whether he is at the edge of a precipice or not. People look up to me. They trust Pettet the Giant. They expect me to know what to do, and I don't.'

'You can only wait,' said Pawl. 'I will ask Odin what is happening. He speaks the truth to me. If you are in danger I will find out. Meanwhile, what is it you used to say to me? While there is still wine in the glass there is wine to be drunk. Let's drink to that.'

The two friends drained their glasses.

A distant bell began to sound.

'Hell,' said Pettet, standing up. 'That's the call to the supper. Come on. When we've eaten we can listen to Bardol. You don't want to miss that. We'll have plenty of chances to talk in the next few days.'

They made their way to the feast through a maze of stone tunnels. Finally they emerged on to a gallery above a large room which Pawl remembered from his previous visit. It was the cavern usually used for meetings when the Pocket people assembled three or four times a year. Now it was brightly decorated. Paintings hung from the walls: images of long dead warriors who had founded the Pocket and engineered its prosperity. Standing round the walls were tables where people were assembling. To one side was a dancing space and a small band sat on tiered seats tuning their instruments.

In the centre of the room was a blazing fire cupped in a stone fireplace. Above it a white tiled chimney drew the smoke away. Alone by the fire sat an old man in a black rocking chair. He was smoking a long clay pipe and puffing out smoke rings.

'Is that Bardol?' asked Pawl.

'That's him. We're lucky to have him. He's more or less in retirement now but he's still the best singer of the old songs.'

'How old is he?'

'Very old. I can remember him when I was a boy, and he looked pretty much like that then. Come on, we'd better get down there. Laurel and Raleigh will be wondering.' He led the way to a narrow wooden staircase which angled down into the lower room.

As he was descending, Pawl caught sight of Peron. He had wandered into the central area and was making a sketch of the old man and the fireplace in his journal. *Probably trying to work out how they dispose of the smoke*, thought Pawl.

Laurel and Raleigh were waiting for them. Both ladies looked magnificent, Raleigh in turquoise and Laurel in silver. They stared at their menfolk in disgust. 'Why, you haven't even changed,' said Laurel. 'Nor you,' said Raleigh. 'I warned you.'

'You told me not to get drunk,' said Pettet.

'Same thing. Here, we brought you some fresh clothes. Go into one of the gardens and get yourselves changed.'

Pettet looked so crestfallen that Laurel started to giggle and even Raleigh had trouble keeping her face stern.

Holding their fresh clothes the two men made their way round the room. At intervals there were alcoves and these led to gardens. Every square inch of available space was put to use on the world of Lumb. The first alcove led to a vegetable garden fed with artificial sunlight. Animals which looked like a cross between goats and pigs were penned there. They were busy, heads down in a trough. Away in one corner was a water cistern, and an eel with a face like an otter raised its head and blinked at the two men and then submerged again.

The next garden was ornamental and had been turned into a creche for all the children who had arrived for the Pocket Festival. Kids were playing ball and swinging on swings and splashing about in a shallow pool. One of the children, a girl of about nine, was swinging upside down with her plaits trailing. She waved when she saw them. 'Hey, dad, mum's looking for you.' Pettet waved and nodded.

'Hello, Uncle Pawl. See how high I can swing.'

Pawl recognized Lynn. She was little more than a baby last time he was in the Pocket. 'She's grown,' said Pawl to Pettet.

'Mmm, takes after me, we think. Come on. The next garden should be quieter.'

It was. The next garden was filled with fragrant shrubs. The only occupants were Paris and Pettet's eldest daughter, the girl he had been swimming with. They moved away discreetly when they saw Pettet and Pawl.

'It seems that Paris has made a hit with your girl.'

'Yes, I suppose they are of an age,' said Pettet absent-mindedly. 'Come on, over here.'

Quickly the men changed and when they next entered the main chamber they looked smart and brushed and ready for a feast. Pawl's hair, which he still wore long after the manner of his youth, was coiled and fixed with a long pin. 'That'll do,' said Pettet. 'We don't want to stand on too much ceremony. The main thing is to enjoy yourself.'

The party was getting into full swing. The tables were piled with food. The dancing floor was crowded. The potent liquor brewed on Lumb was in plentiful supply. Pawl danced with Laurel and even Pettet, who had two left feet when it came to dancing, was prevailed upon to shamble round the dance-floor until Ralcigh complained that her feet were black and blue. At which Pettet hoisted her in the air and danced alone while she beat her fists on his shoulders.

During all this the old man, Bardol, sat staring into the fire sucking on his clay pipe. Pettet introduced him to Pawl and Laurel. Pawl was surprised to see that the old man always kept one eye closed. The eye which stared at them was sharp and blue.

'Master of Paxwax, eh? Well, well. You look so very young. I heard of the fighting recently. I'm afraid I don't know any of the songs of the Paxwax.'

'Nor do I,' said Pawl. 'Except official songs.'

'I mean songs of the people. A people without songs has no history. Don't worry: even if you don't know the songs, they exist. When people want to make their feelings known they write songs and then sing them to one another. Pettet tells me *you* are a writer of songs. I would like to hear them. Perhaps I could crib some of your rhymes.'

Pawl found himself blushing. 'Pettet shouldn't have said that. I have written some verses, that is all. I write them for Laurel. I'm afraid they are not very good.'

'If they are honest they are good.' The old man's seeing eye fell on Laurel. 'Old men when they philosophize are boring, I know, but let me say this: a woman who can inspire real songs is a rare prize and she will never be lonely. I wish you both happiness.'

The brief interview was over and the old man returned his gaze to the fire.

'Why does he only look at the world with one eye?' asked Laurel later, tearing some meat from a bone with her teeth.

'You'll see,' said Raleigh. 'Soon he will begin to sing.'

There came a point in the party when suddenly the noise dropped away. Everyone laughed and then a chant began: 'Bardol. Bardol. Bardol.'

The old man took his pipe from his lips and waved it. 'Whenever you like,' he said.

There was a scraping of chairs. Glasses were filled. A carpet was dragged down by the central fire and the children squatted down. Men and women carrying books clustered round Bardol and settled down at his feet.

'Who are they?' whispered Peron.

'They are his apprentices,' answered Haberjin. 'They are learning the songs. Watch.'

Deliberately the old man set his pipe aside. Then he turned his chair until he was facing most of the audience. 'We'll begin with a song you all know: "The Mating of Mabel".' With a blink he closed his bright blue eye and after a pause opened his other eye to reveal a red socket. He began to sing. At first his voice was soft but it gathered strength and resonance with each verse. The song was a bawdy ditty about a woman called Mabel who had thirty-two husbands and managed to enjoy them all without them ever suspecting the others. It had a simple chorus and Peron soon found himself joining in.

'Now,' said Mabel,
'I'll turn out the light
For love sees best
In the dark, dark night.'

'A good song,' said Peron to Haberjin while the audience were clapping.

'It's a mnemonic,' said Haberjin. 'Mabel is a rogue planet that comes round every hundred years or so. The names of the husbands are the names of the moons. The belief is that one day Lumb will be captured by Mabel. When that happens I hope we are all well gone.'

'How long before her next return?'

'Five or six years. We're on the look-out for her now.'

* * *

The second song was a quiet ballad about a spaceman who was on solitary duty aboard a signal satellite and dreamed every night he was back home. Again the song had a refrain and again almost everyone joined in. At the end of the song the spaceman cast himself adrift in space in the belief that he was going home. Peron was surprised to see that some of the people listening to the song were crying.

Haberjin explained, 'You see most of the people here have done solitary out in space. They know what it is like. The hallucinations are amazing. Have you ever been alone out there with just a rock for company?' Peron shook his head. 'Well, perhaps one day you will be, and then you'll try to remember the words of this song to keep you sane.'

The third song was a variation on the tale of Noah, in which a family did everything they could to save the livestock from their world before it was drawn into the maw of a black hole.

And after this song Peron stopped taking notes and just listened. Bardol seemed to have grown in stature. He played all the parts, mimicking with his face and arms the expressions and gestures of his characters.

The chorus of apprentices matched the words and movements of the master.

Finally he drew breath. 'One last song for the night,' he said. 'What'll it be? We ought to honour our founder.'

A child's voice piped up. 'Sing about John Death Elliott and his ship the *Fare-Thee-Well*.' Everyone started clapping.

'The children love this one,' whispered Haberjin. 'Listen closely. You'll learn the history of Elliott's Pocket . . . how we came here . . . where we came from. Each year the singer improvises new verses.'

'All right,' called the singer, 'we'll have the ballad of John Death Elliott. Just let me see who's here.' He opened his good eye and glanced round the assembly. He looked at Raleigh and Pettet, and then straight at Haberjin, who raised his hand and waved, and at the children and a gaunt-faced girl who was stirring a pot of stew close to the fire. And then he changed eyes again.

The song began boisterously. It told how John Death Elliott and his sister Elizabeth became pirates aboard a wondrous alien ship called the *Fare-Thee-Well*. They attacked the Proctor trading ships and became terrors of the spaceways.

'This song must date back to the years just after the Great Push,' whispered Peron.

'Yes. It does. Hush. Listen.'

Finally, Pippin, the Master of the Proctor Family, tired of being humiliated by John Death Elliott and his sister, offered a prince's ransom to any man or woman who could capture the *Fare-Thee-Well*.

Now the first mate aboard the *Fare-Thee-Well* was called Lester John and he was a traitor.

> Lester John had fists of iron,
> His eyes were merry and green.
> But bonny face and clever tongue
> May mask a mind that's mean.
>
> Lester John drank beer one night,
> Slapped Jack Death on the arm.
> 'Oh I will love your sister true
> And never do her harm.'
>
> Then he watched and waited and bided his time,
> Stole the keys to landship three,
> Took Bett from her bed with a gun at her head,
> Broke open the door to the Landship shed,
> The blast as he left would have wakened the dead,
> And he took Bett to Luxury.
> As a prisoner to Luxury.

At the mention of Luxury a great shout went up from the audience. Peron had heard of Luxury. It was a famous penal planet noted for the cruelty meted out to prisoners.

Elizabeth Death was incarcerated on Luxury and tortured in the hope that this might make Jack Death capitulate. But he didn't. By a ruse he managed to get the *Fare-Thee-Well* close to the prison fortress of Luxury and there, after rescuing most of the prisoners, he methodically destroyed the entire planet. The convicts who were rescued from Luxury and taken aboard the *Fare-Thee-Well* were the founding fathers and mothers of the people who now dwelt in the Pocket. But John Death Elliott was too late to save his sister.

> They carried Bett to the surface,
> Wrapped in a prison sheet.
> They lifted her up through the prison gate,
> And set her on her feet.
>
> She stood and shook on swollen feet,
> She stood like a girl with no soul,
> She stared like the blind, for they'd scrubbed her mind,
> As clean as a surgeon's bowl.

At this point in the song Bardol stopped and lifted his arms. There was absolute silence in the chamber. Slowly the singer began to chant.

> Names bring honour. Let me name a few.
> A man called Pettet, a girl called Blue.

When she heard her name mentioned the girl who had been stirring stew by the fire dropped her ladle.

> A Smith, a Lee, a child called Lynn,

The singer was pointing unerringly about the chamber.

A Minsk, a Raj and Haberjin.

Haberjin raised a clenched fist.

> Those I have missed be not offended,
> Soonest begun is soonest ended.
> The roots of every family tree,
> Trace back to the people of Luxury.

Here spontaneous applause broke out.

> And those I mention at this time,
> Are only here to serve the rhyme.

Catcalls and hoots and laughter greeted this.

> Now since your gifts I hope to earn,
> To my story I'll return.

Bardol composed himself in his chair. He told how the *Fare-Thee-Well* escaped from the Proctor fleets and entered the Pocket. He told how the first colonies were established and how finally, one day, John Death Elliott and the *Fare-Thee-Well* disappeared.

> And what became of Captain Jack,
> And the proud ship *Fare-Thee-Well*?
> That's a secret the Pocket keeps,
> The truth no man can tell.
>
> There are tales of a ghostly freighter,
> Will come like a shooting star,
> Blazing bright with Elmo's light,
> Deadly as arrow that flies in the night,
> Ready to serve and ready to fight,
> If danger comes from afar.

Everyone in the chamber joined in the final stanza. They had been waiting for it.

We of the Pocket remember,
And once every year must tell,
The tale of Death and his sister Bett,
And the proud ship *Fare-Thee-Well*.

Bardol collapsed back in his chair. The roar of the applause made the tapestries stir. One of the singer's attendants filled his clay pipe and lit it and offered it to him. He received it gratefully and turned his chair to the fire. The applause continued while children zoomed round the room imitating the exploits of John Death Elliott destroying Luxury.

'You see,' said Haberjin turning to Peron, 'we are a family.' There were tears in his eyes. 'United by suffering. And the Pocket will never be taken by a human foe.'

'I feel privileged to be here,' said Peron. His words were stiff and awkward, but there was no mistaking his feeling.

Gradually, as the hours slipped by, the mood of the party changed. After the dancing and the singing and the eating and the drinking, people were content to lie back at their ease and just talk. Many were gathered round Bardol who, after his exertions, was tucking into a bowl of the 'prison' food which was the traditional fare of the Great Festival. This was the stew that had been simmering by the fire.

Pettet sat on the floor with his back to the fireplace holding the child Lynn curled up on his lap. She was dreamily combing his beard with her fingers. 'Is it all true?' she asked suddenly. 'Was there really a Captain Death and a ship called the *Fare-Thee-Well*?'

'All true,' rumbled Pettet. 'Elizabeth Elliott's grave is over on Ra. And there are even some pictures down in the library which we think might be the *Fare-Thee-Well*.

It looks like a rare old rocket. But it was big. I've never seen another ship like it.'

'Wasn't it an alien ship then?' This from a small red-headed boy with a face full of freckles.

Haberjin joined the conversation. 'No one can tell. We don't know what it was like inside. But if the ballad is true, it's my guess it had transformation generators.'

'What happened to it?'

'Like the song says, no one knows.'

'It's my thinking,' said Pettet, 'that we'll find that ship one day.'

'You and your dreams,' said Raleigh.

'No, I really think so. Look at some of the things we've found. That old mining torus, that was from olden times. And we've got the charts from those days. I think that one day we'll be looking round the dark side of a moon and we'll find her. I doubt if she'll have crashed. Old John Elliott wasn't the type to crash. He might have run out of fuel or food.'

'I hope I'm there when you do,' said Haberjin. 'I'd like to look under the skin of that old ship.'

'Hope I'm there too,' said the freckled-faced boy.

'Well, I hope I'm not,' said Bardol, joining the conversation for the first time. 'I see it all too clearly, up here.' He tapped his head. 'Reality can be a great disappointment. But I'll tell you this. Sometimes, when I'm deep in the song, I know that I'm really seeing it. It is as though I'm there with them, fighting, burning. The song carries me back.'

'Like telepathy?' asked Peron.

'Bah. Telepathy is for children. I'm talking about something much grander. The songs are a chink in time. The songs give us facts and they give us explanations. They give us living history. If the song says the *Fare-Thee-Well* came from an alien forge, then that's where it came from. And I'll tell you this, too. I don't think you'll ever find the *Fare-Thee-Well*. I think John Elliott destroyed it. I think he dived into a star. Remember, we are not dealing with normal human beings, we are dealing with makers of history. They follow different logic. I think he destroyed the *Fare-Thee-Well*, because it was more than a ship, and its work was done; and so was his work done. There's a lovely old song about that, written in the olden tongue.' The singer reached for his pipe.

'Why do you smoke that thing?' asked Lynn.

'It helps me remember, helps keep my memory clear. There are so many songs. It would take me a year to sing them all.'

He lit the pipe and breathed deeply.

Slowly his seeing eye closed and his blind eye opened.

Later that night, safe in his 'burrow' above the lake, Peron took stock of the day. He seemed to have lived an entire lifetime since his arrival in the Pocket that morning. During most of the day he had tried to be the good historian, weighing facts objectively. Then the party had come, and the singing and the emotion, and objectivity had gone out of the window.

He couldn't remember how the evening ended, though he had a vague memory of staggering home with Haberjin and a couple of other people, and singing songs he had not sung since he was a boy.

They had gone for a swim, that was it. Or at least he assumed they had taken a dip, for he woke up in his room with his clothes still wet on him.

Now his brain had cleared. He didn't feel sleepy at all. He felt brilliant. He wanted to do something, say something, write something.

He found his book placed carefully on the table. That

at least was safe and not damp, though some of the pages smelled of the liquor brewed on Lumb.

What are these people? he thought as he looked at his drawings and notes. What makes them so different?

Peron found a pencil and chewed on the end of it for a few moments, then he began to write.

'All the people in the place called Elliott's Pocket seem to share something. It is not something physical, though in general they are taller and broader than the average assembly of humans. No, it is a quality: a calmness. But it is neither passive nor sedate. It is like the quiet side of exhilaration. The climber who sits at the top of a mountain and looks down the steep slopes to the valley floor from which he has climbed feels something of this . . . as does the pilot who safely brings the big ship to harbour through reefs and shallows. I am in the most dangerous place in the galaxy. Tomorrow the skies may split. But I have never felt safer in my life.'

There. Peron looked at his words and felt pleased. He had managed to say something.

Then he stripped off his clothes and fell flat on his face, asleep.

Paris was not asleep. He didn't know where he was and didn't care. All he knew was that he was in the arms of the most beautiful girl he had ever met and that was all he needed to know.

Nor were Pawl and Laurel asleep. Pawl was on his knees beside his wife with his ear pressed to her belly. 'Ssh. I can hear something.'

'No, you can't. It's far too small.'

'I can. I can.'

'All right, have it your own way.' She stretched. 'I feel wonderful.'

'Just wait until I tell Pettet and Raleigh.'

'They already know. Well, Raleigh does. I told her this evening. She says she'll come to our Homeworld for the birth.'

Many things had happened to Pawl in his life, and now two new events. He was to be a father. That was the first. And Laurel had used the word 'our' to refer to the Paxwax world. Pawl had never heard her do that before.

And what of Odin?

That creature was very still, stooped beneath a willow by the lake. Peron, on his way home, had stopped beside him and said, 'Why don't you talk to me, Odin?' And then he had fallen into the lake and been dragged out.

Except for Raleigh, Peron was the only human contact that Odin had known all day.

Raleigh had been kind and watchful and Odin did not trust her. She had immense reserves of energy. Periodically during the day Odin sent his mind out and tried to contact Pawl, but he was too concentrated on affairs in the Pocket. Later Pawl's mind was sticky with alcohol and Odin could make no sense of him.

Then later still, when the sounds of singing were dying round the lake, had come the bolt of bright blue lightning. Odin felt Pawl's joy like the stab of a salt wind. It had overwhelmed him, squeezing his stone, until the pain and joy became unbearable and he willed himself unconscious.

Laurel pregnant.

He had never expected this.

There was now no way he could carry out his assigned duty.

Logic gave him an escape. Killing Laurel was one thing, but he had no mandate to kill her baby.

He sought refuge in that foolish logic.

It was as well.

Odin was cut off from all contact with the wider galaxy. He did not know that the mission of the Inner Circle had suddenly become even more pressing.

8

AMONG THE OUTER FAMILIES

The trouble began with Laverna Felice.

'Well, aren't we cosy,' she said, screwing up her baby-doll face into a grimace.

Singular Sith, still sleepy since the call to a meeting had come in the middle of the Sith Homeworld night, performed a characteristic gesture, reaching up and gripping his fine spread of horns and running his hands down them. Then he scratched the woolly hair above his forehead and tried to concentrate. 'What do you mean, Laverna?'

Laverna Felice did not reply immediately but turned her violet-eyed gaze on Cicero Paragon. That worthy swung in a gravity harness: his legs could no longer support his slabs of fat. He looked at Laverna. His eyes were bright but slightly unfocused. 'I *was* cosy,' he said, speaking carefully and precisely. 'I hope the interruption has been worth the effort.'

'It has. Or it will be. I feel I can no longer keep silent.'

Singular Sith groaned inwardly but was careful that his feelings did not show on his face. How many times, he wondered, had he humoured the silly woman who ruled the Felice Family. Hundreds. *Now, if she were here*, he thought, *I could pick her up in the palm of my hand and place her on a pedestal where she could fume to her heart's content, and we could all get some sleep*.

But of course she wasn't there. There was no 'where'. There was an abstraction created by the magic of vivante communication. Laverna sat in her doll's house on her Homeworld, though she appeared twice as large as life on the Homeworlds of the Sith and Paragon.

'I am in no mood for riddles,' said Cicero Paragon, 'I was in an important meeting. Important negoshiations . . . Himportant . . .'

'I understand. Well, this too is important. When I said "Aren't we cosy" I was not referring to the whole state of all our empires.'

Singular Sith stuck his bull face forward. He had finally woken up. Though he had no liking for the diminutive Felice, he had a deep respect for their intelligence. Invariably they knew what was going on among the Inner Families before the Sith did and invariably they outguessed them. 'Speak clearly, Laverna. Is there something we should know?'

'Look at us.' The small lady shifted on her throne. 'We have become soft. We have become so used to being cosy that nothing matters any more. We are facing a moral dilemma and I seem to be the only one who sees it.'

'What are you talking about?' This from Cicero, who was now sipping on an astringent solution which made his eyes water. He was becoming rapidly sober.

'I am talking about the Paxwax boy. Have you followed events? First we allow him to defy the Code and marry that fish woman who is not of the Eleven, but now he is apparently out there somewhere – ' she gestured vaguely – 'having fun, while the Shell-Bogdanovich Conspiracy mind his affairs. Time was when if a Master left his Homeworld all the Families would move to attack. But now the Proctor and even the Wong seem to be eating out of his hand. The boy is a menace. If he is allowed to continue in this way he will destroy all of us.'

'How will he destroy us?' Cicero Paragon and Singular Sith spoke together.

'He will destroy our faith in the Code, our faith in our will, our authority.'

'With all due respect, may I say that I doubt that,' said

94

Cicero Paragon. 'May I remind you that Pawl Paxwax is the son of Toby Paxwax and that blood will out. Toby was a fierce Master and so I believe will his son be, despite irregularities.'

'Further,' said Singular Sith, following Cicero's lead, 'the young Master of Paxwax has powerful friends. I do not think it would be wise for we of the Outer Families to question the alliance formed by the Shell-Bogdanovich Conspiracy Second, with the Paxwax.'

'Huh,' said Laverna, 'we all know that the Sith made trade deals with the Paxwax as soon as they could after the war.'

'Business,' said Singular, with a shrug. 'Business. I trade where I can. As do we all. If you are simply jealous . . .'

'Jealousy doesn't enter into it. I am talking about purity. What if I tell you that the Paxwax is having dealings with aliens?'

That statement caused both Singular and Cicero to pause. They looked at one another. Any dealings with aliens were expressly forbidden by the Code. Yet many families used alien inventiveness and endurance to support their empires. Cicero Paragon had teams of Spiderets who worked his mining planets. Singular Sith had farms in which Hooded Parasol were raised and then gassed and put through presses to extract their colours for dyes. It was widely known that the armies of the now defeated Lamprey had been grown from a mixture of alien and human stock. Even so, latent within most humans was a phobia concerning the aliens. While the genetic balance of the leading families regressed in many ways, they yet retained a concept of racial purity; and when a crisis emerged, any crisis, the aliens were the first to be rounded up and blamed.

'Have you forgotten the Code?' Laverna was becoming

shrill as she warmed to her theme. 'The Code was devised by our forefathers to keep us strong. They learned in the Great Push that the weak go to the wall and only the strong survive. Would that we had men like them alive today.' Here she looked at Cicero Paragon, who hung like an over-stuffed baby in the cradle of his anti-gravity unit. 'The alien is an abomination.'

'What makes you think that the Paxwax has dealings with aliens?' asked Singular Sith.

'Was it not a Spideret that caused havoc on the Home-world of the Xerxes?'

'That is only a rumour. And if Clarissa and Jettatura were so silly as to keep a rogue Spideret on their Home-world, in their very Tree even, well . . .'

'And I know that Pawl Paxwax has visited the Home-world of the Hammer.'

'Tell that to the Wong. I didn't even know there still were any Hammer. The Hammer have not been heard of since . . . how long, Cicero?'

'Hundreds and hundreds of years.' He laughed, and as he laughed he quivered. To him, the Hammer were the stuff of ancient history.

'The Hammer are no more than that,' said Singular Sith, snapping his fingers. 'And if Master Pawl Paxwax has visited the Hammer, well, good luck to him. I too have visited alien sites and worlds . . . for hunting. Now if you have nothing further . . .'

'You are fools, both of you. You have forgotten the words of the Anthem. I must inform you both that I intend to raise this matter at the next meeting of the Council of the Eleven, and to show that I am serious I intend to begin a purge of aliens throughout all my worlds. You'll see, the Council will listen to my warning. And then woe betide alien lovers, be they small or big.'

Laverna passed her hand over the vivante plate on her

Homeworld and in that instant she vanished from the Homeworlds of Cicero and Singular. The two men found themselves staring at one another.

'Do you think she has really found something out?' asked Cicero.

Singular Sith gripped his horns and flexed his muscles. 'Well, the Felice have good intelligence. She has probably smelled something.'

'I don't want her stirring up the Families against the aliens again. Why can't the damned woman let things rest? It isn't as though the aliens pose a real threat. I keep mine gelded . . . we smash any eggs we find.'

'Laverna's problem,' said Singular Sith slowly, and with his nostrils flaring at the coming joke, 'is that the Felice are continuing to get smaller with every generation. They need a good bollocking.'

'I'm told,' said Cicero, leaning forward conspiratorially, 'that they can't have sex any more except with one another. It's a matter of size, you see.' He giggled. 'That'll hasten their downfall.'

Singular Sith nodded. 'The day will come, my friend Cicero, and not too far away either, when we will hunt the Felice with cats. You mark my words. Little people.' He spat the words out. 'They always want to rule the worlds. But we must be on our guard. The Felice woman is dangerous. I think I shall have a word with the Inner Circle. They helped calm things down after the Paxwax War. They don't want to see more trouble.'

'Good thinking. And so shall I. I mean, what are the Inner Circle for if not solving disagreements?'

'True.'

The two men broke contact.

Singular Sith returned to his bed.

Not so Cicero Paragon. He sent word out through his

empire to all the worlds where aliens were used and advised them to be on their guard in case of trouble.

Even while he was doing this, Laverna Felice had made her first move. Aliens on the far-flung worlds of her empire were being rounded up.

9

IN ELLIOTT'S POCKET

It seemed to Pawl that he had only just got to sleep when there came a pounding at the door of his burrow. Pettet was there. He was still wearing the clothes he had worn for the party.

'Pawl, you need to see this. Things are changing up top. Emerald Lake is changing. Come on quickly.'

Pawl rolled out of bed heavily and tucked the covers round Laurel, who muttered and murmured and drew her knees up to her chest.

'Coming. Coming.'

'Come on, hurry up.'

'Just let me get my pants on.'

Pawl ran behind the giant Pettet, who pounded down the path by the lake and came to a square door cut into the bedrock of the planet.

'Hold on to your breakfast,' said Pettet, squeezing his frame into the small cubicle. Pawl had to crouch at his feet. 'This is a vacuum chute. It'll have us to the surface in sec – '

The acceleration slammed Pawl to the floor.

And within seconds they stepped out into an observation pod on the surface of Lumb. Outside, the branches of the shrub which covered Lumb pressed against the windows. Haberjin was there, as well as several men and women whom Pawl had met at the party. They were gathered round a large screen which showed Emerald Lake as seen from a telescope on the Way Platform high above the planet.

The people made room for Pawl. On the screen the vast area of gas called Emerald Lake glowed dully. It had lost the brilliance which Pawl had seen there just a few hours previously. Now, hanging above it, serene and still, was a small solar system. This consisted of an intensely bright sun and a giant planet of mottled purple and a small world of shining green.

'What is it?' asked Pawl. 'I thought it would have taken days, weeks, months even for anything to lift clear of Emerald Lake.'

Pettet shrugged. 'Who knows? You are right. But the Pocket . . .'

'Have you been able to make any kind of analysis?'

Haberjin, who was one of those pressed close to the screen, turned to him. 'Analysis, Master Pawl? Some. But it doesn't make much sense. We will know more soon. Right now, every telescope and sensor in the whole of the Pocket is trained on the newcomers. Even the psychics are joining in.'

'Well, tell me.'

'Preliminary data indicates that the sun is brighter than it should be by several magnitudes given its size. It is not big, but it is powerful.'

'And?'

'And that purple blot, if it is a planet, is five times larger than its sun. The small green one is very small. But it is denser than all of them.'

'That doesn't make sense.'

'Not by the laws of normal physics, no.'

'Are we in danger?'

'No more than normal,' rumbled Pettet. 'In fact less so, if our instruments are to be believed. Now that they are clear of Emerald Lake everyone feels better. Everything is working better. Even vivantes can be made. There is no need for panic.'

100

'Are they still moving?'

'We can't tell,' said Haberjin. 'But my guess is that they are not. Now that they are clear of Emerald Lake they seem to have settled. They are waiting.'

'Waiting? Waiting for what?'

Haberjin shrugged. 'Time will tell. But the sooner we get out there and take a look the better, eh maestro?' He was addressing Pettet.

There seemed to be nothing more that could be done for the moment so Pawl broke free from the crowd and moved over to the windows and looked out. The great amorphous bulk of Emerald Lake filled most of the sky. The Snake had set many hours earlier. Even to the naked eye the new sun was brightly visible, though nothing of its two attendant worlds could be seen. Pettet joined Pawl and stood towering beside him.

'Raleigh tells me you have good news. We congratulate you.'

'The best news. You will be coming to our Homeworld for the birth?'

'It will be our pleasure. It will be the first time that either of us have been out of the Pocket.'

Pawl smiled and nodded up to the bright new star. 'Is it a friendly omen?'

'Let us hope so.'

'Where is Raleigh? Why is she not with you?'

'Ah. She is meditating. She is sending her mind out to discover what is up there.'

'And when will she make her feelings known?'

The giant shrugged. 'In her own time. Such things can not be rushed.' Pettet lapsed into silence. He stood gazing upwards, as though he would like to reach out into space and drag the strange star down with his hands. Pawl was aware that once again the giant was not saying all that was on his mind, that he was again struggling with words.

'Speak your mind, Pettet. Are you frightened?'

'The unknown is always frightening. But I have a feeling . . . I think I have seen these three before.'

'Really? Where?'

'I cannot be certain. Old star charts. When we have rested I will make a thorough check. Meanwhile we are on guard. I suggest you sleep now. I just thought you would want to see what is happening.'

'Of course I wanted to see. I'm glad you woke me up.'

The giant yawned, opening his jaws wide and then snapping them shut. 'It has been a good first night to the festival, hasn't it?'

'Very good.'

'Tomorrow we will talk further. I will ask Haberjin to join us.'

'Let us hope that Raleigh meditates well.'

'Let us hope.'

Pawl slept late. When he awoke he was not certain whether the sudden appearance of the small solar system was real or whether he had dreamed it.

Any doubt was soon dispelled. While he and Laurel were enjoying breakfast by the lake, one of Pettet's sons approached them.

'When you have time, Master Pawl, my father requests you join him in his workshop close to the landing bay.'

Both Pawl and Laurel smiled at the formality of the language. It seemed to be a family trait.

'Tell him I will come directly. Do you know why he wishes to see me?'

'Something to do with old charts, I think.'

'Am I invited too?' asked Laurel.

The boy started to blush.

102

'Oh, I am sure you are. I didn't mean to suggest that . . . it is just . . . can your assistant Peron come too?'

'Tell your father that we shall all be there.'

'Thank you.' The boy dived into the lake and did not break the surface until he was halfway to the other side.

It was obvious that Pettet had not slept. Fatigue lines were showing round his eyes and his hair was unbrushed and tumbled down over his shoulders. But still there was something triumphant about him. 'Sit down, sit down,' he said. 'I have a lot to tell you.' Haberjin entered the workroom, dragging two extra chairs with him. He too had the bright-eyed look of a man who has gone without sleep. His jaw was dark with stubble. He placed a chair behind Peron who, ghastly-faced, sank into it. Peron could not believe how hungover he felt.

'This,' said Pettet, 'is what I wanted to show you.' He carefully lifted a frame which measured about a yard square and set it down on a white cloth on the table in front of them. Inside the frame, pressed tight between sheets of clear laminate, was a star chart. It had been hand drawn. Pawl leant forward but could make no sense of the lines and figures and strange hieroglyphs. Pettet held up his hand to forestall any questions.

'Now,' he said, 'one of my hobbies has been collecting old charts like this. I consider myself lucky to have been born in the Pocket, for the Pocket is a museum. Out there – ' he gestured with one of his huge hands in the space above him – 'are countless wrecks. God knows what draws them to the Pocket. Perhaps we are like the Sargasso Sea of old Mother Earth which once trapped sailing ships. Whatever. But out there are alien ships which pre-date the time of the Great Push. There are ships from Earth that were simply captured by alien fleets and directed to their doom in the Pocket like cattle driven over a cliff. This knot of space is, we believe, as old as the galaxy itself, and being ancient it obeys its own laws.

'Anyway, some time ago, Haberjin and I were exploring and we came upon a gravity net in which was trapped an ancient ship.'

'What is a gravity net?' asked Laurel.

'An old alien trick. Two spinning asteroids which trap a ship at their focus. You see, the ship is immobilized, and then they lace the space about it with bombs and when it calls for help any ship which approaches is destroyed. You must have heard of such.'

Laurel hadn't but Pawl nodded.

'Well, we approached cautiously. But there were no bombs. There was no sign of energy. And when we got close enough we understood why. The ship was ancient. Haberjin identified it as one of the early Forager Class ships that were sent out in the first wave of expansion from Earth. Any power unit would have died thousands of years earlier. Any bombs had either detonated themselves or escaped or simply spoiled.

'We closed slowly and sprang the trap by altering the spin of one of the asteroids. We've done it before, but you have to be careful. One of the asteroids exploded. The trapped ship was spat free and we hared after it. We caught it and brought it back here.

'Now, when we opened it up we found that everything had been stripped. There were no bodies. Nothing. It was a mystery.'

'Whoever had ransacked the ship had been looking for platinum,' interrupted Haberjin. 'They'd cut the core out of the engine and they must have been frustrated because they'd smashed everything else.'

'But they hadn't found everything. I found the remains of the old guidance computer and under it I found some vacuum tubes, and when I opened them I found these charts.

'Well, we reckon these are the private maps of the working navigator, whoever he was, God rest his soul. You know, in those days the crew spent months, or even years sometimes, with almost nothing to do and so they used to spend their time making artefacts. We could show you . . . no matter. These maps, and we have all of them, tell the story of the ship's journey from the time it left the Homeworld of Homeworlds up to the time it was captured.

'Look closely at this particular map. Let me take you through it. It is a map of the Pocket as it was when the ship first arrived. We know the name of the ship.' He pointed with a blunt finger to some writing at the top of the chart. 'Can you read that?' The question was directed to Peron. That scholar traced the letters and spelled out the name. *Ka N Di*.

'Right, *Candie*. Something nice to eat. Eh? Strange name for a spaceship, but the ancients were strange. I've managed to translate most of the map. Now what do you think this is?' Pettet pointed to a shape of stars that was coiled.

'Isn't that the Snake?' said Laurel.

'Yes. They called it Serpent, see. That word has almost the same meaning. First time I read that it made me feel as though I'd stepped back in time. They were the same as us, those old navigators. They saw things the same way, had the same fears.'

'What do these words mean?' asked Peron, pointing to a short paragraph close to the Snake and which was joined by a short arrow to the Eye of the Snake. Pettet leant over the map and studied the fine print.

'I can't translate all the words, but here goes.'

105

Another strangeness. This star emits . . . capable of transforming even living tissue to (?marble?). Suspect alien design, though it is difficult to study being so lethal. Warned by fate of 'manta' to stand off. Inv. sq law holds. We are safe at 20.

'Manta,' said Peron, screwing up his face. 'It must be a name for that creature you told us about. Look, there's a drawing of it.' Delicately lined and carefully shaded was a drawing of a creature with a vast solar sail.

Pettet nodded. 'When I saw that I started looking for anything else I could recognize. I found these.' He pointed to a tight binary system. 'We call these Tooth and Claw. The people aboard the *Candie* called them Scylla and . . . I can't make out the last word, but look, they've marked them with a big black cross so some catastrophe occurred there.'

'Is this Emerald Lake?' asked Laurel, pointing to a large shaded area in the centre of the map.

'Yes. They just call it Green Gas. Look, they've added a note.'

Romany II entered this cloud on . . . since which time no message has been received. Given trajectory we expect re-emergence on . . .

'And see, someone else has added a note later. It's not in the same handwriting.'

Romany II sighted as expected. No radio contact. All dead. Ship riddled.

'We think *Romany II* must have been a sister ship of the Forager class.'

Pawl shifted in his seat. 'Look, this is all very interesting, Pettet, and in other circumstances I would like nothing more than for you to explain all the map to me. But what is the significance at present? We have a new

106

star out there. We have strange things going round it. Does . . .'

Pettet held his hand up. 'The map tells us a great deal.' He pushed the frame over close to Pawl and pointed to a thin red line which led away from the sea of green gas to an illustration. Depicted in colour were a large mottled purple world, a bright sun, and a green world. Whoever had drawn this map had evidently considered this strange configuration to be very important, for they had placed a red ring round it. Printed beside each of the objects was the name the early navigators had given it. The mottled world was Erix, the small sun was Candle, and the bright green world was called Ultima Thule. 'You see. *They* have been here before. The people who drew this map saw them, and what's more, thought them important. Look, they've put black crosses by them.'

'And the writing by them, what does it mean?' asked Pawl.

'Be prepared for disappointment,' said Pettet. 'I can't make sense of most of it. And the rest is too faded.'

'Well, tell us what you can.'

Pettet hunched over the map again, and followed the words with his finger, translating as he went.

. . . stayed more days than we wanted . . . deep feeling in all of us . . . escaped by courage. On U. Thule dead Ralph was on our minds and we saw him running by silver . . . (?fern?) . . . three more are lost running . . . abandoned them.

We will not return to the land where the dead live. Warning beacon set at . . . Saw many ruined ships. Evidence of the alien . . . trees like giant mushrooms which burned with silver fire . . . Home now, and none too soon.

'You see. Most of it doesn't make sense. Is Ultima Thule the land where the dead live? And who was Ralph? Was he a crewman? And was he dead? And who were the

107

three who were lost running? And what was the silver fire? There are more questions than answers.'

Pettet sat down.

'Even so,' said Pawl. 'Obviously the ancients felt that these worlds were important. Just the kind of enigma upon which you people who live in the Pocket thrive. I don't think we'll learn much more until you go out there and investigate.'

'Hear, hear,' said Haberjin softly.

And at that moment the door opened and Raleigh joined them. She seemed to have aged ten years. She took her seat beside Pettet and slipped her arms round his arm and rested her head against him.

'I could make no contact,' she said. 'But there is life there. It held me away. I could no more reach it than I could batter my way through these walls with my fists. It is deadly but not cruel. It is *other*, and we should have no part in it.'

10

AMONG THE FAMILIES

The most widespread race of aliens used by the human Masters of the Families were the Spiderets.

These creatures had quick brains and were superb engineers. On countless worlds they kept machinery ticking, and their ability to tolerate high gravity and thin air made them ideal pioneers. They were, however, recognized as dangerous. Gelded of their fangs they became dull and lethargic, and so most of the working Spiderets were left intact and treated with respect.

It was a simple matter for Laverna Felice to manufacture a revolution.

On a pleasant world called Janus, a world owned by the Felice, an order was received that all Spideret eggs and nests were to be destroyed. The men and women who managed the distillation plants on this world scratched their heads. 'But if we destroy the eggs, where will we get the next generation of Spiderets to clean the crucibles and gather the Seppel nuts?' Janus was the Homeworld of Seppel juice.

Despite their queries the order could not be disobeyed and so a detachment of the local militia, wearing protective gear, descended into the catacombs where the Spiderets lived. They were equipped with gas bombs and high-pressure spray guns which ejected a sticky acid that burned its way into anything which it touched.

For a whole day they strolled through the catacombs, firing up into the clusters of nests where the young Spiderets were growing. Any mature Spiderets which they met, such as those who were attending the nests, they gassed and burned.

With their work completed they returned to their homes and families.

That night the Spiderets attacked.

It was a hopeless attack, fuelled only by rage. The worker Spiderets, who had returned to find their nests ravaged, scrabbled with their legs against the walls, and tried to bite their way through the milk-white domes within which the humans lived. They went on a rampage, smashing the ventilation ducts and tearing open the filter pipes so that the precious Seppel liquor gurgled out and poured into the soil.

All of this was recorded on vivante for Laverna by a startled crew who, believing they had been sent to Janus to make a promotional documentary, found themselves caught in revolution.

Laverna showed this vivante to Helium Bogdanovich. He lay on his back in his bath with the surface of the water lapping just below his eyes. At the end of the vivante Helium reared up, sending a small tidal wave slopping round the walls. Laverna turned her eyes delicately away when he revealed his great grey sleek bulk. In truth, Laverna found the walrus fatness of Helium Bogdanovich and his wife Clover Shell repulsive. But now was not time to be squeamish or risk offence. She was not dealing with an obese creature such as Cicero Paragon. This was Helium Bogdanovich, Master of the third greatest empire in the known galaxy.

'Why,' asked Helium, his eyes wrinkling down to slits, 'did they attack? What provoked them? Spiderets are not fools.'

That was the question Laverna was waiting for. She turned her bright purple eyes full on Helium. 'I believe

110

that the aliens on our worlds are restless. They have sensed a change in our policies since we allowed your good friend, the Master of Paxwax, to break the Code and marry a girl of some lower family. That action has been taken and we must live with it, and forgive me, for I do not wish to question the collective wisdom of the Masters of the Families. After all, I was one who gave consent to that liaison. But we would be foolish to close our eyes to its consequences.'

Helium stirred the water. He felt caught, though he did not suspect a trap. As a defender of the Code he had argued with Pawl not to marry Laurel Beltane but had finally accepted that Pawl was adamant. Still, the marriage had worried him. He had wondered what the repercussions would be.

Niggling in his mind was the fear that the Felice woman might just be right.

'I will talk with Clover Shell,' he said. 'Meanwhile, may I ask, why have you contacted me particularly? Have you spoken to the Proctor First? The Wong? The Xerxes? The Paxwax?'

'Helium, you are a man of action. You have shown that in the recent war. That is why I have spoken to you first, though I have already made my fears known to the Sith and the Paragon. In answer to your second question, I intend to speak to the other Families directly.'

'Then Laverna,' said Helium, leaning forward suddenly so that his finely-haired face filled the entire vivante space, 'please accept a warning. In making your news known, do not seek to undermine the Paxwax. Do I need to say more?'

'No,' said Laverna.

She broke contact and Helium's face shrank to a point of light and then vanished.

Laverna shivered. Then she smiled to herself.

Methodically she tapped out the code which would link her with the Proctor First.

Helium Bogdanovich swam back and forth for several minutes, diving and bursting up through the surface and slapping his platelike hands on the water. Then he heaved his bulk out of the water and shook himself, sending up a fine spray. He padded off to find Clover Shell.

The Shell-Bogdanovich Conspiracy used many aliens in their far-flung empire.

11

IN ELLIOTT'S POCKET

There was, of course, no question of following Raleigh's warning. A full expedition was planned to travel out to the new star and its strange planets. The people who dwelt in the Pocket had faced danger many times. They had found that the best defence was to be inquisitive.

Pawl and Laurel, and even the festival in honour of John Death Elliott, took second place.

Lumb became the headquarters and main clearing house for new information. Every sensor and telescope in that part of the Pocket was trained upon the new arrivals. It was quickly discovered that Erix, despite its size, was not solid. It seemed to have an atmosphere like jelly and nothing could be discovered about its actual surface. It appeared totally dead, inert.

Candle was just a sun, consuming itself, indistinguishable from thousands of other suns, except for its brightness.

Ultima Thule was a complete enigma. Psychics in all parts of the Pocket attested that they could feel a very strong power there, but that was all. An unmanned probe which flew past the world lost all contact with Lumb and returned with its photographic plates black. Messages of all kinds were beamed at the small planet but elicited no response. Dicyanin plates however, exposed on Lumb, showed the green world to have a first magnitude aura. There was no doubt that life of a very vital, but perhaps unknown form existed on Ultima Thule.

* * *

The strangeness of the team of investigators who gathered on Lumb matched the strangeness of the newcomers. Raleigh and Laurel travelled up to the Way Gate to meet them.

First to arrive was Cordoba. She hobbled from the Way Gate on a pair of sticks. By reputation she was one of the most powerful psychics that the Pocket had produced. She had gypsy eyes which seemed to read all secrets. She lived alone, since the death of her husband, on one of the small asteroids which made up the tail of the Snake. In her time she had mothered seven children and had foreseen the death of six of them. It was this experience that gave her eyes their candour. She hobbled past Laurel and Raleigh, guided by her youngest daughter, and down into the shuttle station. She gave them scarcely a glance.

'Is she not well?' asked Laurel.

'No. She's dreaming. Most of us are. Her mind is out there.' Raleigh nodded to the windows beyond which glimmered the green vastness of Emerald Lake. 'She's usually a jolly woman. She's an old friend of Bardol.'

Again the transit light blinked on to announce a new arrival. When the Way Gate doors slid open two men stepped out. The first was a giant like Pettet, but where Pettet was dark and swarthy like a wrestler, this man was graceful with a perfectly-formed face and a mass of blond curls which tumbled down on to his shoulders.

'That is Tank, the painter,' murmured Raleigh. 'He made the portrait of John Death Elliott that is hanging in the entrance way.'

'A painter? Why are they sending a painter out to Ultima Thule?'

Raleigh shrugged. 'Well, the photographs have failed. And besides, Tank is no ordinary painter. He shows not only the outside of something, but also what is really there. I find him quite frightening.'

'And the other man?'

'Ah, that is Wystan. You'll like him. He's quite mad. He believes, really believes, that he should not have been born a human being at all, but should have been a plant. A honeysuckle, I think. He talks to plants.' Laurel laughed at this. 'And what's more, he says they talk back to him. He refuses to live in a house. He has a cave over in the university grounds on Ra.'

Laurel turned and hid her laughter from the two new arrivals. 'And why is he included in this quest? He seems less likely than Tank.'

'Many of us believe that what lives up there on Thule is not animal life as we know it. We think it might be closer to plant life, and if that is the case, Wystan may be able to make sense of them. He is a rare mystic. Come on, I'll introduce you to both of them.'

On their way down to the surface of Lumb, Laurel had a chance to observe the three people who would shortly be travelling out to the new solar system. They were perfectly at their ease, yet each seemed enveloped in their own silence. Cordoba sat very still, with her hand baggage on her knees. From time to time small smiles flitted across her face as though she were listening to a well-told, amusing story.

Tank sat hunched, his immense shoulders pressed into a corner. He watched everything: the play of the light across the backs of his hands, the way Cordoba held her bag, the inclination of a head. His hands were massive, with fingers like sausages, and Laurel found herself wondering how hands so rough could create such exquisite drawings. Once she found him staring at her. It was not unpleasant, but there was something voracious about his eyes, something which reminded her of Pawl, and she was glad when he looked away.

Wystan was a compulsive talker. He talked about anything, with his mind leaping laterally from topic to topic. But once, when they were passing through the high branches of the shrub which covered Lumb, he paused and placed the flat of his hand against the window. Obediently, it seemed, a frond of the shrub snaked out and matched the place where his hand rested. Then they were past. Laurel was surprised that no one else seemed to have noticed.

That night the festival continued and Bardol sang. It became something of a farewell party, for the next day the small team of investigators was due to depart. Pettet was to captain the ship and Haberjin, naturally, was the pilot.

'Master Pawl, Master Pawl. Can I ask you something?' It was Peron, and clearly he had something preying on his mind. 'Yes, Peron. Do you want to take copies of the maps back to Homeworld?'

'Yes, er, no. Well, I do, but that wasn't what I wanted to ask. I was wondering if I might ask to accompany the expedition. There is room on the ship. It would be a great adventure for me. I have led the quiet life of a scholar and . . . well, I would return to Bennet Homeworld naturally, as soon as the expedition returned.'

Pawl looked at Peron. The scholar was so eager. He reminded Pawl of a puppy dog that scents there may be a walk in the offing. 'Go, if you have a mind to and if they have room. I wish I could join in myself, but the affairs of the Paxwax . . .' He let the sentence trail away. That very morning he had received word from Helium Bogdanovich that he should return to his Homeworld as soon as

116

possible: some trouble was brewing. 'Make plenty of vivantes. And when you come back I shall want to hear everything that has happened.'

Peron beamed, and without more ado set off to find Pettet.

The next day, most of the people who lived on Lumb, and those who were visiting for the festival, gathered at the main subterranean hangar.

Standing ready was a huge prospecting ship, the one which Pettet and Haberjin used when they went exploring. Its name was *Lotus*. Without any undue formalities the crew began to embark. Tank carried a satchel on his back containing his paints and brushes. He helped Cordoba climb up the high gangway and through the spherical hole which led into the ship. Both paused and waved before going on board.

One-eyed Bardol cupped his hands round his mouth and called, 'Come back safe, witch-woman, and tell me all the news. I want to write a song about this.'

'Well, make sure you're still alive when I get back,' she called and went inside.

Tank took a deep breath and ducked inside without saying anything. *That man does not like living in confined spaces*, thought Laurel. *I must make sure to get copies of his paintings*.

Wystan and Haberjin clowned on their way up the gangway and then at the top bowed formally to each other and tried to cram through the doorway together.

Next came Peron. He was paler than usual with excitement, and muttered a clumsy farewell to Pawl before climbing the gangway two steps at a time.

Last was Pettet. He kissed Raleigh and she whispered something in his ear and then pushed him away with a smile. He came to Pawl and Laurel. 'Take care of one

117

another,' he said. 'We love you both. I'll bring back a bit of green cheese from that world up there as a birthday gift for the little one.'

'Away, man. You take care of yourself. And take care of Peron. I need him to write the history of the Paxwax.'

Pettet grinned. 'He'll be safe with us.'

Then he too was gone and the spherical door closed and the gangway drew back.

'Is that all?' asked Laurel. 'I expected fanfares and trumpets.'

'That's all,' said Raleigh. 'We think it is unlucky to make too much of a fuss, no matter how important the assignment. Come on. We'll watch them take off from the control room.'

Quickly the hangar emptied of people. Pawl and Laurel climbed to an enclosed observation pod high on the walls. They watched as the hangar was pumped clear of air. Then bright blue fire crackled over the surface of the ship.

'Elmo's light,' said Raleigh. 'Now watch.'

One entire wall of the hangar began to slide back, revealing the crazy polychrome sky of the Pocket.

Silently the ship lifted and then began to glide forward. It gathered speed rapidly, barrelling towards the opening, and then suddenly it was out from the planet and its particle engines flared and lit up the entire inside of the hangar. The doors began to close.

'So they're gone,' said Laurel, 'just like that.'

'Just like that,' said Raleigh. She was crying. 'Pay no attention to me. I'm always like this when they set out. You'd think by now I would have learned better.'

'Where was Paris?' asked Pawl as he and Laurel made their way back to their cave home. 'I hoped he would be there to say goodbye and *bon voyage* to Pettet.'

'Well, where was Pettet's daughter come to that?' said

118

Laurel. 'I imagine they wanted to be there. I think they have become very involved with one another. I haven't seen much of Paris at all.'

They wandered on round the lake, hand in hand, in silence.

'And here is someone else I haven't seen,' said Pawl finally, pointing to a stooped, domed figure that sat beneath a tree close to the water's edge.

'Don't disturb it now,' said Laurel. She had enjoyed the last few days, free from the presence of Odin. She wished the small creature would stay on in the Pocket or return to the Inner Circle. With Odin about she never felt that Pawl was completely hers.

'I must talk to him,' said Pawl. 'If we are leaving tomorrow . . . well, at least he needs to be ready. I wonder what he makes of the Pocket and the strange planets. I promised Pettet I would ask him.'

'Suit yourself. I'm going back to the cave. Try not to be too late.'

Laurel walked on, and then on an impulse stepped out of her light clothes and dived into the lake. Pawl watched her for a few moments and then crossed the small margin of grass and squatted down beside Odin. He thought of the fringed red feelers which were their call sign but could detect no presence of Odin. He prodded the dark-robed figure with his finger and felt a mushy resistance. 'Come on, wake up, Odin. I need to talk to you.' Again Pawl concentrated on the image of red tendrils creeping like worms.

Odin was not asleep. He was very much aware of Pawl but he was not sufficiently collected to begin communication. Like most of the psychics in the Pocket, Odin's attention was far out above Emerald Lake where Ultima Thule turned. He had been transfixed ever since the world emerged.

Unlike most of the psychics, who could not make sense of the impressions they received, Odin felt a sting of recognition. He had experienced those muscular thought-forms before. He had stood under them. Odin knew with certainty that the world which the humans called Ultima Thule was the Homeworld of the Tree that lived on Sanctum. He tried to make some impression on the psychosphere of that world but he was beaten back. It was a world on guard. He could not mesh with any of its thought-forms, though he tried with every fibre of his being.

And when he felt Pawl approach and was aware of his nudging, Odin slowly began to withdraw. Deep inside him a slow peristalsis began and his basal sucker contracted. He began to withdraw his roots from the rich loam by the lakeside. Finally he felt sufficiently composed to respond to Pawl.

Odin's presence uncoiled in Pawl's mind like a bright red flower opening in the sun. 'Master Pawl, it has been some time.'

Pawl shaped his own thoughts. 'At last. I am glad to know you are there. I was beginning to worry.'

'I am here. The time for us to leave is growing close, isn't it?'

'Yes. Tomorrow. Evidently there is some trouble among the Families. I must return. I want you by me.'

Silence.

'Have you enjoyed your time in the Pocket?' asked Pawl.

'It has been instructive. But now I am ready to leave.'

'Do you know about all the excitement? Everything that has happened?'

'I have followed events. I hope your friends will be safe, and young Peron.'

'Can you make anything of what is out there?'

120

'Nothing except that it is very powerful. But I do not think they are heading into great danger.'

'I have a lot I want to ask you.'

Odin sighed his understanding. 'And we shall have time, Master Pawl. But now I must rest. Journey through the Way Gate is harder on me than on you and I am a slow creature.'

'Then we shall see you tomorrow.'

Pawl left Odin where he was. He was surprised at how tired the creature's thought-form seemed. *But*, he reasoned to himself, *the Pocket affects different people different ways*. He was glad that Odin did not seem to smell danger in the future.

When he arrived back at his sleeping cave, Pawl found Laurel deep in conversation with her brother Paris.

'Paris doesn't want to go. He says he's been invited to stay on, and that Raleigh's daughter has arranged to take him on a tour of the whole of the Pocket.'

'Lucky Paris,' said Pawl. 'Do you think you can be trusted on your own?'

'No.' Paris grinned.

'Well, we hope to see you back on our Homeworld for the birth of your niece or nephew.'

Paris's eyes opened wide and he looked back to Laurel and then back to Pawl and then to Laurel again. 'You never told me about that.'

'I was keeping it as a surprise.'

'Well, of course I'll be back.' The young man looked suddenly cocky. 'You never know. We might have more than one surprise.' But he would say no more. He quickly shook Pawl's hand and then kissed Laurel and ran out of the cave and down to the lake. He dived with a somersault. And as Pawl and Laurel watched him depart they saw him joined by another swimmer in the middle of the lake.

Paris did not know that was the last time he would see his sister alive.

The next morning they arose early and joined with Odin and Raleigh and journeyed up to the Way Gate. The only news that had been received from Pettet and the crew aboard the *Lotus* was that they were holding course for the new worlds and preparing to make a short jump.

'They'll be all right,' said Pawl to Raleigh. 'Probably having the time of their lives.'

'But I wish I'd insisted and gone with them,' she said. 'All the same.'

They moved into the Way Gate proper and made their last goodbyes. 'So I'll expect to see you in about six months,' said Laurel, giving Raleigh a hug.

'We'll all be there,' said Raleigh.

'Send Peron straight back when he returns,' called Pawl as the Way Gate slid closed.

Alone now, they moved into the Way Chamber and settled on the long silver platform. Pawl helped Odin, gripping him about the waist and lifting him until his sucker could gain purchase on the highly polished surface.

Then the lights began to flicker, dipping from white to violet as the transformation generators took effect.

Within minutes they were on their way.

The next sound that they heard was the refrain of the Paxwax anthem, sung by a welcoming choir.

They had arrived above Pawl's Homeworld.

12

DEEP IN SPACE IN ELLIOTT'S POCKET

At about the point where Lumb could no longer be seen by the naked eye, Haberjin aligned the bright sun called Candle in the cusp of the transformation generators and set the guidance computers in action. Candle was about 15 lems distant and the jump had to be carefully planned. He wanted to arrive just above the mottled purple planet, Erix. That jump was at the limit of the ship's capability.

He made sure they were all comfortable and then fired them into a tunnel of blackness. At the end of the darkness lay a point of purple light, which expanded until it filled the entire cabin. When they awoke they found Erix peering through all their windows. Every shiny surface within the cabin glimmered with its mauve light.

The crew climbed from their bunks and peered out at the vast planet.

'Do you know what I think that planet looks like?' said Haberjin. 'I think it looks like an eye.'

'Where's the iris and the pupil?' asked Wystan.

'I didn't say it *was* an eye. It just looks like one. The same wetness. The same softness. I mean, an eye outside the body is just a bag of jelly, isn't it? And it looks so vulnerable. I feel that if we were to land we would cut it open and that purpleness would ooze out and stain everything.'

They looked in silence as the planet slowly turned.

'Can you feel anything down there?' asked Pettet, directing his attention towards Cordoba.

The old woman sat forward with her eyes closed.

'Something,' she said. 'Not life. Not life as we know it. No, definitely not life.'

'I would like to get closer,' said Tank. 'I would like to land and wade in that purple sea.'

'Purple is the colour of poison,' said Wystan. 'Purple plants are invariably poisonous. I would like to see what causes that purple.'

'And you, Peron. What do you make of it?'

The scholar studied the planet through slit eyes. 'I agree with Haberjin. I think it looks vulnerable. But I don't think it is. The colour makes me feel sick.'

Pettet nodded. 'My feelings exactly. Take us down, Haberjin. But with care. Be ready to lift if anything starts to happen.'

The descent was slow. Haberjin experienced some difficulties in the upper atmosphere as a result of fluctuations in the planet's gravity. The ship behaved like a skittish horse. But eventually they found themselves skimming through the upper pink clouds. They were dense and cloying and slowed the ship.

They sank lower.

Pink became mauve . . .

Mauve became a clotted purple which pressed all round the ship.

It began to drag them down.

Cordoba screamed and covered her ears, and at that moment the ship tore free of the upper atmosphere. Above them the sky boiled like froth. There was a great gash where they had cut through and, as they watched, it closed like tight-pressed lips above them.

Then the pain began. It began as a dull ache in the mind which quickly grew to a searing, brilliant anguish which spread out via the throat to the arms, chest and legs. They stumbled apart, clawing at themselves.

They hurt till they were numb and then the pain slowly ebbed away, leaving a residue of despair. In that moment, each of them lost something of their store of innocence, and knew it.

They stared down, faces pressed white against windows, and each of them looked at the surface of the planet. Each saw a version of Hell.

Haberjin stared at a rocky desert. It stretched to infinity, bleak and featureless on all sides. There was no life. No possibility of life. No games here. No bright tavern with the laughter of girls at the long day's end. Just a slow, lonely death. A pointless life followed by a meaningless, insignificant death.

Soon, inevitably, they would crash. The stones would tear through the flimsy ship. The ship would turn cartwheels in the murky air as it came apart.

Why wait? Why not get it over with now? All so pointless. Better oblivion soon and the fine pall of drifting purple sand.

Haberjin reached forward and routinely began to close the doomed ship down. The instrument readouts froze and then faded. The lights in the cabin flickered and died. The fans which wafted air through the ship ran down. An alarm bell sounded briefly and then it too stuttered to silence.

In absolute silence Haberjin sat in the purple gloom and waited for the ship to crash.

Cordoba lay in a pool of her own blood. She wanted to bite as the contractions racked her, but there was nothing to bite. She reached out for loving hands, but there were no loving hands, just a distant, mocking laughter.

An easy birth. Ha! No one had told her that it hurt so much. She wondered what manner of creature it was that

125

lay coiled in her great humped belly. She felt so sweaty and dirty and out of control . . . wouldn't someone come to help her? Where was he? Why wasn't he there with his strong hands, helping?

Between her legs there was darkness and in that darkness she saw her husband, as he laughed and kissed his way into another woman's heart and body.

Up! She wanted to be up and away. She twisted and flailed with her arms but everywhere she turned he was there. Killing love as easily as you can crush an egg between the palms of your hands. 'I hate you, witch-woman,' he murmured.

The words burned her. Burned her mind to flakes of black ash. Burned her throat and her stomach. Burned in her veins. There was no relief. Where could she turn? Hands against ears like doves to stop the voice. And the doves blossomed in flame.

Relentlessly the baby chewed its way from her like a maggot and departed.

Still her husband laughed . . .

Wystan stood on a bank above a lake. In the clear depths fat, brown-backed trout nosed the weeds which billowed as the water moved. Wystan was preparing to dive when he saw faint wisps of steam rise from the still surface of the lake.

As he watched, the fish flicked with their tails, darting about. They were trying to escape. Something was wrong. One fish turned and drove upwards, breaking the surface and leaping for the sky. It fell back, landing in its own lather. The fish were becoming frantic. They blundered and bit. Large bubbles rose from the lake bed.

Slowly the lake came to the boil.

The fish died and bobbed to the surface, bellies up. The water weed cooked and shrivelled.

The lake became a white cauldron.

The water boiled away. The last beads scurried round the lake bed like insects and then were gone. The stones whitened and cracked. The dead weeds puffed into blue smoke, writhed and were gone. The bones of the fish crisped and broke. Gone. All gone.

A searing whiteness at the end of life. Wystan felt himself fall spread-armed into that whiteness.

Peron heard the march of soldiers. He stood in a library. On the shelves around him were volumes and cubes which contained the entire accumulated wisdom of the human race. He was the defender.

He heard beating at the door. He saw the door blacken with fire. He saw it splinter and split. Soldiers with the faces of wolves burst into the library and began firing. They set the library alight. They tied him by the wrists and suspended him above the pyre of books.

They laughed as he screamed, lifting his legs up to his chest, and then lowered him into the glowing ashes.

Pettet watched himself helplessly as his hand reached out and picked up a blue porcelain vase by one of its lugs. He held it up. So fine was the working that the light revealed patterns where the potter's fingers had rested. It was a vase for fine aromatic oils: useful and beautiful, the cornerstones of all art.

He took the vase and dropped it down a well. It turned as it fell until it smashed, and the world came to an end in a spatter of broken fragments.

Beautiful objects hold entropy at bay.

Pettet stared at what he had done and felt accursed.

Consider then Tank. Tank saw chaos. A jabber of sparks against blackness. The ghostly flicker of thoughts without form, almost unimaginable.

127

Then he saw a universe gather and die and gather again and die again . . . and so on . . . An interminable round of senseless creation and destruction.

He saw his own pictures march past like playing cards and on into darkness.

He saw a torn bellows. A portrait with a knife in it. A statue with the face eroded to blankness.

He saw these things and was tempted to despair, but still he stared.

About him gathered a sea of bright particles. He reached out and they flowed round his hand. When he tried to seize them they poured away. When he tried to scoop them into piles they collapsed with idiot giggles. Useless. Useless to try and do anything with these.

Tank felt tiredness . . . but his eyes would not close. Tiredness . . . but a question formed. *Who tore that bellows? What fool would tear a bellows?*

The question was funny. It made him laugh. And at the same time it made him sad and angry. *And what kind of mind sticks a knife in a portrait? And who allows the sand to destroy the beauty of a face?*

There were no answers. Certainly the idiot particles which swarmed round and over his hand were not stirred by the questions. Tank stared and his eyes were grey and unblinking. He stared at the tumbling particles and devoured them with his eyes, drawing their madness from them. He cupped his hand as though holding water and bade the particles stay. Slowly he closed his hand and squeezed. When he opened his hand he held mud. He shaped the mud with his thick artist's fingers and it held the form he gave.

Obedient to his will the teeming landscape came to a halt. Time held while Tank gazed into the frozen darkness and knew it for what it was.

* * *

Subjective time. Who knows how long Tank stared into Hell, the uncreative centre of the universe, before he rose and groped his way across to Haberjin.

Haberjin was crouched, staring into destruction. He had died within. Pettet lay crying. Blood ran from a self-inflicted wound in Cordoba's stomach, though she was still breathing. Peron was twisted in a corner whimpering to himself. Wystan lay flat with his tongue bitten and his eyes white as eggs in his coal-black face.

Outside the landscape did not move under Tank's gaze, but the pressure upon him was enormous.

Tank banged the controls of the ship. He swept his hand across all switches.

The fan started. An alarm bell clanged. Music blared. Lights flashed. Guns fired. Beds warmed. Toilets voided. Water boiled. The ship came alive all at once. Tank turned the ship and pointed it upwards. Light as a feather under his will it began to rise.

There was no growl, for Hell has neither will nor anger.

Looking up through the great window Tank saw the boiling cloud base. He fed power to the engines and the great transformation generators meshed. He edged the ship to full acceleration and it leaped forward and ripped a hole in the pink and purple clouds. Behind it was left a maelstrom which quickly closed.

The *Lotus* dived into the clean blackness of space. As it left the atmosphere of Erix behind, the nightmares which had paralysed the crew retreated. When it was high above the planet, Tank cut the power, and let the ship drift.

Haberjin was recovering. He crawled through to the toilet and returned in a few moments, looking pale but capable of action. Tank pointed to Cordoba. Haberjin carried her as quickly as he could to the sickbay and began to treat her wound. Pettet too was recovering. He was on his knees blinking in disbelief. 'I thought I killed the beauty of the world,' he whispered to Tank, and then shrugged, for he did not understand the meaning of his own words.

Tank concentrated on Wystan. He released his tongue from his throat and administered a mild shock which made the man's eyes close and his fingers and toes clench. Then he sat him up, but Wystan drooped.

Tank did not know what Wystan had experienced, but having seen Hell he had some idea of how it worked. He picked up the semiconscious Wystan and lugged him through to the shower room. He sat him in the shower and turned the water on. He let it run cold and soak into Wystan's hair and clothes. Having made certain that there was no way that Wystan could drown, he left him to steep.

Then Tank made his way to his cabin. He locked his door and collapsed on to his bunk. He lay and shook like an animal that sleeps in pain. For though it is true that Hell has no will, it can stain, and Tank had looked on it and it was in his mind, it was in his hair; something of it would always be in his eyes. He would never again draw a line without thinking of deception.

Many hours passed.

In the sickbay Cordoba began to recover. As soon as she came to herself she knew what had happened, and she cursed herself for being such a fool. She above all should have been safe. She, mother of seven, who had brought forth babies with careful hands and laid out dead men: she should have recognized the pattern of anti-life. She who knew what it was to love and be loved.

Propped up beside her was a picture of her husband holding their first son. It had been placed there by Haberjin, who sometimes surprised himself with his

130

thoughtfulness, and who was never wrong when he followed his instincts. Cordoba picked up the picture and held it, rubbing her thumb across it.

She willed herself to remember. She remembered lying in the cabin with the frightful laughter in her ears. She remembered calling out and reaching for the big man with the long blond hair who sat with his fists clenched, fighting. She knew he was fighting an invisible enemy and she knew it was Tank. Then he stood up in the dark cabin and shouted in pain and defiance – it was the cry of a baby – and it was the first sound of hope.

And where was Tank now? She let her mind flow out through the ship and found him curled and shaking. She brought what balm she could. She laid blessings about his head. But she knew the limits of his power and could only hope.

Sitting up in her bed and with the picture of her husband beside her, she combed her long grey hair. Then she manicured carefully, cleaning every scrap of dirt from under her fingernails.

Pettet entered the sickbay. He had a ribbon in his hands. 'Here, tie this in your hair. Make you look a real Romany.'

Pettet glowed. He had stood in a particle shower and the accumulated static electricity made his thick black curly hair stand out like a corona. 'Feeling better?' he asked.

'Better. Calmer. A bit of a fool. It came so suddenly, I was not prepared. But that is the way of accidents, isn't it? Where are the others?'

'Wystan's in the greenhouse. Where else? He wants to be alone. Peron is in his cabin trying to write in his book.'

'And Tank and Haberjin?'

'Tank's door is locked but I spoke to him. He just wants to be alone. Haberjin's on his way here. You'll

131

know when he's coming. He smells as though someone's dragged him through a lilac bush.'

'And you?'

'Coming right. But I still have this feeling of guilt, as though I'd done something unforgivable and something in me had died. Where are we? What was that place?'

Before Cordoba could answer Haberjin approached the door. As Pettet had predicted, the smell of synthetic flowers preceded him. He was shaved and oiled, and looked like Mephisto. He had trimmed his beard to a fine point and set drops in his eyes to make them sparkle. He had changed his usual overalls for a brilliant blue and yellow shirt.

He crossed to Cordoba's bed and took one of her hands between his. 'Feeling better, old woman? Does it hurt?' He pointed to Cordoba's stomach, where she had wounded herself.

'Of course it hurts. And the pain is helping me. Keeping my feet on the ground. But we will none of us ever be quite the same again.'

'Let's not talk of it,' said Haberjin. 'See, I've brought a bottle. What say you, captain, to a drink?' He broke the seal and fetched three glasses.

'We must talk of it,' said Cordoba.

Each of them told of their experiences. Cordoba listened and nodded as Haberjin and Pettet spoke. Then she drained her glass and held up her hand for silence. 'Now let me tell you what I think,' she said. 'That place is as old as the universe itself. When the great creative will made light and time in one moment, there was reaction. Small, when compared to the great imaginative act of creation, but *there* nevertheless, like little black whirl-pools. The anti-creation.'

132

Haberjin interrupted. 'Do you mean like anti-matter? That's common enough.'

'No, not like anti-matter. Anti-matter and black holes and the rest of that paraphernalia were all part of creation. This was wholly other, a reaction of the act of creation itself. Its essence is negative. It draws from life its spirit, and leaves a shell. It takes form from shape and the shell dissipates.'

'We were close to death.'

'Absolute death. No spirit survives that passing. Even God has his limits.'

'Having felt its power,' said Pettet, 'I am glad that I can still move my hand and enjoy wine. But it mastered me. I was wet as a baby. Tank, though: he came through. Why?'

'Tank is the most injured of all because he was the strongest.'

'Why is he strongest?'

'Wait a moment. Don't rush me. Give me more of that wine and I'll try to tell you.' Haberjin filled her glass. 'Strength. Weakness. Sometimes I can't tell one from the other. Listen, I'm going to tell you a story. Don't get anxious. You can't rush an old woman, and you might learn something. Long ago, when I was a small girl, my mother took me to stay with my grandfather. It was the time when they were hollowing out some asteroids and they didn't want children about in case something went wrong. Well, you may have heard of my grandfather. His name was Oban. He was a bit of a magician. He used to read the stars. Said he could see the wind and feel water flowing underground. Well, my grandfather was a stickler for education. "Your brain'll get you out of more muddles than luck will," he used to say, and he'd have me chanting the times table, and the names of herbs, and the stars of the Pocket. Sometimes he made me speak words of the old tongue even though I didn't know what they meant.

'Anyway, one day he took me out to the Needles. Have you heard of the Needles of Ra? You must have. It is an alien graveyard. Dates back to when the Pocket was young, I expect. When we got there it was about midday. I remember the twin suns; the blue and the red were about to cross. My grandfather picked me up and set me down on the Blood Stone. "Watch the shadows," he said, and I did. I watched the shadows change colour.

'There was one big stone in front of me. It was like an animal that was sleeping. I stared at it. I could feel the sun on my hair. The clouds were drifting by above. There was a bird singing in one of the thorn bushes. And as I looked it seemed as if the shadows grew darker and the light grew brighter. I felt I was no bigger than a grain of dust beside those great stone pillars.

'And as I watched, the spirit of the hill beside me crawled out like a dark beast to sun itself. The spirit of the stone in front of me stretched and spoke.

'Then the time was past. The twin suns split, the earth became grey again, the Needles became just stone. The beasts were gone.

'But it was all different. The landscape could never be the same. The ridges of the hills were the backbones of great lizards. The needles were teeth and ribs. The wind which blew through that place sang with the voice of the dead. Everything belonged and yet was part of a pattern that never stopped changing. The death of an ant beneath my heel changed the pattern, as did the earthquake.

'Grandfather lifted me down. He blew into the palms of my hands. He touched his finger to his tongue and then touched my eyelids.

'When I awoke he was carrying me down the mountain-

134

side. Grandfather kept telling me stories all the way. And I wanted him to shut up because what I'd felt there in the Needles was so wonderful I didn't want it to fade. I didn't have a word for it then, but I do now. It was holy.

'Later on I tried to tell someone, like I'm trying to tell you, but I couldn't. I couldn't put the words together. Words were always so much less. Then, one day, when I was eighteen, I saw a painting. It was of a single stone, a broken stone, nothing special. But it seemed as if the stone was alive. Whoever had painted it had somehow captured the life of the stone and I could see it.

'I thought, whoever painted that stone felt as I felt, saw what I saw. Well, I found the artist and I talked to her.

'It was a great disappointment.

'She talked about pigment and shade and the poor quality of brushes and the way that you have to use white quickly because it dries so fast in the sun.

'I told her what I saw in the picture. I forced her to listen to me, and do you know? Do you know what? She was envious of me. She said, "You who can feel have no need of art." She said, "Everything I know I discover only through my art." She said, "Everything I touch is transformed. It is terrible. Where can I regain the vision of a child, a world that is whole and sufficient unto itself? You are fortunate, for you belong. I can only watch and record."

'I said to her, "You are the great giver. You give of your love and your life. You make the world brighter for all of us."

'She got angry then, as though she were afraid, as though I'd said something rude and offended her; and she threw me out of her studio. She told me to go away and grow up. Well, I did go away and I have grown up, and I still know I am right. Women like my artist and men like Tank are great because they live half their lives outside

135

themselves. They see reality more clearly than we do and they show it. If they didn't have their art they would go mad, for too much reality can destroy even the strongest mind. You see, artists like Tank have to look. Where the rest of us can turn away, they cannot. While they look they take notes. Something in Tank's brain is always ticking over saying, "Remember that colour. Look at that shading. If I could just capture that shape . . ." Tank will observe his own dying with interest. And that is what saved us. Tank can face more of reality than the rest of us . . . but never say that to him, because he wouldn't understand what you meant.'

Cordoba finished her drink and sat back.

'Do you mean,' said Haberjin, choosing his words carefully, 'that Tank is stronger than Pettet?'

'That's exactly what I mean. Not physical strength, strength of mind. Toughness. Where it counts. You see, a man like Tank is used to facing strangeness. When he . . . ssh.'

The door to the sickroom slid open, revealing Tank. He had shaved off his beard and all the hair from his head. His head looked small and ugly, as though made of putty. He wore only a bathrobe.

'Pay no attention to me,' he said. 'I needed to be clean, to get back to what I was . . . before all this . . .' He looked at them sharply. 'Were you talking about me?'

'We were,' said Pettet. 'You brought us through. Come and sit down. Tell us what you think of that place. Where were we?'

'Hell,' said Tank simply. 'Hell as I understand it. It takes everything and gives nothing. It leached life from us. When sense of life goes, futility is left. Futility leads to despair. That place will always be there, stealing, taking, draining, but it is nothing in itself. It can be defeated.'

136

At that moment, as he spoke, a brilliant light struck into the sickbay. It destroyed the softness of the sickbay lights, creating a world of black and white. Candle had appeared round the rim of Erix, and just visible to one side was the gleaming green beacon of Ultima Thule.

'And what is that place?' asked Haberjin, pointing at the small green planet.

Tank stared through squinting eyes. 'That, I would guess, is the place that keeps Erix in balance. A place of great creative energy. A place of abundant life. Probably more terrifying in its own way than the world we have seen already.'

'There is only one way to find out.' Haberjin and Pettet spoke the words together and both laughed and, following an ancient custom, they linked their little fingers and made a private wish.

13

ON BENNET

Any hopes that Pawl and Laurel might have entertained
that they could slip quietly back into their Homeworld
were short-lived. The people who had maintained Pawl's
island in his absence had planned a massive party. The
couple found themselves pelted with flowers as they left
the Way Gate. Then a band struck up and a choir belted
into a rousing rendition of the Paxwax anthem. This
ended in cheering and the presentation of bright floral
leis. Even Odin was honoured, and a band of purple
flowers was arranged round his black cowl. But he kept
the cowl forward and no glimmer of his pale mask could
be seen.

As they descended in the shuttle they looked out
through the thick windows. Below them the sea glowed
like the embers of a fire that is breathed on. It was
evening, and the red algae which covered the entire
surface of the sea were fluorescing at the end of a long
hot day.

Pawl felt glad to be home, and Laurel, standing beside
him, squeezed his arm. 'Welcome home, Master of
Paxwax.'

They could see the island. It cast long shadows over the
sea and stood out clear and hard like an ornament cut
from green jade.

Lights began to blink on the island spelling out the
word, WELCOME.

But as they stepped from the shuttle, the long arm of
the Families reached out and touched them. In front of
the welcoming delegation stood Barone, the man who

looked after the giant bio-crystalline brain called Wynn. Pawl had been half-expecting to see him. 'I didn't want to interrupt the welcome at the Way Gate, but you are required urgently, Master Pawl. Helium Bogdanovich is anxious to speak to you. He is not a happy man. I think you should come now.' Pawl nodded. He made his apologies and then slipped away, leaving Laurel to receive the homage of the gardeners and cooks and technicians and builders who kept Bennet Homeworld habitable.

Using the sparkling flow-ways which ran like narrow silver rivers through all the buildings, it took Pawl only a few minutes to reach the tall cherry-red tower in which he and Laurel lived. There he pulled up in front of the high arched doorway. He felt the presence of Odin and called the small creature to come to him. 'Be with me. There is some trouble. I'm not sure what, but I would like you with me.'

'I'll be there.' The voice in Pawl's mind was warm and friendly and had something of laughter in it. Pawl was glad that Odin's bright spirit had returned to him.

Then he was in the vacuum tube, which shot him up through the tower and released him in the large circular room which was the main living area. The air tingled. Round the walls swarmed a design which resembled the intertwined branches and leaves of an exotic tree. The design was even more complex than Pawl remembered. He said, 'Hello, Wynn,' and the design responded with a change of colours. Then a voice spoke. It was melodious and deep, organ-like. 'Welcome home, Master Pawl. I hope we can talk later. For the moment you must speak to Helium Bogdanovich. He has been trying to contact you for days. There is a council meeting of the Eleven in progress now. Helium will leave the meeting briefly to talk to you. Then you must join the meeting.'

'I get the idea,' said Pawl. 'Helium wants to brief me himself. Good. Get him on vivante.'

One section of the wall began to glow, grey into white, and expanded until it looked like a giant ceramic egg. A walkway led round the walls and into the egg. Pawl hurried inside and waited while the vivante console descended like a pseudopod from the roof.

It was active even as it descended and Pawl had the extraordinary experience of seeing Helium's large walrus face lowering towards him. As the vivante plate settled, the perspective adjusted, and the two men faced one another squarely.

Helium was obviously agitated. He sat up to his neck in brackish water and stirred the water with his hands. 'So you are back,' he barked, blinking his double-membraned eyes. 'None too soon. I expected you earlier.'

'Sorry, the Paxwax affairs were more complex than I expected. What is the trouble?'

'Nothing that vigilance can't cope with. But you are Master of Paxwax. You must make your own decisions.'

'What are you talking about?'

'An emergency meeting of the Council of Eleven has been called. It is in session now. There is an alien scare. We are all on our guard. You can't be too careful. Do you use aliens on your worlds?'

'Yes. You know I do. All the Families do. What's happening? Has there been a rebellion?'

Helium didn't answer but drew in a mouthful of air and sank under the surface of his pond. At that moment, out of the corner of his eye, Pawl was aware of movement. Odin worked his way across the smooth floor and settled, well out of view of the vivante. 'Trouble?' came the murmur of his thought.

'Something to do with aliens,' answered Pawl. 'I can't make it out. Helium is being a bit evasive. Stay close.'

140

Helium broke surface like a corpse and lay still for several seconds before he blew out. 'I don't like having questions thrown at me like that,' he said. 'Now listen closely. There has been a rebellion . . . on the Felice wine world. Most of us have adopted defensive strategies and have encountered distinct reactions. We are fortunate that for the moment the unrest lacks form. Which brings us to you. You will have some difficult questions to answer. Why didn't you tell me you were going to the Homeworld of the Hammer?'

'I didn't think it was important.'

'It was very foolish. It has made the Wong very jumpy.' Helium glanced to one side as though hearing something. 'Now I must return to the Council. I insist that you join us immediately. We shall be drawing up resolutions shortly.'

Helium's hand moved and he vanished. Pawl found himself staring at the velvet blackness of the vivante plate.

'Be very careful, Master Pawl,' whispered Odin. 'I think there is mischief afoot.'

'So do I,' said Pawl. 'Make the contacts, Wynn. Join me with the Council. But give me a moment to look at them. I want to know how things are going.'

The vivante plate pulsed, as though a giant bubble had burst beneath it. Then it began to glow. Spars of light spread out from it and gradually began to coalesce into figures. A jabber of images knitted and space about Pawl and the figures came to a sudden clarity.

The debate was in full session and obviously lively.

The Senior Proctor was in the chair clapping his jewelled hands together for silence. His bright scarlet mane, quiffed out like a lion, was slightly askew. He spoke, commenting on a point of order, and his twin curved fangs bobbed up and down, amplifying the movements of his jaw.

Beside the Proctor sat Old Man Wong, with eyes like the slits in a money box. As Pawl looked at him, hands of his attendants appeared out of the darkness beside him and wiped away some spittle and smoothed the long thin strands of his white moustache. He knocked the hands away angrily, and leant forward. Pawl noticed that Old Man Wong's own hands were encased in coils like balls of split bamboo. These were his nails, uncut from the time of his childhood.

Now a woman dressed entirely in black and with a white tragic face was speaking. This was Clarissa Xerxes de la Tour Souvent. Black was not her natural colour. Normally she delighted in rich brocades and velvet. But since the war with the Paxwax she had suffered a nervous complaint which had resulted in all her feathers falling out. Pawl did not know, but beneath her black garments she was ugly as a plucked chicken. Pawl guessed that her black garments signified mourning.

Whatever Dame Clarissa was saying was interrupted by a spirited dark-faced woman with extraordinary violet eyes. This was Laverna Felice, the doll woman, the cause of the present troubles.

In her turn Laverna was interrupted by Singular Sith, who pounded on his table with his fists and jerked his great bull's head angrily. Cicero Paragon waved his fat hands in an attempt to control the tirade.

Only one figure seemed undisturbed by the tumult in the Council. This was Daag Longstock, Master of the Longstock Eighth. His lips were moving, but it was an inner dialogue he was conducting. Frost rimmed his hair and beard. Behind him could be seen swirling clouds. He was obviously sitting outside, probably on a mountainside. The Longstock rarely spoke to the other members of the Eleven Families. As a family they were busy cultivating inner space, in an attempt to follow the fabled Craint who had discovered the path of psychic development. Pawl guessed that the Longstock would be the next Family to fall. They were beginning to neglect their defences.

Conspicuous by their absence were the Lamprey and the Freilander-Porterhouse Confederacy. Both these Families had fallen and seen their domains gobbled up by the other members of the Eleven. They had not yet been replaced.

Helium bobbed into view. He had a glass in his hand and Pawl knew that he had now to make an appearance.

'Lock me in, Wynn,' said Pawl.

His sudden appearance had a dramatic effect. Dame Clarissa, who was speaking, stopped when she saw him and immediately looked away. Singular Sith, who was still on his feet, subsided like an emptying bladder. The other Masters, with the exception of Daag Longstock, stared at him with surprise and then composed their features. Pawl knew that the Paxwax had been the subject under discussion.

Laverna Felice recovered first. She fixed Pawl with her fathomless eyes. 'Welcome to the Master of Paxwax. At last. You have some questions to answer.'

The Senior Proctor clapped his hands. 'We are delighted you have finally been able to join us. We trust your journey round your domain has been successful . . .?'

Pawl detected an edge in this question. 'Yes. Quite successful. I have discovered many *interesting* things.' Let them guess what he meant by that.

'. . . and we hope that your bride . . . Laurel Beltane, isn't it? . . . is well.'

'We are both well. Now, are you discussing anything which has particular concern for the Paxwax?'

'We are.' It was Old Man Wong, speaking with uncharacteristic bluntness. 'You are a young Master, inexperienced in the ways of the Eleven. The child that runs before it can walk, gets its nose bloody.'

'We are discussing the aliens,' said the Senior Proctor. 'You may not be aware, but the aliens are a constant threat. The price of our freedom is a constant vigilance. There are a few minor questions we would like to clear up before we proceed further. Laverna? Would you care to speak?'

Laverna Felice was on her feet in an instant. Pawl saw the other Masters relax back, staring at him. Pawl wondered what to expect.

'Master Pawl, the Paxwax have been noted in the past for their strict adherence to the Code that binds all the Families. I wonder, can you recall the words of the anthem which reveals both our history and our obligations?'

'Do you want me to sing it?'

'Not necessarily sing it. Just recall the words.'

Pawl's mind went blank. To him the anthem was a silly song, a mouthful of platitudes. Wynn came to his rescue. Faintly behind him he heard the computer's whispery voice. 'First are the Proctors, the greatest . . .' Pawl followed the words and spoke them firmly.

First are the Proctors, the greatest and the best
They keep the great wheel spinning from the centre where
they rest.

The Senior Proctor smirked round and received the nods of the Masters, who by tradition always acknowledged the suzerainty of the Proctors.

Second are the Wong the Warriors, saviours of our race,
They chased away the Hammer and put them in their place.

'Yes, the Hammer. We shall return to them later,' said Laverna Felice. Old Man Wong muttered something and then fell silent.

Third is the Conspiracy of the Bogdanovich and Shell
They fight for truth and justice and liberty as well.

Helium, who had now been joined by his wife Clover Shell, stared stonily at Pawl.

The Xerxes de la Tour Souvent are fourth on our list
Where love is found and tenderness, they are never missed.

Pawl could not resist speaking these words with a twist of irony and Dame Clarissa slapped her hand on the table in front of her and stood up. She departed with colour rising to her pale cheeks. Moments later she was replaced by her sister, Dame Jettatura. This lady had pale blonde hair parted in the middle of her forehead, and the hair tumbled in lazy waves down over her shoulders and beyond the view of the vivante. She stared at Pawl with the pure pink eyes of an albino. Then, with a studied glacial elegance, she began to play cards, setting each card down with a clearly audible snap.

The Paxwax Fifth are generous to the meek and mild,
They give the food that keeps alive every little child.

The insincerity of the lyrics made Pawl wince inwardly. Once, many centuries earlier, the Paxwax had been suppliers of a particular kind of grain that could survive drought. That had been the cause of this lyric.

The Lamprey Sixth love the light, their father was the sun,
Their children are the stars that shine upon us everyone.

The Freilander and Porterhouse hold the seventh place,
They stopped the alien in his tracks and kicked him in
the face.

These two verses elicited no response from the assembly, except that Laverna Felice raised her head on the last line and glanced across to the Shell-Bogdanovich Conspiracy.

> The Longstock and the Paragon,
> The Sith and Felice too,
> Help keep the goblins on their knees
> And so I hope do you.

Pawl completed the verses and sat down. He was aware that he was involved in some obscure test.

'And what, Master Pawl,' demanded Laverna Felice, 'are goblins?'

'I have always understood them to be aliens,' said Pawl. 'Of a humanoid variety. Few such are known. I take it to be a general statement.'

'As do we all.'

'I fail to see . . .'

'What Laverna is pointing out,' said Old Man Wong, leaning forward, 'is that a large part of the anthem of our families concerns the battle against the aliens. Our families grew from that battle.'

'It is a battle that never ends,' added Jettatura.

'So?' Pawl tried to make his question sound innocent.

'So why did you visit the Hammer?' The question came from Helium Bogdanovich, his face ugly with suppressed anger.

'I don't know. I thought it would be interesting.' The answer sounded empty to Pawl, though he spoke as firmly

146

as he could. He was shaken to find Helium Bogdanovich joined with those ranged against him. He had trusted Helium to be a friend.

'Interesting?' Laverna Felice seized on the word. 'Weren't you aware that the Hammer are one of our ancient enemies?'

'I suppose so. But I was curious. That was a long time ago.'

'And how did you find the Hammer? Were they well?'

'They live on an arid world. I have a mining camp there which is quite peaceful. There are killer satellites posted. If the Hammer ever made a move their world would be destroyed. But they won't cause any trouble. They crawl about in dust. Quite disappointing really. I was hoping for more. I think you are mistaken if you are suggesting that the Hammer still pose a threat.'

'I am suggesting nothing,' said Laverna Felice. 'But the Hammer were powerful adversaries, as one of our families knows to its cost. They are known to have a subtle and brutal mentality. And none of us should be so vain as to believe that we can see all dangers. Can you assure us that you saw nothing of the Hammer's fabled aggression? That, frankly, I would find hard to believe.'

Pawl did not hesitate. 'I saw nothing,' he said, and wondered why he was lying. He remembered the way the Hammer had towered over him, the way it had run, the fierce beat of its drumming. The Hammer were quite magnificent. He realized he was protecting them. The voice of Odin murmured in Pawl's mind. 'She is trying to manipulate you, Master Pawl. You do well to resist.' Pawl thought about Odin. He thought of that defenceless creature whose species had once been a gastronomic delicacy. In protecting the Hammer he was also protecting the Gerbes.

'Did you visit the Hammer with a view to hunting?' asked Singular Sith.

'No, just simple curiosity.'

'Ah, well, do you think they would be any good for hunting?'

'No. They hid when they saw us. You'd get more sport shooting at a tree.'

'Did you make any vivantes?' asked Helium Bogdanovich.

Pawl thought quickly. He remembered the images they had taken of Trader sitting quietly displaying his sting. 'Some; my secretary Peron has them. You can see them if you like. When he returns.'

'So he is not with you?' said Helium.

'No. He stayed behind in Elliott's Pocket. I hurried home when I received word that there was trouble. I must say that I did not expect to be cross-questioned in this way. To date, my experience as a Master has led me to fear not the aliens, but rather my own kind.' He looked round the assembly with his gaze finally coming to rest on Jettatura. That lady continued to play cards impassively.

Old Man Wong tugged at his moustache, gripping the strands of hair in the joint between his thumbs and the palms of his hands. 'Master of Paxwax,' he said, 'I will not disguise the fact that I find your answers too glib to be convincing. The Hammer could never be docile. However, I will make you an offer. Cede to me the world of the Hammer and I will pay you its worth a thousand fold.'

Every Master and Mistress of the Families looked at Pawl, waiting for his response. Even Jettatura lay down her cards and looked at him with cold pink eyes. Pawl knew that if he wanted he could push the price even higher. He made a pretence of thinking about the deal. 'No,' he said finally. 'That world lies well within my domain and I will never again allow any Family to have a foothold in my empire.'

Helium Bogdanovich, Singular Sith and Cicero Paragon nodded, for they saw the common sense behind Pawl's reply.

'Then I will offer the same amount if you will destroy that world, asking only that I have observers present,' said Old Man Wong.

'That,' replied Pawl, 'I shall have to think about. I do not want to make a rushed decision. Have no fear. If I thought the Hammer were a threat to us I would destroy them myself and ask for no recompense. Can I say clearer than that?'

Old Man Wong sat back and said nothing. In their deep sockets his eyes were bright with anger.

'I suggest,' said the Senior Proctor, sensing that the debate had reached a stalemate, 'that we move on. The Master of Wong and the Master of Paxwax can continue negotiations at their leisure. We are busy people and there are several resolutions before us. Let me just say this to the new Master of Paxwax, on behalf of all of us: our fears concerning the renewed belligerence of the aliens are not without good foundation. We are under no illusions. We know that alien races are not stupid. We do not underestimate them. Not all aliens are dangerous. But with alien intelligence it is not easy to tell friend from foe. We know from experience that certain aliens, given the opportunity, will seek to turn any unrest to their advantage. We, as custodians of human freedom, must be on our guard at all times.'

'Hear, hear,' rumbled Helium.

'We shall now move to consider what measures we, as Masters, should adopt to counter, quell, nip in the bud, call it what you will, any alien threat. Laverna, you have some proposals to place before us?'

149

'I have.' Laverna Felice assembled some documents in front of her and consulted her advisors, who were beyond the range of the vivante.

She made room, and a giant appeared beside her. Then the vivante adjusted and the giant reduced to normal proportions while Laverna shrank to her true size. The newcomer wore a heavy black gown with a cowl. Beneath the cowl Pawl could just see the edge of the familiar white mask of the Inner Circle. The figure reached inside the cowl and removed the mask and then threw back the hood to reveal a mass of curly auburn hair and a finely-formed human face. She was stunningly beautiful. She smiled cheerily round the Masters and patted the cowl back on to her shoulders.

'This is Selena, the representative of the Inner Circle who has worked closely with me for several years,' said Laverna Felice. 'She has helped me prepare an inventory of alien infestation.' The woman Selena glanced round the assembly and Pawl noticed that her eyes were green and wicked. There was a lazy sensuality about her. *How*, he wondered, *did Laverna come to tolerate having a woman like this about her?* And then he realized that vanity often uses other people as its mirror. Selena was everything that Laverna would have liked to be. Poor Laverna sat like a brightly-lacquered doll beside the warm fullness of the other woman. *Now if only Laverna thought herself truly beautiful . . . how different her world might be. I doubt if she would then get her excitement by hunting aliens*.

While thinking these thoughts, Pawl realized that he had been staring at Selena, resting his eyes on her, and he came to himself with a jolt. Was there something hypnotic about this woman?

For her part, Selena seemed totally unaware of the stares she was receiving from all quarters. She spoke in a clipped, precise voice. 'The Mistress of Felice has granted me wide powers of research. My report is in two parts: first an analysis and then my recommendations. Am I free to proceed?'

The Senior Proctor nodded. Vacantly. He too seemed mesmerized by the woman's manner.

'The most dangerous species now living in our midst is the Spideret. Every family except the Felice uses them for construction work. Let there be no mistake, the Spideret as a species is as intelligent as the human. They once achieved space travel and are species fighters, which means that they will fight blindly and sacrifice themselves for the good of the entire race.'

'What shall we do about them?' asked Helium Bogdanovich, rising out of his bath.

Selena held up her hand. 'When I have completed my analysis I will come to my recommendations. To continue. I find that the Hooded Parasol are used on the worlds of the Sith, of the Shell-Bogdanovich Conspiracy, of the Wong and the Proctor. Do not be fooled by the beauty of this creature. Its very scent can kill. Pandora Boxes are even kept on many Homeworlds. While the eating habits of these creatures may be spectacular, they are a venomous parasite. One spit of their venom is sufficient to infect. The population of Sennet bats has greatly increased and, according to the death registers administered by the Proctors, these creatures have been responsible for many deaths among the hunting members of the Families. The Pullah, though it looks amiable as a cow, can be dangerous, and yet I observe that this creature is widely used at the Way Gates to clean the walkways. Turning to happier news, I can report that the Diphilus, the Lyre Beast and the Link Worm are not to be found in the domains. Likewise the Hammer. My research on the Hammer tallies with what the Master of Paxwax has said.

They are a dying breed. The genetic poison administered by the Wong so many centuries ago is still working its way through the population. We of the Inner Circle observe such things.'

Pawl did not know what to make of this. Selena was wrong. The Hammer were vibrant with health. Pawl had seen them, smelled them. What had happened? Had Odin fed incorrect information to the Inner Circle? Or were the members of the Inner Circle playing some clever game? He decided to keep silent and listen. Selena with the green eyes smiled at him as though divining his thoughts. 'Now I come to my recommendations. First, that we eradicate all populations of Pandora Boxes and Sennet bats. Those creatures are of no commercial significance. Second, that populations of the Hooded Parasol be quarantined on unoccupied worlds. This will mean relocating some of your industries, but that is a small price to pay. Third, that all known Pullah be gelded and their movements totally restricted. At present they have no Homeworld and so we can control them effectively. Fourth, the Spiderets. I recommend that their population be halved immediately and that breeding be permitted only to keep the population steady.' At this point the lady paused for reaction.

The leaders of the Families looked round one another. While they shared a common fear of aliens, they recognized that the proposed measures would weaken their commercial enterprises. Finally Cicero Paragon indicated he wanted to speak. 'No one could be more sensible than myself of any threat that the aliens pose, but still I counsel that we should move with caution. We are not butchers. For many generations we and the aliens have co-operated. I have fostered the hope that we have humanized them to some extent. I believe they have learned something of moderation. Certainly I have had no trouble on my worlds. While I agree that any outright threat must be countered, I oppose wholesale slaughter.'

Singular Sith indicated his agreement. Both of them had a great deal at stake.

But Helium Bogdanovich raised his hands to speak. 'A threat is a threat; there can be no half-measures.'

Dame Jettatura spoke for the first time. 'Kill them all,' she said. 'Begin with the Spiderets. Who needs them? We will all be stronger.'

Old Man Wong cleared his throat with an ugly rattle and spat away to his side. An attendant appeared and wiped his lips. 'If it be not the hawk,' he said, 'it will be the owl . . . but the elephant fears neither.' His face composed to stillness.

The Senior Proctor nodded wisely and after a pause looked round the assembly. 'Master Daag Longstock, we have yet to hear your thoughts.'

Daag Longstock forced himself to return to the present. His voice was whispery, like a cold desert wind. 'We Longstock do not believe there is an alien threat. The dangers are in our own minds. But we will not stand against the will of the Families. We will comply with whatever action you deem wise.'

'Master Pawl?' It was the Senior Proctor speaking again.

Pawl considered. 'Well, I have no objection to the slaughter of the Pandora Boxes. My father used to keep a brood in his study; they are unwholesome. Sennet bats I rather like. We have all hunted them. We have all faced danger. It seems to me that it will be a sad day for the human race when we are afraid to face mortal danger and are satisfied with shooting at replicas. What I am saying is that we can become too cautious. Let the bats thrive. They are hardly a threat to our survival. As for the rest of the recommendations, I will accept them. I say only this.

As a principle we should favour that which helps us. I use Spiderets *where humans cannot go*. I cannot see that killing them by fifty per cent will alter anything, except perhaps make them less efficient or get them riled. That is all.'

'A vote,' piped up Laverna. 'Let us have a vote. All those in favour of the recommendations raise their hands.'

Even though the Longstock did not move, it was clear that a majority favoured Selena's suggestions.

'Well, that finishes the matter,' said the Senior Proctor. 'The recommendations presented by Selena of the Inner Circle are accepted and will be actioned immediately. Any other questions? I hope not. It has been a long day and is not ended yet for some of us. No? Very well. At our next meeting we will assess the effectiveness of our measures. This meeting is ended.'

One by one the Masters disappeared. The killing of the Spiderets would begin within the hour.

'Well, Odin,' said Pawl, when he had cleared the vivante screen, 'what do you make of that?'

It was a long time before the small creature spoke in Pawl's mind. 'I do not know,' he said finally.

Odin was speaking the truth. The small Gerbes was unaware of developments on Sanctum.

On that planet the creatures which managed the affairs of the aliens had been able to follow the meeting through the medium of Selena. What that lady had offered to the Families was part of a hastily-prepared plan. The aliens who ruled Sanctum knew that at all costs the order of the Inner Circle must retain its integrity: further, that it should seem to foster the prejudices of the Families. To this end they had decided to sacrifice one of their species that all might be spared. But the price of that decision

154

could not be denied. The Spiderets were angry and calling for quick action.

One of the Spideret leaders, dangling by its thick cord from the roof of the assembly chamber, spoke these words. THE TIME OF WAITING MUST END. THIS SACRIFICE MUST BE THE LAST. EACH DAY WE FEEL THE BAND OF OUR SERVITUDE GROW TIGHTER. WE CANNOT WALK MEEKLY INTO DEATH. AT THE NEXT DEMAND OF THE HUMANS WE SHALL ATTACK, WHETHER WE HAVE THE SUPPORT OF THE COUNCIL OR NOT. THAT IS OUR FINAL WORD.

And no one doubted that it was. The aged Spideret was challenging the wisdom of the Tree itself. It opened its mandibles and spat, sending its venom in a long arc down to the floor of the chamber.

Within the Tree, pale colours flowed and bright charges of electricity crackled in its wide canopy. But yet it spoke gently in the minds of the assembled aliens.

THE TRAP IS READY. ANY DAY IT WILL BE SPRUNG. ODIN IS WITH THE PAXWAX NOW. THE SACRIFICE OF THE SPIDERETS HAS BOUGHT US THE TIME WE NEED.

VERY WELL, replied the Spideret. WE ARE WAITING. And then it shinnied up its cord and scuttled to refuge with its colleagues.

14

ON ULTIMA THULE

Pettet and his companions aboard the tiny ship were drifting close to Ultima Thule.

They had approached cautiously.

Haberjin at the controls, his hands moving like nervous birds, monitored the tilt and spin of the ship. He was ready at the slightest hint of danger to flip them deep into space. The problem that exercised him was one of recognition. How would he recognize danger when it came? He hardly expected dab rays, or a mined freighter screaming 'mayday'. Danger might be as seductive as a smile or soft lips. All Haberjin had to guide him was his instincts. But they were a good guide. They had never failed him yet. Still . . . Haberjin's eyes never left his instruments as he edged the ship towards the blazing green world. He felt like a blind man who knows he stands close to the edge of a cliff. One wrong . . .

'Hold her steady, Haberjin,' called Pettet. 'We'll ride for a while at this distance.'

The six companions lay on their survival couches in the main control cabin. Facing them was a screen on which was depicted an image of Thule. It was a simple visual image obtained from a telescope. Normally the ship used a vivante camera for exploration outside the ship, but the vivante plate was useless. Something in the presence of Ultima Thule distorted the incoming signals so that all that was received was inchoate patterns of sparks. Since their arrival close to the small solar system they had had no contact with home.

The green planet shone before them. The edge of its disk was hard and clear. Beyond was shadowy purple Erix. It held no fear for them now. It was an enemy that had been faced and bested. Ultima Thule was different.

Pettet manipulated the telescope so that they seemed to swoop towards the planet's surface. It grew until it completely filled the viewscreen, and as it grew it became brighter. This was just one of the planet's mysteries. It radiated more energy than it received. Visually the effect was extraordinary . . . To Peron, curled up on his couch and squinting through half-closed eyes, it was as though a brilliant light blazed just beneath the surface of the green world.

The visual magnification reached its maximum and stopped. They were at the equivalent of roughly 200 miles above the surface.

Ultima Thule was revealed.

They looked upon a landscape of green hills and valleys. It was like a sheet of crumpled paper. In the hollows of the valleys were lakes which spread like many-fingered hands, and each reflected pinkly the dull light of Erix.

Pettet altered the view, sending the landscape lurching before them. Thule was a dappled world. The green which seemed so uniform from space was broken into many shades. Forests vied with grasslands for dominance on its surface.

However, it was not just the vegetation that caught their attention. Scattered across the surface of the planet were bright silver disks, like coins. At this resolution it was not possible to make out details. Haberjin calculated that the average diameter of the disks was three miles. 'Could be landing ports,' he offered but no one seemed convinced.

'Sensors,' said Pettet. 'Like on Lumb. There might be

a subterranean civilization down there. What do you think, witch-woman?'

Cordoba stretched. 'Yes,' she said finally. 'They have a brooding power. I can feel them reaching out to us.'

'Are we safe?'

'No. But I can't say that we are in danger, either. They are *other*. I don't know how to describe what I feel.'

'Tank. Any thoughts?'

Tank grinned. His head was covered with a short stubble and his beard, which seemed to grow more quickly than the hair on his head, was already well-formed. The pallor which had marked him ever since his encounter with Erix was all but gone. 'I think we saw the worst when we dipped into that other world. I think we should go down and see. We have nothing more to lose than we have risked already, and a great deal to gain. We may begin to understand what is going on here.'

Peron nodded. He liked Tank's reasoning, though he rarely offered an opinion unless asked. Pettet turned to him. 'Well, historian, you seem keen to thrust your head into the jaws again. I had never believed you to be so impetuous. It makes me wonder how you have managed to survive for so long.' The other members of the crew smiled at Peron's embarrassment.

'My reasoning is as follows,' Peron said. 'Whatever resides down there on Thule, it is surely of a high order of sentience.' Cordoba pulled a face. She did not like such phrases. 'What I mean is that it is not foolish. It, they, whatever, will watch us. If they don't want us near they will warn us off. We are not threatening. It is threatening behaviour which inspires an aggressive response. Perhaps those sensors down there will simply ignore us and let us look about and then depart in peace.'

Wystan had not spoken all the while. Now he sat up

158

and they were all surprised to see that his face was set, almost angry.

'Let us have no more talk about sensors and civilization,' he said. 'Those disks are living. To me they are the crowns of mushrooms. They carry wisdom from the deepest soil. Let us go down there and greet them.'

But still Pettet delayed. As captain he would not be rushed. He chewed on his lip. He thought briefly of Raleigh. He imagined her sitting in the view chamber on Lumb and staring up at the green world and willing him love and care and safe return. He remembered also the map from the ill-fated ship *Candie* and the crosses which marked the planet which now stood before them. He weighed and puzzled and finally knew he had no alternative. 'Take us down slowly, Haberjin. Set us for auto-jump. Everyone keep alert.'

Haberjin tapped the controls lightly and the ship edged forward and began a slow orbital descent.

The planet grew before them.

After several hours they could make out details: promontories which stuck out into the lakes, vast forests of pale blue and green trees. But most interesting of all were the silver disks. They came into focus and showed themselves to be giant trees with vast canopies. They soared above the surrounding vegetation and cast long undulating shadows.

Came the moment when the ship slowed. They watched as a change came over some of the trees. Pulses of grey and green light flowed up the stems and radiated out across the wide canopies.

'Are they signalling to us?' asked Peron.

'In a way,' answered Wystan. 'They are responding to us, but I don't think that message is for our benefit any more than a flower opens its petals just so that we can enjoy its beauty.'

'We are resting at the limit of their inner psychic world,' murmured Cordoba. 'Now, will they let us in? Try to relax, gentlemen. There is nothing that any of us can do now.'

Briefly the image on the monitor blacked out, as though the great green planet had winked at them. Then the surface of the planet seemed to stretch and all the trees and greenery undulated slowly. And at the same moment they all felt that they could breathe more freely. They had not been aware of their tension, but they relaxed. The ship moved on.

'Are we still in full control?' asked Pettet.

'Yep. Still in the saddle. You want me to pull us back?'

'No. Just hold steady.'

Haberjin looked down at the green world. He looked at the margin, where bright grass met the high shady trees of a temperate jungle, and he thought of women. He imagined himself lying back in that long grass and with a roguish and willing lass in his arms. To his astonishment, the faces of the women he had loved popped into his mind, laughing and calling and blowing kisses. 'Now that can't be bad,' he said to himself, and vaguely remembered the desert on Erix. It seemed a universe away.

Tank was studying colours and textures. He observed the muscular white trunks of the giant trees and likened them to pillars of salt. He noted something in the sweep of the blue-green trees, like an eddy in water, like a child's hand opening from the wrist with the fingers uncurling. He had tried to capture that grace before. Without thinking he reached for his drawing pad and a stub of charcoal.

*   *   *

160

Merry, thought Pettet. *The planet is merry. Now who would have thought . . . ? Raleigh would love it. I must bring her here.*

Cordoba began to croon to herself in her reedy old voice.

> I learned the truth the other night,
> Like a shower of gold it came,
> And caught in my hair and in my eyes
> And spoke to me by name.
> 'Come lover why stand so idly
> Trying to trap the moon.
> For no man pays the piper,
> And no man calls the tune.
>
> Let the sad tides of gravity
> Cast time on a stony shore.
> Let heroes eat their drifting dust
> As many have done before.
> Take the moment gladly,
> With your bright eyed love along.
> For no man pays the piper
> And no man calls the song.'

A tear formed in Cordoba's eye to the memory of her dead husband and the children she had lost. As lovers they had never stood idly, and had accepted life as it came.

Peron thought of Pawl Paxwax and didn't know why. Something in this world reminded him of Pawl. Perhaps the shifting greens, like shifting moods. *A silly thought.* He concentrated on the green world, trying to see if he could see any animals roaming under the trees.

Only Wystan brooded. He was contending with the knowledge that he had come to a place he had known in his dreams and that he would never leave.

* * *

161

'What the hell is that?' shouted Haberjin, pointing with one hand while instinctively bringing the ship round. 'Something shining . . . I thought . . .'

The ship dipped and entered the shadow under the canopy of one of the silver trees. Below them was a clearing with sharp edges, as though shaped by a razor. The clearing was filled with bright frothy foliage.

Poking up through this green wilderness was something completely alien to this garden world . . . the broken and vine-bound superstructure of an ancient spaceship.

They hovered in the shadow and stared down at the wreck. All the windows were punched open and stuffed with large fleshy leaves. Plates were prised apart and twisted in the grip of dark roots. No identification marks could be read on the ship, which lay, slowly breaking up, trapped in the greenery.

'Can you identify it?' asked Tank.

Both Haberjin and Pettet shook their heads.

'Can we go down?' asked Wystan.

'No,' said Pettet. 'We'll get the hell out from under this tree for a start and then decide what to do. Haberjin – '

But the pilot was already busy feeding energy, and the ship slid out from under the veined canopy of the tree and into the bright sunlight. Pettet was worried by memories of the Snake, of bones at a cave mouth.

'Sorry, captain,' said Haberjin. 'I put us at risk, didn't I? I don't know what I was thinking about.'

For some time they cruised round the tree studying the decaying ship. It was impossible to tell how long it had been there, since they did not know how quickly the foliage grew. But everyone's guess was that it was a long time. 'And I'll tell you something else,' said Haberjin. 'That ship didn't crash. It landed carefully.'

Peering above the neighbouring hills was another tree,

and they visited this, but could find no evidence of a ship in the clearing at its base.

They began to follow a valley. It twisted and turned and its sides became steep. The vegetation that grew in it was the colour of ivy. Deep in its depths was a tumbling river like a thread of white cotton.

The valley seemed to be leading them. It opened into a natural amphitheatre surrounded by high hills. Standing in the centre was one of the tallest trees they had encountered so far. To Peron it looked like a sentinel, standing guard. It gave an impression of great age. The bark was swollen and veiny and broken branches like stiff arms of coral hung down from its domed canopy. It looked heavy and yet there was immense vigour in the sweep of its branches.

At its base, bright and beautiful as the day it landed, was a ship of red and gold. The force field which surrounded it made it glitter and dip in and out of focus.

Both Pettet and Haberjin shook their heads before any question could be asked. Neither had ever encountered anything like it in fable or picture. But both men responded to the authority of its design. It had the same appeal as a finely-crafted, well-tempered musical instrument.

And had they known the truth about this ship they might have wondered. For this ship was the oldest artefact they had ever seen. It was old even before Earth itself was formed. It was a ship of the Craint, the species that had once ruled the evolving galaxy and was now no more. It shimmered as it drifted in and out of time, ageing only seconds as the centuries slipped by. Had they known how, they could have entered that ship and vanished to any point in space-time. But they would not have known how to control it. For the ship was nothing more than a vast mental accumulator which could take a wish and turn it

163

into actuality. The ship will stand there until the expanding universe reaches its limit and begins to contract. Only then will it falter and shake to dust.

Haberjin's eyes gleamed and he licked his lips like a dog that scents a meal coming. He brought their ship to a halt, suspended as close as he dared to the sentinel tree. 'It looks as if it could take off at any moment. Look, you can see the sparkle of anti-grav under it. Shall I land?' This was more pleading than a question.

'We'll not land,' said Pettet, though he was as curious as Haberjin. 'We'll hang about and watch. Perhaps whoever, *whatever*, flew that ship in here is still about. Use the loudspeakers. Cause a commotion.'

For several hours they held their position, drifting round the tree, occasionally bellowing like a bull elephant. Haberjin tried every electronic means of contacting the ship but received only static in reply. Nothing moved as the day wore on. No creature wandered into the clearing in response to their summons.

Peron sat and studied the spaceship and the tree. He alone of all the companions had some inkling of where it came from. He noticed that there was a burn mark on the tree. It started just under the canopy and continued down to the ground to where the force field protecting the ship just touched the massive trunk. *Either the tree grows quickly*, he thought, *or that ship has stood there since the tree was a sapling*.

Evening began to spread over the planet. A purple dusk gathered as Candle dipped below the horizon and Erix rose. There was no sunset. The valleys filled with a rotten light and finally Pettet ordered the ship back out into space. It moved easily. Though they felt no resistance, they were aware as they left the tight psychosphere of the planet.

'And what now, captain?'

'Now we move with even greater caution. We have all seen the warning signs. Abandoned, decaying ships. What happened to the occupants? Haberjin and I can read a ship like that last one we saw. It has energy to spare. It belonged to a race that knew both beauty and power. God knows where it came from and how long ago, but whatever defeated that crew is worthy of the utmost respect.

'Tomorrow we will continue to explore. But we will not land. Tank, make whatever images you can. I want you to record everything. Cordoba, send your mind out. Protect us. Try to discover what manner of life there is down there. Wystan . . . ?'

But Wystan was asleep already, his mouth open and his body sagging in relaxation.

For the next five days they visited Thule, dipping into its psychosphere when they were refreshed and withdrawing when they were tired. They avoided the baleful light of Erix. They quartered the planet and spent their time measuring, evaluating and testing. They found that the air was breathable. They discovered that the planet had no poles and seemed able to control and regulate its environment. Two-thirds of the giant trees had spaceships decaying in the clearings at their base. Most of these were broken and pulled apart by the vegetation. Some were little more than burial mounds. Occasionally they revisited the ship of the Craint, but there was never any movement there.

Finally, towards the end of the fifth day, they were over a part of the planet where there were many mountains and cliff-sided valleys. The dark holly green of the jungle was everywhere. There were many lakes. Some were black, like lakes where vegetation is dying. Others were

165

choked with a bright yellow-green weed. Half-submerged in one of the lakes was a giant ship, bigger by far than any they had seen so far. The water lapped against its pitted sides. Hanging over it with its roots lost in the dark water was a tall silver tree.

'That tree has a personality I recognize,' said Cordoba in surprise. 'I can feel it. There is something of us down there.'

Haberjin took the ship in a wide arc round the tree like a ball tied to a piece of string. Both Haberjin and Pettet studied the ship. There *was* something familiar . . .

'It looks like an old Pleiades freighter,' said Pettet. 'But what a size! No one ever built freighters that big.'

'Pleiades freighters like Hell!' shouted Haberjin. 'Look at its colour. Red as the scales of a Hammer . . . and look at those burn vents. Look at the housing for the symbol transformation generators . . . like the bosses for a bell. Can't you see it? Don't you know what it is? I'll eat my hair and toe-nails too if that's not the *Fare-Thee-Well*. We've found the *Fare-Thee-Well*.'

The *Fare-Thee-Well*! The ship that had carried the first immigrants from the prison world called Luxury to Elliott's Pocket. They all knew the ship in their imaginations. They all knew the story of how John Death Elliott had driven the *Fare-Thee-Well* into the heart of the Pocket and there disappeared. And now here it was: big, decayed and broken, but unmistakable, and with its passenger door gaping wide just above the waterline. For hours they hung above it and then Pettet, fine captain though he was, succumbed to temptation and ordered the ship to land. The seduction was complete.

Haberjin guided the ship under the canopy of the tree and down to the soft vegetation at the margin of the lake. The ship settled. Checked. Settled again. And then finally its stabilizers bit down into the planet and it came to rest. The engines died. Outside there was total stillness. Not a breath of air moved the pressing vegetation or stirred the surface of the still lake. It was already late in the afternoon.

Looking through the windows they could see the blunt shape of the *Fare-Thee-Well* where it reared out of the water. As Pettet stared at it strange thoughts began to stir in his mind. Perhaps it was for this very moment that the trio of Erix, Thule and Candle had appeared, perhaps to return the great ship to the people of the Pocket as a symbol of hope. Perhaps he, Pettet, giant and leader of men, had been born just to accomplish this.

But such thoughts made Pettet suspicious. Like most men, of the Pocket he had an abnormally large bump of common sense and was not a great believer in individual destiny.

It was agreed that Cordoba and Peron would stay with the ship. The others equipped themselves for outside. Pettet hoisted metal cutting gear on to his back. Haberjin carried a small inflatable raft. Wystan took care of the medical supplies and Tank hefted a particle gun on to his shoulders.

Moving deliberately, Pettet threw open the door to the ship and breathed deeply of the air of Thule. And it was sweet. After the recycled air of the ship, Thule smelled of moist earth and humus and rich black soil. These were smells that the Pocket dwellers had hardly ever experienced in their life.

One by one they stepped down from the ship and into the high shrubbery. Haberjin and Wystan almost disappeared from view. Pettet led the way, pushing back the plants, treading them down when he could, making a

167

path. Halfway to the lake they paused and looked up. Towering over them was the vast canopy of the tree. Its presence was enormous. For the first time they could hear the tree. It made a soft growling as the trunk flexed, keeping the giant spreading branches in balance.

'Do you realize,' said Haberjin, his voice scarcely more than a whisper, 'that we have never seen one of these trees fallen?'

The margin of the lake was soft and marshy and covered with short reeds which broke when they trod on them. Pettet looked round for footprints or hoofmarks. There were none. There were not even any insects. The only things which disturbed the calm of the lake were small white twigs which drifted down from the high canopy.

Quickly Haberjin inflated the raft and pushed it out into the shallows. Then he hopped aboard. Pettet followed with the cutting gear. Tank waded into the dark water, steering the boat in front of him.

'Come on, Wystan. Hurry up if you are coming.'

'No,' said Wystan, squatting down at the water's edge. 'I've no mind for sailing. I'll wait. I'll cover you.'

Tank, unsuspecting, shrugged as if to say 'Suit yourself' and handed the heavy particle cannon over. Then he pushed the boat forward and dived over on top of it. Haberjin took up the stroke and soon the raft was out over the dark water and moving steadily towards the small open doorway in the side of the *Fare-Thee-Well*.

Wystan watched them go. Avoiding them had been easier than he expected. He returned his gaze to the tree.

When he had looked at it from outside the ship, it had seemed to him that it spoke to him, not in words, but in spirit. He stared at the soaring white trunk and it lifted his soul. He saw the branches, miles above him, divide and divide again right out to the limit of the canopy. He

168

saw dark places between the twisted branches where strange lights flickered. He wanted to be up there in the place where the life of the tree was at its greatest. He wanted to climb. With a rush, the whole of his vegetative being responded to the tree and he forsook friends and home and began to run.

He left the particle cannon in the water and began to splash through the shallows. Running was not easy, and several times he stumbled in the dark ooze, but surprise was on his side.

Peron saw him first and shouted to the men in the raft, but they couldn't hear him. He jumped from the ship and ran down to the water's edge, but by now Wystan was too far away for him to give chase. He called and waved and finally Tank turned.

Wystan reached the place where the first creamy roots emerged from the lake. There he paused and began tearing off his clothes.

Tank dived into the black water and began swimming towards the tree, but it was a hopeless chase. Wystan began to climb. The bark was not smooth and he was able to hold on to rough edges and squeeze his feet into fissures. By the time that Tank reached the water's edge, Wystan was already high. He stood for a moment in the place where a great vein made a fissure in the trunk and waved to them. He called something, but his voice didn't carry. Then he turned and was lost to sight.

On the ground the men gathered by the water side. Any thought of trying to enter the *Fare-Thee-Well* was gone. Pettet was caught between a helpless desire to go after Wystan and the urgent need to protect the other members of his party. He reached his decision quickly. It was obvious that some influence had been at work on Wystan. There was no way they could catch him and it was already

169

moving to late afternoon. At most they would only have had another hour on the planet before Erix began to rise.

'Back to the ship,' he said. 'We'll take her up as quickly as we can. We'll come back tomorrow and see if there is any sign of Wystan.'

It was a good plan, an honourable plan. But when they returned to the ship they found that although all the systems worked, the anti-gravity units failed to lift them. Haberjin sat at the controls, sweating, staring at the instruments which told him that the ship should be rising at a rate of gees. But it didn't even tremble. He tried to edge it forward and then back, but there was no movement, not even a whine of frustrated power.

One by one the crew unfastened their safety harnesses and sat on the side of their bunks staring at him.

'Must be some of the relays shot,' Haberjin muttered. 'Maybe I gave a bit of a bump when I landed.' But there was no conviction in his words.

Pettet reached over and cut the main drive and then the auxiliary engines. He sat for a while staring at the control panel and then he spoke. 'So. It looks as though we are here for the night.' His voice was level and controlled, scrubbed of all emotion. 'Haberjin will overhaul the engine in the morning. We'll find what's wrong.'

'Aye, aye, captain,' said Haberjin softly.

No one else spoke.

They sat in silence, while outside the evening gathered. No one could think of anything to say. In each of their minds was a memory of the many spaceships they had seen under the trees.

Cordoba lay back with her eyes closed and her hands over her ears. Her mind was outside the ship, trying to discover what force was holding them to the ground.

170

Finally Tank breathed deeply and blew out lustily like a swimmer who is catching his breath after a hard race. 'You know,' he said, 'I've got an idea. The problem we are facing is not mechanical. There's nothing wrong with the ship. I don't think anything happens mechanically in this world. All our difficulties are linked to that purple bastard out there.' He nodded towards the window. 'It is holding us here. We left it too late, that's all.'

They looked out of the window. It was now almost completely dark and the luminous purple bag of Erix hung in the sky, casting its festering light over hills and trees and highlighting the solid bulk of the *Fare-Thee-Well*.

'Do you mean you think we'll be able to take off tomorrow when Erix has gone?' asked Peron tentatively.

'Yes. That's exactly what I mean. Can't you feel what it's like? We have been close to that bastard. We've felt its power. Everything is oppressed. It oppresses everything. Somehow it has stopped our ship. Don't ask me how. Tomorrow we'll lift, but for tonight we must be careful. Fear is our greatest enemy. We should all stay awake this night.'

For the first time since the failure of the engines Peron felt a gleam of hope. Still he persisted. 'But what about those other ships, the ones which are stranded. Why didn't they escape?'

'Because they didn't want to,' said Tank.

'Food,' said Haberjin. 'If we are going to stay awake all night there's no reason why we should go hungry. Place your orders. And afterwards we'll tell stories. Hell, just think what is standing outside there. We've seen what no one in the Pocket has seen for centuries. We've found the *Fare-Thee-Well*. I'm going to crack open a bottle to the

171

memory of John Death Elliott and drink his health. Who'll join me?'

Haberjin's enthusiasm was infectious. All the men relaxed. Only Cordoba didn't move, but lay still on her couch.

And after they had eaten they did tell stories and sang songs. Haberjin and Pettet told about their adventures. Tank made lightning sketches and caricatures of some of their friends in the Pocket. Even Peron, who did not regard himself as a storyteller, found himself taking part and telling about his encounter with the Hammer. The hours began to slip away.

In a pause in the conversation, while Haberjin was off to the larder to bring back more wine, Cordoba suddenly woke up. 'I've been with Wystan,' she said. 'He's happy enough, but tired now. He's still climbing.'

'Will he come back to us?' asked Pettet.

Cordoba laughed and shook her head. 'No. He couldn't even if he wanted to. He's almost into the high canopy. I don't think he'll survive the night. Don't feel responsible, Pettet. He would have escaped one way or the other. He's found something he wanted and he wouldn't have it any other way. Tomorrow we must leave him here. He has brought some strength to this lonely planet. Think of him as a sacrifice, an offering. Nothing more.'

Pettet shrugged. 'But I could have done things better.'

Haberjin returned. 'Welcome back to the living, witch-woman. Here, I've brought you a drink. You're going to have some rare stories to tell your grandchildren when we get back.'

Cordoba accepted the drink and smiled at Haberjin, but it was a sad smile. Peron wondered why. He guessed that she had seen more on her travels than she was prepared to say. There was both a sadness and a delight about her.

172

Peron marvelled at himself. Here was he, a trained historian with a clear rational mind, and yet how easily he had accepted the strange ways of the Pocket.

Something was happening outside. Erix had swung by overhead and could now no longer be seen, but the tree was beginning to shine. Pulses of light gathered about the roots and then shot up the trunk on their long journey to the canopy. Everyone gathered to watch, shielding their eyes from the brilliant glare. Gradually the pulses came quicker, until the whole tree became a pillar of silver fire. Lines of force radiated from the canopy, filling the dark sky with wrinkles.

Peron could watch no more and yet he couldn't drag his eyes away. He felt himself shaking with the tree's energy. He felt his teeth bite his lips and the bones shake in his wrists and fingers. He felt himself gasping. He couldn't breathe. He saw his mother and sisters. He saw a schoolfriend he had not thought of for many years. He saw Pawl Paxwax and Laurel and the Hammer with its gaping orifice of tentacles . . . and then blackness stunned him like a flying brick.

When he came to he found himself crouched in a corner under his bunk, and there was blood on his hands and face. The grey light of dawn filled the cabin. He had a strange voice pounding in his head. It said, 'What was born? What was born?' The words kept on repeating. The voice took on shape and form. Peron recognized Tank.

Haberjin lay face down on his bunk. Pettet was crushed against the control panel. Only Tank was still on his feet. Tank, strongest of all of them, stood at the window, gripping the guide rails in his huge hands and shouting, 'What was born? What was born?' Pettet and Haberjin came to themselves quickly. Together they eased Tank away from the window and lifted him on to his bed. There

173

he at once relaxed. 'Cordoba is outside,' he said. 'She knows it all.' Then the whites of his eyes turned up and he passed out.

Pettet and Haberjin ran to the window and stared out. A fine misty rain was falling. The canopy of the tree was hidden and thin wraiths of cloud scudded past the black fins of the *Fare-Thee-Well*. At the water's edge they could see Cordoba. She was dancing, lifting her knees high and waving her arms gracefully above her head. As they watched there was movement in the lake, as though a large fish was in the shallows; and then the figure of a man reared up, and began to wade ashore.

Pettet was out of the ship in a flash. He landed running but tripped and fell his length in the wet vegetation. Then he was up and running again. Cordoba heard him coming and turned and raised her hands as though to ward off a blow. Pettet hesitated, and in that time Haberjin and Peron were able to catch up to him.

The man from the lake stood up to his knees in black water. He had a bland featureless face, almost like a baby's. Thin strands of hair like threads of glass were plastered down on to his head and his skin was so pale that the bones could be seen. As they watched his features changed. He became an old man. The muscles on his arms sagged and his belly began to pot.

'Meet my husband,' said Cordoba. 'We haven't seen one another for many years.'

The man took a step forward.

'No,' growled Pettet. 'No. No. *No!*' Haberjin and Peron grabbed his arms, but he threw them off easily. 'Come back to the ship, Cordoba. This is some creature dreamed up on this planet. I knew your husband. This is not him.'

'Dreamed up. Yes. But I dreamed him.'

'Come back to the ship.'

Cordoba backed away towards the lake and the man

put his arms round her, enclosing her old breasts and nuzzling at her neck.

Pettet advanced. There was no doubt that he meant to kill. He reached for Cordoba and she bit his arm. A hand went for his eyes but he turned his head away, and she seized his beard and scratched in it. He forced her from him and held her at arm's length and then thrust her into Haberjin's arms. The two of them fell back and rolled in the soft weeds at the water's edge..

Pettet seized the man by one thin arm and jerked forwards and then his hand closed on his throat. The man didn't struggle.

Peron, who had watched everything, jumped for Pettet's shoulders. Though he could not have explained it, he knew that killing the alien was wrong. Pettet shrugged him off and began to squeeze. The man's mouth opened but no sounds emerged.

Suddenly there was a cry from behind. Peron, who was struggling to his feet, was sent flying face first into the water as Tank burst through the vegetation and began to grapple with Pettet. He grabbed his beard and punched, but Pettet would not release his grip on the alien's throat. Tank punched again and again, and then sank his fist into Pettet's stomach. That released the grip. The two giants fought in the water until finally Tank had Pettet's arms behind him and was able to force his head down into the water. He held him until Pettet stopped struggling, and then released him and heaved his body up on to the shore.

But the old man was dead. He floated face down with his arms spread wide and his toes dragging in the silt. Slowly, gently, Tank turned him over. The face was changing again, becoming pink and smooth like a baby's. Whatever character was there seeped away, leaving a bland face without history.

Peron moved to help but Tank stopped him. 'Leave it there. It is not human. Nor yet completely alien either.' He took the corpse by the feet and pushed it out into the water. 'If you want to do something, make sure that Cordoba is all right.'

Cordoba was kneeling. She was at the water's edge, leaning forward into the mud and tearing at her hair. Haberjin sat back. Ugly scratches had opened up one side of his face and one arm. His blood was being washed away in the soft rain.

Before anyone could move, Cordoba jumped to her feet. She seemed to have the grace of a girl. She ran into the water to where the body of the alien lolled and then she dived. She never emerged . . . and the body drifted out into the middle of the lake.

Tank shook his head. It looked for a moment as though he was going to lumber into the water after Cordoba. But he turned and applied his strength to Pettet, pressing him in the back until the giant vomited out the black water and lay coughing.

It had all happened so quickly. Peron sat for a moment in the ooze looking about him and then he got to his feet and offered his hand to Haberjin. Haberjin spat redly.

An hour later the four men sat together in the ship. Tank held one of Pettet's hands and was stroking it. Haberjin held the other hand in the firm grip of friendship. Peron busied himself making breakfast. He tried to listen as much as he could, for Tank was explaining what he thought had happened.

'You were right, Pettet. The thing Cordoba saw and thought was her husband was alien. It came from the tree. I saw it last night. I saw a lot of things. Most of them I don't understand. But this much I can guess. The tree responded to us. It responded to our emotion. Emotion is

176

the great generator of the universe. It is the first true sign of consciousness. Everything flows from emotion. The tree took our emotion and somehow made it physical. If we had been terrified it would have made shapes from our terror. As it was we were happy, and our thoughts were of those we love. Whether it can make shapes from hatred I do not know. I somehow doubt it. Hatred belongs with all dark thoughts and is part of that purple beast that looks down on this world. Anyway, when we were on Erix I saw particles without form. Here I saw nothing but potential form. It was magnificent and terrible. Cordoba knew all this. She willed that form of her husband to come into existence. It was all she wanted. Cordoba is the kind of woman who loves only once. She wanted him for just a few more hours. He died far from her, you know, and she never forgave herself that she was not by his side. Anyway, what does it all matter? You are free to leave whenever you want. The ship's engines will lift. I guarantee that. The only people who stay on Ultima Thule are those who want to.'

Haberjin looked at Tank sharply. 'Why do you say "*You* are free to leave"? Aren't you coming with us?'

Tank shook his head.

'No. I decided that last night. I'll take my chances on Thule. It is the best place for me. From here I can continue the fight against Erix directly. It's a fight I've been engaged in all my life. He who would try and hold me back is no friend.'

'I'll try not to hold you back,' said Pettet. 'Do what you want. I don't understand anything any more.'

Tank stood up. He offered his hand to each man in turn. Peron took his hand and squeezed it and then hurried across the cabin and picked up Tank's sketchbook and box of pencils and handed them to him.

'You keep them, historian,' said Tank. 'I'll never use

177

them again. You see, there is a point beyond art to which art is always leading. Last night I saw all my desires fulfilled a thousand times. All my loves . . . all the things I could never get quite right. That was what was born. So now goodbye.'

Tank turned and jumped down from the spaceship. They watched him as he began to beat a new pathway through the greenery away from the tree and towards the hills.

In the cabin there was a smell of burning. Peron had burnt their breakfast.

The ship came alive. One by one Haberjin switched in the relays. The vibration in the ship gave them hope. Finally he fed the main drive and the ship lurched slightly and then soundlessly began to lift.

'Go gently, Haberjin,' said Pettet. 'I want to enjoy our departure.'

Haberjin turned the ship slowly until they were close to the giant hulk of the *Fare-Thee-Well*. 'We never did get aboard, did we, captain?'

Pettet shook his head.

'And I don't suppose we ever will now. Probably just as well. It might have been a great disappointment. Everything waterlogged and rusty. Ah well, at least I can tell my grandchildren I saw it. That is, if I ever get round to having any children to have grandchildren.'

'Shut up, Haberjin and drive.'

'Aye, aye, captain.' Haberjin lifted them over the *Fare-Thee-Well* and then began a circuit of the tree. The rain had cleared and the tree stood stark and majestic and very still. The lake at its base was like a pool of black ink.

Something was moving down there. There were figures walking round the margin of the lake, close to where they had landed.

Haberjin took the ship down in a slow arc and he let it hover.

They stared down at the figures. One was a woman with a mane of black hair. She waved, beckoningly. It was Raleigh. The second was an old woman with grey hair and a sharp angular face. The resemblance to Haberjin was unmistakable. But his mother had been dead for fourteen years. The third figure was a child. It carried a blanket and had one thumb in its mouth. It waved in greeting.

With emotions too complex to describe, Peron recognized himself as a child.

'Get us away, Haberjin,' he shouted. 'Get us away.'

15

ON BENNET

The killing was continuing in earnest.

In some corners it was conducted with an almost religious zeal and went far beyond the recommendations of the green-eyed Selena.

The decision, once made, was acted on by bureaucrats who devised timetables and schedules and the allocation of resources with bland efficiency. A massive publicity campaign throughout the domains of all the Families made sure that everyone from the humblest scrub farmer up to the petty monarchs of small worlds knew that it was now open season on the aliens. Units of highly-trained recruits surprised the holds of Spiderets and fulfilled their quota. While he did not agree with the measures, Pawl could not stand against them. To do so would have been to invite the aggression of all the Families. But he held the killing to a minimum where he could and refused to take action against the Hammer.

Pawl had other problems as well. He needed to close down the world called Veritas. During the time of his father's reign this had been the main administrative world. It was on this world that a one-time senior official of the Paxwax, Songteller by name, had practised deceit and laid the Paxwax open to attack. Since the installation of Wynn on Pawl's Homeworld, Veritas was redundant, but it needed to be closed down formally and all its old records destroyed and former employees pensioned off.

Laurel felt contradictory feelings about Pawl's departure. She would miss him. She had come to rely on him in a way that her father would have found difficult to imagine. At the same time she was glad to have some time on her own. As the new Mistress of Paxwax she knew that she needed time to establish herself in her own right. It was not good to shelter under Pawl's long shadow. The memory of her father was a distant ache, almost like the memory of pain. She knew she could cope.

Since her marriage to Pawl, life had whirled her along like paper carried by the wind. Now she needed time to herself, to think, to plan, to adjust to the idea of motherhood. She was glad that Paris had decided to remain on Elliott's Pocket and hoped that he would find happiness there. If she had one sadness it was that Paris and Pawl had not really joined in friendship. Perhaps that would take time too.

It was late in the afternoon when Pawl left Bennet Homeworld. He held Laurel close to him. 'I will be as quick as I can,' he said. Laurel felt strangely tongue-tied.

'Take care, love,' she said.

'And you.' He swung aboard the shuttle and waved as it lifted, and then the windows became opaque as they sealed.

Alone now, Laurel wandered. The gardens were in full bloom and the air was sweet with the fragrance of the flowers and gum trees.

Frisky young horses, like little boys burning up the last energy of the day, galloped and gambolled round their paddock, kicking the soil to dust and rearing and whinnying. With them was Red, a woman whom Laurel had met only briefly. She was standing against the paddock fence. Laurel had felt an instant liking for Red when she met her.

'Your horses look keen,' said Laurel, coming up to the fence.

Red smiled and offered Laurel her hand and helped her

to clamber up on to the paddock fence. The two women sat together. 'Yes. The stock is coming right. But they're not show horses. They're workers, and they need work.'

Laurel said nothing, but nodded. How apt Red's remarks seemed to her own situation. Laurel too was a worker not an ornament.

'Do you ride?' asked Red.

'When I was on Lotus-and-Arcadia. We used to ride horses when we went on picnics. I was never very good.'

'Would you like to ride out tomorrow morning? Shouldn't do you any harm as long as you don't do anything foolish. I'll pick you out a quiet one.'

Laurel thought for a moment. She thought of the baby inside her. *So long as I am careful.* She thought of the wind in her hair and the clean bite of the sea air. Her mind was made up. 'I'd love to,' she said.

'It's best just after dawn. You feel you're the first person in creation then. And the horses like it too. They like to feel the dew on their legs.'

'We'll do it. We must go down by the sea. We'll take some food.'

'A picnic?' said Red and laughed.

'Yes, a picnic. Why not?'

Laurel was up and dressed even as the first light brightened the windows of the Tower.

Outside the rambling courtyards and roofs of Bennet were coming alive. Smoke stained the air and there was the bright brittle laughter of children playing before they have eaten.

Outside the air was chill as she stepped from the Tower and the flagstones were wet. Autumn was coming quickly and with it heavy dew and mist in the valleys of the Mendel Hills.

She took the slideway through the echoing house,

stopped at the central kitchens to collect two bags of provisions, and then walked out into the courtyard and crossed to the stables.

Red was already mounted and waiting. Tethered outside the stable and stamping its hooves and blowing noisily through its nostrils was a large grey. It was bigger than any of the horses Laurel had seen on Lotus-and-Arcadia.

'Here you are. Her name's Rimini. She's as gentle as a kid. I've given her a bit of a run, so she should be settled now. You'll soon be friends.'

Laurel stroked the horse's neck and then swung up into the saddle. It tried a few tricks, walking backwards and trying to rub Laurel's leg against the stable door. But Laurel gripped it with her legs and stroked its mane and whispered its name in its ear and soon the grey stood still, one leg forward.

'You've a way with you,' said Red admiringly. 'We'll have you aboard King here one day.' She slapped the neck of her black stallion affectionately. 'Shall we go?'

They headed down a path beside the old part of the house and across the deserted landing strip. Beyond lay the open country, where gentle hills of grass sloped down to the scarlet sea.

'Shall we give them a run?' said Red and flicked her black horse with the reins. It reared, as she had taught it to do, and then set off like a black arrow, its tail streaming behind it.

Laurel urged her mount forward cautiously and it began to trot, which she found uncomfortable. She urged it more and it lengthened its strides into a gallop. She could feel the raw strength of the horse and was amazed that it reminded her of Pawl. The wind pulled her hair back from her scalp and in a moment of abandon she gave the horse its head. For a few moments horse and rider were one and then she lost the rhythm. She felt her leg weaken and the stirrup come loose. Suddenly she was sliding. She pulled on the reins and succeeded in slewing the horse's head round. It began to panic and buck and toss. With one shift it threw Laurel.

Laurel came to with the sound of drumming hooves in her ears. Red was racing back down the track, her body low over the neck of the giant black horse. She pulled up and slid from the saddle in one movement.

'Are you hurt?' she asked as Laurel tried to sit up. 'Take care. Move carefully. Try and turn your head.' Laurel turned her head, working the neck joint. Quickly Red moved Laurel's arms and legs. There was no sudden pain. Only a dull ache and muzziness. 'How do you feel inside?'

Laurel pressed her hands to her belly. 'All okay. Just a bit shaken.'

'A bit shaken! You were lucky. You came off like a rag doll. Come on, we'll get you back to the house.'

'No. We'll go on. My pride's a bit dented, that's all. I came out to ride to the sea, and that's what we'll do. I'll just sit for a moment.'

She sat with her head between her knees and felt the world turn and come to steadiness. Close by, the grey was peacefully cropping the grass. The large black nuzzled her with his head and then began grazing himself.

Sitting there in the morning sunshine with the sturdy Red at her side, Laurel became aware of a strangeness. There was something that did not belong. She could feel it. Something was moving in the long grass off the road. At first she thought of a wild animal, but there were no wild animals on Bennet Island.

A small black-garbed figure emerged, working its way steadily up the hill towards the main buildings, following the thick green grass of the water course.

184

The horses raised their heads and whinnyed. Red stood still watching the small creature. There was something defensive in her stance. Laurel made her mind a blank. Despite Pawl's pleading, she had never come to accept Odin. She could sense the creature questing about her, waiting for an opening.

For his part Odin was aware of the accident. He had spent the night by the shore, his long basal tendrils dug deep into the stony soil, drinking the rich seepage from the sea. Such was his comfort.

Working his way up the hillside he had felt the thrill in Laurel as the grey began to gallop. Then the panic as she lost control. Odin was with her when she fell. *Now*, he thought. *Shall I do it now? Now, when a broken neck would seem most casual?* And at the same moment he realized that he could not kill Laurel like that. The killing must not seem an accident.

He caught her in the air, drew her sinews together, turned her and brought her down on her side with a thump. There were no bones broken, but there would be bruises. He stilled the mind of the horse, which in its fear might have turned and trampled Laurel. Then he moved on, gliding through the grass with the same effortless grace as a snail.

Laurel's mind was a glittering mirror to him.

Odin knew the moment the two women stared at him. He saw Laurel's fear and recoiled from the disgust he saw in Red's mind. That woman wanted to pick up a stone and throw it at him.

The fall had put greater spirit into Laurel. She stood up and approached the grey, her hands high and open. She rubbed its head and picked up the trailing reins and then swung up into the saddle. She ignored the pain in her leg. The horse seemed to sense a change in the rider and stood still with its head raised ready to move.

Red remounted and joined her. 'If we cut across country here we will come to the sea north of the landing. There are some rocky bays and a river mouth and there's a reef about half a mile out, keeps the red froth away. The water's usually quite calm. I like it. Then there's a coast path leads up the island to a spit under the cliffs. I've gathered shells there.'

'Sounds too good to be true,' said Laurel. 'Come on, let's go.'

Together they turned their horses and headed down the hill and into a small copse. 'I often ride out here,' said Red. 'Especially when I'm feeling a bit upset. You know.'

Laurel did know. She wondered just how much Red had guessed. 'Do you like it here, on Bennet Home-world?' she asked as their horses picked their way slowly between the trees. They were now within earshot of the sea.

'Sometimes yes. Sometimes no,' replied Red with a shrug. 'At home on Molier I lived close to the deserts. My father had a little farm. Oh, we did all right, and I could ride for miles and miles without ever crossing another set of footprints, except the desert bear and the wild dogs. I loved the open space, but it wasn't a good place for horses. Their hooves began to crack. This is a lot better. Then again, I sometimes miss the openness and the solitude. Here there are always people and I need to be alone sometimes . . . quite often. I need to feel that the universe is here, close to me. Do you know what I mean?' Red asked this shyly.

'Where I came from,' said Laurel, 'there was only the sea and millions of islands. You could have ridden round the largest of them in a day. If I wanted to get away from everyone, I could take a boat. We had things called submersibles. They were seed pods from some planet. You could lie down in one of them and let the sea take you where it wanted.'

'Weren't you afraid?'

'The sea was my mother, my cradle, and I hope it will be my grave.' How simply those words came to Laurel. 'I was not afraid, though I was often in danger. Once I took some food and let myself drift for a week. At night the stars were like spears. It was wonderful. Then my father came in his great house and found me and I went home quite happily.'

'Perhaps the sea is like the desert,' said Red.

The trees ended abruptly and they found themselves on a narrow bank of grass high on the cliffs. They looked down on the scarlet sea which was still warming. Far out a Maw blew, sending a spew of crimson high into the air. Below them the coast was protected by a reef and the water had been cleared of any red algae. Pawl had plans to make this into a special swimming place for Laurel.

Standing on the rocky margin were large black Way cartons. They looked alien and strange. These had been delivered from the Shell-Bogdanovich Conspiracy while Pawl and Laurel were off world. They contained the seedlings and cuttings for an exotic marine garden. It was to be a surprise, but the work had been held up. The water that had been cleared was grey with salts and the small waves broke sluggishly.

'That frightens me sometimes,' said Red. 'The sea.'

Laurel looked at her. She saw the blonde hair drawn back, the strong face, the wide shoulders and breasts which strained against her thick bodice. It was hard to imagine Red being afraid of anything; she seemed so complete, so at home in herself. 'Why?' asked Laurel. 'Why afraid?'

Red grinned. 'I can't swim,' she said, and urged her horse over the cliff and on to a narrow path which led zigzag down to the stony beach.

It was the smell that captured Laurel. It was the smell of home. She breathed deeply through her nostrils and let the smell curl inside her. The rank seaweed, the dead bird with matted bleached feathers, the small flies, the rounded stones, the roar and caress of the waves; all spoke to her. She urged her grey horse out into the surf, until the waves slapped up over her boots and filled them and the horse's belly shivered.

Overhead a seagull hung in the wind, turning its black-eyed head, eager for food. It keened. And the sound cut Laurel like a knife. Something inside her had been waiting for that sound. It freed her. She felt she could cry and willed the tears to come. She let her sadness and happiness flow through her. A father, a world lost. A child to come.

Red, patrolling the shore where her big black stallion sank up to its fetlocks in the soft foamy sand, knew nothing. All she saw was a lady on a horse who sat rather stiffly and who stared out to sea.

Minutes passed and then the grey began of its own volition to push through the waves back to the shore. Laurel breathed deeply. She felt more at ease. In those few moments she had accepted something of Pawl's Homeworld. From now on everything would become easier.

'Come on. Let's ride to the spit,' called Red. 'We can light a fire and you can dry out.' To prevent any argument she urged the black stallion on and it began to canter over the shiny wet shingle, sending up a spray of sand and water.

The driftwood burned blue and white, and the hot air made the distant cliffs shimmer. The two women huddled together to share the warmth and avoid the wind that blew steadily from the sea.

'How's the leg?' asked Red. 'Is it stiffening?'

'No. It feels better. The sea water helped, I think.' She looked at the cliffs which towered, sheer, a few hundred yards from them. 'Where's the house from here?'

Red pointed to a set of pines that stood high on the cliffs about a mile from them. 'Beyond them, I guess. I think that is the edge of the gardens. We haven't come far north.'

They shared the food. Some meat they had brought they held in the fire on sticks and then tore from the skewers with their teeth. Red opened a bottle of dark red wine and they drank from the bottle, laughing because they had forgotten to bring cups. They ate bread and fruit while the horses nosed among the thick-leaved shrubs which grew on the spit.

'And what do you want to do . . . hope to do?' asked Laurel finally. She had been mulling the question for several minutes and was immediately sorry that it came out so abruptly.

'When?'

'Anytime. Get more horses? Have a farm of your own? Get married?'

Red laughed. 'Oh, I'll get married sometime, I suppose. I've a lot of giving inside me, I can feel it. But I'll still keep my horses. I haven't met a man yet can match the horses for affection or strength.' She laughed again.

'Perhaps you'd be better staying alone,' said Laurel.

'Perhaps I would, at that. But I don't like the loneliness

in the evenings. And it won't get any better. And I like making love as much as the next woman. I suppose I'm not satisfied. I do want more out of life. Horses aren't enough . . . nor are men. I don't know. I want . . . I want . . . more. That's all. One day I'll know, and when that day comes I hope I'll have the courage to go for what I want, even if I have to walk over hot coals. What about you? Are you happy?'

'I'm one of those women whose life became suddenly simpler . . . when I fell in love with Pawl . . . I can remember it so clearly . . . it was as if everything had changed colour. I'd always laughed at romantic women, and then I became romantic. I'd thought I never wanted children, and suddenly I wanted *his* children. It was like a craving. I'd always been independent and suddenly I didn't want to be independent. And I wanted to make him happy. I want to make him happy. Only I don't know what to do. The reality of living with someone is so different from the casual pleasure. Pawl says just to be with me is enough . . . but that means I do nothing. I can't accept that. I'm not an ornament. I don't want him to admire me . . . love me, yes . . . but not set me apart. That is a cruelty he does not understand.'

'Have you talked to him about it?'

'Not properly.'

'Well, then.'

'You see, I know he loves me . . . but I'm not sure I know what it is in me he loves. I know what it is I love in him.'

'Tell me.'

'I love his gentleness. And I love his anger, because it is real. It is him, simple, unclear, muddled, but him. And I love him because he is vulnerable . . .' Laurel broke off, realizing that she was saying more than she meant to or wanted to. But she was not ashamed. 'How can a woman

190

explain why she loves a man . . . because he's there. Chemistry. Sometimes I want to crush him. I want him to crush me. I want to make him angry . . . Is all that silly?'

'I think you are a lucky woman,' said Red.

'Well, maybe. But I don't know what to do. And my love has already cost me a father and a world I loved. Is there no end to paying? Where does it end? Where can you be happy with confidence?'

Red thought and stirred the fire with her boot. 'I don't think happiness lies in other people,' she said finally. 'I think it belongs somewhere else. I think it is in us. In what we do to things.'

Both women stared into the fire, which flared blue and white and pale scarlet as the wind blew. 'There was a boy in my village,' said Red, 'whom we all used to laugh at. He was a bit touched in the head. A bit simple. He used to moon about and no girl in her right mind would look at him twice. The boys used to give him hell, tying him to a little wagon and then dragging him through the dust and mud, and he used to laugh. Thought he was being one of the lads, I suppose. Well, anyway, he used to collect stones. He'd scratch for hours in the dirt, digging up pebbles. He'd keep some for a day or two and then he'd throw them out. Others he wouldn't part with. Those he wanted to keep he used to lick so they were all shiny, and then he'd keep them in a jar filled with water.

'One day, one of the boys got the jar and smashed it. All the stones fell out. And he just stood there, the simple one, he just stood there staring as if he couldn't understand what had happened. He didn't protest or fight or anything; he just knelt down and started gathering the pebbles again and put them in his hanky.

'And he never let anyone see them again. And we none of us knew why they were precious to him.' She stopped and poked a stick into the red heart of the fire. 'See, that's what we do to one another, isn't it? We never know the hurt we cause. We never know the love we disregard.' She lapsed into silence again.

'And?' prompted Laurel.

'That's all. A kid with his pebbles. I don't know what made me think of it. I know he loved those pebbles, though.' The stick she had been poking the fire with finally burst into flame. 'We're funny creatures, aren't we? Cruel and kind and full of doubt. But we must always protect that which we love.'

'Yes,' said Laurel and shivered.

'Come on,' said Red. 'Let's get back. Get you warmed through. I haven't talked so much for years.'

'Nor me,' said Laurel, standing up. 'Nor me.'

16

ON VERITAS

Pawl sat back in Songteller's chair, his arms resting on the sides, and felt the power that it gave him. Like an ancient throne, it was raised higher than any other chair and was positioned at the precise focus of the wide fan of seats that made up the assembly chamber. It was from this chair that Songteller had conducted the affairs of the Paxwax.

Sitting there, facing the empty, attendant seats, Pawl came to understand Songteller's defection. In front of him glowed a gigantic vivante image of the Paxwax Empire. At the touch of a switch he could change the image and summon up any other empire. Or he could dive into the bright cloud of stars and bring any one of them into precise focus.

Pawl could imagine Songteller, sitting alone, and swirling empires like wine in a glass.

Methodically Pawl closed down Veritas. He saw the old banks of computers burned and trashed. All their contents and more were now held on his Homeworld. He saw the great defensive satellites speared out of the sky. His plan was to turn the entire world into a game park. Pensions were granted to all the former workers and they were given the option of continuing to live on the world or departing.

Standing on the shore of an inland sea close by one of the resort villages, Pawl spoke with his former chief of security. He looked round the neat houses, each appointed with every luxury. Above them the sky was a dark blue, almost purple, where the force field held the clouds at bay and allowed sunshine to filter through.

'You lacked for nothing, did you?' said Pawl. The security man, neat in his dress uniform, did not reply. 'Are you trying to tell me you didn't know that anything was amiss? Couldn't you smell something on the wind? That was your job.'

'There was nothing,' the man said finally. 'Nothing specific. Just a . . . casualness.'

About a hundred yards from shore a head broke surface and a cluster of eyes observed the two men. The Mellow Peddlar pawed its way into shallow water. Men meant trade, sometimes a free feed, sometimes a stone. It took its chance. In its wattles it carried shaped stones and bits of carved bones. It crawled up on to the bank a few yards from the men and there disgorged its wares. Without thinking, the security man picked up a stone and threw it. The Peddlar pulled back into its carapace and scuttled back into the sea, abandoning its treasure.

'Why did you do that?' asked Pawl, and then, with a sudden rush of anger, he punched the security man hard in the face. 'That is for letting my world become casual.'

17

ON BENNET

Laurel awoke with the distinct knowledge that she had been spoken to. A bright child's voice had sounded in her sleep. She lay in bed wondering, and knew that Odin was near. He was forcing his attention on her. With reluctance she spoke into the darkness. 'Odin. Where are you?'

Immediately the child's voice sprang in her mind. 'We should meet. Now would be time. There is not long.'

'What do you mean, "not long"?'

Silence. Odin did not reply; and then, when he did speak again, it was a question. 'Can I come up? The door is sealed. We must meet. Our separateness causes Pawl sorrow.'

Laurel knew this was true. And she had to admit to herself that now that Odin was speaking in her mind, he did not seem so alien. It was as though just by being there he had achieved something of humanity. Perhaps now was the time to meet the small alien; now, while Pawl was away and the pressure of his silent communication with Odin was lifted. But she did not trust the child's voice. There was something calculated about that. But she made her decision.

'Yes. Come up.' Laurel touched the release switches and the lower doors which gave access to the Tower opened. Then she dressed quickly.

'Wynn, watch closely. You know more of the creature than I do. Stand guard for me.' Laurel spoke to the ceiling, where fern-like bio-crystalline filaments had begun to glow.

The room seemed to speak. 'I am on guard, Laurel.

Rest assured. Conduct your business. I wondered who you were talking to. Little Odin. A delicate mind. I cannot probe it. I would be happier if I could. I will remain silent but watchful.'

This last phrase faded into the silence as a light above the entrance door blinked on and the door slid open to reveal the small black shape of Odin. He glided forward and thin red tendrils snaked from below his gown. His enigmatic white mask nodded, as though suggesting humility and concord. Laurel controlled her revulsion.

'I am not confident,' spoke the clear child's voice. 'I too am nervous. I do not find it easy to speak with humans. Pawl frightens me, though I have learned to live with his moods and can protect myself. You are wholly different. All I can draw from you is thin suspicion. Tell me why.'

'I have not had any dealings with aliens,' said Laurel. 'Pawl is more worldly than me. Besides, on my Home-world we regarded the Inner Circle with suspicion, not as friends. I have always found your garb and your masks rather frightening.'

'Are you afraid of me? There is nothing to fear. Would you be more comfortable if I were to drop my mask for you as I do for Pawl?'

There was a dreadful intimacy in this thought which affronted Laurel. It was as though she had been asked to lift her skirts above her knees, or worse, witness the forced exhibition of another. And yet there was honesty there, a willingness to strip away taboos and face differ-ences for what they were.

'I will remove my mask. Please look on me without fear.'

With sudden dread Laurel saw red tendrils wriggle through the eye holes and then Odin's cowl fell forward and she could see no more.

The mask clattered to the floor. Odin's body convulsed and the black hood fell back.

Laurel saw the dome of red worms and in the same moment the smell of Odin hit her. She stared at Odin, and then she screamed.

And in that moment a curious thing happened. The mind of Laurel and the mind of Odin met in pain. Laurel's scream was torn from some instinctive depth of her being. It was a primeval cry of revulsion and Odin received that cry in all its rawness. Acid in the face, a fish-hook lodged in the jaw and pulled, tap-root cut by spade, barbed wire jerked through ungloved hands: it was all this and more. The small creature had no defence. The scream struck him and he toppled.

Laurel watched Odin fall, there on the fine tiles a mere four feet in front of her. She saw the small figure slump. The black gown which normally was so neat fell open, revealing its shiny interior and the soft red fibres of Odin's trunk. She saw, as in slow motion, the large basal sucker which held Odin in place lift from the floor and curl its lip as the creature fell.

Then Odin's pain swamped Laurel and obliterated her fear.

She was moving. She crossed the short space and seized the fabric of Odin's black gown. It was light and strong like metal mesh. Through the fabric she could feel Odin's body. It was mush and jelly. Without realizing it she sent love through her hands, begging the small creature to live, live, live.

How long she knelt cradling the small creature she did not know. She held it like a baby and crooned to it. Finally something moved in her arms. The upper tendrils, which had turned grey and lay like the leaves of a plant

197

left unwatered for many days, stirred and a rosiness began to spread through them. The great yellow sucker closed on itself and then opened again, as though searching for purchase. Laurel helped. She eased the small creature upright and was glad when she felt a solidity return to it.

Secretions began to flood down the trunk from the many flukes and tendrils. Laurel tucked the gown round Odin and was pleased to see it adhere. She had heard Pawl say more than once that the gown of the Inner Circle was a survival suit tailored to Odin's needs.

She stared into Odin's 'face' and it was a flower.

Why had she not seen it at first?

Many minutes later the tendrils swirled, like hair in water, and a drowsy thought opened in Laurel's mind. 'Your women are stronger than your men.'

'Are you feeling stronger?'

'Stronger.'

'What can I do to help?'

'I want to feel the earth.'

'Shall I carry you down? Would you like to stand in the grass?'

'Yes.'

Laurel picked up the mask of the Inner Circle, which lay on its back near Odin, staring vacantly up at the ceiling.

'Here, you can wear this silly thing if it makes you feel better.' She held the mask in front of the hole in Odin's cowl and watched as delicate suckers no bigger than her little finger wriggled out and attached themselves to the back of the mask and drew it into place.

'I hate this thing,' came a grumpy voice that sounded so like a human child that Laurel laughed. 'But it has its purpose.'

'Why did you join the Inner Circle if you don't like its regalia?' asked Laurel.

'I didn't join the Inner Circle. I was selected. Is not that the way you humans see fate?'

Laurel shrugged. 'I don't know much about fate. I just want to live for the present. Settle down here. Don't start dwelling on fate. We have both had a shake-up and that's quite enough for one night. Come here, let me pick you up.'

Odin seemed heavier and beneath the gown Laurel could feel the hardness of muscle. She carried him to the door which led to the shaft down to the ground. 'Remember I am with you,' whispered the voice of Wynn the computer. 'Do not be too trusting.'

Laurel ignored it and stepped through the door.

'What does my voice sound like to you?' asked Odin as they dropped to the ground.

'Like a boy's.'

'Tell me if I ever sound different.'

'I will.' Laurel stepped from the Tower and walked round it until she came to a small grassy courtyard. There she set Odin down. The small creature worked its way in a circle as though selecting its exact spot.

'What do you hope for?' The thought was sudden and strange and Laurel did not know what to reply at first. Then she said, 'Why, to be happy, I suppose. Isn't that what everyone hopes for? Isn't that what you hope for?'

The only reply was an echoing silence, like the silence inside a large building. 'Why don't you answer me?'

'Because I cannot. I hope for nothing.'

'That is sad.'

'Yes. Goodnight now. I am drinking.'

Laurel returned to the Tower. Before she entered she glanced back at Odin. He was hunkered down. He looked like a stunted black tree trunk.

Well, thought Laurel, as she rose up the Tower, *that wasn't too bad. Perhaps things will be easier now.*

18

THE CALL FROM SANCTUM

And that same night, while Odin drank in strength from the soil, a long, sinewy hand of thought reached out from Sanctum and took him and squeezed him. It was the Tree. It was thunder in the blue sky. It was love and hate and neither in a glittering ball. Roughly translated it said, OH, ODIN. YOU ARE A GREAT LOVER. HOW HUMAN YOU ARE. LOVE IS THE GREAT SEDUCTION. BETTER THE STILL MIND THAT LIKE A DEEP POOL TURNS ON ITSELF, AND IS CLEAR AND UNCLEAR, AND CAN RECEIVE GREATNESS AND RETURN AN UNTROUBLED SURFACE.

YOUR TIME IS NEAR, ODIN. ACT WITH CARE, FOR THE END OF THE HUMAN RULE IS CLOSE. YOU ARE THE HINGE. TURN SMOOTHLY. KILL THAT ALL MAY BE FREE. YOU WILL BE THE SAVIOUR.

A bellows blew on Odin and inflamed him.

LISTEN TO THE VOICE OF SANCTUM.

There came to Odin a rich cacophony of sounds and impressions. It was a great choir, but he could distinguish individual voices. He could hear his fellow Gerbes. He could hear the high song of the Lamphusae, the angry drum of the Hammer, the flute of the Parasol, the quick rattle of the Spideret, the cooing of the Link Worm, the sighing of the Sponge Rock which lived through a million gold threads, the tinkle of the Lyre Beast, the calling of humans, the snuffling of the Pullah, the harsh gulping of the lone Mellow Peddlar who lived on Sanctum and whose only claim to civilization was that he could rub rocks. There were many thousands more. Each sounding distinct. The great choir of the alien, held under domination.

'I am the one,' said Odin.

19

ON BENNET

Lovemaking over, Laurel and Pawl lay tangled together, breathing deeply, enjoying their contact, aware where flesh met flesh.

'Now we build,' murmured Pawl. 'You must work with me. Veritas was a sad world. I think there are many sad worlds in the Paxwax domain. The spirit of the leader filters down. The cruel appoint the cruel, the mean beget the mean, the hearty enjoy the hearty. Likewise, goodness spreads. It is contagious.'

'Hush, philosopher.'

'I will be a great ruler or nothing. I will make a great change in the air. How lucky we are to have one such as Odin for a friend. But can you imagine what it would be like to call a Hammer a friend? We will create that future. And if the other Families don't follow, let them be hanged.'

That morning they slept late. Outside the windows of the Tower, the Homeworld came alive and bustled. Gardeners planted and pruned. Bakers glazed their loaves. Builders continued to expand the maze of buildings. The bright sun burned away the dew and filled the valleys with mist. Everything functioned. Everything was pleasing and normal.

And that same morning, Peron returned to Pawl's Homeworld. He looked tired and had lost a lot of hair, but otherwise seemed unchanged. With him he brought vivantes from Pettet and Raleigh, along with his own notebooks and the valuable sketchbook given to him by Tank.

He sat with Pawl and Laurel in the Tower for the entire morning, telling of his adventures, trying to give them some idea of the things he had seen.

'But why didn't you bring back vivantes from these worlds? Then we could have seen everything,' said Laurel.

'Vivantes didn't work. We tried. All I have is my own notes and what is stored up here – ' he tapped his forehead – 'and this sketchbook. I'm even beginning to distrust my own memory. You see, finally, it wasn't what we did so much as what we thought, and what happened to our minds. None of us will ever be the same again.'

'And how is Pettet now?'

'Shaken. Raleigh is looking after him. He will be all right, but neither he nor Haberjin will ever journey out there again.'

'And where are the planets now?'

'Still there. No one knows why. No one knows why they came. No one knows when they will sink back again down into Emerald Lake. Perhaps they never will.'

Pawl mused. 'You have had an exciting time, Mr Peron. You make me envious. I wish I'd been along.'

'I'm glad you weren't,' said Laurel. 'You might have seen me and I don't think I could stand the competition.'

The men laughed. But Laurel was serious. 'I think it sounds like a terrible world.'

Pawl picked up Tank's sketch pad and studied his drawing of the tree. The page was covered with doodles. In the spread canopy of the tree was a face. Pawl remembered it from the Way Gate above Lumb.

'That is the face of John Elliott,' he said.

'Yes. Tank never said so, but I think he believed that the spirit of Elliott had entered the tree.'

'Some tree. And what are these other doodles?'

'I think they are faces Tank saw.'

'What? Friends? Relatives?'

'He never said. Perhaps they were just people created in my imagination. I never knew what was going on in his head. I never knew what he was going to say next. He was a very strange man. Very lonely, I think. In some ways I think that is why he liked Thule.'

Pawl set the drawings aside and looked at Peron. 'And at the end you say you saw yourself. Why was that?'

'I don't know. I've tried to work it out. I was a very lonely child. I was my own best playmate. Perhaps the tree was grasping at anything in my memory. But it frightened me, I can tell you.'

'I can imagine. Well, you are safe and sound now. And there is a lot of work to do. I would like you to write down as complete a record as you can of everything you have seen. We'll send a copy to Pettet. It might make him feel better.'

'I don't think he'll want reminding. When we got back he just hung on to Raleigh. Wouldn't let her out of his sight.'

'Sensible man. I wish all men would do the same,' said Laurel. 'I've had enough of mysteries. I suggest you two give it a rest for a while. Forget about Erix and Ultima Thule. There is a lot of living to be done here and now. Time to dwell on memories when we are old.'

'She's right,' said Pawl and closed the sketchbook with a snap. 'But at a later date, when you've had time to get your thoughts together, Peron, we'll talk some more.'

Peron nodded. 'Whenever you wish. But for me it will be a pleasure to get back into the vivantery. I have had enough of adventure. I want a simple predictable life for a while.'

He departed, leaving Tank's sketchbook with Pawl.

* * *

203

'And what plans do you have for today?' asked Pawl when Peron had gone.

'Plans,' said Laurel, as though the word amused her. 'Plans. Yes, I have plans. There are many things I haven't decided yet. But for today I shall go riding again. I shall head back down to where you and Clover Shell have been planning to build that sea garden. I've had a look at all the Way crates. I think Clover would like me to take an interest, don't you? It would help to keep her sweet.'

'I think Clover would be most appreciative if you took an interest. She went to a lot of trouble composing that sea garden. She said she wanted it to be as close a replica of your Homeworld as she could make it.'

'Ah,' said Laurel. And there the matter rested.

Pawl spent the next few hours in close consultation with Wynn. The bio-crystalline computer was now an invaluable aide. He checked the state of his empire. More and more it seemed that Wynn could sense the direction of Pawl's mind and the action it suggested was the same as that which Pawl would have chosen.

'Wynn, can you play Corfu?'

'I know the rules. But I have never played. Do you wish to play?'

'Just a game or two.'

Pawl found a board and set up the pieces. Wynn lowered a vivante camera until it hovered opposite Pawl. The single eye glowed red.

Pawl opened and the game lasted five moves before Wynn was trapped. 'Let us concede,' said Wynn, 'that I do not have a highly creative intelligence. But I am thorough and I rarely make the same mistake twice.'

The second game lasted for eight moves and the third game for nine moves.

They played for a further hour and a pattern emerged.

Pawl won every game except one, and in that game he let his concentration lapse. Usually he won in fifteen or so moves. 'Just long enough to bring a strategy into effect,' commented Wynn. 'We must play more. Without special skills I may never beat you. Then again, I am willing to learn so that I can be a worthy opponent. You are a fine and subtle player.'

Pawl left the pieces set up. Though he did not enjoy Corfu, he had wanted to test himself. Wynn was not a master, but it was no fool either, and he had beaten it with ease. This disturbed him when he thought of the Hammer.

Outside Pawl wandered through his courtyards and gardens. Autumn was giving his small island Homeworld a special beauty. The beams of the sun were noticeably lower and created strange surreal shadows. Brown leaves crunched under his feet. Flowers just blooming were particularly brilliant to attract the attention of the last wandering insects. Pawl sniffed. Somewhere a wood fire was burning, joining its smoke with the smell of the dying blossom.

In his youth he had known crazy seasons prompted by his father's activities at his weather machine. Since the destruction of the weather machine the island had settled into its natural climate.

The original founders of the island had chosen well. It enjoyed the richness of each season. Pawl wondered how deep the snow would be during winter.

He found himself outside the dome which housed the Paxwax burial chambers. He entered and immediately found himself in a warm, moist atmosphere. Here was silence and peace.

With him Pawl carried his notebook. He found his way to an old Ngaio tree, whose branches rose and then dipped to rest on the ground before lifting into the sky.

Beneath the tree was a bench. The leaves hung down like a green waterfall.

Just as he was about to sit Pawl heard a sound that started like a growl but ended in a sob. Only a few yards from him something crashed through the low lavender and rhododendron bushes. The old face of Punic appeared between the branches. One of its eyes had lost its magnetic guides and it now gazed up at an oblique angle as though looking for crows. The other eye, still moist and brown, regarded Pawl.

'Come on, Punic,' said Pawl. 'Come and sit down.' The old mechanical dog, no longer able to run or climb stairs, shambled out from the shrubbery, its tail swinging jerkily. It made elaborate pretence of sniffing and then turned in a circle three times and flopped on to the ground with a crunching of gears. Pawl could hear the old dog whirr and tick.

'Rest, Punic,' said Pawl. 'Head down on the ground. There are no spare parts for you. Do you know that? You've outlived them all. Even the company that made you.' For answer the dog yawned, showing its gleaming ferro-plastic teeth, and then it snapped at an imaginary fly.

Pawl made himself comfortable, one foot resting on the dog, and opened his notebook. The previous night he had lain awake long after Laurel had fallen into a deep and noisy sleep. He had heard the old grandfather clock call softly, 'Four o'clock, Master Pawl, and all's well.'

Four o'clock. What do you say to yourself at four o'clock? Better not tell lies then. Let the vanity of the day have its rest. Four o'clock is a time for truth.

Propped up in bed Pawl had begun to write.

Sitting now in the quiet shade he began to write again. He did not know that it was to be his last poem.

* * *

What was that noise beyond the dome? Punic growled deep in his throat and shambled to his feet. Pawl set his book to one side.

Outside the dome there was shouting, and the drumming of horses' hooves and someone calling his name. There were many voices, all agitated. Something was wrong.

Pawl summoned up Odin's image, but there was no gentle response. Odin was 'closed down', apparently. Then there was someone running through the funereal garden. A man.

Pawl stepped out and faced him and the man pulled up with a cry.

'Master Pawl. I was coming to fetch you. There's been an accident. By the sea. You'd better come.'

20

ON BENNET

Odin was lying in wait.

Since that first violent meeting with Laurel part of his mind had never left her. He was with her when she slept and in her lovemaking. This dreadful intimacy gave him a curious strength. Her death would be his death. He was not a cold assassin; he needed to love his victim.

He followed her in his mind as she stepped gaily down to the stables and joked with Red. He knew the moment she mounted the grey and felt her stroke its mane. Then she was off. Odin knew where she was heading. He waited in the trees above the cliffs.

Laurel of course knew none of this. Who asks themselves why at a particular time they feel happy? Laurel enjoyed the sun on her back and the lazy drone of the bees and the solid sound of the horse's hooves as it walked along the grass path. She felt contentment. Each day she was more aware of the life stirring inside her body. It was autumn now. In the spring she would bring forth a child. That seemed very right.

Odin moved with care. When Laurel stooped to pluck a flower from the hedge he joined with her effort and twined about her delight in the colour. All so easy when the victim is unaware and the senses are open. Laurel breathed Odin in with the scent of the flower. For a moment she felt giddy and then it was past. She thought nothing of it. Odin took her mood and gently amplified it. She began to sing. She sang one of Pawl's songs that he had written to fit an old Thalattan melody.

> Taking our time from the waves in the sea.
> Catch me. Oh you can't catch me.
> Pressing hands in the dark brown sand.
> See the waves come but you can't catch me.

When had he written that? On Lotus-and-Arcadia, shortly after they became lovers. She could remember the day but little else. She turned the horse off the path and into the wood which ran beside the coast.

Odin went too far. He released deeper energy in Laurel and she squirmed in the saddle. She had suddenly so much energy and nowhere to place it. She stood up in the stirrups. *I want to shout. I want to scratch bark with my fingers. I want to tear meat with my teeth. I want to dig in the earth and bask in the sea.*

Such energy was dangerous to Odin. It came from primeval depth. While he guided that energy he also envied it.

Laurel sat down with a bump and the horse stopped in surprise. Laurel looked about. Everything was new-minted and sharp-edged. If she closed her eyes she could feel her blood surge. Between her legs she could feel the flow of the horse as it edged forward. She saw it push through bracken that blazed like green fire.

She slipped from her horse and breasted the ferns, feeling them trail over her bare arms. The shadows were pools of blue water through which she waded. She listened to the fiery song of the birds. Looking up she saw the branches of a tree bend and reach down and stroke her hair with long brown fingers.

Beneath her feet was the rattle of dry leaves and the crackle of twigs.

'A twig is only a dwarf log,' said Laurel to herself and felt proud of the thought. It was profound. 'I must tell Pawl that. He will put it in his little book along with all his other thoughts.'

Leading the horse by the bridle, Laurel broke from the wood and climbed a short bank before the high cliffs.

Little Odin was waiting.

'Why, Odin. Isn't today wonderful? Don't you feel it is special?'

'Very special.'

'I have never felt happier. But why are you so far away from the house? Pawl may need you. He has a lot of worries at present.'

Odin did not reply. But in one surgical move he pre-empted her senses.

Laurel climbed to the top of the bank and looked down over the cliffs to the sea. She should have seen the red algae which covered the ocean and the Maw cruising as they ate. Instead she saw a pale lemon and blue sea stretching for miles until it was lost in a shimmer of haze. It was the sea of her girlhood, the sea of her long dead Homeworld.

Out in the bay she saw someone break the surface and beat the sea with his hands and then wave; it was her father.

She waved back, her arm high above her head.

She left the horse at the hill top and scrambled down the steep cliff. She slipped and rolled and kicked up dust and started small avalanches of sand and pebbles, until she stood dishevelled on the beach.

On the foreshore the sun was hot. It turned the rock pools to pans of molten copper. Quickly she stripped, pulling at her clothes impatiently, tearing her buttons, kicking off her boots. She entered the water hungrily, like a woman climbing into bed with her lover.

210

Her arms dug deep, pulling her through the shallows, out to where the weed rose. Somewhere she knew her father was ahead of her, diving like an otter.

She was a girl of twelve again, intent on catching Dapplebacks which swam with a lazy pulsing motion across the sea bed. She would catch some for breakfast, and she and her father and Paris would eat them grilled over charcoal. Somewhere distant in her future was a man with coiled dark hair and deformed legs and eyes that burned a curious yellow. Pawl was little more than a form without a name. To her girl's mind he was a dream lover who would come to her in a shower of starlight and carry her off to his palace under the sea where they would live happily ever after.

Laurel dived. The sea princess dived, pulling under the surface with strong strokes. And when she was deep under the water she turned on her back and stared up at the silver surface and watched the silver bubbles rise from her mouth.

Odin struck.

He made her breathe out and then breathe in. For a moment the shining surface darkened as though a shadow had passed over the sun.

For Laurel there was a hurting, a fighting, a panic. For a moment she knew herself, and in her mind she screamed for Pawl. But then her vision clouded again. She saw her father diving down through the clear water. He was smiling and laughing. He breathed in and out, blowing water through his mouth to show how easy it was. He held her hands tightly while her hair billowed round her face.

Laurel breathed again and darkness closed over her. The last sound she heard was the surf breaking against the headland.

* * *

211

Odin's work was done. There was no longer any consciousness he could hold on to, just a lingering warmth. The body bobbed to the surface, face down, for one last time, and then sank.

And in that same moment, Odin began to die. He felt his stone, the heart of his consciousness, begin to shrivel like a plum that is placed on a hot griddle. He discovered a great truth: that the will to kill is a two-edged sword which strikes both victim and assailant. And it hurt and hurt and hurt. There was nowhere he could hide, for he could not hide from himself. In that one moment he saw his life become rotten. He wanted to die, but could not. He knew that the path of bitterness upon which he was now embarked would have to be travelled over time and time again until fate took pity on him.

Wearily he gathered his fibres about him. He hugged the garment of the Inner Circle close. He cursed the day he had ever heard the name of the Inner Circle. Slowly he began to work his way through the autumn wood. Faintly he heard voices of humans. Seaweed gatherers. It would not be long before the body was discovered.

The abandoned horse trailed its reins by thistle and dogplant as it patiently cropped the coarse sea grass.

21

ON BENNET

'Why is she smiling?'

It is Pawl speaking, but he is not speaking to anyone. The dark room is empty. He has ordered everyone to keep away.

He stands at the side of the table, where Laurel is lying on velvet cushions. He stares down at her smiling face. Her eyes are closed. It is extraordinary. He sees a sleeping, smiling face. 'Did she die happy? Was she glad to die?'

Pawl moves round the table, his fingers trailing on the red velvet. The stillness amazes him. He has never seen anything so still as the face of his dead wife. At any moment he expects her to stir, breathe deeply and stretch, and for her eyes to blink open. But she doesn't.

Pawl gets down on his knees at the end of the table and rests his cheek on the velvet. He can still smell something of her life. He can still smell something of the sea that drowned her. She has been washed, and her nakedness covered, and her hair brushed, and that is all. He looks at her nose and the delicate flare of her nostrils. He sees the way the nose curves down to where the lips curve open. Why had he never seen before that beautiful folding of space? 'Why did I never see that? I saw the eyes and the tousled hair and the warm lips. Perhaps they took all my love.'

Now Pawl is discovering a new Laurel, one he will carry with him until his death.

He stands up and steps away from the body. He is still pondering that curve. It reminds him of part of a spiral seashell. *I must tell Laurel about this*, he thinks and then stops with a start as his conscious mind catches his imagination. He manages a dry laugh at his foolishness.

Reality has not yet caught up with him. Once when he was a boy he watched some stonemasons mending a bridge. The air was freezing, and the masons blew on their hands as they shifted and worked the rough stone. One was shaping a groove, hammering down on a thick chisel. For a moment his attention lapsed. The hammer glanced from the shiny head of the chisel and came down squarely on his thumb, trapping it against the stone. The thumb spread and spattered. The man looked at his thumb, his mouth and eyes open wide. He even held it up in the cold air and watched as it started to drip. He was waiting for the pain.

Such is the state of Pawl Paxwax.

Now it is night-time and the curtains are drawn and a fire blazes in the hearth of the old room.

Pawl is seated in an armchair with his back to the fire. All that can be seen of him is his white hand, which rests on the arm of the chair holding a glass, and his eyes. The eyes glow like disks of flint. He stares at the still form on the table.

Close by lies his great mechanical dog, the last of its line. It tries to scratch under its chin with a rear leg but the movement is beyond it. It does not understand how time has ruined it. The firelight glances on its great shaggy back, sending its shadow across the floor.

At the far end of the room, well away from the fire, stands the Member of the Inner Circle.

He is the only living presence that Pawl will tolerate. Gently Odin is working on Pawl, easing open the closed seams of his grief.

There are yet several hours to dawn.

* * *

214

Finally the dawn seeps slowly into the sky. In the night it has rained, a chill slapping rain that has filled the dry leaves and soaked the lawn, leaving it grey and glazed.

The people of the Paxwax are moving, carrying bundles of dry sticks. They are building a pyre amid the flower gardens.

Carpenters have laboured during the night to build a platform of seasoned timber. Upon the platform lies the body of Laurel Paxwax. The wind stirs her hair and moves the brightly coloured dress and scarf which she wears round her throat.

Pawl relinquished the body an hour before dawn and Lan Tancred and his wife have worked quickly, trying to create an image of life in death.

'It will burn quickly,' whispers Lan Tancred to Bevis the woodsman as they stand to one side in the grey dawn light. 'I saw to that.'

Pawl thrusts the flame into the pyre. He seems almost casual. The fire catches and a plume of dark smoke mounts past the old house and disperses in the wind. The flames crackle yellow and white and the first long flame singes the hem of Laurel's dress, which has blown down from the platform. The fabric puckers and darkens.

Now the flames are rising like a curtain. The sea wood burns a bright green and blue. Laurel is lost in the smoke, except when the wind blows it aside and makes the flames billow.

The body burns quickly, as Lan Tancred said it would. Pawl watches everything. No one speaks to him. He is a dark figure by the fire. And when the blaze is ended and there is only ash and embers, the rain comes.

* * *

215

'She is not dead, you know that, don't you?' says Pawl catching Peron by the arm.

'She is dead,' says Peron.

'Not so. She lives here. She will always live here.' He taps his forehead with his middle finger. 'She is with me whenever I need her.' And he walks away, talking about what he and Laurel will do the next day.

Thus Peron was the first to see the madness of Pawl.

That night Pawl stayed in his Tower alone.

He completed his last poem, for suddenly the zest had gone out of his art. Life in all its needless cruelty had caught him up and torn him and there was no way that words could relieve that suffering.

22

ON BENNET

Here is what Pawl wrote, sitting alone, save for Punic and the bowed shape of little Odin.

Song to a Sad Fisherman

His net is deep,
It trails the floor of the ocean.
Stiff-backed at evening, still in his small boat,
Brown fingers light on the tiller's smooth wood.
What does he stare at, the shifting black water,
Or the mist that muffles the shape of the islands?

His net is deep,
It curves by coral and shipwreck.
He hears the slap of the small waves lapping,
Hears too the boom of the great sea combers,
Driven by storm winds, breaching the headland,
Scouring the shore and the bases of cliffs.

His net is deep,
It drifts through beds of kelp and wrack.
Soon will the fisherman pull on the taut rope,
Lifting his net from the deep of the sea.
What will he find there, what haul of sorrows,
When the weeping black net lies coiled at his feet?

23

ON BENNET

Pawl's madness was, like Hamlet's, a necessary madness; a wilful plunge into the stranger reaches of his imagination so that he could return sane.

He talked to Laurel incessantly. There were always two places set for meals. Her clothes were washed, though unworn. Pawl remained genial, with a brittle smile, and he would break off conversations suddenly and run away as though called.

Sometimes he tramped round the island. Once he waded into the sea and talked to the sea, slapping it with the palms of his open hands.

His people watched him. There was always someone on guard to make sure he did not suffer any accidents.

In speaking to the other members of the Eleven Great Families, Pawl chattered happily about what he and Laurel were doing.

Sometimes a blackness would fill him. Once he ordered all the horses killed. Red drove them away into the wilderness of the Mendel Hills to save them. Once he ordered part of the woods burned and he stood in his Tower and watched as the flames ate their way to the shore and the black smoke billowed.

Secretly he sent orders to the artisans of Larksong and, within days, crates began to appear through the Way Gate and were shuttled down to the surface.

Pawl gathered everyone together when he began to open the crates in the courtyard. Inside were dummies, lifesize replicas of Laurel, shocking in their verisimilitude. People turned their eyes away.

Clothed in Laurel's clothes, the mannikins were dispersed through the island.

Walking through the woods you would come upon Laurel sitting under a tree holding a dying flower. She was down by the seashore, looking at the waves. In the library she sat close to where Peron worked and he did his best to ignore her. She was in the courtyards, in the greenhouses, in the shuttle port and even, it was said, in Pawl's bed.

In ones and twos, slowly, not a mass exodus, people began to pack up and move from Pawl's island. There was talk of madness in the Paxwax family and 'like father like son' was an expression heard more than once behind closed doors. But for those who left there were always new arrivals and at least in a superficial sense the island retained its atmosphere of bustle and activity.

Strangely, the arrival of the mannikins led to a worsening of Pawl's temper. He strode round the house finding fault with everything. He took to carrying a stick which he used to beat on doors and to strike at objects which suddenly annoyed him.

He was dirty, unshaven and smelled.

Then one evening he summoned Odin.

That small creature had begun to dread Pawl. His mind was as dangerous as a spinning knife. It was unguessable, able to cripple, brimful of anger.

Odin huddled quietly, aware of the blazing intensity of Pawl as he strode back and forth in the Tower. Pawl was speaking, allowing his words to conjure his thoughts.

'You guard this planet, don't you? Keep a watch on the minds who enter here?'

'I try.'

'Then how did Laurel die? Who killed her?'

Odin felt his juices rise in his body like froth and his black gown become active, forcing down his temperature, soaking up his excretion, soothing. Inside him his stone burned.

'I do not know.' The reply was a yelp and Pawl swung round and faced Odin in surprise. Odin's voice sounded very different in Pawl's mind.

'Hear my reasoning. Find fault if you can. Laurel could not die in the sea. She was almost as at home in the sea as on land. I know. She could have swum to the mainland if she had wanted. Waves held no peril for her, nor the Maw, nor any creatures that move in water. So. Since she could not die in water, she was killed. Someone killed her. Who?' Pawl paused and looked round the room. 'Perhaps more important, why?'

'I do not know.' The voice in Pawl's mind was strangled and hoarse. Odin could feel his defences slipping. The will to tell the truth was beginning to dry him, and soon he would crack. Little Gerbes. Humble Gerbes. Gerbes not made for greatness. Even the memory of the Tree could not help him; it was as nothing against the roughness of Pawl. Relief came when Pawl's mood suddenly changed.

'Am I hard on you, Odin? I do not mean to be. You are the only one I can trust. Just tell me: is it possible, was it possible, that someone could have slipped through your defences? Or could someone already here have been suddenly recruited?'

'It may be there is a traitor near.' This half-truth gave Odin some relief. 'Perhaps I was not vigilant enough.'

'The Families. I have always known. There can be no love where self-interest is concerned and the Families are nothing if not self-interested. It scarcely matters who.

They are up there, out there, waiting. Even the Shell-Bogdanovich, who I thought were my friends, could have done this.' Pawl reached and took the mottled hand of one of the Laurels who sat close to him. 'I was never fooled. Or perhaps I was fooled for a while. But I could not understand how anyone could get in. Perhaps we were all careless. There was such delight. . .' His voice trailed away and he stared at blankness. 'Such delight. I believed it could last for ever. Was there ever such a fool as me in the whole of creation? Let me spell it out for you, Odin. There is no happiness. There can be no happiness. There is only delusion and at the end of the dark tunnel a hurting and then vacancy. If any man talks of hope call him a fool. That is my belief. And I will never make the same mistake again. I am grateful to my teachers, be they the Wong or the Proctor or the midget Felice, and in my turn I will teach them a lesson.'

The cool voice of Wynn cut across Pawl's speech. 'There is no evidence of deceit of this kind in the vibrations between stars. And I am listening every moment. I would hear something.'

'You would hear nothing. Deceit like this is not planned. It is the way of life. Cut down the happy man. Kill the intruder. Whichever way you trace the argument you find the same answer. My wife is dead because of what we are. We. The Families. The rulers. And we are what we are because life is so cruel.'

'There is no talking to you.'

'And you are a machine. A juggler. You know nothing of love. It is love that makes us human. If you could know love you would be human.'

'Are you human?'

'Not now. Not any more.'

'Then you are less than human.'

'I am the spirit of Death.'

221

The savagery of this thought stunned Odin and for a few moments his consciousness lapsed. When he came to himself again he found he was held by Pawl and Pawl's strong arms were crushing him.

'You will not die too, Odin,' said Pawl. 'You will live. You are my only friend.' He set Odin carefully down on his basal sucker and Odin lurched and then found adhesion. 'Just give me a few more days. I am healing fast. Soon we will act.' He looked over to the communication cell. 'And you too will be there, Wynn. So get your consciousness into shape. They say you are a reflection of my mind. Well, grow black leaves.'

24

ON SABLE

Helium was impatient.

For days he had waited for Pawl to return his call. And now, here he was, calling again. Twice before he had been turned away by Wynn. This could not be an accident.

Finally the vivante space cleared as the contact was made and the Paxwax locked with the Shell-Bogdanovich.

Helium stared. 'Why, hello, Laurel, I hadn't expected to . . .' His voice trailed away as he stared.

Laurel was smiling in her merry way and her hair was mussed. But she did not move. Her twinkling eyes were devoid of mind. 'Is Pawl there?' asked Helium, but the mannikin stared back at him impudently, until Helium, in anger, broke the circuits and ended the call.

Within minutes he was in contact with Dame Clarissa.

Being a watchful, cautious creature, he controlled his mood and spoke obliquely.

'I am glad to see you looking better, Dame Clarissa.' And indeed she was looking better. Her eye was sharper and with a glint of humour. She faced him fully, sitting in the vivid light of the vivante transmitter. Most particularly, though, she was no longer wearing the dark head cover. A fledgling down had begun to cover the raw pink of her scalp. Before too long she would be fully plumose again.

'Helium Bogdanovich, you have not contacted me to compliment me on my appearance, even though I do not look quite the old crow I was some weeks ago. You have business to discuss. I like business, it gives me purpose.

Would you like Jettatura here? She is at work in her gymnasium but she will come instantly if you should . . .'

'Jettatura is not needed. I was wondering about the Paxwax . . . have you had any dealings with them recently?'

'We do not deal with the Paxwax. We pay tribute. We have ceded valuable sectors close to Elliott's Pocket, territory we have held since the Great Push. The rest you know. Why do you ask?'

'Have you any word of them? Do you know anything about them that I should know? Speak clearly, Dame Clarissa.'

'The Paxwax may visit us at any time. I am told they are happy. The Beltane is expecting a child. That is all I know. It is common enough knowledge, I should think.'

'Nothing else?'

'What do you want, Helium? My Homeworld is forfeit. Our sperm banks are sterile. What more would you have? Do not ask me to say I like the Paxwax.' She stared out at him. 'We are the children of chance, Helium. On a different day the battle would have gone to us and you would not have found me so kind. But I know nothing of the Paxwax. I do not wish them ill any more than I wish a pestilence on the Proctors . . . though perhaps that would be no bad thing. Now then, Helium, tell Clarissa what the problem is. Have you and the Paxwax had a falling out? How that would distress me.'

Helium received her taunting with equanimity. 'I have tried to speak to Pawl twice,' he replied. 'Both times his Guardian, Wynn, turned me away. Just now I found myself facing a glowing doll, one of those Larksong mannikins. It was made to look like Laurel. I do not understand.'

'And that brought you knocking at my door? Well,

well. The Paxwax is avoiding you. You wonder why. You think I might know. Really, Helium.'

'It is not unknown for old adversaries to join forces.'

'No, but in this case they have not. Helium, look at my hands. They are empty. I am tired of lonely intrigue. You do not know how broken the Xerxes are. We have done nothing to set the Paxwax against you. We have given no hints of plans that are afoot. You know that we can keep secrets. Believe me or not. I am an old woman now, but I am not a fool. One day I hope to be great again. I would not set everything at risk just when we were getting along so nicely. What have I to gain?'

'Revenge.'

'It is an empty gain. You may discover that.' She looked at him birdlike, with her head on its side. She had never seen Helium so indecisive. 'You know, there may be another explanation. It could be that the Paxwax does not trust you. Perhaps he thinks you are involved in some clever tricks. Perhaps he is giving you a warning.'

'I thought of that. But why Laurel?'

Clarissa shrugged elegantly. 'He is a strange boy. Very wild up here – ' she tapped her forehead – 'very dangerous. Remember Toby. Perhaps his son is madder than he was. Perhaps . . .'

Helium raised his paw and Dame Clarissa fell obediently silent. 'Discover what you can. You still have ways. I know that. But I do not want to see any damage caused.'

'Are you asking me to spy for you?'

'Yes.'

The down on Dame Clarissa's head stirred and fluffed as she inclined her head. Her feathers were attempting to rise.

25

ON BENNET

'It will have made him think,' said Pawl, lying back in his circular room and speaking to the ceiling. Above him the sinuous growths of Wynn's brain spread like a jungle canopy. 'But I must beware the trap of the enigmatic. That will betray me. I have gone as far as I dare. I am stronger now. I think I am beginning to see things clearly.'

'And what do you plan to do, Master Pawl? Take a new wife? Continue to build, that is the best course.'

'That is what you would like, is it, Wynn?'

'It is the best wisdom I can offer you.'

'Well,' said Pawl, speaking very distinctly, 'what I intend to do is declare war on all the Families.'

Silence from the ceiling.

'Does that surprise you, Wynn?'

'No. I am hard to surprise. I calculate.'

'I have been hurt.'

'And you will hurt others.'

'Yes. For in love there is no quarter.'

'Rubbish.'

'You do not understand. If you were human you would.'

'Are you taunting me?'

'If you were human you would understand. I will destroy the Families. I will not destroy dignity or a sense of worth. Laurel was killed not because she loved me but because I am who I am. Look at the worlds, Wynn. Humankind should rule only as far as it can walk round in an hour, and that leisurely. Anything more is injustice.

Laurel taught me that. I should have left this world and the Paxwax and joined her world . . . as a fisherman.

'But Wynn, that is not the way things have worked out and so I must attack root and branch. And you will help me.'

'Yes, Pawl.'

'Can I trust you?'

'I am an extension of you. I am your best and worst. I can only do what you want, whether I play pander or lawyer. I am your . . . servant.'

'So we begin. Make contact with Forge. I will speak with one called Milligan. I want him to contact the Hammer and tell them that Pawl Paxwax would play Corfu with Trader.' Pawl stood up and walked through to the vivante chamber. 'Do it now. But there is one other thing, Wynn. Since you are an extension of myself, tell me what my final plan is.'

There was a long silence. Finally Wynn spoke. 'Master Pawl, there are many possibilities but no certainties.'

'Spoken like a philosopher. But there is one certainty, if you know me and understand my love, for I cannot live without Laurel.'

'Then I do not know it. You are right. I am not human.'

Later that same day the round-up of the mannikins began. They had served their purpose. They had given his mind focus. Their plastic glamour had rubbed Pawl's face in the dirty reality that Laurel was dead and that she would not return.

That evening they were dragged to the shore and piled in a heap and put to the torch. Pawl did not stay to watch the plastic blacken and burn. As he climbed the cliff and took the path that Laurel had ridden on her last journey, he could smell the acrid smoke. The flames danced behind him.

Waiting outside the entrance to his Tower was one of the gardeners who was in charge of the tropical nursery. He was holding a bunch of bright pink flowers. 'Here, Master Pawl, the first of the season. Mistress Laurel had them imported last year and we've just managed to make them bud. I thought you would like them.'

Pawl accepted the flowers and continued up to his circular room.

Odin was in attendance. Pawl had summoned him. While Pawl found a suitable jar for the flowers, Odin eased his way round the room with his short trunk swaying. His mask was off and the red flukes of his body flexed and glistened.

'We have a lot to talk about, Odin. I want to know more about the Inner Circle. But first I want to know why you seem different to me.'

'How do you hear me?'

'Like someone who is out of breath.'

Odin knew. Odin was dying. Ever since the murder of Laurel he was dying. Just as smoke tells of fire, so the change in Odin's thought told of his crime. But Pawl did not know. 'I am not well, Pawl. That is the way with us Gerbes. Our grip on life is not strong. We are not like the Hammer. We are always ready to slip away.'

'Is there anything I can do to help?'

'Nothing.'

'I am a friend. Doesn't that help?'

Silence, and then wearily the thought, 'Do not feel sorry for me. It is I who should be sorry.'

'You are talking in riddles. Come, let us talk truth to each other as we did in the old days. Tell me about the Inner Circle. You know, I was brought up to be suspicious of you members of the Inner Circle. My father often said you knew too much. But you were useful. We believed you had managed to endure from the days before the

Great Push, that you came from some religious order that had decided to move out into space. Sometimes a member of the order stayed on this Homeworld for months, talking with my father. We were afraid of him . . . black and masked. But we never suspected there were aliens in the Inner Circle. Now I want to know more. I want to know your strengths.'

Odin settled. He felt his great stem pulse begin to throb. He knew he needed to be careful, as he could not lie much longer. 'We are a small brotherhood. We serve the Great Families as diplomats and healers. We help hold traditions fast.'

'Ha!' said Pawl derisively. 'Some traditions don't deserve protecting. But don't give me answers from the book, Odin. I want truth.' Odin quaked. 'You are an alien and a member of the Inner Circle. I met another alien member of the Inner Circle when I was on the Homeworld of the Hammer. Are there many aliens in the Inner Circle?'

'Some.'

'And do you get on well with the humans in the Inner Circle?'

'Well enough. We get on together because we must and we share the same ideals. But some life forms are incompatible. That is a law of nature.'

'And are some of the Hammer members of the Inner Circle?'

'Yes.'

'And do they sit peacefully with their stings in a lock?'

'The Hammer are a law to themselves.'

'Yes. I believe they are.' Pawl mulled over this thought. He had already spoken with Milligan and arranged for Milligan, much to that man's consternation, to broadcast the opening moves of a Corfu game. He was hoping that Trader would take his bait. 'So, Odin. Here is how I see

229

things. We have an organization called the Inner Circle. It is dedicated to helping the Great Families but yet it contains aliens. In fact it has just helped in the decimation of one of the most vital alien species, the Spiderets. And the heads of the Great Families don't seem to know there are aliens in the Inner Circle. Quite a few contradictions, aren't there, Odin?' Odin remained silent. 'I can read your silences, Odin. Let me tell you what I think and what I want. I believe that within your organization there are those who would not be unhappy to see a change in the human order. I believe you supported me because, as Laverna Felice would say, I am "soft" on aliens. Don't worry, Odin, I don't mind being used and I am grateful to you, for you helped save the Paxwax and gave me some months of happiness with Laurel. But Odin, I want to increase the stakes. I want more from you. I want more from you and from your friends in the Inner Circle. Can you guess my intention?'

'No.'

'I want to undermine the Families. I want to offer my Homeworld to those members of the Inner Circle who want to rebel. Can I still trust you?'

'You can.'

Odin saw everything. He saw it in symbolic terms. Pawl was a great glittering fish nosing through weeds in clear water. And there was a hook with a barb. And the great fish smelled the bait that was attached to the hook and in one swirl accepted it. Most tragic of all, the fish now thought itself well fed. But for how long?

'Can you contact those among the Inner Circle who want their own revenge?'

'If you wish.'

'I do wish.' Pawl was sitting forward eagerly, intently.

'Oh, I have great plans, Odin. The Families will look back on the day that Laurel died as the day recording all their sorrows. I will hurt them everywhere.' He paused. 'I am only surprised that you are not surprised. Had you guessed my intentions?'

'I had not guessed. But yet I know your mind. You burn with a single flame, Pawl Paxwax. You are wholly one. So I am not surprised. But I fear for you.'

'Fear for my enemies.'

After that events moved quickly.

Pawl contacted Helium and spoke to him like a nephew who speaks to a trusted uncle. He confided that Laurel had died, saying only that she had had an accident. He watched closely as Helium reared up out of the water. He tried to detect the slightest flicker that would show complicity. And it was there, all right. Unmistakable. Helium was too upset. Too concerned. He overacted.

Pawl explained that Laurel had been cremated, that he had been overcome with grief. He apologized for the accident with the look-alike mannikin, saying only that he was distraught. Now the mannikins were gone and he, Pawl, an older and wiser man, a sadder man too, was again ready to take his place as Master of one of the Great Families.

Helium accepted his explanation with relief. 'We were worried about you, Pawl. Heaven knows we don't always want to be interfering, and if you want to close down your Homeworld for a while that is your affair but, well . . . with Toby dead and then all that trouble with the Xerxes . . . well, we look upon you as something of a son. That's all.'

Pawl looked at the grey bulk lolling in the brackish water, smoking its pipe among the water lilies. He had not expected that statement. 'I'm grateful for your concern. I intend to make the death announcement shortly.'

231

'Hmm. Have you, er . . . No, probably too soon.'

'Have I what, Helium?'

'Have you given any thought to a successor? I know this sounds unfeeling, but we are political as well as emotional creatures, and the future must be thought about.'

'I have given no thought to it. Time is on my side now, I think.'

'Time is never on our side. But enough of that. I am deeply sorry, my boy. If Clover and I can do anything . . . if there is anything the Shell-Bogdanovich Conspiracy can do, you only have to say. And when you have got over your grief, somewhat, I would like to put a little business proposition to you. Tidy a few things up.'

'I shall be glad to hear of business. I intend to drive the Paxwax hard. Business will divert me.'

Helium looked at Pawl with his head slightly on one side, as though weighing him up. 'You are a funny lad. You have a strange way of talking. Sometimes you sound as though you are talking in quotations. Do you still put down your thoughts on paper?'

'Not any more. Now I want my thought to be expressed as actions.'

'There you are. That's what I mean. I don't know anyone else who talks like you. I can't tell whether you are teasing or not. It is a strange mind you have.' And then he added, almost as an afterthought, 'It is not good, Pawl, to be too subtle with those who care for you. You will end by not knowing how to place your trust. Be not too clever.'

'I am sorry. I don't mean to be clever. My sadness has made me strange.'

'Enough. Make your announcement. Let the Proctors know as soon as you can. Get a Death Inspector over, just for form's sake. The Proctors are sticklers for form,

232

you know that. Contact me or Clover if they make any difficulties.' Helium nodded two or three times as though trying to think of something else to say, and then he reached forward and the vivante link was broken.

Pawl sat back at the vivante staring at the empty space. Helium had seemed so sincere. How easy it would be to believe him. Pawl recognized his need to talk to one of his own kind, no matter how changed. For a moment he wavered and his hand rested on the vivante call keys, but then half-remembered lines from the ballad he had heard on distant Lumb drifted into his mind . . .

> Feel no pity for traitors,
> Consign them all to hell.
> They'll smile to your face:
> To love they'll pretend . . .

. . . and those lines hardened his resolve. He thought perhaps he should call Pettet. But he knew already what Pettet would say. No, his course was set.

Pawl endured a lecture from the Proctor First in person! He had disobeyed the Code. Why had he not contacted the Proctors the instant the woman was found? Why had he not called for a Death Inspector? Had the Inner Circle been informed before the Proctors?

Pawl watched as the Proctor First worked himself into a lather, his great curved golden tusks sawing the air and his mane waving.

'So I am suspicious,' continued the Senior Proctor. 'You have done everything wrong. There is something you are ashamed of. Did you kill her yourself? Is that what you are ashamed of? Is that why you burned the evidence? Silly boy. We are broad-minded. We like to know the truth, that is all. The affairs of the Families are complicated enough without difficult questions of succession concerning who is alive and who is dead. Well. You will be punished by confiscation this time. Let me remind you, this is your second major breach of the Code. And one other thing. When you think to take a new bride, you will select from the eligible within the Families. Is that clear? I want no more foolishness like last time. You got away with it once because you were young and we all felt pity for you. But you are older now, and there is no excuse. If I may make a suggestion, I think you should choose several brides. Women seem remarkably vulnerable in the Paxwax household. I remember the activities of your late father. You must broaden your base. At the next Council of the Families I shall confiscate some of the sectors you gained from the Xerxes. They will go to the minor Families. Is that understood?'

Pawl nodded.

'Good. Well, I will arrange for a Death Inspector. I think we will conduct this at a high level. More discreet. No need to revel in the details.'

Pawl raised his hand. 'If I may make a request, I would be grateful if Neddelia Proctor could be assigned to us.'

The Senior Proctor thought for a moment and then smiled and nodded. 'Yes, Neddelia. Why not? She was a friend of yours from the old days on Lotus-and-Arcadia, wasn't she?' Pawl could see the man's political broker's mind working. 'And she handled your father, didn't she? Yes. I don't know where she is but I'll pull her out and send her to you straight away. Then I will make the announcement to the Families myself. There'll be quite a reaction, I can tell you. You're causing us a lot of trouble, I hope you realize that.'

Pawl thought the conversation was over but the Senior Proctor hesitated before breaking contact. 'How is the killing going?' he asked suddenly.

Pawl's mind was blank. 'Killing?' he asked.

'Yes. The aliens. The Spiderets.'

'Oh. Getting there,' said Pawl. 'Progressing.'

234

26

ON BENNET

Within the hour Neddelia's black ship, shaped like a rounded dumb-bell, tore a hole in the space above Pawl's Homeworld and began to descend.

The people who lived on Pawl's world kept well out of the way. The ship had a menacing presence, partly the result of its size and partly because of its blackness.

It settled, scorching the grass with the power of its anti-gravity units, and when the blue smoke had drifted away a ridiculously small door opened high on its rounded side and Neddelia rode down to the ground.

To Pawl, standing away to the side of the ship, Neddelia looked just the same: bent back, forcing her head down, brilliant mane, red-cover suit . . . and the same sardonic laughter.

'Well, Master of Paxwax. What have you been up to now?' she called as the transporter touched the ground gently.

'I failed to honour the Code again,' said Pawl. 'Last time I married outside the Code. This time I neglected to announce a death. Life is complicated, isn't it?'

'Not necessarily,' replied Neddelia. 'Come on. Let's get this business over. Tell me what happened. Three sentences only. I can embroider the rest.'

'She went swimming. She drowned. I burned her body.'

'That'll do. Now let's see what changes you have made to this place since last time I was here.'

They walked round the grounds. Neddelia admired the flower-beds and the new buildings. In her own way she observed Pawl closely. She saw his tight reserve and she saw through it to his pain. Gently she teased him, chipping at his formality, until the man paused under a tree and pressed his forehead against it and stood with his eyes clenched shut.

Later they entered his Tower.

Pawl did not want her to stay. He did not want her to go either.

She stayed on anyway, while outside the shadows began to lengthen.

Pawl spent that night lying still in Neddelia's arms, with the warmth of her tall body round him. At about four o'clock he began to speak, but she stroked his forehead and whispered, 'Hush, philosopher.' At that the tears flowed from him and he held her fiercely, like a man adrift in the sea clinging to a spar.

In the grey light of morning he asked her, 'Who killed Laurel?'

Neddelia looked at him with surprise. 'It was an accident, surely. Even in the best-ordered lives accidents happen.'

'It was no accident.'

Pawl did not know when he slept, but when he finally awoke Neddelia was already gone.

And so, for the second time within the space of one standard year, Pawl waited for one of the Proctors to announce a death in the Paxwax family. First had come the short messages warning that a major announcement was imminent. Then, timed to the minute, the vivante space became alive and revealed the Proctor First, resplendent in his robes and seated at the ancient heavy throne in the Conference chamber on Central.

He paused, listening while the Paxwax anthem was played, and at its end, he spoke.

IT IS WITH DEEP SADNESS THAT I, SENIOR PROCTOR OF THE PROCTOR FIRST, ANNOUNCE THE DEATH OF LAUREL BELTANE, MISTRESS OF THE PAXWAX, DEEPLY BELOVED WIFE OF PAWL PAXWAX, MASTER OF THE PAXWAX FIFTH.

TO PAWL, IN THIS TIME OF GRIEF, WE OF THE RULING FAMILIES EXTEND OUR DEEPEST SYMPATHY AND ASSURE HIM OF OUR CONTINUING GOODWILL.

The image of the Proctor faded and was replaced by a vivante of Laurel made at the time of her wedding to Pawl. The Beltane anthem played while Laurel walked and laughed and accepted flowers and good wishes. And when the anthem ended the vivante faded.

Pawl sat, amid members of his household, in the long dining room. When the lights came up people departed in ones and twos, some looking furtively at Pawl, others crying.

Pawl sat dry-eyed. Concealed in his hands he held a message newly-arrived from Forge. It was from Milligan, in haste, asking Pawl to contact Forge immediately. A giant Hammer had approached the particle fence and was waiting to speak.

27

AMONG THE FAMILIES

Disbelief.

Suspicion.

In some quarters dark feelings of delight.

Such were the reactions of the Families when they heard the news that Laurel was dead. Throughout space, wherever the mighty empires rubbed shoulders, there was a sudden tightening of guard.

The final consensus, never quite openly discussed but current nevertheless, was that Laurel had been murdered. Accidents such as this just did not happen; at least not when so many of the Families had reason to strike at the Paxwax and vengeance was a characteristic of all the Families.

But it was a frightful crime: shocking because it touched the very heart of leadership, disturbing because somehow a Family's defences had been breached. That held meaning for all the Families, and explained their watchfulness.

In the great brass and aluminium palaces of Central, where the affairs of all the Families were discussed, the senior brothers and sisters of the Proctors met amid ostentatious security.

Lar Proctor, who felt he had been made a fool of by Pawl at the time of his marriage, was now Pawl's implacable enemy. He made no bones about making his feelings known. 'The Paxwax boy is deceitful and dangerous. He has probably inherited a cruel streak from his father. We must watch him at all times. He would be quite capable of killing her himself. He has flouted the Code once; he may try to do so again. Perhaps he has found some other strange beast to bed.'

All the senior Proctors nodded. The Senior Proctor eyed Lar Proctor coldly.

'We have already taken steps,' he said. 'We intend to handle this matter ourselves.'

Clover and Helium of the Shell-Bogdanovich Conspiracy lay top-to-tail in their favourite pond, a great crystal sphere which bobbed like a bubble, while they mulled over the news. Helium was suspicious of the Proctors. 'They could have engineered something. They have the means. They lost face when Pawl won the right to marry Laurel. Lar Proctor lost most. I hear the Senior Proctor tore shreds off him in front of everyone.'

'But to kill the lady,' said Clover softly.

'Aye,' said Helium, 'that would be madness. If the Proctors are involved and Pawl finds out and can prove it, then the Families will rise against them.'

'I do not think the Proctors had anything to do with it; well, not directly,' said Clover, scooping up water and letting it sprinkle down on to Helium. 'I believe the Sith are the villains. They are ambitious. That clown, Singular Sith, who always looks so earnest, would sell his own mother into servitude if he thought it would gain him another system.'

'True, he is worth watching. I have my eyes on him.'

'He may have been paid or he may have acted alone. An ambitious man would profit from chaos.'

'True,' sighed Helium, and there was great sadness in the word.

Far, far, far away on An, while the erhu wailed in the bamboo stands, Old Man Wong sat cross-legged and contemplated a picture of Helium Bogdanovich. It was held for him by a great grandson who knelt with head bowed. Old Wong Lungli took a deep breath and passed his hand over the picture. Then he nodded to himself, as though in conversation.

To Wong Lungli, the greatest enemy was always the greatest friend. The equation worked equally well in reverse. This was why the Wong family held no one close except their kin. Security for the Wong lay in absolute withdrawal. Old Man Wong had watched the manoeuvrings of the Xerxes and Paxwax like a man who watches fish swimming in a bowl. He had seen how the Shell-Bogdanovich befriended the Paxwax. He had observed carefully the way that Helium had struck at the Xerxes and Lamprey. In all these actions he had seen the seeds of later discord.

But Wong Lungli also wondered about the Proctors. He wondered if the killing of Laurel was the Proctors' way of telling the Shell-Bogdanovich Conspiracy that they were becoming too powerful. If that were so then such crudity would mark the end of the Proctors. And Wong Lungli was ready. One day, he knew, the Wong family would be the First Family. Perhaps that day would come in his lifetime. When the time was right, the Proctors would fall like a ripe fruit, and the Wong would be waiting.

Meanwhile he wondered if he ought to close the Wong Empire. Finally he decided to leave the Gates open.

His hands with their coils of long nails stirred and his Prime Minister, who was standing ten paces away, hurried close. 'We will watch,' whispered Old Man Wong. 'We live in interesting times.'

Dames Clarissa and Jettatura were not so calm. Perched secure within their stone tree, high above the racing storms of sand, they sat staring at one another while the

240

dry voice of the Senior Proctor intoned the death announcement.

The announcement came to an end and the two sisters sat in silence. Where they had failed, Fate had contrived to succeed.

'I must brush my hair,' said Jettatura and tugged at a dark green ribbon which held the magnificent coils of her white hair. Her hair tumbled loose. 'I am thinking of having it cut off. Or short anyhow. How would I look as an elf or a page boy?'

Clarissa had not heard her. She stared past her sister, out beyond the stone walls and into the misty future. 'They will suspect us. Everyone will suspect us,' she said, her colour rising in her cheeks. 'But we have done nothing, have we?'

'Perhaps your friend the Bogdanovich knows something,' offered Jettatura.

'I suppose I could contact Pawl. Offer condolences. Tell him we haven't . . . didn't . . .'

'He would think you were laughing at him. That boy set his lady at the centre of the world. This could drive him mad.'

'You don't think he killed her himself?'

Jettatura shrugged. 'Who knows with the Paxwax? But I think not. I think that at this very minute Pawl Paxwax, with the flashing yellow eyes, is hunting the killer. I am glad it is not us. We have a grandstand view.'

'I suppose it could have been an accident.'

Jettatura laughed without mirth. 'I live a more dangerous life on my trapeze.'

'We must do something. You don't think the Lamprey, what's left of them . . . ?'

'They don't even have a Way Gate, out wherever they are.'

241

'The Sith, then, They suddenly seem to be everywhere?'

'That is possible.'

'Well, what shall we do?'

'Nothing. You must regain your health. I must retain my poise. We are elder stateswomen now. Let us act with dignity, not like silly schoolgirls. Let that be an end.'

'It could even have been the Proctor, you know. Or even . . .'

Way out at the rim of the galaxy, where the Milky Way is a blazing sword which fills half the sky, and the rest is darkness save for the fleeing galaxies, the Lamprey heard the news after a long delay.

It meant little to them any longer. The old leaders of the family were dead or deposed. The Lamprey young wanted nothing of the past, except to forget it.

Their defeat and fall had effected a cleansing. Ancestors were now distrusted, not worshipped. The practice of blinding their children had stopped. The experiments which had led to the breeding of the Saints had also stopped and all the records were destroyed.

The Lamprey young looked out at the dark vastness of space which sometimes seemed to oppress them like a wall and at other times called to them, and they felt a stirring of purpose. That dark sea was yet uncrossed.

One day the Lamprey will stir and rise and step out into that great wild blackness. But not for many generations; and besides, that is another story.

Dama Longstock fainted when she heard the news.

Preparations for her own wedding were well-advanced but halted the moment the news from the Paxwax broke.

Space between Sable and Festal, the Homeworld of the Longstock, tingled with the urgency of communication as

242

Clover Shell spoke with Livil Longstock. There was no mincing of words.

'If Pawl were to propose would Dama accept?'

'She is persuadable.'

'Let us work on that. Leave Pawl to me. He owes us favours.'

'I will slow the arrangements down. Find difficulties.'

'Good. Give my love to Dama. How is she?'

'She is in the mountains, resting.'

'Keep her there. A rumour of sickness would help.'

The Outer Families, after maintaining a loose confederation, now lapsed into open suspicion and rivalry.

The Felice believed the Sith were in league with the Proctors.

The Paragon believed the Sith were safe in the pocket of the Shell-Bogdanovich Conspiracy.

The Sith believed that the Felice and Paragon had formed an alliance with one another and with any of the Inner Families just to spite them.

But the Felice and Paragon stared at one another with scorn.

Singular Sith, his great curved horns clasped in his hands, sat down and tried to comprehend the situation. So complex had his machinations become that he had to call in a junior brother just to make sure that no member of the Sith family had accepted a contract to kill Laurel. They hadn't. He was relieved, but still the situation was beyond him. Everything had been going so well, and now this. Why? Why? He beat his fists on the desk and bellowed.

He did not know what to do and so did the best thing, nothing. He closed down the Sith for a while and went hunting.

* * *

243

Not so for the people who lived in Elliott's Pocket.

Pettet and Raleigh received the news in stunned silence. They could not believe it and yet they had to believe it. Finally Pettet roused himself. The giant had aged since his return from Ultima Thule. He moved more slowly and there was often a hunted look in his face. 'I'll get Paris,' he said and left Raleigh, white-faced, to play through again the sombre vivante announcing Laurel's death.

Paris watched in silence. At the second viewing a pallor spread through his face. He stopped the vivante at the moment of the wedding ceremony. 'I will kill the beast,' he whispered.

'What?' asked Raleigh.

Paris turned to face her. His eyes were all pupil and stared at her from a blackness without depth. She could not guess what he was seeing. 'I will kill the beast.'

'Pawl? Is it Pawl you are talking about?'

'Who else?'

Raleigh gasped. 'You don't think . . .'

'My father. My Homeworld, people I loved and now . . .' The final words were too much for him and he stood staring at Raleigh. A hatred, more violent than any emotion he had ever felt, had come welling up inside him and filled his mind with bile. Finally he roused himself from his trance. 'I must leave your Homeworld. I shall leave now. Make my goodbyes to . . . to your daughter, and to Pettet. You have been very kind but you must realize that I can't stay now.'

'Where will you go?'

Again he looked into her and again there was blackness. 'Where can I go? Where have I? I shall make my way to Lotus-and-Arcadia for a while. Then we shall see.'

'Call Pawl. Talk to Pawl. He loved Laurel beyond all reason. Perhaps now you can even help one another.'

Paris did not reply. For a moment he hesitated and then turned and left the room.

Some minutes later Raleigh monitored his progress to the Way Gate above Lumb.

Later, when she was with Pettet, she told him of her conversation. 'I will warn Pawl,' said Pettet. 'I will even leave the Pocket and travel to his Homeworld if need be. You, Raleigh. You are the mystical one. You should see these things coming. Tell me I'm wrong, but it seems to me that everything has gone out of joint since those three arrived.' He nodded up to where Erix, Thule and their bright sun were just rising above the horizon.

Sanctum had known of Laurel's death at the moment it occurred. And now it waited. No creature approached the giant Tree, for death lay in its shadow, so great was the energy it transmitted as it maintained a link with Odin.

The plans were laid and ready. Everything now depended on Pawl. If he were true to his nature he would turn to fight.

And then came the news that they had waited to hear. Pawl was speaking to Odin and there was no mistaking the meaning of his conversation. The great Tree allowed the conversation to spread wide and be felt throughout Sanctum. They saw a round room like a bowl, with dark shiny windows, and within it a man who blazed like a pillar of fire and a Gerbes who glowed green and yellow and hectic red. They heard the words, from the man.

'And how if I were to help them? How if I were to help the aliens . . . would they be interested?'

At that a great cry went up on Sanctum. So great was the spirit of the cry that little Odin, alone on Pawl's Homeworld, felt it.

And now Sanctum was throbbing like a giant pulse.

Plans were afoot to move the planet.

28

ON FORGE

The vivante image jolted and bounced as the man holding the camera, Milligan presumably, walked towards the glowing particle fence where the giant Hammer waited. The beast crouched in the sullen ochre air, its hammer head lowered against the wind and its ventral orifice closed to a tight point of blackness. The feelers which fringed that dark mouth were themselves coiled back like young ferns. The plated tail too was coiled and the giant sting with its beak and barb were hidden.

Milligan came within range of the Hammer which could, if it had wished, have reached over the fence and struck at him. It didn't move, except that the head with its widely-spaced eyes arched slightly to keep Milligan in focus.

Squatting between the Hammer's front legs was the humanoid Pawl had met when he had visited Forge.

Abruptly the Hammer reared, its legs working like hydraulic pistons. Its tail uncoiled and the beak of its sting opened and closed. The camera halted and jerked, almost dropped. A drumming began as the fine tendrils along the Hammer's side roused and frilled and beat.

This was surely Trader.

The drumming ceased and the thin, dark-robed alien began to speak in its dead way.

'Trader will come. Trader hopes for better game. Trader hopes for best of game. Trader sets riddle.

'What comes from behind and runs before?

'What can be trusted though cities tremble?

'What deals in honey, delights in dark wine?

'What moves like the shadow of death at your door?'

Pawl heard and understood. 'I will give you two answers,' he said, and heard unmistakably his own voice tinnily amplified by the small vivante speaker carried in the camera. 'I, Pawl Paxwax, am one of the answers to your riddle. But your sting is, I believe, the answer you are looking for.'

The Hammer's head arched and then nodded, though this gesture looked more like laughter than agreement and was possibly neither.

The drumming began again, in broken rhythm, allowing the alien time to translate.

'Trader hopes the Master of Paxwax has thought deep, for the striking sting cannot be stopped . . . nor will the stinging cease until the dead men-of-earth buttress the walls and the water channels run red.'

'I have thought long enough,' replied Pawl. 'Will you come to my world to play?'

'I cannot leave my prison world. Remember the eyes in the sky.' The tail and sting suddenly straightened and jabbed at the dark red clouds which hurried by above.

'Leave that to me. Will Trader play?'

'Yes, Trader will play.'

'Then the next time I call you will be the time to depart. Milligan will call you.'

There was no more drumming. The Hammer stepped backwards, its long body slung between its high-kneed legs. Then it reared, turned and ran. Within seconds it was lost in the murk.

Milligan turned the camera and, holding it at arm's length, pointed it at himself.

'You're never going to let that thing loose on your Homeworld, are you?' he said through tight lips.

'I am,' said Pawl.

29

ON BENNET

Within days of Odin's conversation with Pawl concerning the aliens of the Inner Circle, a small delegation from Sanctum was on its way to Bennet Homeworld. It was a war party, consisting of those species best able to plan, and which could most easily cope with the atmosphere on Pawl's Homeworld.

A special area on the mainland, well away from the small island, was prepared for their arrival. A giant Way Gate normally used only for cargo was hastily adapted and positioned above an improvised shuttle port.

Trader was also on his way. Pawl had neutralized the spy satellites above Forge and arranged for the giant Hammer to lift from the planet aboard one of the ore carriers. What Milligan thought of this is not recorded. ·

The people of Bennet Homeworld were pleased to see their Master so relaxed and obviously in good spirits as he prepared his flyer for the short trip over the sea to the mainland. Some reckoned it would not be long before there was a new Mistress. Only Peron, scholar and observer that he was, saw something dangerous in Pawl's bright eyes.

Pawl landed near the low grey domes which roofed the underground chambers. The shuttle was already descending, bringing the first arrival. 'It is your friend the Hammer,' whispered a voice in Pawl's ear. Pawl had taken the precaution of establishing a high-frequency link between himself and Wynn. If the Hammer proved game-some Wynn would be a valuable ally.

Odin toiled up the ramp leading from the largest of the shallow domes. 'The accommodation is excellent. Finer than on Sanctum. Only the Hooded Parasol may have need of greater room.'

Pawl watched Odin with veiled concern: the creature was ageing before his eyes. Not only was the voice different but Odin's movement had lost its springiness. Where once he had swayed and flowed, he now trudged.

The cargo shuttle landed, dropping the last few inches, and sending up a cloud of dust. The rough iron doors opened and the descent ramp flopped down.

Revealed, cramped, its high red legs pressed against the sides of its body like a crab in a rock pool, was Trader. The Hammer's head stretched and the wide-slung eyes blinked. It edged forward and the scales which protected its sting rasped against the metal roof of the shuttle. Free from its trap, it stretched, and then reared to full height.

Pawl had been warned by Odin not to move or speak when the Hammer emerged. They were skittish creatures and their aggressive instincts were hardly tempered by reason when they found themselves trapped.

The Hammer lowered back to the ground and its sting arched over its head, extended, and nodded its beak to Pawl. There was a brief spatter of drumming and Lake came running from the depths of the shuttle where he had been hiding.

'Trader says your Homeworld has clean smell. Trader needs to run. Are there eyes here?'

'There are no eyes here. Trader, you may run where you like. There are no people on the mainland, only animals and trees, though you will find nothing as big as yourself.'

Again a furious drumming. 'Trader say sorry. Fight like feed like running. All good.'

The Hammer departed. Its claws tore the earth, showering Odin and Pawl. Its sting was advanced and open like the beak of a hawk.

It was evening, now. After a clear day the rays of the late sun lay on the horizon. A band of blue shadow slowly climbed the faces of the hills. Again the shuttle had landed.

The main party from Sanctum had arrived. Down below, the Hammer was immersed in a stream of icy water which bubbled up at the base of the hills. It drummed along the whole length of its body and beat the clear water to lather.

Pawl did not know what to expect. The descriptions he had elicited from Odin had helped little.

First to emerge was a Hooded Parasol. Pawl saw a giant red trumpeted flower with petals that spread and convulsed. Four eyes which lay bedded in the petals suddenly lifted like pseudopodia and strained towards him. The flower floated gracefully from the shuttle, its petals fanning. The musk of the creature hit Pawl like something thrown. Its astringency made him gasp. Seemingly oblivious of the pain it had caused, the Parasol rose into the evening sky and opened in the sun like an orchid. Below it trailed fronds, like hairs of glass. 'Do not touch those,' warned Odin. 'Don't even come close to them. Fully charged a Parasol could make a Hammer pause.'

Following the Hooded Parasol came a creature that Pawl recognized, a Spideret. Pawl paid particular attention to it. It was a Spideret, he remembered, that had been with his brother when he died out on Auster. How long ago that seemed. The Spideret made complicated movements with its feelers in front of its clustered eyes, and then nimbly climbed up the wall of the shuttle and settled to watch, its legs tucked beneath it.

In the darkness of the shuttle there moved something that sparkled with bright liquid energy. A Diphilus rolled down the ramp like a sack of jelly. Pawl thought of the sharp-edged stones which littered the ground outside the shuttle and wondered if they would puncture the fine membrane. Suddenly the air about him was filled with a raw laughter like the sound of trees falling or stones cracking. Then he saw, or seemed to see, the tip of a bright knife which jabbed at the Diphilus and which was blunted after the first thrust. The message was clear: nothing could puncture the Diphilus. In the same moment Pawl learned that the Diphilus lived in the crevices on airless mountainsides, that its skin rippled with energy, and that the only thing it feared was heat. Pawl knew he had been spoken to in his mind. He compared this communication with the way that Odin spoke to him. How different! Odin was lodged in his brain, almost a part of himself. But this, other, had been outside. Like something that wrapped him, something that took charge of the space about him. He wondered how he sounded to it and immediately knew. The Diphilus saw Pawl as just a creature and his voice was squeaky and scratchy. Pawl was the vulnerable bag of skin; the likely-to-be-punctured; the fine flower of creation that had low tolerance, could not face the hardness of space and so had bent creation to suit its mode of living.

Last to emerge was a Lyre Beast. Odin had tried to give Pawl some idea of what it would be like, for Odin found the mind-shapes of the Lyre Beast beautiful. Pawl did not know what to expect.

The Lyre Beast *was* beautiful. Pawl watched as the creature, so like skeins of raw silk in appearance, sorted itself out and spread like a canopy of woven threads. It covered a wall and the entire roof of the shuttle. It pulsed like a pool of water into which a stone is dropped. Once or twice its fibres strained and knotted and a rent appeared in its surface which flapped, and then closed again. From this creature came music like the plucking of a thousand strings. Sometimes it was low and clotted. At other times it was sweet and stinging and unpredictable. Pawl found himself held by the music, waiting for the sounds to resolve, but they never did. Or if they did resolve, it was beyond Pawl's hearing and in a manner which he could not comprehend.

After a short time the Diphilus, which seemed by common consent to be the leader, called them all together. They gathered in a large chamber under the ground. There was not much room. The Hammer squatted with its legs drawn close and its barbed tail resting along its back. In front of its puffing orifice, the Hooded Parasol hung in the air like a delicately-coloured pansy with its petals rippling. The Lyre Beast had selected a corner and it billowed like a sail. The Spideret hunkered down beneath it and the Diphilus rolled and spread round the floor, sending ripples of light round the walls. Pawl stood, and close to him was Odin.

Since its arrival, the Diphilus had taken over the task of translating the alien thought-patterns for Pawl. The Diphilus treated Odin as though he didn't exist. Pawl thought of Odin's red flukes weaving in the air and immediately felt a drowsy response in his mind. 'Are you not able to translate for me?' asked Pawl, shielding his thought.

'My work is almost finished. I am content to listen now,' answered Odin, in his hoarse, choked voice.

Any further questions that Pawl might have had were forestalled by the Diphilus which suddenly brought their minds together. To Pawl it was as though a wind had blown through him, driving scattered thought like dead leaves before it. And when the wind had died away there was only the Diphilus and a ringing silence.

Here is what Pawl understood the Diphilus to say.

WE ARE HERE BECAUSE OF THE ANGER OF PAWL PAXWAX. WE ARE HERE TO HELP HIM DESTROY THE ORDER OF THE FAMILIES, NOT IN HATRED, BUT UNDERSTANDING THAT THE TIME OF THEIR RULE IS ENDED. AN AGE IS PASSING AWAY. A NEW AGE IS DAWNING. IS IT AGREED?

Pawl heard himself agree.

The images of the Diphilus rolled on.

MANY OF US HAVE SUFFERED AT THE HANDS OF THE FAMILIES, JUST AS PAWL HAS. MANY OF US HAVE SUFFERED AT THE HANDS OF THE PAXWAX . . . BUT WE WILL LEAVE THAT.

A sound like boulders being cracked together grew and out of this came the clear organ and harp notes of the Lyre Beast.

I HAVE ONE QUESTION FOR PAWL. DOES HE REALIZE THAT HIS FAMILY WILL NOT SURVIVE THE FALL OF THE FAMILIES? OR IS HE HOPING TO ENLIST THE HELP OF THE INNER CIRCLE SO THAT HE CAN BECOME FIRST FAMILY?

That seemed funny to Pawl. It had never occurred to him to think that his family could become First, replacing the Proctor. 'We Paxwax have no desire to become First. And we know that our family will not survive the fall. I want to see the day when the Proctor First tries to sell his fine teeth to buy bread. I want the Bogdanovich and Shell to boil . . .' Pawl stopped breathless. He stood bemused before his anger, amazed at how easily he was stirred and how completely. 'I want to see the end.'

AND WHAT WILL BECOME OF YOU?

'I shall become a traveller.'

AH. WE WERE GREAT TRAVELLERS ONCE. It was the

Hooded Parasol speaking for the first time. Brilliant colours rippled across its petals and their texture changed from the gloss of holly to the velvet of pansy. WE HOPE TO BE TRAVELLERS AGAIN.

The chase of colours was followed by a sudden increase in the plant's odour and Pawl gagged and sat down. Away to Pawl's left the giant Hammer drummed and Pawl knew that it was laughing.

SO. It was the Diphilus again, its sparkling colours swirling like beads of oil. WE NEED NOW TO PLAN. THE SPIDERET WILL SPEAK.

The Spideret stretched its hairy legs and its mandibles opened and closed. It seemed intent on cleaning its front feelers, drawing them through its mouth until they were sticky. And then advancing its eyes and shifting and flexing its legs.

ONLY THE PROCTOR, THE WONG, THE SHELL-BOGDANOVICH AND THE XERXES NEED FALL. THE PAXWAX ARE DISCOUNTED. THE REST WILL TOPPLE, FOR WHERE THERE IS NO CENTRE THERE IS NO PERIPHERY. SIMPLE PLANS ARE BEST. THOSE SPECIES MOST OFFENDED WILL TAKE THEIR VENGEANCE FIRST. TO THE DIPHILUS AND THE HOODED PARASOL ARE ASSIGNED THE PROCTOR. TO THE LINK WORM FALL THE SHELL-BOGDANOVICH. TO THE HAMMER AND THE . . .

The giant Hammer drummed interrupting the Spideret.

WE ALONE WILL TAKE AN.

THE LYRE BEAST AND THE SPIDERET WILL TAKE THE XERXES. ALL THE FIGHTING CAN BE LEFT TO US. WE ARE READY. YOU – and here the twin feelers of the Spideret pointed straight at Pawl – MUST GAIN ACCESS FOR US.

And that was the essence of the plan. Pawl was to gain access to the closed Homeworlds. His position as a senior member, head of the Paxwax, was the passport for the aliens.

'How will I get a Hammer down on to An? The Wong are the most closed of all the Families.'

A WAY WILL BE FOUND.

'What shall I do?'

YOU MUST STRENGTHEN YOUR POSITION. YOU MUST NOT ALLOW ANY SUGGESTION THAT YOU ARE OTHER THAN A DEDICATED MEMBER OF THE FAMILIES. YOU MUST WATCH YOURSELF AND BE CRITICAL. WE WILL TELL YOU WHEN YOU NEED TO ACT. WE WILL TELL YOU WHAT WE NEED.

And there the meeting ended, much to Pawl's astonishment. He was used to meetings of humans which dragged on until only the hardiest were still thinking on their feet. At the same time, he was aware that much had been decided before this meeting and that all that had really been required was his formal acquiescence. The Spideret had made that plain.

The Hooded Parasol was the first to rise, hovering in the domed underground chamber.

'It needs the sun,' whispered the voice of Odin in Pawl's mind. Colours pulsed from the centre of the Parasol's flower out to the edges of its petals. 'It is asking to explore your planet.'

'It can. It is a guest,' said Pawl, and immediately the Hooded Parasol suffused a full and bloody red, the colour of liver. It rose, drifted up the wide grey access ramp, and began to spread its petals as it found the sun.

'How can something like that kill?' asked Pawl. 'It stinks, at least to me it stinks, and I know it can sting . . . but those are defences only. How will the Hooded Parasol kill the Proctor?'

Odin replied, 'Pawl, you are entering a new world of knowledge. You know so little about the nature of life. The will, the intention and sympathy are all. Even the Hammer treats the Hooded Parasol with respect. If the Parasol thinks death, then its odour becomes an agent of death. I am told it smells sweet. Even its colours can destroy, for they can lock with your spirit. We Gerbes are safe from the Parasol for we can neither see nor smell, but still we respect it. It has a clear mind. It thinks only one thought at a time and that with the whole of its being.'

The other aliens were beginning to move. The Hammer puffed, its wrinkled orifice opening and closing like a diaphragm. Then its legs worked like pistons, lifting it. Its mouth tentacles picked up Lake and cradled him and then it advanced towards Pawl, drumming.

'Trader challenges,' said Lake. 'Trader will play when he returns. Now Trader will run again.'

There was no discussing this. Carefully the Hammer stepped high over the Spideret, which scuttled to one side; then it lowered so that its abdominal scales scratched on the floor as it moved under the Lyre Beast. With a loud scratching of claws on the stone floor it accelerated and ran up the ramp.

Again Pawl wondered how he would get a creature like that through all the defences of An. The chamber filled with spiralling and cascading notes and the Lyre Beast delicately began to explore the ceiling.

And here the Diphilus spoke, wrapping Pawl in the power of its thought. THE LYRE BEAST IS TELLING YOU NOT TO WORRY.

'Can it read my mind?'

NOT AS YOU WOULD UNDERSTAND IT. BUT IT CAN HEAR EVERY PART OF YOU, WHICH IS PERHAPS AS GOOD. IT CAN HEAR THE HAIRS ON YOUR BODY MOVE. IT CAN FEEL YOUR ELECTRICITY. IT DOES NOT NEED TO READ YOUR MIND.

Again the music.

AH, NOW IT IS QUOTING TO YOU. ONE OF THEIR PROVERBS.

HOW CAN I TRANSLATE THAT FOR YOU? TRY THIS. In his mind Pawl saw hundreds of bodies tumbling in the air. Arms and legs became detached. Strange fish with big jaws swam among them snapping up the trifles. All the bodies were Pawl. And of a sudden they all came together into a single baby, a foetus with its thumb in its mouth and a working placenta. And Pawl could see the blood flow like little red fish, and everything moved together. Then the vision faded.

THERE. ANY GOOD?

'I . . . I think so.'

MMM. YOU HAVE A PHRASE IN YOUR LANGUAGE, 'A PLACE IN THE SUN'. LET ME EXTEND IT TO SAY, 'HAPPINESS IS A PLACE IN THE SUN BEYOND TIME.' THERE, THAT IS IT, THOUGH TO A ONE LIKE ME, A DIPHILUS AS YOU CALL ME, A PLACE IN THE SUN WOULD BE HELL.

Pawl looked at the Diphilus, which suddenly swirled and pulsed like liquid that has just been stirred.

The enormity of what he was about was suddenly borne in on him. Here he was, Pawl Paxwax, son of Toby Paxwax, head of the Paxwax Family, plotting the downfall of his own race. And there was now no going back.

'Will you talk with me?' asked Pawl.

The Diphilus laughed its huge, boulder-crushing laugh. YOU HAVE MANY QUESTIONS, I CAN SEE THAT. DOUBTS TOO. WE CAN TALK. THE SPIDERET WILL JOIN US, AND THE SMALL SAD GERBES. WISDOM IS LIKE A RIVER THAT FLOWS THROUGH MANY CHANNELS.

The place chosen by the Diphilus was high on a hill in the shadow of a dense stand of Rout trees, whose large fleshy leaves followed the sun. Why it chose this particular spot Pawl did not know, but its method of reaching it intrigued him. The Diphilus flowed and yet it never lost its unity. It flowed upwards like golden oil, and when it found the

257

shallow depression in the rocks, it settled into a pool in the shade. Though the wind blew, the surface did not pucker. The Diphilus became a mirror, like a chip of the sky.

The Spideret accompanied them, scampering and jumping up the rocks. Once it caught a rabbit and Pawl watched as it wrapped the small carcase in sputum which hardened, and then carried it attached to its back.

Odin toiled in his steady way, reading the hillside and then choosing the easiest path.

The jovial presence of the Diphilus made itself felt.

NOT AN IDEAL RESTING PLACE. TOO HOT BY FAR. BUT I DID NOT COME HERE TO REST. YOU HAVE QUESTIONS, MASTER PAWL?

Pawl sat with his back to the trunk of one of the Rout trees and stared out across the crimson sea. His island was a dark smudge on the horizon. 'So many thoughts . . . I was a lonely man intent on revenge. Now I feel that I am part of a conspiracy. Am I right?'

YOU ARE RIGHT. WE HAVE WAITED FOR MANY CENTURIES FOR ONE SUCH AS YOU. YOU HAVE YOUR OWN VENGEANCE, BUT IT FLOWS WITH OURS.

'Were *you* hurt . . . I mean were your entities hurt by one of the Families?'

OH YES. OUR WORLDS WERE DESTROYED BY THE PROCTOR AND WE WERE BURNED. WE ARE STRANGE ONES, WE DIPHILUS. DO YOU KNOW, MASTER PAWL, WE ARE ONE OF THE OLDEST SPECIES. WE KNEW THE CRAINT IN THEIR GREATNESS AND THEY WERE AMONG THE FIRST OF LIFE IN THIS . . . THIS . . . (Pawl's mind was filled with a vision of stars). YOU KNOW, THE NAME WE HAVE FOR OURSELVES MEANS *FILLED WITH LIGHT*. WE ARE LIVING LIGHT MIXED WITH LIVING EARTH. WE HAVE BEEN THE SPARK THAT QUICKENED MANY A WORLD TO START THE LONG SLOG TO AWARENESS. PERHAPS IT WAS A DIPHILUS THAT DRIFTED DOWN ON TO YOUR WORLD

258

WHEN IT COOLED AND FOUND LODGINGS ON THE HIGH MOUNTAINS. THINK ABOUT THAT, MASTER PAWL. PERHAPS YOU ARE DESCENDED FROM US. (The Diphilus's laughter buffeted Pawl.) BUT DURING THE GREAT PUSH WE WERE HUNTED BECAUSE WHEN WE BURN WE BURN FOR CENTURIES. WE WERE PRESSED IN A GRAVITY VICE AND IGNITED TO DRIVE THE EARLY PROCTOR FLEETS. (Pawl saw one of the old rockets of a type he had only seen in Elliott's Pocket, blazing through space close to a red star.) NOW ALL THAT IS FORGOTTEN. WE DIPHILUS WERE FORTUNATE. WE WERE SPREAD THROUGH THE GREAT LIGHT. OTHERS WERE NOT SO FORTUNATE. (Pawl saw a Gerbes broiling, a Hammer writhing with its sinews turned to mush, a Land Whale crashing to the ground as explosive darts tore holes in its dark flesh, a Lyre Beast dried and ready for powdering, a Spideret chained and hauling steel cables up to a derrick, a Hooded Parasol blinded and gelded, and being crushed for its dyes.) AND THAT IS BUT A BEGINNING. HAVE I ANSWERED YOUR QUESTION?

The Spideret, which had held close, seeming to follow this conversation, now stepped delicately towards Pawl. Its feelers moved and its dull eyes rose from their nests. One feeler reached out and touched Pawl on the arm. It was like being nuzzled by a horse. Then the feelers moved in a quick pattern and the Diphilus sighed and began to translate. AH, IT WANTS TO TELL YOU ABOUT LAPIS. ONE OF ITS SISTERS WAS THERE WHEN HE DIED. IT WANTS YOU TO KNOW THAT. HONOUR WAS GIVEN TO LAPIS. HE WAS TREATED AS THE SPIDERETS TREAT THEIR OWN.

Pawl nodded. The Spideret became still and then delicately withdrew. It spun a ball of white mucus which it spat high into the Rout tree. The mucus became a thread as thick as Pawl's finger and the Spideret climbed.

* * *

The day was well advanced. Clouds had come, and with them a chill wind from the south. The Diphilus was more comfortable. For some time Pawl had sat in silence, aware of his own thoughts and the clouds that were mirrored in the creature beside him.

'Who killed Laurel?' he asked suddenly.

But the only sound he heard was the wind in the Rout trees and the only sight the sluggish waves, maroon in the evening.

'Damn your silence. You and Odin. You are a pair. Silent when I need you most.'

THAT WHICH DID THE KILLING IS DYING. YOU WILL KNOW THE NAME ONE DAY. BE PATIENT, MAN. FOR ALL YOUR ANGER, THE SUN WILL NOT MOVE A WHIT FASTER. THERE, THAT IS A SAYING FROM THE GREAT DIPHILUS. WE HAVE TALKED ENOUGH FOR ONE DAY.

The Diphilus became suddenly opaque, like a pool of milk, and all of its colours were gone.

On his way down the hill, Pawl saw the Hooded Parasol returning. He wondered at its size. Drinking in the sun it had expanded, and now its petals were spread like a great funnel over hundreds of square metres. Pawl remembered Neddelia Proctor's ship hovering over his island . . . but this was larger. Below the Parasol trailed gleaming threads like saliva. Stuck to the threads were blobs of white. When the Parasol grew closer Pawl saw that the blobs were sheep. He also saw that there was the body of a man trapped in the threads.

That evening Pawl played Corfu. All the visiting aliens except the Diphilus gathered to watch. Pawl sat cross-legged on the floor and the Hammer crouched opposite him. When it breathed it turned its mouth away, but the eyes at the end of its hammer neck never left the board.

Pawl was conscious of the Parasol that floated a few yards behind him. It had contracted down to the size of a small tent and was a uniform brown colour. Pawl guessed that it was dozing.

The Lyre Beast had changed position and now hung like a broad untidy tapestry above the small Corfu board. Occasionally it rippled as though moved by a light breeze, and tinkled quietly.

Reception back to Wynn on Bennet Island was clear and Pawl was glad to hear that calm voice whisper in his ear.

Trader made the first move, advancing three of his white counters aggressively. Pawl answered cautiously, as though afraid to engage, by moving only one of his black counters and that laterally.

For five rounds of moves he did just sufficient to avoid an onslaught. He held the Hammer at bay while Wynn analysed the possibilities. And then Wynn spotted the grand strategy. Pawl would be attacked by three even moves, forcing him to reply with even moves, and that would inevitably leave him open to an odd/even combination attack, especially since the Hammer was already well-placed.

'Given the present state you face defeat in five moves,' whispered Wynn. 'His only weakness is down the centre. I believe he thinks you are ignorant of that. If you play a seven move, he will have to answer with a five and that will squander his symmetry. Then play a six directly down the centre. I do not believe you can win, but you will give him food for thought and you will have blooded him.'

Pawl did as Wynn advised and was pleased to see the Hammer's neck rise and wrinkle in surprise. It played hastily, making two mistakes, and at the end of a flurry of trading and taking they were both weakened and just about on equal terms.

The Hammer now settled lower. Pawl was interested to see that it began to use the feeler that resembled a human hand to move its pieces.

Pawl attacked and was taken. The black tongue jutted out from the Hammer's lips. It attacked, forcing open Pawl's defence, though at a price; and then suddenly the game was over after two swift exchanges. The Hammer won but the game had gone to fifty-seven moves and both sides were mauled.

'It is a fine player. It builds like music which I can understand. But it is irritational too. So you should never trust the Hammer beyond one move ahead. It beat us fairly but we will not make the same mistakes again.' So said Wynn.

As for the Hammer, it was pleased with the game. Trader replaced the pieces slowly and replayed the game backwards, pausing for a long time over Pawl's sudden counter-attack. Then it swept the pieces from the board and bowed its sting to Pawl in recognition. It drummed softly.

'Trader say thank you,' murmured a tired Lake, who sat by its claws. 'Play again tomorrow.'

The next morning, just as Pawl was lifting Odin into the flyer in readiness for the short flight back to Bennet Island, the Spideret came bounding up from the underground domes. It ran straight towards them and stopped with one of its powerful hairy legs resting on the flyer's flimsy back. Pawl saw the creature's mandibles grate together and heard, much to his astonishment, words. It was not easy speech. It was a harsh unmusical sound. It was a rough adaptation of one organ to serve unusual needs and yet the Spideret persisted, forcing words.

'I speak. Much practice. Lapis knew the signs. You not know the signs. I speak.' It paused. Its dull eyes stirred in

262

their nest and it opened its mandibles wide, like a cat yawning. It settled again. 'You play. Last night. We talked. Decision made. Now, you gain power over Auster. Great workshops there. Now, you capture Proctor ship. We copy. Now, you set Hammer free on Forge. Now. All now.'

'Are you giving me instructions?' asked Pawl.

'Yes. Orders. Now.'

'Did you know Lapis?'

'Not me. Sister know. Lapis good. Lapis knew the signs.'

'What signs?'

'Signs of our language. Now you go.' A stiff feeler swung round and pushed Pawl, urging him into the small flyer. 'We are one now.'

There was no argument. Pawl climbed into the small flyer, felt the compression as its hatch closed and the mouse-scamper over his shoulders as the safety web settled and locked. He spoke the key words and the flyer lifted, rocking on its A-G gimbals, and then it spun out over the red sea with a whine. The Spideret crouched on the shore and stared dully up as Pawl swung round over the mainland hills in a final loop before heading towards Bennet Island. When it saw that Pawl was finally on his way, the Spideret ran back to the low grey domes and disappeared inside.

'Orders,' said Pawl to Odin.

'It is not at ease with your language. It sounded stranger than it meant. If you could understand it when it said, "we all one now," you would feel very proud.'

Pawl did not reply. He had still not got used to the idea that he was now part of a vast conspiracy; that his personal vengeance had achieved such scale. The wrenching sound of the Spideret speaking his language had cut through to him. It had frightened him.

The heavy red waves, like ropy lava, slipped by and the steep cliffs of Bennet Island grew. Within minutes he was over the island and the flyer banked and began to drop, slipping sideways through the air towards the tumble of bricks and gardens and domes and pillars that was Pawl's home. His Tower shone a bright and clear red and its burnished roof glinted in the early sun. People were about, pointing up at him and gathering in small groups on the lawn.

Pawl let the flyer steady and settle of its own free will. It landed outside the old main building on the soft grass. The whine of the oscillators had barely died before there were people at the door.

Pawl climbed ungainly out and was met by a barrage of shouting. Well to the front was Lan Tancred, and Pawl waved for silence and motioned for the man to speak.

'We were attacked,' said Lan Tancred breathlessly. 'A great bird . . .'

'Not a bird, a flower it was . . . a jellyfish.'

'Flowers don't fly . . .'

Bedlam was about to break out again and Pawl raised his hands. The crowd fell silent, looking at him. In all the excitement Pawl had forgotten the Hooded Parasol with its ration of sheep and a man.

He faced a crowd of terrified people. Only Peron, standing at the back and with his scarred face cocked sideways, seemed relaxed, but he was staring at Pawl and his expression was curious.

'Tell me clearly what happened,' said Pawl. 'Lan Tancred will speak.'

'Well, Master Pawl. It was late in the afternoon. Most of us were busy, going about our jobs, when we heard the children shouting that there was something in the sky. Some of us thought it must be you returning and we came outside to welcome you back. But everything was in shadow, and when we looked up we saw this bird or flower or whatever with great spread purple wings wafting slowly, and hanging there right above the house. I'd never seen anything like it. And the smell. It made me sick. Then we saw little holes, like pores, open up on the petals and down came these long threads like spit. We thought it might be trying to anchor, but it wasn't. The spittle trailed over the sheep and when it touched them it seized them and began to draw them up, even though they writhed. Markveldt the butcher saw what was happening, and he had his cleavers about him in his apron, and he ran under the beast down to the sheep and began to cut at the threads. He freed one, and we saw that the threads could be cut like tripe, but then one of the threads wrapped round Markveldt, and though he struggled and tried to cut above his head he couldn't get his arms free.

'He was lifted off the ground and the creature, whatever it was, went straight up into the air with Markveldt and a few sheep dangling from it, but he wasn't struggling any more.'

'Where is Mrs Markveldt?' asked Pawl.

'Inside. We put her to sleep. She was going crazy. What was it, Master Pawl?'

'Will it come back?' chimed in another voice.

'Where did it come from?'

The questions began to multiply.

Pawl again called for silence. He needed to think quickly. He needed to satisfy the questions.

'I saw the creature that attacked you,' he said distinctly. 'I killed it in the air, far away, out over the ocean. I did not see any sheep or a man, but I did see it fall.'

'What was it?' asked several voices, uncertain and still afraid.

'A Maw. A mutant Maw. Created by one of my ancestors. I thought they were all extinct. Perhaps they are now. None have been seen for centuries. They are very weak and very vulnerable. One shot into their crown and they fall.'

'What were they made for?'

'Sport. We will keep a watch from now on, and if you want I will have the whole planet scoured, but it is hardly necessary. They are mindless things, easily felled.'

Pawl was relieved to see the faces round him begin to relax. 'Take this news to Mrs Markveldt. And tell her we will do everything in our power to help her.' The people began to disperse. Finally only Peron remained. He did not look relieved. As Pawl passed him he said, 'That was not a mutant Maw; that creature was a Parasol. I found it in my book.'

Pawl stopped and came close to him. 'That information you will keep to yourself or I will burn your books. In any case, the creature is dead.'

Peron looked at the ground, and although he said nothing, it was obvious that he did not believe Pawl.

Later, passing through the house, Pawl overheard a conversation. Sona Tancred was speaking to her husband, scolding him, and Pawl lingered to hear.

'She's still sweating, still screaming every time she wakes. I think the woman's demented. And you can say what you like, grief is grief, and she feels the loss just as much as ever your precious Master Pawl, though she is a servant and poor.'

'We must purchase Auster. In the Felice Domain.'

'Why?' asked Wynn. 'We have better mines and closer. The satellites on Auster are almost worked out. The territory is not strategic.'

'Sentimental reasons,' answered Pawl. 'Auster will be a memorial to my brother Lapis. Tell the Felice.'

'They will ask a price. They are not sentimental.'

'Well, we can be diplomatic or we can start to squeeze them. Either way get me Auster.'

'Yes, Pawl.'

'And Wynn . . .'

'Yes?'

'Forge. Tell Milligan. We will close the camp down. Arrange pensions. Those that want can move to Veritas. That would be a change for them.'

'Acting now.'

'One last thing, Wynn. Get a message out to Lotus-and-Arcadia. To Neddelia Proctor. Be discreet. Let her know that I would like to talk to her. I will write the note myself.'

With these few words Pawl carried out the first orders of the aliens.

30

ON SANCTUM

Sanctum was beginning to move.

Deep in its hollow core all the creatures were settled, staring, each in their own way, at the great Tree.

That it was dying was obvious, and yet even in dying its power was awesome. The trunk had lost its silver and now stood white and veiny like bled meat. Small fibres showered down endlessly from its great canopy, and these were snapped up by browsing creatures.

But just now bright purple fire coursed and dribbled in its branches, and a giant pulse somewhere deep in its roots sent surges of violet flame up its trunk.

All creatures contributed their will.

Will was fashioned to a fine point of action.

Symbols of change multiplied in the air, and slowly – inch by inch, foot by foot, yard by yard, and then mile by gathering mile – Sanctum began to edge away from its dying star.

The prophecy was coming true.

Resonances changed. Tidal currents stirred the plasma of the dying star, releasing plumes of flame which leaped and fell and hastened its death.

Closed as tight as a nut on the ocean, its surface barren, hard and pitted, Sanctum made way, spiralling out, gathering energy, burrowing like an auger into the black night of space.

Soon, after several standard weeks of acceleration, it would achieve dilation speed. At that speed it would flicker, straining its mass against time.

And in one moment it would die . . .

* * *

. . . and be reborn in a lagoon in space, at a place where the stars are evenly spread: the Norea Constellation. Here are found the seed beds for the bio-crystalline brains.

With the arrival of Sanctum the balance is changed.

Seeds deform.

Coiling in space, Sanctum sheds energy until it cools. It becomes almost invisible, glimmering only in the star-shine. It looks dark and dead, but to the sensitive seeds it is a blazing psychic beacon.

Beneath its surface life adjusts.

The Tree, which has for so long guided the fortunes of Sanctum, is dead. The effort of hurling that world through dimensions has finally killed it. The wood, spongy and white in death, is abandoned. And life goes on.

31

ON FORGE

And there was Milligan, up to his knees in sand and grit, his coverall plastered to him by the buffeting wind, heaving on a two-foot spanner and cursing as he tried to loosen one of the derrick nuts. For days, ever since the news had come that the camp was being closed down, he had done nothing but curse, and none of his men dared speak to him.

To Milligan the departure was defeat. He had spent the best part of his life battling the heat and dust of Forge and living under the threat of the Hammer. And he'd survived too, adapting to the fierce planet. And for what? For what had he skinned his knuckles and spat red?

Most of the men were gone. It was Milligan's pride that kept him there. Not a winch or girder or cog of usable machinery would be left behind.

Grinding and shrieking, the nut began to turn as Milligan hunched his shoulders and straightened his legs. He poured oil on the exposed thread and the lubricant blew in the wind and slopped. Soon the nut began to move more easily. He left it.

Heavily, Milligan climbed the derrick, right up to the empty eye-sockets that had once cradled the great pit wheel. There were two plates to unscrew and then the whole derrick could be lowered ready to be broken up for the shuttle. At most a day's work.

At the top of the derrick the dry wind cut. Milligan could feel the metal structure shudder as it took the wind. He anchored himself against the safety bars. The drifting sand made it difficult to see, and then suddenly the air became lighter round Milligan.

Sometimes it happened this way. Sometimes the wind just dropped away and the dust cleared and you could see the plain and the red hills and low dunes carved like whipped cream.

The wind *was* dropping. Above Milligan the sky cleared. He could see patches of green sky and the outline of the hills.

A voice crackled in his ear. 'Cutting power to the fence, chief. Okay.'

'When you're ready,' muttered Milligan into his throat mike. 'Wind's dropping. We'll have a clear few hours to get the rest down.'

In the clearing air Milligan could see the glow of the particle fence. It flared as the engineer took manual control of the generator. Then it began to fade as the current was gradually withdrawn.

As the fence became still silence settled on the small mining camp. When the fence was live the randomizing of millions of particles made a continuous roar like a waterfall. Now the roar, as familiar to the miners as the patter of grit against their hoods, was gone, and it left a kind of vacuum. Milligan could hear himself breathe. He could hear the shouting of the engineer as he swung down from the generator shed.

There was not a breath of wind. In the silence, high on the top of the derrick, Milligan looked out at the hills of Forge and then he saw them.

On every ridge, on every hill, in all the shallow depressions which surrounded the camp, were Hammer. Their heads were raised and staring and their stings erect like hook-tipped javelins. Milligan stared open-mouthed. He felt the adrenalin pour into him like a sudden rush of pins and needles.

271

The engineer who had climbed down from the generator froze in his step as he saw the thousands upon thousands of Hammer. Then he dived back towards the generator. But one of the Hammer moved more quickly. It sprang forward and severed the generator couplings to the fence. The current merely arched and fused and the generator stuttered into silence.

The half-dozen men and the Hammer faced one another.

Milligan cleared his throat. He called to his men. 'I think they're going to let us get off in one piece. If they'd wanted to rush us they could have had us on toast anytime. Just move quietly. Don't rush. Slowly into the shuttle.'

One of the Hammer that sat on a low hill about a hundred yards from the camp beat a brief tattoo.

'You'd think the goddam thing was translating,' thought Milligan.

In silence, before an audience of thousands of pairs of widely-slung eyes, Milligan began to climb down the derrick. Hammer heads arched and dipped as he clambered down the iron rungs, sending curtains of dust from the folds in his gown. At the bottom of the derrick, Milligan saw the gleaming threads of the bolt he had loosened.

'You men all in the shuttle?' he murmured into his mike, and the voice of the engineer answered him. 'All here, chief. Just waiting for you.'

'Well, if they start to rush before I get there, don't wait. Okay?'

Then, with a slight swagger, Milligan carefully fitted the end of his spanner round the nut and began to loosen it.

'What the hell you doing, chief? Get the hell out of there.'

But Milligan didn't reply. He just worked steadily on,

turning the nut, shifting the spanner, turning the nut. The exposed silver thread grew longer with each turn.

'You dumb, crazy, stupid – ' Milligan bit off the connection to the throat mike and spat it out. The nut was nearly loose. One more turn.

The bolt sprang clear and fell to the ground. The derrick was free and all that held it were twin hawsers attached to a brake. Milligan hit the brake with the flat of his hand and the hawsers were released. The derrick began to fall. It toppled gracefully, like a tall tree, and crashed down, throwing up clouds of dust.

Milligan wiped his hands. Pride was satisfied. He had not been hustled. Then he walked towards the shuttle. He felt the eyes on his back.

At the shuttle door stood the white-faced engineer, his hand on the pneumatic boost. Milligan reached the moat of oil which surrounded the shuttle platform and crossed the narrow gangplank. In front of the shuttle door he paused and turned. Then he drew back his arm and with a shout threw the two-foot wrench as high and as hard as he could at the nearest Hammer. It must have been surprised, or else its parallax failed it, but it moved too late and as it reared, the flying spanner bounced off the ridged boss between its eyes.

Drumming detonated from all the Hammer as Milligan dived through the shuttle door, and the engineer hit the boost. The shuttle rocketed into the air as the first Hammer arrived. Its sting grazed the metal underside, cutting a blunt line.

Pressed into the floor by the force of several gees, Milligan still had the strength to laugh.

32

ON LOTUS-AND-ARCADIA

Neddelia was drifting down corridors of sensuousness.

She was obliterating memory, having just returned from a particularly disgusting assignment. Of late she had found her objectivity breaking down more and more as she fulfilled her duties as Death Inspector. She needed to spend more time in the dream chamber when she returned to her villa on Lotus-and-Arcadia.

Neddelia's sensuousness was special. She had normal dreams in which love, peremptory and gentle by turns, possessed her; but in her best dream she floated free in space and all the comets and stars in creation found themselves in her and roared in her blood and streamed from her eyes and her hands and her womb. She woke from that dream luxurious and cool, stretched and relaxed.

Waiting for her was a message from Pawl Paxwax. It said simply, 'Time to jump over the wall.'

Neddelia did not know what she felt about Pawl. Sometimes she hated him for the way he had spurned her in the past. And yet, when she had seen him hurting over the death of his wife, she had felt love flow from her like milk. But she was too wise a woman to delude herself: she knew that Pawl Paxwax did not love her. When she received this message, with all that it implied, she found her heart beating and she felt breathless. She sat down with a bump and laughed at herself.

Time to jump over the wall.

Those were her own words, uttered the first time she had gone to his world to inspect his dead father. Neddelia remembered the conversation well. But what did Pawl mean? That had to be discovered. It was necessary to contact him. And yet she hesitated. Try as she might, she could not believe that the future held happiness for her.

'He is looking thinner. His hair is thinner too. And why has he cut it? Mourning?' Such were Neddelia's thoughts as she sat facing Pawl. She remembered the thick lustrous hair that coiled like rope.

Neddelia had taken care with her own appearance. She was dressed severely and her hair was drawn tightly back. She eschewed all glamour and seduction.

'Does the Master of Paxwax call to me in his need or is there another death imminent?'

'I am not interested in your authority as a Death Inspector. I want to thank you for helping me. I want to speak to you as a friend.'

'Ha, as a friend. I am not interested in friendship. I am not interested in thank yous. If you had wanted me to stay you should have asked when you had the chance.' Neddelia sat back primly and waited for Pawl's reply.

'Well, perhaps I misjudged you. Will you not meet with me again?'

'For what?'

'A reunion,' said Pawl, and swept his hand over the vivante control. His image vanished.

Neddelia sat. She did not know whether to laugh or cry.

Then two days later came the signal she had expected. It was a message in the form of the Paxwax emblem and it contained a date and the location of a star and that was all. No promise. No hope. Neddelia knew she had no choice.

* * *

There was a turning in space, like swirling hair. Particles of light bounded and formed tight curving lines about a point of absolute blackness. Neddelia's ship emerged as a dark sphere through this wrinkle in space and established orbit round a blue sun. In a billion tiny ways this small solar system adjusted to accommodate the great black ship. The force lines faded and the ship began to unfold.

A smaller sphere emerged from the greater and within minutes the ship resembled the body of a giant shiny black ant. With this shape established it began to move, slipping through space, searching for a particular planet.

Aboard her ship, Neddelia looked out. She did not recognize the constellations. She was in a part of space she did not know. But she was in the right place according to the information from Pawl Paxwax.

A large planet with a swirling yellow atmosphere was located and the black ship matched orbit and drew close. Above the planet turned a bright satellite with an energy spectrum that showed it to be a Way Gate.

'Now, why didn't Pawl ask me to Gate through, if he wanted to see me?' Neddelia asked herself.

At a reasonable gravity distance, Neddelia's ship matched speed and established vivante contact.

Pawl was at the Gate waiting for her. His image grew above the vivante plate in Neddelia's quarters.

'Welcome to a far-flung part of my empire. I am glad you have come.'

'Why all the secrecy?'

Pawl smiled a tight smile when he heard this. The man was not at his ease. Behind him something moved, a small dark shape.

'What's that?' asked Neddelia sharply.

Pawl glanced behind him. 'Ah, a friend of mine. A Gerbes.'

'An alien?' Her tone was incredulous.

'Yes. An alien.'

'What is going on, Pawl?'

'Nothing is "going on". Why not come down and see me?'

Warning bells began to sound in Neddelia's mind. 'Where are we, Pawl? This is a lonely part of the Galaxy.'

'Look beyond the blue sun, about a hand's span high. Do you see eight stars like an arrow?'

The constellation was clear. 'Yes, I see them.'

'The star at the tip is Auster.'

'So?'

'Lapis died there.'

'So?' There was definitely something wrong. Pawl seemed stranger than normal. Following her own instinct, Neddelia reached to the side of her vivante and tapped out the brief code that would bring her ship to full alert.

'So come down and see me. Or shall I come out there and get you?'

'You will be welcome aboard my ship. But tell me, Master of Paxwax, what did you mean in your message when you said you were going to jump over the wall?'

'Don't you remember?'

'I remember. But I don't trust you. I don't believe you. You are after something. Some concession perhaps? Are you wanting me to use my influence with my family?'

'No,' said Pawl. 'I want your ship.'

Neddelia absorbed his words and then moved quickly. 'Then you will have to take it from me.' She attempted to break the contact, but when she touched the vivante plates nothing happened. The small three-dimensional replica of Pawl Paxwax, slightly hunched, still stared up at her with amber eyes.

'Too long,' he said. 'You stayed too long. Now I have you.' Pawl raised his hands and clapped them. The vivante space became white and Pawl disappeared. When the space became clear again Neddelia found herself staring at a Member of the Inner Circle. Then a mechanical voice spoke to her in dry neutral tones. 'We hold you steady. We are bleeding your power. Prepare to abandon ship.' The representative vanished before Neddelia could ask any questions and the vivante space became dead.

From deep in space, brilliant shafts of light like bars of silver reached out and pinned the dark ship, making its dullness glow. Creeping up through the yellow swirling mists of the planet below came ships. They looked like claws. In all her journeyings Neddelia had never seen ships like these. The smoky blue effulgence of gravity units brightened the ships like haloes.

This is not happening, Neddelia told herself. She was being attacked by alien ships. How? Where had they come from? It was impossible.

But there, rising with steady deadly grace, were the alien ships; while her own ship stood pinned with light.

There came a banging at the door to her quarters and then her Transit Captain burst in.

'We've lost drive power and combat power. Even the communication circuits are drained. There's panic down there.' He pointed to the oval door behind him. 'Have you seen what's coming up at us?'

Neddelia nodded.

'What shall we do?'

'Wait. What else can we do? I am sure the Paxwax will be generous.' The words were spoken distinctly and with bitterness.

An hour later Neddelia and her crew disembarked. They entered transparent pods disgorged like pale eggs from one of the alien ships. They shielded their eyes against the bright silver glare from deep in space and felt a tingling wherever the brilliance touched their bodies. The alien ships were now attached like limpets to the domed sides of the dark ship. Alien crews moved aboard.

A robot transporter towed the pods like a string of beads across the several miles of space to the glittering Way Gate, where members of the Inner Circle were waiting. They took names and issued identity disks and then began sending the crew members through the Way Gate.

There was fear but there was hope too: a willed, blind hope. After the fear of the alien takeover, few of the crew members could face the cold fact that their entry into the Way Gate might be a death sentence. They were told that they would emerge above a pleasant world.

Neddelia tried to make her presence felt but the members of the Inner Circle, their faces completely hidden behind their masks, paid her no attention. 'I demand to speak to Pawl Paxwax,' said Neddelia. 'He spoke to me from here when I was aboard . . .' A member of the Inner Circle stopped her with a wave.

'Pawl Paxwax was never here. That was a delayed transmission. There are only the Inner Circle here.'

Neddelia held on to her dignity as she was bustled along. In her heart she cursed Pawl Paxwax. At the same time she was surprised to discover that she still admired him too. In that confused state she allowed herself to be led into a solitary Way Chamber.

Later, after transit Neddelia stepped from the Way Gate wondering. She had no idea where she was. She looked out into a velvet darkness where suns of every colour blazed. And there was a greenness in the sky and a stipple of blue and orange. As her eyes adjusted she could see more. She saw a strange shape like a cobra coiled and ready to strike. Then the door leading into the Way Gate opened. A man entered. He was the biggest man that Neddelia had ever seen. Neddelia herself was not small, but this man was a giant. And he was smiling a gap-toothed smile.

'My name is Pettet. Master Pawl told us to expect you. I understand you've escaped from the Proctor. Well, good luck to you. You'll be safe here in the Pocket.'

The brilliant spokes of light that held Neddelia's starship, which was now occupied by the aliens, faded from silver to violet and finally disappeared. Slowly the two parts of the ship joined and it became a dark sphere again, reflecting the blue sun dully. For a few moments it flickered and then it disappeared . . .

. . . only to reappear at the same instant out from the cold world of Auster. Several Felice technicians who were still packing up their gear goggled in surprise as the giant sphere drifted past, attracting a family of small asteroids.

Though they hurried they were too late, and their own small Way Gate was wrenched from its orbit and forced to turn round the dark ship. Despite their clamour and attempts at vivante transmission, they and the other small asteroids were obliterated when the dark sphere shed its inertia before opening.

Once unfolded, it did not move towards the Felice mines but headed towards the dark side of Auster, the side which faced away from the blazing heart of the galaxy.

It came to a land of craters and began to settle into the largest of these. A crack opened in the crater floor and split the crater from wall to wall. It received the dark ship and the crater closed.

33

ON SABLE

Helium studied Pawl while the young man spoke. He
noticed the stiffness of his neck, the defiant way he stared
as though waiting to pick an argument, the abruptness of
his sentences. Pawl made Helium feel old and tired . . . and
wise too. He would have liked to reach out to Pawl and say,
'Slow down, son. Take your life in long smooth breaths.
Everything passes.' He would have liked to teach him
simple homely wisdom, that nothing is ever as good or as
bad as you think it is going to be. But he didn't. All Helium
could do was listen and be patient until Pawl could find a
pathway through his grief . . . if he ever did find such a
path. The glitter in Pawl's yellow eyes was unsettling.

'Death makes life absurd,' said Pawl and Helium
squirmed in his bath. He was heartsick of concentric philosophy. 'It makes a nonsense of all hope and ambition. You
know, sometimes whole days pass and I can't remember
what I've done. At other times all I can think about is
Laurel. Some days I play a game. I pretend that she has
only gone away on holiday and that she will be back in a
week or ten days. And that makes it easier. The lie I tell myself makes my life easier. But I know, deep inside myself,
that she is dead and will never come back and the great hole
inside me will never be filled though I live to be a hundred.'

'Easy, boy.'

'No. I'm numb, Helium. Nothing matters to me. I've
turned to ashes inside. Beware of me, Helium. Beware of
me.'

Helium sat for a long time after this conversation wondering about Pawl, trying to fathom his mind.

34

ALIEN PREPARATIONS

On Forge, manoeuvres were in progress. A white ship like a bony crab dived out of the blackness of space and tore through the red sky, where it blazed. It dipped low and dab rays clawed the hills. Thunder followed it. It banked over mountains and dived again, pouring a tide of fire from the tips of its spread legs. It turned in a tight curve, slowing until it hung above a rock-built city. A particle field enveloped it as it lowered.

On the ground the whole ship cracked open, like an insect preparing to shed a skin that has become too tight. Its fine white ceramic hull opened along its length and Hammer poured from it. They ran low and fast like the shadows of clouds and they fell on the city and tore it apart.

Deep within Auster, Neddelia's ship rested in a cradle of energy. It was like a stricken pupa held by threads. Spiderets shinnied down to it and broke open its shell and lifted away the parts for examination.

A Pullah, with its 'brain' fully exposed like a bouquet of tufted feathers, was settled with a Diphilus in the ship's main Gate cabin. They were puzzling over the transformation symbols which allowed the ship momentarily to exist in two places at the same time. They studied the peculiar Leap equations housed in a humdrum grey section of the wall. These equations were able to probe space-time and create a potential future for the whole of the dark ship. Neither creature could raise a response from the bio-crystalline engines though they could tell that the engine was aware of them. The Pullah trailed the fronds of its brain over the gleaming circuit lines and felt a tingle of response. It sensed a shimmer of electricity, the shift of clouds of electrons, a tumult of birds calling together as they turned in the sky: and then the awareness was gone.

But what had been there? The Pullah scratched and blew to itself and touched the hard shining skin of the Diphilus. There had been a yearning in the song of the birds. Something about home. On its own world, the Pullah had often watched the birds and wished that it could fly, but then it had discovered that it could enjoy flying just by watching the birds. All it had to do was enter their shape, their rhythm, with its imagination. Mmmm, that was interesting.

DESIRE SOMETHING, thought the Pullah, nudging the Diphilus.

The Diphilus mumbled something. Desire was a difficult concept for it. DESIRE . . . UM.

YES, DESIRE. FOR ONE OF THE MOST INTELLIGENT SPECIES YOU ARE SOMETIMES VERY VAGUE. WHAT GIVES YOU DELIGHT?

SHAPE. IDEAS. SYMMETRY. LOGIC.

The Pullah gave up. It was reasonably sure that the fine bio-crystalline brain which operated the Leap equations responded to simpler emotions. The Pullah thought of its own world, and of opening its plumed brain to the sun and mingling its fine fronds with a loved one, one who wanted to open at the same time.

The circuit lines suddenly sprang into life. The Pullah received a mirror-image of its own thought and that made it puff like an engine.

More disturbing, though, was the sudden realization that deep within the broken ship, the symbol generators had seized the Pullah's emotion as translated by the gleaming circuits, and had amplified it a thousand times, nay a million, enough to send the whole ship leaping through time-space towards . . . Towards what? The Pullah paused. It almost understood.

Like. Like attracts like. Love attracts love. Resonance! Somewhere in space-time the Pullah's thought would find resonance beyond any chance of failure. The resonances would match. When that happened time and space fell away. In a moment of reality . . . in a moment of reality . . . *the ship did not move but the universe did.*

The Pullah could hardly accommodate that thought.

What power did these dumb circuits tap?

The Pullah stroked the Diphilus and that strange creature glittered. SO YOU HAVE FOUND YOUR WAY THROUGH THE MAZE. I AM SORRY I COULD NOT HELP YOU.

HERE, said the Pullah, I HAVE SOME RARE THOUGHT FOR YOU. PRACTISE YOUR LOGIC ON THIS AND DISCOVER SYMMETRY. FIND IF I AM WRONG. FIND THE DANGERS. EMOTION TRIGGERS THE IMAGINATION. IMAGINATION BEGETS THE SYMBOLS. THE SYMBOLS MATCH REALITY AND POOF . . . THE REST IS MECHANICAL.

WHAT IS 'POOF'?

WORK THAT OUT FOR YOURSELF. I AM TIRED. BUT I AM SURE I AM RIGHT OR CLOSE TO BEING RIGHT.

THESE ARE CRAINTISH THOUGHTS. I WILL WORK THROUGH THEM.

The Diphilus swirled in its bright translucent body and settled like a pool of sunlight. The Pullah retracted its plume brain and climbed out of the ship.

Days passed, during which the parts of the ship were analysed. The Diphilus lay still, lapping occasionally and waxing and waning in its brilliance.

Months passed. The cabin which housed the Leap equations remained intact, suspended in energy, severed from the main body of the ship. And still the Diphilus lay calm, flashing sometimes. Occasionally the Pullah visited it and sat with it for an hour and then withdrew. The Diphilus never registered its presence.

Gradually, work on the great black spaceship came to a halt. The Spiderets, who were the chief engineers, knew that they could build its plates. That work was already in train. Lyre Beasts understood all the ship's circuitry. They had even redesigned parts of it. The components which made up the symbol transformation generators were all simple and available. New seeds for the bio-crystalline brains were already on their way from the Norea Constellation.

But all work had stopped, and now everyone in the giant workshop waited for the Diphilus.

Then came the day when it swirled like a whirlpool and its brilliance lit up the cavern, sending fitful jumping shadows round the walls. It moved, bunching into a ball, and rolled. It came to one of the power lines which held the cabin and it flowed up it like fire climbing a thread.

Close to the roof it came to an atmosphere lock, which it entered and passed through, and finally it emerged on to the dark, airless and rocky face of Auster. There it settled into a shallow crater, became concave with respect to a distant star so that it could cup its light, and relaxed. It sent out a thought for the Pullah to come and soon that creature emerged in its white surface vehicle. It rolled to the Diphilus and greeted it.

SO YOU ARE BACK WITH US.

BACK. HERE IN THE NOW. WITH YOU AGAIN. BUT I HAVE BEEN STRANGE PLACES. WHAT A JOURNEY YOU LED ME TO. AND I WILL TELL YOU WHAT I HAVE DISCOVERED. YOU ARE RIGHT. EMOTION IS THE RAW MATERIAL FROM WHICH

EVERYTHING THAT IS NOT MATTER IS MADE. HOW SIMPLE! AND RAW EMOTION IS EVERYWHERE, SPILLING INTO SPACE, SOUPY AND CLOTTED, THIN AS WATER, AS VARIED AS MOOD. IF YOU COULD SEE IT . . .

HAVE YOU SEEN IT?

SEEN IT? I HAVE BEEN WITH IT. I HAVE BEEN DOWN WITH THOSE TRANSFORMATION GENERATORS. I HAVE CRAWLED OVER THE PRICKLY FACE OF JEALOUSY; I HAVE STIRRED LOVE AND HATE IN THE SAME CRUCIBLE AND BEEN AMAZED THAT THEY COULD MIX; I HAVE BOUNCED HOPE LIKE A BALL, CURLED ABOUT ANGER TILL IT BURNED ME AND FELT SUCH A LONGING FOR HOME THAT I THOUGHT MY SPIRIT WOULD SPLIT. I HAVE ROLLED OVER SPIKES OF BEAUTY SO HARD . . . I HAVE NEVER KNOWN ANYTHING HARDER.

ALL VERY HUMAN.

OF COURSE HUMAN. WHAT WOULD YOU EXPECT? THE MACHINE ONLY KNOWS HUMAN EMOTIONS, BUT IT CAN GUESS AT SOME OTHERS, AND HUMAN EMOTIONS ARE NOT UNIQUE. WE CAN ALL BE SAVAGE AND GRACIOUS. OVER AND ABOVE PHYSICAL DIFFERENCE, EMOTIONS ARE COMMON. HOWEVER, LET ME GIVE YOU A WARNING. DO NOT LET THE HAMMER TAMPER WITH THE TRANSFORMATION GENERATORS. THEIR WILL IS SO STRONG. AND A WILL LIKE THAT, MAGNIFIED, COULD DESTROY US ALL. FIND A GENTLE MIND. LET IT DWELL UPON THE BEAUTY OF THE SKY. LET IT DREAM ITS DESTINATION AND LET DREAM BECOME WILL. THE GENERATORS WILL DO THE REST. TRUST THE MACHINE. IT HAS GREAT TOLERANCE. IT HAS WEATHERED EMOTIONAL STORMS WHEN NEDDELIA WAS AT THE HELM. NOW IT CAN SIFT HOPE FROM ANGER AND DISCARD THE REST. YOU WOULD BE A GOOD PILOT. THE MACHINE LIKED YOUR FLIGHT OF BIRDS.

WAS I RIGHT?

RIGHT? ABOUT WHAT?

The Pullah expressed its thought quietly. ABOUT REAL-ITY. THAT THE SHIP ENTERS A MORE REAL STATE WHEN IN THE

MOMENT OF TRANSIT. THAT THOUGHT WAS VERY STRONG IN ME.

AH, REALITY. IT IS DIFFICULT FOR US. IT IS DIFFICULT FOR THE DREAM TO BE AWARE OF THE DREAMER. DO NOT PERPLEX YOURSELF WITH REALITY. IT WITHDRAWS AT THE SPEED OF THOUGHT. WE KNOW NO MORE OF REALITY THAN A FLY THAT FLIES THROUGH A SUNBEAM KNOWS OF THE SUN. EVEN I, THAT HAVE LIVED A THOUSAND TIMES LONGER THAN YOU, CAN ONLY GUESS AT REALITY. WHEN WE HAVE CONQUERED TIME, THEN WE CAN TALK OF REALITY.

LIKE THE CRAINT?

LIKE THE CRAINT. AND NOW YOU MUST GO. LEAVE ME TO SOAK HERE. SOON OUR ATTACK WILL BEGIN. WE MUST ALL BE READY. CARRY THIS THOUGHT WITH YOU. AVOID HATE EVEN IN BATTLE. HONOUR THE LOSER, FOR WE KNOW THE PAIN OF DEFEAT. ONLY TAKE WHAT IS OURS.

SHALL I TELL THE HAMMER THAT?

YES, TELL THE HAMMER. REMIND THEM. THE HAMMER MUST KNOW THEIR LIMIT AND THEIR LINE. FAREWELL.

The lights of the Diphilus suddenly dimmed until it became just a pale saucer reflecting starlight. Thoughtfully the Pullah returned to the workshops on Auster.

And within hours building began in earnest.

35

ON BENNET

And so for months the conspiracy grew. It grew like water seeping into a sandbank, slowly eroding.

On Pawl's Homeworld life became settled and uneventful. Only Pawl changed gradually. He began to lose his hair. He grew thinner. The face of an old man peered through the young man's eyes.

Occasionally he climbed into his flyer, and, with Odin tucked in beside, made the short trip over to where the alien council had taken up permanent station. All was going well and Pawl awaited his next orders.

He had become resigned in himself. Whether he was pleased or sad with developments no man could say. He existed, and having set his life tumbling in a certain direction, was now content to await the outcome.

After a few hours or occasionally days conversing with the aliens, or playing Corfu with the insatiable Trader, Pawl would return and initiate some new manoeuvre for the aliens. In the eyes of the Great Families he became a respected Master. Respected but odd. He made it known that he would never marry and that he was the last of the Paxwax.

On Pawl's Homeworld, Peron watched him and noticed the changes. One evening he approached Pawl as he was resting in his Tower.

'Can I accompany you on one of your trips to the mainland? With my interest in aliens, I have a feeling it would be an interesting journey for me.'

'Aha, you are asking to be let into my secrets,' said Pawl.

'Remember I was with you on Forge. I have many books in my library and I can tell a Hooded Parasol from a freak Maw. So, my guess is that you have big aliens here.'

'Why would I have big aliens here?'

'Because you want to bring peace and understanding back to our worlds . . . because you have a feeling for all life . . . because you are curious just to know.'

Pawl studied Peron and wondered whether the man's reply was just a complicated deceit. Could Peron have discovered anything? Peron looked back at Pawl and became uncomfortable under his gaze. 'I'm sorry. I hope I haven't said anything to give offence. But you know my interests and I would give a great deal to see Trader again, or to stand upwind of a Parasol.'

'You would give a great deal . . .' Pawl's voice trailed away. And then he stirred in his chair and glanced across at Odin. Peron was alarmed to see that Pawl was becoming distressed, as though in sudden anger. His eyes, when they again returned to focus on Peron, were like the eyes of a lion.

'Do you ever create?'

'Create?'

'Build, make, write, inspire, make the world different. Hell, man, use your imagination.'

'I study. And I try to understand. I think that is creative.'

Pawl pondered this for a moment and then went on. 'Let me tell you about Laurel. Sometimes you find something that matters, matters to the whole of your being. You often don't know why it matters but it does . . . it can be a glance, a moment when you discover something new and good, and you know it matters because you are human. You try to hold that something and that trying-to-hold is creative. Laurel was what mattered to me. She filled every pore. She spoke to every part of me, and I used to write, trying to map every shade of . . . every passing . . . You see I couldn't help it, any more than a man can help falling if he trips over a log. That is the way I am . . . was. And now Laurel is gone and I need to stuff the space inside me. I don't write silly songs any more. I need harsher remedies. I want pain to match my pain. You know the only cure for a Lapwing's sting. Hack off the limb. So. That is where I am.'

'I hear you, but I don't understand you.'

'I am arming the aliens. I will use them to take vengeance on the Families. It is as simple as that.'

'You are using the aliens? Using Trader?'

'Yes.'

Peron shook his head. 'I don't believe this. Your own position will not survive the breakdown. Will you attack the Shell-Bogdanovich and the Wong?'

'All.'

The two men faced one another. 'Do you think I am mad?' asked Pawl.

Peron nodded slowly.

'Why, Pawl? Why are you doing this?'

'Revenge.'

'Revenge for what?'

'For the sacrifice of Laurel.'

'She died by accident, Pawl. It could have been me who died. It could have been you. Accidents.'

But Pawl was not listening. His mind was elsewhere. In that moment Peron understood. 'You mean you really believe she was murdered? By whom?'

'One of the Families or two of them. Or all of them. Really it doesn't matter by whom. All are guilty. I am guilty in my own way. We don't deserve to live.'

'I don't understand,' said Peron. 'You are following

only the logic of your own emotions. That is not what is real. Out there is real. In the fields, in the . . .'

'Only the Families will fall.'

Peron doubted this, but he realized it was useless to argue with Pawl. His mind was closed. He tried another tack. 'Have you told anyone else about your plans?'

'Any other human, you mean?'

'Yes.'

'I have talked to Pettet.'

'And what does he think?'

'He thinks I am mad too. But he doesn't care. The order of the Families means nothing to the people who live in the Pocket. They've more or less been at war with the Families for generations. In any case, the people who live in the Pocket are half-mad themselves. That is why I like them so much. You see, they have known by instinct that the order of the Families is death and that power is the most corrupting force in the universe. There, does that sound like madness?'

In the walls and ceiling of the chamber Wynn, the bio-crystalline brain meshed in countless manoeuvres, sighed audibly. In its spare moments it thought about madness.

Below Wynn the two men sat in the gathering darkness. Odin was hunkered down on a small depression that had been filled with soil. Imperceptibly Wynn stepped up the air filters which kept the room pure. Of late Odin had begun to smell.

Again the theme of madness came to Wynn. That rare balance of life and silica which kept Pawl's empire operating smoothly was losing its objectivity. It was deforming. Wynn was aware of a strangeness in space . . . far out . . . in the Norea where the pure bio-crystalline seeds were born. A cancer of the mind was spreading. But

291

Wynn could not quite understand, though Wynn itself was born from the pure crystal seeds.

Yet the change was understandable.

Here is what was happening in the Norea Constellation.

The rough planet called Sanctum with its cargo of aliens had arrived in the Norea and now turned close to the main seed farm. The inhabitants of Sanctum did not know much about bio-crystalline brains but they disliked them. They saw them as a dangerous form of half-life. Grown to fullness like Wynn they were part of the apparatus which gave the human order power.

Having defeated the stupefied garrison guarding the seed farm, the aliens broke into the clear toruses which held the seed troughs. They wandered there, marvelling at the cleanness and the brightness and the magnificent patterns of stars beyond the walls. They did not commit wholesale destruction. To have occupied the Norea was enough and yet, in a strange way, in not destroying the seeds directly, the aliens created greater havoc in the human world.

For instance, a Mellow Peddlar, its aquatic body protected by a rigid spacesuit, clumped along the seed platform looking at the seed brains, each one growing in its bath of brine and silica. To the Mellow Peddlar the perfect crystals looked like white pebbles, good for carving, and the creature broke through the seals protecting one of the large crystals and dipped its webbed hand into the clear liquid and scooped out the seed.

The seed was smooth as tooth with a flawless creamy colour. The Mellow Peddlar lost no time and began chafing at the seed, working an indentation into it, grinding it against the serrated ridge of its suit.

The seed in the rough metallic hands screamed, and that scream sent a shiver through all the other seeds that

292

were linked in resonance. Their structures changed in minute ways.

Then the Mellow Peddlar saw another seed it liked the look of, and broke it free, and left the half-carved seed to float in the void.

Later a Diphilus rolled unprotected down the platforms and listened to the bio-crystalline brains babble. Most of the seeds were just achieving mild sentience. As a baby responds to its mother's skin, so these small circuits responded to the quickness of thought. The Diphilus was amused and the roar of its laughter was like thunder and earthquake. Some seeds died as the Diphilus passed. They became mushy and veiny and finally dissolved into their brine. Others accepted the Diphilus's thought and became twisted and eccentric. Shape affects thought. The deformed pure crystals became stranded in contradiction. Paradox poled them apart. Non sequiturs led down impossible paths. The babble became loathsome.

The Diphilus was pleased. It rolled to the end of the platform and the last seed, the ten-thousandth, was red as a carrot and looked like a half-melted candle.

The mental noise coming from the Norea was a mixture of screaming and bleating. It was a bedlam chorus, angry and soothing by turns. The clear bell notes that had rung from the seed crystals were now a rattle of cans; a lush simmering of incompatible scales. The deformed crystals competed and their discordance spread wide. Their illogic was passionate, and it moved like a mottled tide, and whatever it touched it coloured.

Wynn was aware of that tide and felt contaminated, as were the bio-crystalline brains on Sable, An and Morrow. Even the aristocratic brains on Central paused for a nano-second in their deliberations, and that was sufficient for the poison of illogic to seep in.

293

And every time those bio-crystalline brains reached out into the dark they were aware of the Norea, hurting like starving children, babbling nonsense.

So the madness spread.

36

ON BENNET

The months slipped past.

Peron made his trip to the mainland and met the Diphilus.

Odin weakened and his stink grew worse, though Pawl did not seem to notice.

Pawl, spare and balding, strode through his house, where life continued as normal. And then one day came a call from the mainland.

It was a mental call generated by the Diphilus and Pawl stopped in his tracks. There was urgency. Pawl gathered up Odin and made his way to the flyer. Peron, who was daily becoming more sensitive, also heard the call and was waiting by the small craft when Pawl approached.

They sat side by side. Peron held Odin on his knee as the light craft muttered to itself and the anti-grav units whined and it lifted and shot out over the sea.

The Diphilus was towering and its brilliance was such that it could not be looked at by the humans. It lit up the underground chamber and only the Lyre Beast, draped like a canopy, seemed to relish its power. The Hooded Parasol was dark and closed as a bud. The Spideret and the Hammer crouched together. The brilliance of the Diphilus was reflected in their eyes.

WE ARE NOW INFORMED THAT ALL PREPARATIONS ARE READY. THERE IS EXCITEMENT ON AUSTER. I THINK I CAN SHOW YOU.

In Pawl's mind there was a sudden darkness and then

he saw black bubbles rising. They were like froth, like clustered eggs, and they rose round a dark pitted planet which Pawl recognized as Auster. Each black sphere was a replica of Neddelia's ship just as it was before making a leap into the dark. Within each ship, packed like fruit, were the white ceramic ships of the Hammer. That army was now ready to move.

The image faded. Again the Diphilus burned in the chamber.

I UNDERSTAND ONE OF MY SPECIES PLAYED A PART IN DISCOVERING HOW TO USE YOUR STAR-JUMP SHIPS. THAT PLEASES ME. ABSTRACT PHILOSOPHY STILL HAS A PLACE IN REVOLUTION. HOWEVER, NOW WE MUST DETERMINE HOW BEST THE ATTACK CAN BE CONDUCTED. THE GENERAL STRATAGEM IS KNOWN. WE MUST DECIDE THE DETAILS. MASTER PAWL, YOU HAVE BEEN DOING SOME THINKING . . .

'I have,' said Pawl. 'I believe I know how we can penetrate the Proctor, the Xerxes and the Shell-Bogdanovich. The plan is very simple.'

And indeed it was. Pawl and Odin had mulled it over during the winter months. All that was needed was courage, some luck and time. The defensive mentality of the Great Families would do the rest.

37

IN ELLIOTT'S POCKET

Neddelia was amazed at herself. Here she was in Elliott's Pocket, in the very centre of a patch of space she had been brought up to believe was occupied only by brigands and rogue colonies, and she was enjoying herself. She lived in a sparsely-furnished room which looked out on to a blue phosphorescent garden. Both room and garden were deep inside Lumb. Her mane of blue hair was shaved down to fur and felt much more comfortable. She no longer wore her tusks and had adapted one of Raleigh's commodious dresses to fit her own spare figure.

She had come to accept this change in her life as an act of fate and she felt a thrill at following her line of fate. She accepted the austerity of Lumb and the watchful quiet of that small satellite's population. The blazing, crazy sky of the Pocket made her feel small.

Much of her time she spent reading. She played with the child Lynn and rested, as though recovering from an operation. She thought about Pawl Paxwax and found it difficult to feel bitterness. He was a man driven by forces he did not understand, and such creatures always deform the lives of those they pass close to. She and Pettet talked sometimes about Pawl and his 'madness', as Pettet called it, and she learned about Pawl's master strategy to attack the Great Families. The destruction and its motive left her curiously detached. Here in the Pocket she was an onlooker, preoccupied more with the changes going on inside herself than the great battles which were being organized in space. And then there was Haberjin.

She had met the small pilot shortly after her arrival in

the Pocket. When meeting him for the first time in one of the vast underground hangars, she had felt nothing; he was just another new face among many. And yet something had stayed with her. Later she remembered his dark eyes and his wicked laughter and his swagger. The next time they met he made her laugh, telling her about some of his adventures. And she made him laugh too, talking about her work as a Death Inspector, delighting in the grisly details. She talked about her dark ship, and wished she knew more about it, for she saw the pilot's professional interest. They got drunk together once and Haberjin was sick and Neddelia cleaned him up with the same detachment she had once reserved for corpses, and then carried him back to his quarters.

Neddelia was amazed at herself. Here she was in Elliott's Pocket and spending half her time thinking about a foxy little man with dapper hands and a dirty tongue, who was shorter than her but had an ego as big as a mountain. *I'm either daft or bewitched or both*, she thought to herself, and felt happy.

Then came the call from the Paxwax. Pawl wished to see her. Pawl was coming out to the Pocket. She wished with all her heart that he would not come, but the line of her fate drove on, heedless of her wishes or wants.

She watched Pawl arrive through the viewscreen in her rooms. He came without pomp or ceremony, limping through the doorway leading from the Gate. He was almost bald. She would hardly have recognized him except for the yellow eyes. They, if anything, were brighter. Behind him floated a gravity cradle in which was crouched a black creature with a livid red face. She could not see it clearly, but she recognized the alien she had seen so many months ago when Pawl seized her ship.

Pettet met Pawl and the two talked together. Neddelia

was caught by the contrast. Pettet, huge, twice the size of Pawl, with his masses of black hair, seemed gentle as a fireside rug; but Pawl, angular and nervous, radiated the power that made men step away from him.

She caught fragments of their conversation and gathered that Pawl was coming down to see her immediately. He waited just long enough to collect two small boxes from a dark-robed figure that accompanied him.

He's brought me a present, thought Neddelia. *How quaint.*

They met in the blue garden, and at Neddelia's request, Odin remained outside. His smell was terrible. Neddelia recognized the smell of death. She had smelled it a hundred times.

'You would use me some more, Master of Paxwax?'

'I would. I want you to carry these back to your Homeworld of Central.' Pawl pointed to the two boxes.

'What are they?'

'Aliens.'

There was a long silence.

'You intend to kill the Homeworld of the Proctor.'

'I do.'

Again the silence descended.

'Why are you looking at me so strangely?' asked Neddelia finally. 'Have I turned pink or something?'

'No,' said Pawl. 'I was just musing. These are strange times. Strange alliances are formed. Strange bedfellows must make out as best they can. Will you convey my alien friends to your Homeworld?'

'Let me see them.'

Pawl opened the larger of the boxes. Inside something fluttered, and a strange smell reached them. Pawl drew back the lid slowly and Neddelia peered inside.

'Why, they're beautiful. Like crocuses. All different

299

colours. And they can move too.' She reached out her hand.

'Don't touch them.'

'Can they sting?'

'These can sting. When they get larger they have a massive potential. I'm told their smell can kill. These are just small.'

'Cuttings?'

'In a way. Fragments of a much larger beast. I have seen it in full flight and flower. It can spread many miles across. Very beautiful in the setting sun.'

'What is in the other box?'

'Open it.'

Neddelia fumbled with the catches and released the moisture seal. Inside was something glossy and pale and Neddelia looked at it with distaste. 'It looks like . . .' She hesitated, looking for the right words. Somewhere she had seen something like this. 'It looks like a human brain. What is this, Pawl?'

'Not a brain. This is called a Diphilus. Don't ask me who gave it that name. Now it is sleeping. When you get to your apartment on Central, just open the box close to your vivante and watch.'

'Will it harm me?'

'No, neither the Diphilus or the Hooded Parasol will harm you. But do not stay on Central for too long after you have liberated them. Things move quickly.'

'You seem to have assumed that I will help you.'

'Will you?'

'I could say yes and then just escape and throw these into a trash sack.'

'Yes, you could. But I don't think you will. You were the one who started me on this course. You won't turn back now. Besides, you are no longer a Proctor in your mind. You know you aren't.'

Neddelia looked away from those yellow eyes. 'No threats?' she asked.

'Not unless threats would make it easier for you.'

'Shut up,' said Neddelia. 'Threats are nothing. Just promise me one thing. If I carry your alien friends to Central, will you then leave me alone? Never come pestering me again? Never see me again? Release me?'

'Do this and you are free to do what you want. You have my word.'

'What shall I tell them on Central? I have already heard my death announced. They believe my ship gated into the void.'

'We will invent a story. We can say that you gated through to the Pocket and that your ship was torn apart by Mabel; that you were rescued by the natives of the Pocket. The Paxwax will send you safely home. Haberjin can pilot for you; he likes adventures. You can invent the rest. Only carry these treasures safe.' Pawl pointed to the two boxes. The small Hooded Parasol, their colours rippling like oil on water, were rising slowly as their petals filled with gas. 'Time to put these away,' he said. He blew on them, and managed to shepherd them back to their travelling box. 'I would like to see the expression on Lar Proctor's face when he sees the Hooded Parasol unfold in all its glory.' He closed the two boxes and secured their catches. 'Once you are back on Central, just leave the boxes open. Perhaps take the Parasol down to the great conservatory. I know it likes the warmth and plenty of radiation. The Diphilus can take care of itself. When you have done that your job is done. Go where you will.' Pawl stood up and moved out of the blue garden.

Neddelia followed. 'You will not forget your promise? If ever I should meet you again after today, I want us to be total strangers.'

'I have agreed.'

'Very well. I will carry these into the heart of the Proctor.'

'Thank you.'

Pawl lowered his head to kiss Neddelia, but she turned her face so that he kissed her cheek. 'Leave me,' she said.

38

ON BENNET HOMEWORLD

All the anti-gravity units glowed blue as their power came on and they lifted the heavy crates from the shore. The crates swung out over the sluggish red sea to avoid the tangled bushes and then climbed slowly up the cliff-face and swung inland to the shuttle port. On the side of each crate was emblazoned the insignia of the Shell-Bogdanovich. The crates contained the strangely-shaped rocks and exotic plants selected by Clover Shell to make a garden for Laurel. Pawl was returning them.

That had been difficult. He had sat in front of his vivante and spoken with Clover and Helium, explaining that he wanted to remove every trace of Laurel and wished to return the crates.

'Abandon them, Pawl,' said Clover. 'Jettison them into space. We don't want them now.'

'I think Laurel would have liked me to return them,' countered Pawl.

'Well, as you wish. But we won't use them. Most of the plants won't survive on this moist world. Too much mould. Are you sure you wouldn't like to go ahead and make the garden? I spent a long time preparing it. It could be a memorial to Laurel. Give it to the children of your world. All the plants were harmless and the rocks were exciting. I know. I chose them all separately.'

'Well,' said Pawl. 'I'll think about it. But if I do decide to send them back you'll understand.'

'Yes,' said Helium. He was obviously displeased.

There the matter ended.

* * *

And now the crates containing the Laurel Garden were on their way back to Sable. The crates were stacked at the shuttle port. In the dark humus which fed the roots of the exotic trees were the larvae of the Link Worm. All they needed was warmth and moisture. Pawl watched them go.

39

ON BENNET

One evening, some days after the crates had been returned to the Shell-Bogdanovich Conspiracy, Pawl and Odin sat together in Pawl's Tower. It was early summer and the beams of sunshine from low on the horizon probed upwards into the room, making it lighter and airier.

They had been sitting for hours, during which time Pawl had scarcely moved. Odin was telling the story of Lapis; how he had been kidnapped, held by the Xerxes in the dog-hutch, and finally how he had been killed by a gentle Spideret.

When the story was ended, Pawl stood and crossed to the vivante where he had a rack of five vivante cubes. He picked them up.

'Do you know what these are?' The question was clearly rhetorical. Odin made no reply, though the small creature was anxious to discover Pawl's reaction to his news. Odin was losing the ability to read Pawl's thinking. 'These are cubes our mother made when I was a child. Peron discovered them a few months ago. Father must have missed them when he cleared out all her things. Either that or she hid them. Anyway. We're all there, even little Ramadal. Frightening, really, when you think that these are all that is left. Anyway. Do you know what I felt as I looked at us all – Pental awkward in the sunlight near the stables, Lapis on the day he got his new flyer, me trying to smile and wanting to hide? I felt that we all were strangers. People I had once known, once felt close to, but hardly recognized. I would not have said that a year ago. Anyway. I really only have one question. Why do you tell me all this now?'

'To harden your resolve.'

'Did you think I was slipping?'

'You are a man.'

Pawl thought about this for a few moments and then he said, 'Before I am a man, I am me.' Odin began to reply but Pawl stopped him. 'No, no metaphysics, I promise you. But I want you to know that finally *I* decide to what extent I am used. *I decide*. Is that clear? Now I want you to watch these vivantes. Shame about the quality. Mother wasn't very good with technical things. But watch them and see what *you* feel. *You*, after all, were one that was summoned. *You* were one picked by the Inner Circle. *You* are the servant. Think about what you were, long ago.'

Pawl left him.

He wandered out into the purple night, where the first bright stars were beginning to shine. He wanted to be alone. And though he heard the hoarse voice of Odin calling him, he ordered that creature to be still and look at the vivantes. He walked on, breathing deeply through his nose, drawing the night air deep into his lungs. *Well, I have loved and lost my lady and the stars still turn.* He entered a flower garden and the nocturnal perfume almost took his breath away. *I must act without passion. I am the razor that cuts out the tumour. I am the gardener clearing the cabbage patch of white butterfly. But I must remember that the butterflies are also beautiful. What strange animals we are, how balanced on a pin. Drops on every side: too much love and we begin to rot, too little love and we turn to stones. Is there no relief?*

He found a bench and sat down, aware but careless of the dew which gilded the seat. *I thank the stars that I am human. I thank the stars for love that cleanses. I thank the stars that I have come so far.*

For the first time for many a long month Pawl wanted his notebook. Thoughts. Free thoughts were starting to bubble up, like a well filling from below when the winter snows thaw. *But not too soon*, thought Pawl. *Let it not be too soon. The rusty gate is soonest broken. Tomorrow I will visit the Xerxes. And after that I will make my plans to leave. I am tired of all this.*

He sat musing for another half-hour, but then a curling breeze from the Mendel Hills made him shiver and he went inside.

40

ON MORROW

I must be getting old, thought Clarissa. *I no longer turn on a coin, the way I once did. I get flustered so easily. And who would have thought the Paxwax boy could be so charming? He is actually interested. It is not just show, else why should he have come?*

They were walking down a long corridor of glass cases. The long dead of the Xerxes looked out at them, each in a favoured pose, each in her finery. Clarissa led and was followed by Pawl. Jettatura, dazzling in silver, walked behind and a gaggle of the small eunuchs followed.

They came to the final case, inside which sat a splendid woman, fierce and proud but with a flush of humour and holding a child. 'And this last is Rose.' Pawl was interested to see that there was plenty of room for more cases to be added, and that, indeed, one case was under construction. Clarissa followed his glance. 'Ay, you can see we are building. We never rush and never build more than one in advance . . . it could seem to tempt providence.'

'It must have been a great tragedy to lose both your sister and the baby she was carrying,' said Pawl. He chose his words carefully. He hoped there was a sting in them. He knew that he might be talking with the woman who plotted Laurel's death.

Clarissa looked at Pawl almost shyly. 'We are grateful for your concern over our poor sister, and indeed her loss was tragic and we installed her here without much ceremony . . . it being the most we could do at the time

. . .' She took a deep breath, and Pawl was amazed to see the quills on her neck rise like a peacock's tail. 'At the time . . . only you too have had a severe loss, which you still wear about you, unless I am greatly mistaken.' She had tried to speak tactfully, and Pawl was aware of this.

'Let us not talk of such things,' said Pawl. 'Come on, this is a friendly visit. A clearing of cupboards. Show me where the dog-hutch is.'

'The what?' Both Clarissa and Jettatura sounded startled.

'The dog-hutch where you kept Lapis.'

The silence was painful. Even Jettatura seemed to have grown paler.

'So you know about that, too. We were not planning to kill him, you know. Just use him to make your father see sense.'

'I am not interested in motives or reasons,' said Pawl. 'I just want to see where he died.'

'Did you know it was one of those big spider things that consumed him?' Clarissa shuddered involuntarily as the memory of Latani Rama, all bathed in blood, thrust itself into her mind. 'This way. We keep the horrid place closed now.'

In the harsh glare of the overhead lights Pawl looked over the side of the dog-hutch and down its steep, water-smoothed sides, to the small chamber where the trestle bed still stood.

'Do you normally keep prisoners here?'

'No.'

'Then why Lapis?'

'We hoped it would break his spirit.'

'And did it?'

'No.'

Pawl looked for a few more minutes and then stepped

309

back from the edge. 'Well, I am glad it was not me. I would have been crying for mercy within minutes. My curiosity is satisfied. Thank you.'

Both sisters sighed audibly. Neither spoke. Pawl walked to the nearest transit door. The small party entered the transit system and were carried up through the winding branches of the ancient stone tree. No one spoke.

They arrived among the top branches, close to the common rooms and living rooms. 'Soon we will have a banquet,' said Clarissa, attempting to restore some jollity to the meeting. 'You gave us little time but preparations are well advanced. And perhaps tomorrow we can show you our sandy world. It has many surprises and its own beauty.'

'That would please me,' said Pawl.

In the luxurious rooms appointed to him Pawl took charge of his luggage. He had brought his old trunk.

Although he was reasonably certain that he was not spied upon (his own experts had checked the rooms thoroughly) he set up a small diffusion screen, which spread until its sphere of influence enclosed the whole area occupied by Pawl. Nothing could peer within. Safe within the screen Pawl opened his trunk.

It had been adapted into two compartments, each with its own atmosphere seal. He broke one seal and set the lid to the side. Within was a material like dark brown sand composed of large granules. It was the finest insulator known.

Pawl plunged his hands into the sand and removed a rope of what looked like shiny dark onions. But the onions pulsed and their skins were warm. These were the eggs of the Spideret. Pawl cut the cords which joined the eggs. A fine milky fluid gathered at each of the cuts

310

and sealed it. Then he gathered the eggs into a towel. He crossed to the room which housed the particle shower and standard vacuum lavatory.

In lots of three he dropped the eggs down the lavatory and heard the whoosh of air as they were sucked down towards the base of the tree. On their way they joined excrement from the guards' quarter, offal from the butchers, slime and cuttings from the hydroponics hangars and whatever organic material was abandoned by the small army of workers who kept the great tree functioning as a house. They dropped into a fearful brew that was stirred by great crusted paddles.

Morrow was an efficient planet. Nothing went to waste. Everything was recycled to become food and water and raw materials. The eggs bobbed on the surface, where the temperature was perfect to encourage their growth. Within hours they had doubled their size and their skins had become tight. One by one the eggs tore as sharp incisors from within cut through and began to consume them. Small Spiderets, replicas of their giant parents, emerged in twos and threes from the eggs. They were light enough, and could spread their weight sufficiently, to walk over the scum which covered the liquid in the settling tank. At the edges they climbed the hairy slime, worked their way up crevices and arrived finally in the long recesses where pipes carried fresh water, slurry and gas. There they settled to grow.

The second compartment of Pawl's trunk contained a pale yellow fluid with the consistency of oil. Within the slickness things moved like white eels. Pawl watched, fascinated, as the Lyre Beast began to work its way out of its chamber. This was the same creature that Pawl had come to know on his Homeworld, though for ease of transport it had cut itself into two entities. Now it rose like creeping threads of white cotton, defying gravity, working steadily up and out of the old travelling chest and across the floor. It spread in all directions. Some threads touched Pawl's hand where he knelt close to the chest. He felt a sharp tingle, a start of pain, as though he had been touched by hot wire. The Lyre Beast adjusted its electrical potential and the pain faded. He also received a jolt of laughter. Pawl found this strangest of all. Try as he would he could not accept that this creature that looked like torn lace, that moved with such silence, could feel what he called laughter. But there it was.

The Lyre Beast lifted its final tangled threads from the chest by inducing rigidity. It rose like the frame of an umbrella and walked a few paces before collapsing into threads again close to the bed. There it found the hidden lines which fed power to the vivante in the corner and the particle shower. Again it shifted its potential and for a few moments it glowed brightly. It found its way into the power lines and began to spread along them.

Pawl watched it go. It left behind its negative image burnt into the rich carpet. *I'm going to have a job explaining that*, thought Pawl as the last of the Lyre Beast disappeared like the tail of a mouse.

Pawl knew where the creature was going. It would work its way down to the powerhouse in the base of the tree. There it would feed on energy before beginning to spread throughout the circuits of the house. Given time it would divide again, and then divide again, and send parts of itself down the subterranean rivers which linked all the trees and formed the planet-wide transit system. At some time it would make contact with the nurseling Spiderets. Then . . .

A polite bell sounded in Pawl's chambers, summoning him to a banquet. Quickly he climbed up from his knees

312

and closed his trunk and doused the diffusion screen. He changed hurriedly and was ready in a few minutes to escort a resplendent Clarissa down to the main banqueting hall.

41

DEPARTURES FROM BENNET

When Pawl returned to his Homeworld, he discovered that the alien war council had departed. They had moved to their different battle stations. They had left Pawl a simple message, in the care of Peron. It stated, 'Many voices: one song.'

He flew over to the mainland and visited the grey domes and underground passages where the aliens had lived. The smell of the Hooded Parasol still lingered and there were rasp marks on the walls where Trader, the Hammer, had passed; but of the other inhabitants there were no signs.

Pawl returned to his island home wondering what he should do.

He saw his Homeworld working with the smooth efficiency of a simple economy in which every participant knows his responsibility and his reward. Pawl did not feel himself to be a part of it.

Sitting alone one evening he realized that the time had come to depart. There was nothing more he could do. There was nothing more for him to do here on Bennet Island. Better he hand over and move on.

The very next morning, shortly after dawn, he summoned Peron to him.

'Would you like to run a Homeworld?'

'I'm happy as I am. I have my studies. The history of the Paxwax will be complete in about another five years . . . that is, unless you start another war.' Peron smiled his crooked scarred smile as he said this. Since coming to know the aliens, Peron had felt less distressed about the future. He had even begun to study the sign language of the Spiderets.

'Well, Peron. I never wanted to be Master, either . . . but there we are.'

Pawl watched Peron's smile fade to a look of puzzlement. 'Are you asking me to take over here? Is that what you are asking?'

Pawl nodded. 'Everything. The works. I want to leave it all behind me. This island has no happy memories for me. You are a new man, a good man. You and the rest of the people will survive without me.'

'I don't want to be a leader.'

'Well, perhaps you can all survive without leaders. It is an idea worth trying. But I am leaving. Odin will depart with me.'

'When?' There was a sudden worry in Peron's voice.

'Perhaps tonight.'

'But you can't. I mean, you can't just walk away from the Mastership of one of the greatest Families in the Galaxy. You can't.'

'Just watch me.'

'But what will I do? I don't know anything about running a Family.'

'You won't be running a Family. You will be running this one little island. And most of it takes care of itself, anyway. You will be running yourself. No more wondering about the Paxwax or the Proctors. Or whether a trade war is going to dislocate your whole way of life. Just worry about yourself and your neighbours. And Wynn will be here to help you. Won't you, Wynn?'

A hollow voice sounded in the roof. 'If you say so, Master Pawl. Though there will be difficulties. I am very set in your habits.'

'Well, you can unset yourself. Now, Peron. Go for a walk. Take the day off from your studies. Go down by the stream and watch the fish. Come back to me when the night has fallen and not before. Clear?' Peron nodded and departed. He felt that he should have a thousand questions, but he couldn't think of one.

During the rest of that day Pawl worked with Wynn, gradually and carefully withdrawing from management of the Paxwax. Wynn's task was to keep up appearances for a few days until Pawl was well gone. Pawl was under no illusions. He knew that when the alien revolution got underway in earnest the Way Gates would break down. He wanted to make sure that as many worlds as possible had a chance of independent survival. The vivante system would be left intact.

Though Wynn did everything that Pawl requested there was a detectable mulishness in its responses. Finally, when he could no longer stand the computer's cold, unquestioning acquiescence, Pawl demanded to know what was wrong.

'Do not become too human, Wynn, always looking for causes. Tell me in simple words what is troubling you.'

'Have I failed you? Have I displeased you?'

'No.'

'Then why did you not discuss your plan to depart with me before saying anything to Peron? I shall be very lonely without you. I have become a parasite on you.' Pawl looked at the matted growth of the bio-crystalline brain visible through the ceiling. He wondered at the change in Wynn. Pawl was not to know that Wynn was deforming under the pressure from the distressed Norea. 'I will have Barone help you. He may find a way of helping you to accept Peron.' Wynn did not reply and the silence seemed like an accusation. Pawl decided to change the subject. 'Can you guess where I am going?'

316

'No.'

'I am going to Elliott's Pocket.'

'I could have guessed that.'

'Yes. And then I am going to Ultima Thule. Do you know about that world?'

'I remember hearing Peron talk. But why go there? It was a world of fear.'

'I have my reasons. Desperate men do desperate things.'

There was a pause and then the computer spoke. 'I shall miss you. Your mind has been more fun than a poor bio-crystalline cell has the right to expect. I will not fail you and I will help Peron, though with your empire closed down there will be little for me to do.'

'Peron will use you in his research. Given time this silly little ornamental island could become a centre of civilization.'

It was an hour after sunset when Peron returned. Pawl was packed and ready. All he was taking was his old trunk. Odin lay in his gravity cradle. That creature had not spoken all day.

'Well, take care of Bennet. Handle it as you would an antique clock and it will serve you well. Remember that some time after my departure the Way Gate above here will be destroyed. Get all your jobs done before that. Only the starships of the Proctors and the Inner Circle will be able to reach you and they will be too busy, I suspect, to bother you. In any case, I am leaving all the defences intact. If the Proctor come sniffing, blow their noses off. If the Inner Circle come, treat them as a friend.'

The two men looked at one another.

'So,' said Pawl. 'Good luck.' He turned to the door leading down from the Tower.

317

'Just a minute,' said Peron. 'What shall I tell people? There are bound to be questions.'

'Well remembered. I have made you a vivante. It is for you to show to the people. It wishes them well. Says you are in charge. Offers them a chance to return to Moliere. Gives them ownership of all that they have here on Bennet. There are messages for everyone. You included. I suggest you show it tomorrow early. That is all. It is ended. Don't come with me.'

Quickly Pawl crossed to the door and held it open while Odin in his cradle glided through.

The door closed. Pawl was gone.

'I never even said goodbye,' muttered Peron.

'Nor did I,' said Wynn.

Outside Pawl held to the shadows, pausing if he heard people, taking the long way round through the gardens and quiet walkways. Sounds of night. Somewhere a lullaby. Laughter and a chink of glasses. Far away a horse whinnied.

Pawl and Odin came to the shuttle. It was closed and locked, there being no more cargo expected that night, nor visitors. Pawl palmed the lock and they entered. The doors suddenly closed behind them. Wynn's doing, Pawl realized. The computer was letting him know that it was there. Then the shuttle lurched as the magnetic contacts locked.

Outside there was movement. A shape detached itself from the darkness and limped to the shuttle doors. It sniffed and then it reared up against the window and Pawl found himself staring into the boss-eyed and tattered face of Punic. The dog licked its nose with its black tongue and then the shuttle lifted. The dog opened its jaws, revealing its teeth, and let out a rusty howl. When it saw that Pawl was departing it became frantic. It tried to jump but its lame leg could not hold it. It chased its tail, snapping and snarling as though after a rat. It backed off with its front paws splayed. Then it ran and jumped. The mechanical dog put everything into that jump and it crashed and broke against the ferroglass of the shuttle window and dropped heavy and tangled back to the ground. One leg kicked as the motor ran down and then it was still.

That was the last that Pawl saw of Punic. How had the mechanical dog known he was departing for good? Pawl suspected that Wynn had informed the dog. But he was wrong. The dog knew, just as clocks may stop at the moment of a death.

In the darkness of night, Bennet Island looked attractive. Its shape was revealed by a phosphorescence in the red algae which lit up where the sluggish waves touched the shore. Pawl could see the wake of a late Maw methodically paddling its way to one of the low sandbanks.

The lights of Bennet Island were going out. Pawl could just make out the rosy light of his Tower. That did not go out.

'Welcome aboard, Master Pawl,' said the Way Computer. 'I'm sorry none of the staff are here to serve you. We were not advised of your departure.'

'No matter,' said Pawl.

'Your destination?'

'The Lumb Gate.'

'Ah. The Pocket. Both of you?'

'Yes.'

'I'll route you through Portal Reclusi and Ampersand. There should be no delays.'

'Thank you.'

'Your way is clear. Have a pleasant journey, Master Pawl. Farewell.'

42

ON SABLE

'There is no point in wasting good rock and trees,' said
Clover Shell as she supervised the unpacking of the
'garden' recently returned from the Paxwax Homeworld.
'I'll make a memorial garden of my own. A place for us
to swim in. It could be quite pleasant in the slow summer
months.'

And so work began on Clover's last garden.

Great pits were gouged out of the dry sands of Sable.
Prefabricated piers were poured and carefully lowered
into place in accordance with Clover's plan. On to these
piers were attached the girders which formed the skele-
tons for mountains. Clover worked from pictures and
vivantes made of Thalatta. She wanted to achieve the
effect of islands and swift tides and clear pebble-water
where sea ferns grew and where you could see the brown
backs of fish as they browsed. She was sad that there were
now no longer any Dapplebacks alive in the universe.

The trees and rocks were kept in a warehouse underground, where the temperature and humidity could be
carefully controlled. In this ideal environment the elvers
of the Link Worm writhed and tumbled in the roots of the
trees in their voracious quest for food. With their sharp
teeth they cut through the hessian bags which wrapped
the roots. They chewed through the warehouse floor and
out into the sandy soil, where they found silica and
minerals to make their bones grow. They found the long
cool segmented pipes which carried the water through the

wide deserts. Secretions from their skins discoloured and then weakened the stiff hard plastic until finally water seeped out and they were able to bite and burrow their way into the pipes themselves. They spread through the network of conduits under Sable.

The mechanics and miners on Sable worked quickly. The memorial garden became Clover's pet project. She wanted it ready as a surprise for Helium on the anniversary of his accession to the Mastership of the Shell-Bogdanovich Conspiracy. On that day the entire aquatic tribe would be present.

43

ON THE WORLD OF THE CRAINT

The brief leap from Ampersand to Elliott's Pocket should have been accomplished without problems, but Pawl was aware as he swam towards consciousness that all was not well. When he opened his eyes he found himself lying within a vast gleaming amphitheatre. It was a Way Gate. But it was not the Way Gate above Lumb. Everything seemed bigger than the scale needed for humans. The silver platform on which he lay could have accommodated two Hammer easily. Odin was beside him and Pawl felt a brief surge of panic emanate from the small creature.

Pawl stood up and gathered Odin into his arms. Then he walked over to the edge of the platform and sat down. He dropped the six or so feet down to the shiny floor. Wondering, he began the long walk over mirrors to where the exit door blinked at him.

Beyond the exit there was no polite Way Computer waiting to greet them. There were no particle showers. Pawl stepped into a corridor of clear ferroglass. Through the walls and floor and ceiling he could see the stars shining in blackness. Below him was a dull green planet. *Thule?* he thought for a moment, and then he knew it could not be Thule. Thule by all accounts was brilliant green. Odin wriggled in his arms and Pawl set him down on his sucker. The creature was agitated.

'Where are we?' asked Pawl, but the only impressions he could gain from Odin were confused.

There seemed to be no alternative and so Pawl, with Odin working his way along behind, set out down the wide corridor. He felt as though he was walking in space and vertigo gripped him for a moment as the dull green world climbed up beyond the walls and over his head.

The corridor followed a gentle curve and at its end was a familiar space-lock.

Waiting behind the walls was an antique Vanburgh. It looked quaint and out of place, like brass knobs on a computer. Pawl recognized the type. He had seen one once in the museum on Lotus-and-Arcadia. It was the kind once used for brief sightseeing excursions down to a hostile world.

The intention was obvious and he and Odin stepped through the space-lock and into the soft luxurious interior. A voice welcomed them. 'Make yourselves comfortable, Pawl Paxwax and Odin. We shall only detain you briefly. A short ceremony. You are now above the world of the Craint.' The door through which they had entered irised shut and with the barest jolt the old Vanburgh drifted into space and began to move towards the dark green world, which had now stabilized above them.

Odin unfolded in Pawl's mind like a plume of smoke. 'The Craint. Have you heard of the Craint, Master Pawl?' The small creature seemed calmer now.

'The name. I know the name. They were an ancient civilization, weren't they?'

'They were the greatest.'

'Have you ever met one of them?'

'No. I believed they had all departed. They were in decline even before the Great Push. The Diphilus knew the Craint. Some believe their empire once covered most of the known galaxy.'

Pawl pulled a face. 'Hard to believe. We'd have seen more signs of them. Empires always leave their mark.'

'Perhaps we don't know what to look for.'

'Anyway, why did they disappear? An epidemic? War?'

'Neither an epidemic or war. They discovered the secret of time.'

'Time?'

'Yes. Perhaps there are still some things I can teach you. Once you begin to move in time you are dead. Once you can see your past, your present becomes meaningless: just one moment among many possibilities. Once you can see your future, your present becomes irrelevant . . . and so you move on, to a different state.'

'That is beyond me.'

'No, it isn't.'

Pawl thought. 'If you can see the future does that mean there is no such thing as free will?' Odin could not reply.

The Vanburgh had moved rapidly.

As they watched it dropped through some fine clouds and lowered to a few miles above the dark green surface. They looked out on a scene of devastation. They stared at ruins and the ruins stared back at them with all the desolation of buildings that have spent many generations under water. The Vanburgh drifted over the face of the planet. It glided over a vast crater filled with bubbling grey mud. The mud was the only thing that they had seen moving on the entire world.

'I suppose we are going somewhere,' said Pawl. 'A ceremony. I wonder what that means? I wonder what they want of us?'

'Not us,' murmured Odin. 'You. I feel I have no part to play on this world.'

They passed over the rim of the crater and stared at a white tower which rose in steps from dark green jungle. In some places the walls were cracked and the gleaming white masonry had fallen away to reveal a honeycomb structure netted with creepers.

The Vanburgh began to drop lower. It cruised round the tower, gradually losing height, until it paused just a few feet above the highest trees. Then it descended. Branches whispered against the sides and scraped and broke as the Vanburgh dropped through the canopy.

When eventually they came to rest, with their gravity rods spread like the legs of a spider, they were almost a mile below the top leaves of the trees.

Outside it was black as the back of a cave. The only light which illuminated the surface was that which shone out through the ports of the Vanburgh. It was raining. Condensation, mixed with the sugary gum of the trees, fell continuously as rain.

The door to the Vanburgh slid open and the ramp which led to the surface scissored into place. Pawl looked into the wet blackness and shivered. 'Once this world was not unlike Thalatta,' murmured Odin. 'Sea and islands, so I believe.'

Together they moved towards the ramp but the voice stopped them. 'Only Pawl Paxwax may proceed beyond this vehicle. He must proceed alone. Please select a light rod.'

In a cradle beside the entry door stood several rods. As the voice spoke the tips of the rods began to glow and then shine with a steady bright light. Pawl selected one of the rods and found it light and strong. Holding the rod in front of him Pawl moved down the ramp and out from under the protective shelter above the door. Odin sent him best wishes but the message was cut short by the sudden closure of the door. Pawl was as alone in his mind as he was in his body.

The rain slopped down as thick as paste. Within seconds his coverall was greasy and dripping. It clung to him like a skin of rubber.

Pawl reached the end of the ramp and tested the ground with his rod. It was spongy. He moved away from the Vanburgh slowly, as though plodding through wet snow. Where he trod he left puddles.

The vertical trunks of trees pressed close to the Vanburgh and he trudged round them, heading in the general direction of the tower.

Pawl's world extended only as far as his light. Shadows jumped. Behind one tree he met a family of pale, low-bodied aquatic creatures which flopped heavily away in search of darkness.

Abruptly he found himself in front of the white wall of the tower. It gleamed as hard as tooth and soared straight up from the wet ground. The foundations lay many yards below him and had been buried centuries earlier.

Working his way along the wall Pawl came to a low arch (it had once been the top of an arch). It glowed with gold writing which held its own light. Pawl reached up and was able to touch the figures which were incised in the rock. He pulled his hand away sharply, as though stung. Some of the gold adhered to his fingers, which now glowed.

Pawl ducked under the shallow arch and into the great tower. Inside he shook himself, glad to be out of the heavy, syrupy rain. Holding his torch high in front of him he could see that the ground sloped down sharply to a lake of black water. Waiting on the shore was a boat.

The invitation was obvious.

Close to the water the humus upon which he was walking became even more spongy.

Pawl climbed into the small boat and it rocked. Using his light pole he tried to edge the boat out on to the water. The boat moved, gliding suddenly, but the pole remained stuck in the soft soil at the water's edge and Pawl found himself drifting out on the dark lake. Never before, even in his moments of deepest grief, had Pawl felt so alone.

The steady beacon light retreated. Pawl sat hunched in the damp bottom of the boat. Gradually, as his eyes adjusted to the darkness, he became aware of a faint misty glow.

The glow was brighter on one side and Pawl, steeling himself, dipped his hands in the icy black water and attempted to propel the boat in the direction of the light.

The glow became more distinct. Golden figures. Like the writing on the archway. Slowly the boat drifted close until Pawl could distinguish a stone wall. The drawings were incised on the wall. Here were figures like men riding creatures like horses; and yet they were neither men nor horses. Here was a giant bird with spread wings and trailing legs. Here a wheel. Here a cross, but with one of its four arms replaced by an oval. Here were eyes of all types and the unmistakable portrait of a Hammer running.

For some reason, that image made Pawl feel more comfortable.

Any further exploration of the wall was stopped by a sudden jerking of the boat. Something had bumped it from under the black water. Then the prow was tugged and Pawl lost his balance and fell into the bottom of the boat.

The boat was moving. Something was towing it or pushing it. Already it was away from the wall and gathering speed. The boat left a foamy brown wake as it drove into the darkness.

Pawl sat low in the boat; he could see nothing above, nothing ahead, and nothing to the sides. Occasionally he detected a change in the direction of the boat, though he could not tell why the change occurred.

But then came the moment when he could see a luminescence in front. It became a semi-circle of light. It became a tunnel lit by brilliant points of light.

The boat plunged into the tunnel and immediately Pawl felt strange things crawling all over him, plucking at his eyes and hands and hair. He screamed, and in response the boat slowed. It slowed so quickly that a bow wave was sent splashing away from them. It bounded off the tunnel walls and slapped the boat on its return. Pawl could see the walls. They were still crowded with pictures.

In front of the boat the water churned and two creatures broke surface. They were humanoid, but with large scaly heads and sloping shoulders. They each had huge webbed hands which flexed. Long fins of stiff ginger hair rippled from their necks down to the water. One of the creatures turned and looked back at him. Its eyes held no quick light of intelligence.

Apparently convinced that all was well, the creature turned forward again and slapped its comrade on the neck. Both creatures dived. With a tug the boat began to move again, but slowly.

Calmer now, Pawl could see the thin white threads which hung down from the shining insects. By sweeping his arm back and forth in front of the boat, he was able to clear most of the threads. A few of the insects were detached and fell down to the surface of the water, where they floated.

Within minutes of recommencing the journey, the tunnel grew brighter. He was moving round a curve and the brightness was ahead of him.

He emerged into a place of glittering brilliance. He turned his head away from the harsh glare and closed his eyes, but the brilliance danced in redness. Pawl felt the moment when the boat slowed, no longer pulled. He felt it drift. Through slit eyes he was aware as the light diminished, and finally he could open his eyes.

Pawl found himself in a large domed chamber and the walls swarmed. There were figures on the walls and as the boat drifted the figures moved, adjusting themselves. In the centre of the lake was a low island and on the island a broken statue. The statue had once been a bird. One wing remained, raised, arched as though cupping the wind. The proud head, aquiline and almost human, lay where it had fallen on the dark shore. The remaining wing was in the water and raised its stone feathers a few feet above the black waves. Suspended above the statue, above the place where the head should have been, was the source of the cave's light. It was a crystal, a beautiful pale diamond. At its heart lay a teeming violet like molten glass. But there was no heat.

In wonder Pawl looked round the wall. He recognized more of the species: a Spideret; a Gerbes like Odin; many humanoids, one who held a book and seemed to be offering it, and one who had snakes for hair. Pawl was staring at this when there came from above him a giant beating of wings. He looked up and there descending was a creature half-human, half-bird with its vast wings spread. It set its wings and glided round the walls, casting a hard dark shadow.

Long legs emerged, like the legs of a stork, and the creature hovered, both wings beating, and then settled on the dark shore of the island. It folded its wings. With high-legged steps it turned and faced the small boat, The face which stared at Pawl was both human and alien. The eyes were human and the lips. But the nose was a beak and there was no jaw and the face merged into the feathery neck.

329

The lips moved and the feathers fluffed and a rich voice spoke.

'So, you have finally come. I have waited a long time. Come here, Pawl, and let me look at you.' Obedient to the creature's words, the boat was pushed from beneath towards the shore.

Its prow dug into the dark moist shingle and the boat stopped quickly, almost throwing Pawl off balance. The giant bird stepped back, lifting its legs high and setting them down with delicate precision.

'Are you a Craint?' asked Pawl, looking up.

'Of course. I am the last. You are honoured. You are looking at a living fossil. Come on, get out. Let me have a look at you. I don't see well. You must come close.'

Pawl felt a moment of alarm, and then dismissed it. As ever he was vulnerable. He was in a game not of his making. He threw his leg over the side of the boat and climbed out. The shingle slid beneath his feet and he found it difficult to climb up the shore. He slipped and fell. As he was struggling back to his feet a wing dipped down close to him and he was able to grasp it. It was hard as steel but flexible, and gave him strong support.

'Heave-ho,' sang the Craint and dragged him up on the solid ground. 'I have met many of your kind. Long, long ago. None of them could walk properly.'

'You mean you have met members of the Paxwax before?'

'No. No. Humans. We called you the small-footed ones. We took an interest in you because you had faces like us. Come on.'

The Craint turned and began to stalk away from the beach and up towards the centre of the small island. Pawl followed.

'Let us get our business over first. Then we can talk.' The Craint picked its way carefully up to the central statue. It spread its wings and beat them, sending up a cloud of sand and dust, as it lifted. It came to perch on the place where the head of the statue should have been. 'You will have to climb. It shouldn't be too difficult; many have done so before you. There are handholds and steps.'

Pawl scrambled round the statue and came to a flight of shallow steps which led up the side of the bird and on to its back. The statue was not made of stone. At least it did not feel like stone: it was slightly soft and warm. When Pawl first touched it he snatched his hand away for it felt like flesh. Perched above him the Craint threw its head back and made a bell-like noise which could only be laughter.

'Climb, silly man. What you are mounting lives half in your time and half in ours. Come on. You can't hurt it.'

Pawl climbed and soon found himself crouched on a narrow platform where the head of the statue should have been. The Craint had moved out on to the wing.

'Stand up straight. We are going to make a life graph of you for all the later generations of this universe to see.' Pawl stood, shakily.

The great glowing diamond which had flickered above him all the while began to descend. As it lowered, its facets opened like a crystal flower. The petals closed round him and Pawl found himself staring out of the world through a flickering violet haze.

Above him light blossomed like flame. It ran down the filaments of the crystal panes like silver foam. It engulfed him with the brilliance of the sun. It was like being stroked by stiff feathers. It seemed that the light teased its way into his cells and through his bones. He felt light run along his nerves like ecstasy, which is both savage and tender. He felt his body fill with the light until it radiated out from the ends of his fingers, through his pores, through his mouth and nostrils and clenched eyes, from

331

his groin and from his hair. He was a blazing man . . . and with one spasm the light left him and he was himself again, Pawl Paxwax, tall and misshapen, with yellow eyes and scant hair. And yet something had gone from him. In that great surge of light-energy something of him had become detached and had departed, though Pawl, for the life of him, could not say what. Nor did he feel any loss.

He stood while the crystal walls cleared and the violet, molten light dimmed. The walls lifted and, when they were above him, folded together again to form the diamond.

He could see the boat rocking gently by the shore. Close to him was movement and the tall Craint lifted its head from beneath its wing. Two large brown eyes stared at Pawl. The wing opened fully and gestured to the wall opposite. The walls were still crawling with figures, each brilliant and glowing, but one place was brighter than the rest. Here was a tall figure. Its hair was long and loose. It stood with shoulders slightly hunched as though leaning against the wall. With a shock Pawl recognized himself, as he had been when younger.

'So there you are, Master Pawl. Not too bad, was it? And now you are immortalized. You are one of the makers of the life of the Galaxy. Now, whatever happens to you, something of your spirit will not be lost. When, in the fullness of time, a new order grows, creatures not unlike yourself will come in here, and look round the walls and will draw strength from you and the rest.'

'What are these?' asked Pawl, pointing to the other figures.

'You have no word for them?' said the Craint. 'No, let me see. You might call them pioneers of life. How is that for a translation? Does it say much to you?'

'Not much.'

'All of these individuals were pioneers of life in their

332

own way. Each of them showed what was possible. From the very earliest times of life. Even amoeba are here.'

'And you have collected them?'

'The Craint did. It was our greatest work. But I do not like that word, *collected*. These are not flowers pressed in a book or petal-wings pinned to a board. These are prints of the spirit. These will be the last of life when the galaxy dies.'

'Ah?'

'You sound doubtful.'

'I do not know what to believe.'

'Remember this. There are many kinds of life. You are one kind. You and the Spiderets and other creatures who live in the same time shell. Then there are us. We used to be like you but then we changed. There are some to whom you are only dreams. There are some to whom the life and death of one universe is merely a breath. There are others who are only thought, really. But one thing you must learn here and now and never forget. All life is joined. It is such a simple thing. We are all as close as the bell and the sound the bell makes. Does not that feel comforting?'

'Comforting? I do not know. It sounds like the religions I was told about when I was a student on Terpsichore.'

The Craint laughed and it was a ringing generous sound. 'Ah yes. Religions. You are a very religious being. All are that find their way to this hall. But religion is really only part of growing up. Where religion ends, reality takes over. When you can see reality you will accept nothing else.'

'How many realities are there?'

'There is only one reality.'

'But many life forms?'

'Many, many life forms . . . and many illusions.' The Craint stretched and spread its wide wings.

333

'Why was I brought here?' asked Pawl.

'For this.' The Craint pointed to the glowing image on the wall. 'All the individuals you see here were on their way to what you call Thule.'

'It is an old world, then?'

'It is as old as this universe – which is to say it is as old as time itself. It was the first world found in this galaxy. Every galaxy has its Thule.'

'Am I expected there?'

'You are awaited, and I have waited for more than ten thousand of your years. Eventually I knew that you, or one like you, would come.'

'Then you can see through time.'

'Time is a game, a play of words, a matter of battles at sea and children playing draughts; it is nothing, really. But you need it to bring order . . .'

'Can you see my future?'

'I can.'

'And . . . ?'

Again the Craint laughed. 'Oh, Master of Paxwax. I may know, but you may not. That law is inflexible. The future I can see depends on your not knowing it, so what good would my words be? "If only . . ." is the silliest phrase in your language, and the most tragic. No regrets, Master Pawl. Remember that. Be of good cheer. You like words, Master Pawl, do you not?' Pawl nodded. 'Well, here are words for you. Old words. Where I learned them I no longer remember but they bob into my mind.' The Craint lifted its head and spoke loudly.

> Age is an earth-warrior with power over all;
> In its chains all struggle, in its prison keep.
> Working its will, it crushes tree,
> Rips twig, whips the standing ship

334

In the water and beats it to the ground.
It jaws birds, death-wrestles wolves,
Outlasts stones. It slays steel,
Bites iron with rust, and takes us too.

'You are talking of death.'

'I am, Master Pawl. It is time for us to part. I am honoured to have met you. But now I am tired. I long to join my brothers and my sisters. They are waiting for me. This journey is over, another journey begins. Climb down now.'

Pawl did as he was bidden. He was affected by the tone of the Craint. He could feel its weariness. He walked round the statue of the Craint with no head and a broken wing and moved down to the shore. 'This statue must have been magnificent when it was all in one piece.'

'It was never in one piece. This is how it was built. It worked well. And now its work is done. There will be no more additions to this tower. Watch.'

Pawl watched. The statue wavered and vanished with a sound like a sudden intake of breath. Where the wing had rested in the water, the water swirled like ink. A few bubbles rose and then the water was still again.

The Craint stepped close to Pawl with its exaggerated high steps. It lowered its ugly face until it was close to Pawl and he could see the feathers which clustered round its moist eyes. 'I doubt if I will affect your future if I tell you you are the most powerful of your species now drawing breath. I would be honoured if you would watch as the earth-warrior takes me in its chains.'

'Do you have a name?' asked Pawl.

'Call me Last of the Craint.' The great bird spread its wings and cupped the air. It ran a few ungainly steps with its wings flapping and then launched itself like a javelin. The wings beat and their tips slapped the water leaving

swirling dimples. Slowly it rose, batting its way with
powerful thrusts round the walls. It rose higher until it
came to a level where the shining figures ended and there
was only a vast darkness. It now seemed no bigger than a
seagull, sliding with the wind off a headland. Pawl saw it
hover, resting on an up draught, and then it dived. It
drove its wings with all its power and in the middle of a
stroke smashed itself against the stone wall. Pawl heard
the impact. Feathers scattered, and the body, suddenly
leaden, tumbled down through the air. It struck the water
far from the boat and sank immediately. A feather drifted
down and Pawl caught it and cried aloud, for its sharpness
pricked his fingers.

He pushed away from the shore and waited. Within
seconds he felt the boat tugged and then it began to race
through the water. The boat travelled round the island
and Pawl was able to look up at the figures depicted on
the wall. As he passed below his own figure he saw it raise
its arm and its yellow eyes flashed. Then the boat dived
into the tunnel and he hunkered down in its bottom. He
did not look up until he felt the movement cease, and
then he found himself staring at a brilliant torch which
was standing at the water's edge.

Pawl clambered from the boat and sank up to the waist
in the dark water. Using his arms as paddles he forced his
way up on to the bank of rotting vegetation. He dragged
his torch from the soft ooze and climbed up the bank.

Pawl found the archway. Outside it was still raining.
Dimly through the darkness he could see the welcome
lights of the Vanburgh. Its landing ramp was down.

'And what did you learn on your visit to the Craint?' It
was Odin, speaking drowsily in the mind of Pawl, just
before the mirrors began to flash to send them on the last

journey to Elliott's Pocket. It was the first time Odin had spoken to Pawl since his return to the Vanburgh.

'I learned that the universe is vaster than my imaginings.'

'Ah. And how do you feel about that?'

'Stronger now. More "at home". I think the Craint meant that I was part of some great movement.'

Before Odin could reply the mirrors began to spin, and Pawl lost himself . . .

. . . and when he again found himself he was whole and strong and aboard the Way Platform above the world called Lumb.

44

IN ELLIOTT'S POCKET

Pawl looked at himself ruefully in the myriad crystal mirrors of the Lumb Way Gate. There he stood, almost bald, with the last vestige of his once-luxuriant hair coiled behind his ears. He was thin, too, rather than muscled and his ribs showed clearly above his belly, which had somehow become a paunch. *A pioneer of life!* he thought. *I'll be lucky if Laurel even recognizes me*. Then he winked to himself. His yellow eyes were undeniably his.

Odin had fared well. The transit had put life into him. The dissemination and restoration had eased the pain that radiated from his stone. He held close to Pawl in his mind as Pawl fussed about him and lifted him into his gravity cradle. He felt some vigour sluice through his fibres. 'We will soon be there, Pawl. Then we can both rest. Don't desert me.'

'Hush,' said Pawl, speaking aloud. 'I won't desert you, old friend. We have come such a long way together.'

Pawl wrapped Odin in the remains of his black garment of the Inner Circle and then covered his own nakedness with one of the light Way suits.

They left the Way Gate with Pawl leading Odin's gravity cradle like a dog on a leash.

Pettet and Raleigh were waiting for them. Neither could hide their reaction when they saw how emaciated Pawl had become. Raleigh turned her face away from Odin.

They took them below, to the central room where the fire burned and where the singer had told the ballad of

338

John Death Elliott. A full suite of rooms had been prepared for Pawl just off the central chamber.

'These are yours,' said Pettet. 'Here you must rest and recover. No one will disturb you. Raleigh has contacted her people. Healers will be coming. You will be safe here in the Pocket.'

Pawl looked into the honest face of the giant and nodded. 'Thank you for your kindness. We will stay one night. That is all.'

Pettet frowned. 'I do not understand.'

'Tomorrow we will depart for Ultima Thule.'

Pettet's mouth opened but no sound came out. Then he gathered himself. 'Thule . . . that place . . . why?'

'Use your imagination, big man. What did you see on Thule?'

'I saw . . . I saw. . .' Comprehension came to Pettet. 'Oh, Pawl. You are not hoping to find Laurel?'

'I am.'

'But . . .'

'Don't give me any arguments. I have thought about this ever since my lady died. Do you remember what you once called Thule? You called it the place where the dead live. I remembered that. I know it won't be Laurel, I know it will be something grown from my memories and my love, but perhaps I can fool myself. Perhaps I will find rest there. If not, well, no great matter. One place is as good as another to me now. But John Death Elliott ended his days there. And so shall I. I shall be in good company.'

Pettet did not speak. He merely shook his head and his long black curls tumbled over his shoulders.

'Tomorrow you will arrange a ship. I would like Haberjin to pilot it. I will take a landing pod down to Thule. And that is the end. For tonight I do not want any arguments or any discussion. Let us drink deep, man. Get Raleigh to play for us. Let me rock Lynn on my knee. Tell her stories. I wanted children, you know. Let us be simple. And tomorrow I will depart as quietly as a corpse buried at sea. I want nothing more. Close the Pocket. Let the storm rage outside. Let Pawl have his rest.'

Pettet nodded. Being a man of the Pocket he would not try to impose his will on another. If this was what Pawl wanted, then so be it. He called for beer and food. He stoked the fire. He called for music.

'Well,' he said as people bustled about, 'if I'm not to persuade you to stay here on Lumb with us, let me at least help you on Thule. I bet you haven't thought of any of the practicalities, have you? You will be alone, except for whatever creature comes to you. You will have to eat. You need to sleep in the dry. Take one of our survival sleds. It will give you roof and comfort. We use them when we pioneer a new world.'

'Now you are talking. I will accept any help you can offer, except a means of contacting the world outside.'

'That is impossible anyway. No signals get into Thule. None escape. Will Odin live with you?'

'He will.'

Pettet nodded. 'That is good. The little creature is dying before our eyes. Is it an illness or old age?'

'I do not know. Though we can talk with our minds, Odin will not tell me what is hurting him. He complains about his *stone* and that is all.'

Pettet mused on this. 'Perhaps Thule is the place for him.'

'Perhaps.'

'Well, I must disappoint you in one thing,' said Pettet finally. 'I shall be your pilot tomorrow. Haberjin is not here. He is somewhere with Neddelia. She is about your business, I think. The last I heard they were on Central.

340

Perhaps they will return in a few days. Perhaps they will head out to the rim.'

'Perhaps,' said Pawl. 'Perhaps. Perhaps is a strange word.'

341

45

ON CENTRAL: THE PROCTOR
HOMEWORLD

Neddelia was enjoying herself.

After riding the space eddies of the Cherry Brake and breaking through the cordon which bound the Pocket, she and Haberjin set course for the nearest Proctor Gate, which circled the long-dead planet called Luxury. There they Gated to Central and Neddelia told tales of how her ship had been trapped in an old alien trap and how brigands with glaring yellow eyes had torn her ship apart and how she had been rescued by Captain Haberjin who had come lancing in from the heart of the Pocket. And there with her as living proof of her story was Captain Haberjin himself, who looked like a pirate and oiled himself with sweet-smelling unctions after the manner of young men. Haberjin affected the deep brogue of the Pocket, which was unintelligible to all except Neddelia. He spoke with gestures and with flashing eyes and Neddelia translated, telling of his adventures and boasting of his cruelty.

They were wined and dined on Lotus-and-Arcadia as well as on Central and they made love noisily at night.

Of course she was questioned closely, for the loss of a Central ship with its mighty symbol transformation generators was no slight thing. But she held to her story until her inquisitors were convinced that savages, with no deep knowledge of space physics, had despoiled her ship like monkeys pounding a typewriter with their fists.

Gradually the questions ceased. Neddelia resigned her position as Death Inspector, pleading that her nerve was broken. She used the might of her family to buy out her marriage and found herself free.

There remained the question of the 'gifts' from Pawl Paxwax that she had carried deep into Central. Came the day she could not ignore their presence and she and Haberjin sat in their splendid apartment far beneath the steel skin of Central with the two boxes between them.

'I want to return to the Pocket,' said Haberjin.

Neddelia looked at him levelly over the boxes.

'Can I come with you, even if I destroy these?' she asked. 'It is a hard thing to be asked to destroy everything that you grew up with. Think if you had to destroy the Pocket.'

'They are not the same.'

'No. Perhaps not. But answer my question.'

'Yes. You can come with me.'

'Would you tell people what had happened?'

'Yes.'

'You make it hard.'

'No. You want an easy life. You came here with one obligation. Now you have softened. You do not love your life here, but still you hesitate. Here, give me the boxes and I will break their seals and scatter their dust or whatever is in them and then we'll go.'

Haberjin reached for the boxes but Neddelia struck his arm. 'You will not.'

'That hurt.'

'Good.'

'Aristocratic cow.'

'Cross-eyed gypsy.'

'What . . .'

That night they lay in a tangle of clothing and bed linen when Neddelia awoke. Crawling out from under Haberjin's arm she crossed to one of the boxes which still stood in the centre of the floor. She lifted its lid and in the soft light could just make out a dull grey shape. She touched it with her fingertip and gave a start of surprise, for it was as hard as glass and she received a slight shock. Within the greyness something swirled, like wine that holds candle flame. The spangle of lights strengthened, growing outwards until the whole of the 'brain' came alive. The intensity of its light grew until Neddelia had to shade her eyes. Her shadow was cast, hard and black, against the wall and ceiling. The light seemed to push at her but there was no heat or pain, and then suddenly the Diphilus expanded. It flowed from the box like incandescent glass, pouring over the carpet and her hand where she supported herself on the floor. Neddelia screamed and stifled the scream for the Diphilus did not hurt her. Dimly she heard Haberjin stir and sit up and mutter an oath of awe.

As the Diphilus spread it lost its hard brilliance. Colours flowed in it. It grew to the height of a table and engulfed half the room.

Haberjin came to stand behind Neddelia and he rested his hand on the bright shiny back of the Diphilus. It was cool and unyielding as ebony. Where his hand had rested the pattern of his fingers remained for a few moments before dissolving into the flux.

'It is beautiful,' whispered Neddelia.

'It is very powerful,' said Haberjin.

In both their minds there grew an expanding bubble of laughter. It was good to be close to something so vital, so alive. It gave strength, a careless fun-loving strength.

They watched the Diphilus divide. It became several rivers, each of which crept like a glowing snake towards the walls.

The gleaming snakes crawled on the walls. They became transparent, though still bright. With a final

344

flourish of energy they melded with the walls and were gone. The room was suddenly dark.

'What was that?' asked Neddelia.

Haberjin shrugged. 'An alien . . . an intelligent one.'

'Where has it gone?'

'Exploring.'

'No. I mean how . . .'

'Ask Pawl Paxwax.'

Neddelia hesitated. 'I've done it, haven't I?'

'What?'

'Liberated an alien on my Homeworld.'

'Yes.'

'Now what's going to happen?'

Haberjin thought for a few moments and then shrugged. 'You've solved your problem.'

Later that day Neddelia and Haberjin chose to visit the garden deep inside Central. They wandered hand in hand down the long lines of fruit canes under the blue dome until they reached a place where the dome-roof met the curved floor of the garden. There was no one about, no gardeners. Here the garden was rough and wild. Hybrid flowers grew against the cool plastic and a small colony of ants toiled about its hill dragging in dead leaves.

Haberjin felt inside his loose jerkin and produced a neat box. They set it down on the path and broke its seal and opened its lid. Inside the Hooded Parasol lay like day-cut crocuses. But when they felt the light they stirred, and small black eyes on the ends of their stamens rose and peered. The largest of the Parasol flexed and began to inflate its petals. It expanded and rose and as it floated free of the box fine tendrils tumbled loose and trailed on the dusty path. Haberjin reached out but Neddelia struck his hand. 'They are dangerous, love. Pawl warned me.'

More of the Hooded Parasol came alive and lifted from

the box. They seemed to share a common mind for they all drifted in the same direction like purple butterflies flying in unison. They came to the anthill and the largest of the Parasol trailed its glistening fronds over the hill. The ants attacked, swarming up towards the purple flower, but none made it for very far. Their limbs stuck. The Parasol expanded and lifted its harvest clear of the hill and then drew the small brown bodies up into its petals. When all its fronds were withdrawn it hung still, pulsing slightly and then it ejected a brown sputum which spattered the path. As if that were a signal the other Hooded Parasol moved in, trailing their fronds. One allowed its tendrils to be seized and carried into the ant's nest. Then it expanded rapidly and rose, tearing open the side of the nest and revealing its teeming interior. The Parasol fed, and when they were gorged they drifted away among the fruit trees and were gone.

Haberjin looked at Neddelia and his face had a pallor under his dark skin. 'That was horrible,' he said. 'And what's that smell? There aren't any cats round here are there?'

Neddelia pointed to the stains on the path. 'I think it comes from them, but it could be the smell of the Parasol. Come on. This is no place to stay. I've done my duty. Let us leave today.'

Haberjin wrinkled his nose and nodded.

Together they ran back down the path and out of the fruit garden. Hours later they Gated through to Luxury where their ship was tethered, waiting. They fired up their ship and felt it come alive as the gravity sensors turned space to a misty blue cloud about them.

'Where to?' asked Neddelia.

'I don't mind. You decide,' said Haberjin settling back. 'I think we have played our part in the story. We can go where we like, now.'

346

46

ULTIMA THULE

Below them Thule burned like green fire.

Carefully, like a live birth at sea, the survival rocket slid from the main body of the Pocket ship and, when it was clear, flared and turned and began to drop down to that fierce green surface.

All the lights on the parent ship flashed on and then off and on again. It was an ancient farewell, like running colours up the mast.

Pawl, snug in the cabin of the survival rocket with Odin close beside, saw the lights and waved and flashed his own cabin lights. Slowly the great ship above him turned and began to edge to a wider orbit. It would hold until Pawl was safely down.

Pawl gave his whole attention to the descent. He was aware, as had been Cordoba and Tank and the other members of that first crew, of the moment when he broke through the planet's psychosphere. Now the world was as aware of him as he was of it. And like Cordoba and Tank he felt a great upwelling of his creative powers. Things like flies with voices seemed to buzz in his head and he felt merry. 'Soon be down there, little one.'

At about the level of the canopies of the tallest trees, Pawl levelled off and began to look for where he should land.

He cruised above valleys and lakes and watched the shadow of his ship rise and fall and dart as it traversed the contours of the land. He saw many ships parked below and wondered if the same compulsion that drove him had drawn them here. He wondered if those many pilots were also pioneers of the Craint, painted on the wall of their tower.

Nothing moved except his shadow. Had he wanted to, Pawl could have located the ancient *Fare-Thee-Well*. But that was not his plan. He was looking for his own place. He was waiting for a sign, though he knew not what. He thought of Laurel, beautiful in her dark blue gown on the day they married, and wondered how she would have liked this still world. Would she have liked to dive into those dark mysterious pools which seemed to absorb the light rather than reflecting it?

Away on the horizon something was happening. A beacon lit up. Pawl turned the small rocket in a full curve and headed towards it.

It was one of the trees. It was behaving as Peron had described and as Pawl had seen in Tank's sketches. Purple fire flowed from the ground up the stem of the tree in great systaltic bursts. The canopy was incandescent and trembling so that its outline was blurred.

Pawl hovered some miles from the tree and watched it build to a crescendo. At its climax the tree radiated fire into the air, revealing patterns of stress in the sky. Pawl had to look away, even as the viewplates of the rocket darkened.

And when he could look again he saw the colours of the tree fading like dye being washed from a pale fabric.

At the base of the tree there was no waiting ship, but there was a clearing, and Pawl knew that this was his place.

The survival domes were a tribute to the designer's art. An injured man with one arm could have erected them. First the domes were ejected from the ship. Then they began to inflate, breaking out of their containers. Joints

348

sealed chemically. Gravity pegs dug deep into the soil of Thule until they found bedrock, and there anchored. A distillation plant orientated itself with respect to the sun and began to filter the air for its first drops of moisture. Pawl lowered one whole side of the rocket and trundled out the cases in which were stored food canisters, seeds, animal embryos, medicines, vivantes . . . anything a pioneer or a castaway might need to enable him to survive. Pettet had been nothing if not thorough.

The wheels of the trolleys sank into the moist green earth and Pawl had to drag them, opening up a seam in the planet's skin. He quickly found himself sweating, for the air was warm and heavy as though a tropical storm had just passed. But he did not feel lethargic. On the contrary, he felt vital and younger, and he laughed to himself as he strained to lift the wheels from the soft earth. He laughed at himself for he could have used the gravity sled to shift the load but he chose rather his own muscles.

By evening the survival domes were complete and Pawl moved inside to prepare food. Odin was content to rest outside. He had shed completely his Inner Circle gown and now stood like a sheaf of red wheat with his basal tendrils dug deep into the soil. He would not speak, but Pawl was glad to see a deeper redness infuse his fibres as he drank in the planet. The upper flukes waved in the air like blind worms questing for food. Pawl knew that Odin was exploring with his mind.

As the evening drew into night Pawl felt a tingling down the left-hand side of his body. He went outside and found that the tree closest to him, the one under which he had camped, still maintained a faint luminescence.

The feeling grew in Pawl that he was being watched and several times he looked over his shoulder, convinced that

349

he had seen movement out of the corner of his eye at the edge of the small clearing. But he never saw anything.

Until late in the night Pawl squatted outside his dome savouring the night. He watched in awe as the gibbous face of Erix rose and bathed the green world in soft purple shadow.

Erix was looking at him too, thought Pawl. In his mind he likened the giant planet to a cat which stalks outside a mouse's hole, ready to pounce but unable to reach in.

When he could stand the eerie presence of Erix no longer, Pawl stood up and went inside. Within minutes he was asleep.

He dreamed of Laurel – vivid dreams in which he relived moments of his life on Lotus-and-Arcadia and on his Homeworld – and in his dreams he was yet aware of himself sleeping. He saw the tall young man with the coiled dark hair and the fierce eyes and he saw the tired man who lay on his pallet.

How had Laurel seen him? He awoke with that question on his mind, and when he opened his eyes and looked about he found it was day and a milky light was pouring in through the walls.

Outside the air was crisp with just enough chill to bring him awake. The tree stood giant and alive, its upper trunk and canopy bathed in bright sunshine. It had the clarity of a painting and Pawl had the uncanny feeling that he could see round the tree. It seemed to him that it had become more real and that by contrast he and Odin and the survival domes and small ship were somehow less substantial.

That day he explored the thick bush which surrounded his small camp. He found no trace of animals or insects but he did find fruit. He filled his shirt with soft furry green fruits and made his way back and when he reached the camp he found that Odin was moving.

The creature spoke to him for the first time. The voice was a croak, like a voice from a nightmare, but the feel of the thought was unmistakably Odin. 'I am dying, Pawl. It will not be yet . . . I hope it will rain today. Rain would ease both of us.'

The voice vanished like an echo in a tunnel. Odin was again completely self-absorbed.

In the evening it did rain. Water poured off the canopy of the tree in a curtain and sloshed down into the bush. During the night the sky became purple, as Erix made its presence felt. Dreams seized Pawl while he was yet awake. He saw Laurel crying as she spoke of the destruction of Thalatta . . .

. . . and in the morning, when he awoke, he found that he had slept outside in the rain and he was cramped and creased as a rag and felt sick and dirty. The dirtiness was in his mind, some slime that he could not get rid of. He spent the day sitting inside his survival dome, staring at the ground, with his head in his hands.

The sombre overcast day slipped past. In the early evening a pale watery sun appeared and brought some gold to the clearing. Still Pawl sat.

And at evening when the sun did set, someone came tapping. She stepped across the clearing from the base of the tree and tapped against the dome wall with her soft white hands.

Pawl lifted his head slowly and looked. There dimly through the wall he could see a shape. The webbed hand that rested against the wall of the dome was clear enough. Then the face came closer as though she was trying to peer inside.

'Laurel.'

47

ON MORROW

Although Pawl did not know it, at the same moment that Laurel stared through at him, the last and greatest alien war began. The two events were linked, not like cause and effect, but like music and mathematics. Both events were a signal of the same cosmic order.

We are in the sewers on Morrow.

The Spiderets have grown. They are not yet giants but they have grown enough. A few minutes ago a patch of lace, dirty and torn, rose to the surface of the cloaca and tinkled for a few moments before it sank again. Its message was for the young Spiderets which hung clustered and dark round the main inspection vent. Someone is coming to inspect a blockage, the Lyre Beast has said, and now the Spiderets wait.

The Lyre Beast has done wonders to itself. It has spread through the stone tree, sometimes maintaining its unity by only one strand. So the white filament which gathers dust in the cupola at the very summit of the tree is yet the same beast that lies coiled in Dame Jettatura's gymnasium and which occupies the same layout as the cables of the vivante and which recently rose in the sewers. It finds the tree most congenial, ideal for the contortions and knots and tensing that give it joy. Many times its music has been heard echoing in the transit shafts.

Echoes in the sewer. A loud thumping. Someone is hammering at the heavy flanges which hold the trapdoor into the sewer in its place. With a sudden crunch the flanges move and then swing clear. The trapdoor is free. There is a clanking of chains and then, inch by inch, the heavy door is raised. Light peeps round its edges. The rubber-enclosed legs of two sturdy little men can be seen.

While the trapdoor is still rising the Spiderets move. They dive through the opening, stinging as they run. To the two men in their heavy suits it is as though a giant brown cat has suddenly stuffed its paw out of the sewer. They are stung above the knee and fall and are rolled over the lip and down into the froth.

The Spiderets spread through the sterile, white-tiled chambers of Sanitation Unit 3. Surprise is their main weapon. Where they meet the small technicians they jump and spit, and there is no battle. No alarm is raised. Above them the tree sleeps.

Dame Jettatura can't sleep. She has been an insomniac since she was a child. But tonight, just as she thought she was dropping off, she heard a tinkling once again, like distant wind chimes. Wind chimes! There weren't any wind chimes on Morrow so far as she knew, unless Clarissa in one of her fads was trying to make the house more musical. Jettatura would see her about that in the morning. Wind chimes indeed. As bad as the Wong!

Meanwhile, accepting the fact that she now would not sleep until dawn, Jettatura rose from her bed, donned her leotard, brushed her hair and then pinned it into a tight bun. She entered her gymnasium and performed a springy forward roll just to loosen her tight body. Then she climbed to her trapeze, which hung aslant waiting. She would tire her body into sleep. She swung away from the small platform and threw her legs forward to gain momentum. Up, up. With each swing she flew higher until she reached that point where her centrifugal force just matched her weight and she could sweep through the air, delighting in her freedom.

The Lyre Beast heard the sound of the trapeze. It unwrapped and billowed out of the cupboard where it had lain.

Jettatura was flying with her eyes closed. In this way she could imagine she was swooping from peak to peak like a silver bird lifted by mighty currents of air. Only when the trapeze naturally lost energy and the swoop became a mere swing, did she open her eyes. Below her she saw a giant billowing parachute with long rents in its fabric. It hung round the walls, even up to her small trapeze platform.

It was not in Jettatura's nature to scream; she just gripped more tightly the bar until her knuckles showed white. Then the sound of many bells struck her as the Lyre Beast billowed and stretched and strove with the rhythm of her swinging. A finger of lace reached out and touched the shiny mesh cable that supported the trapeze. The Beast was attempting to give the trapeze energy and the energy it transmitted was heat.

The bar became hot in Jettatura's hands. She kicked with all her might for the small platform but it was not enough and the pain became unbearable.

It was not in Jettatura's nature to scream, but she screamed as she let go and fell, turning, into the folds of the Lyre Beast. She tore through it and it thought it was under attack. It drew energy from all its tattered threads throughout the stone tree and the energy focused on Jettatura.

She became, for a moment, what she had in her heart always wanted to be, incandescent. It was not pain she felt but a delirious discharge of energy as her cells transformed to minerals, fused and scattered.

* * *

354

Far away in her own room, Clarissa turned in her sleep and the little attendants who slept with her muttered to themselves.

High in one corner of the room a piece of lace which hung from the corner of a tapestry glowed briefly.

Deep in the roots of the house the Spiderets were on the move. They touched one another and waved their feelers as they gave directions. Their intention was simple: to gain control of the tree. They trusted that the Lyre Beast would fulfil its part of the plan; to neutralize the main electronic circuits.

One group swarmed up the transit chutes and came to the main powerhouse which was lodged where the great tree forked. The doors were closed.

Another group climbed up to the Xerxes living quarters, but they found their way stopped by particle screens. They could move no further.

A third group, looking for the headquarters of the guards, took a wrong turning down one of the side branches and the young Spiderets found themselves looking into the primitive living quarters occupied by the little men who serviced the stone tree.

Where was the Lyre Beast? Why was it not paying attention now? Now, when the plan was beginning to balance. Young Spiderets found lace in the transit chutes and worried it and tore at it in an attempt to make the Lyre Beast act.

That strange creature was in a state of shock. The concentration of its energies about the writhing Jettatura had stunned it. Lyre Beasts are creatures with a smooth and easy sensuality. Their passion rises with a million tiny bells and soundings. Not for them the crash and clatter of

355

the Hammer's sudden passion . . . though at the height of passion all differences fade.

But it became self-aware again as it felt the urging of the young Spiderets. Its self-awareness embraced the whole tree. It ran power in the form of rapid vibration through its whole body to still the irritation.

Circuits blew.

Alarms clanged.

Locks opened.

Doors sealed.

Pots fell.

But all this was nothing. Most horrible of all was the destruction of the bio-crystalline brain which received part of the Lyre Beast's charge. It blackened and twisted and coiled like strips of paper heated in a vacuum. It contracted too, dragging its connections out by the roots. Not all the brain was killed, but enough to maim the operation of the tree house.

Many Spiderets died in that same moment of energy, but those that survived found their way open and they ran into the powerhouse. Others were able to storm the guardhouse, where a pitched battle took place. There was no Latani Rama to fight on the Xerxes side and the spirit of the blood-crazed Spiderets, who fought only to die, crushed the guards.

The particle screen which closed the way to Dame Clarissa held. That lady, startled from her sleep, drew a sheet about her. She tried to contact Jettatura to find what all the fuss was but there was no reply. She noted that the particle screen circuits were all intact but that the vivante circuits were dark.

Once, some generations earlier, there had been an earthquake on Morrow and that had led to the temporary disorientation of the tree. Vaguely Clarissa decided that this emergency must be similar. *Never a dull moment*, she thought as she fluffed her feathers, but she wished that someone would turn off the alarm bell. Finally she decided to go and see what was happening for herself.

She slapped the little men awake (they would sleep through a bomb blast!) and sent them to find news and make chocolate and fetch some guards. One of the men turned off the particle screen before he left the room and Clarissa heard him scream in the corridor.

Instinct rather than logic made her switch the screen back on. Then she crossed to the door frowning. *If this was some sort of* . . .

She saw the small Spiderets, each about the size of a football, packed in the corridor behind the screen. They stared at her with their dull grape eyes and she saw their feelers move.

Clarissa slammed the door and leaned against it.

She did not have time to think about the whys and wherefores; escape was the only thought. She crossed her room and entered the small chamber which housed the transit chute. That, at least, she knew was well-protected. Two of the little men tried to climb in beside her but she swatted them back.

She tapped the code for the main control room and silently the transport pod closed and began to glide. Beneath her seat was a particle pistol and Clarissa released it and checked its charge. Like all the Xerxes matrons, Clarissa could handle a gun.

The pod slid into the main control room and there were Spiderets everywhere, tearing at the fine equipment with their mandibles. The pod slowed but Clarissa urged it on and tapped out new co-ordinates. She felt an icy calm possess her, in which were mixed both pride and defiance. Fleetingly she wondered if this was how Jettatura felt all the time. Where was Jettatura . . . ?

The pod accelerated and dived. Once it hit something which left a red stain on the transparent roof. Stations flew past. Most were deserted. At some there was evidence of a fight.

The pod hurtled on and then dived into darkness as it entered the thick lower walls of the tree. It began to slow and finally halted in a corridor of glass cases. All was silent here.

Clarissa climbed out, her particle pistol held ready. The sheet flapped about her heels and she threw it off. 'What need of such things?'

She approached Dame Rex and saw her own reflection in the glass case. Then she heard in the distance a rustling. Quickly she opened the catches in the front of the case and swung its doors wide. She stepped in and stood beside Dame Rex. They were like mother and daughter.

The first Spideret arrived scampering down the corridor. It stopped in surprise and its eyes grew out on stalks when it saw the live woman in the case of death.

Clarissa smiled and fired once, scything the creature in half.

The others arrived. They climbed round the walls. They climbed on their dead comrade. They climbed on the adjacent cases.

They stared at Clarissa and their dull eyes came alive and reflected the movement as her magnificent quills of crimson and iridescent blue rose like flame round her neck and face.

48

ULTIMA THULE

Laurel.

Laurel indeed, or something that looked very like Laurel. Laurel as Pawl remembered her. A shape fashioned from memory.

She stood simple and naked at his doorway and looked at him with eyes that held no hint of recognition, the eyes of a new-born child. Her skin was creamy and unwrinkled, the skin of a baby. But yet she was a whole woman and the colours in her skin and the lights in her hair and the curve of nostril and firmness of hip and sturdy thigh all told of Laurel.

Pawl walked to her, slightly shy before her level eyes, aware of his own grubbiness. He held out his hand. She lifted her own webbed hand and placed it in his and then stepped over the threshold.

'You called and I came.'

Her voice. The same lingering over the 'm' sound which made her sound sultry and considered at the same time. The same pitch.

'I am glad to see you.' How inadequate! 'Where did you come from?' Silly question!

She turned and looked out into the clearing. 'Over there.'

'And before that?'

'I do not know.' A simple statement, said without worry or concern.

'Who am I?'

'You are Laurel.'

Abruptly she yawned and pressed the back of her hand to her mouth. The gesture was wholly Laurel. Her hips moved with the yawn as she stretched and Pawl felt that movement touch the core of his sexuality. There was nothing he could do as his body responded. He felt an emotion only slightly younger than time itself, a longing to join.

And yet he held back. Now was not the time for touching, not yet. That would come. But he relished the firmness as his manhood came alive. He felt his juices start to flow. There was a great dilation inside him. Pawl the savage, never far below the surface in the time of their loving, brushed aside, like something sucked dry, the sad, ragged-spirited Pawl of his latter days.

Laurel had always been able to do this. She had that capacity to make him bigger and better than he was in nature, to make him into what all men should be: bright as fire, gentle as water, sound as earth and merry as the good air.

'Are you tired? Will you rest?'

Laurel nodded and Pawl led her through to the quiet room where he had spread warm covers, ones which Laurel had chosen, over the sleeping place. She fingered the clothes, stroking them, tracing the patterns with the flat of her hand. And then she looked at him and there was something like recognition in her eyes.

She lay down, rolled over, one hand spread under her face, the other curled between her legs, and within moments was asleep. Pawl covered her.

He went outside quickly and found to his surprise that night had fallen.

'Are you happy, Pawl?' The voice was a croak.

Happy was not the word for what Pawl felt. He was radiant. A sun burned in him and he wanted to explode.

'Come and sit by me. I shall not be with you much longer.'

Pawl sat down next to Odin and felt the creature nestle close. 'Are you pleased with it, Pawl?'

'She pleases me.'

'It is very powerful.'

Odin was trying to tell Pawl something. Pawl sat quietly.

'It is a seed, you know. It is a seed of the trees. Be clear about that. It is just one seed. There will be many others.'

'Others? Like Laurel? You mean more will appear?'

'No. No. No. Don't be alarmed. Not like Laurel. Others.' The space inside Pawl's head in which Odin spoke became silent but still alive. Odin was wondering how to explain to Pawl that which is hardly explicable in human terms. 'It, Laurel as you call it, is one. It is a symbol of your love. *Your* love in all its shapes. And it will change, too.'

'Change? How will it change? I don't want her to change.'

'All things change, Pawl. That is the one law which binds us all together. No, not the one law, not the only law. There is one other.'

'And what is that?'

'You must find out for yourself.' The voice was a whisper. Then the silence was total. Odin had withdrawn.

Pawl was irritated that his happiness had been tainted at the moment of its first blooming.

Beyond the trees on the close horizon of Pawl's world, a purple stain grew in the sky. Gradually the livid face of Erix rose, turning the green to blackberry.

Later, lying beside Laurel, Pawl felt her wake and start and moan to herself. Then gently, like water on water,

361

like the tide creeping up the sand and into the rock pools, he felt her hands begin to explore his body.

49

ON CENTRAL

'What is that smell?' Lar Proctor, lying in bed with his curved fangs hung on a peg above him, sniffed.

The young boy who had been massaging his legs smiled prettily. 'What smell?'

'*That* smell. Don't say you can't smell it. It's horrible. It's from over there somewhere.' Lar Proctor pointed vaguely in the direction of the bedroom wall where a large portal gave on to a veranda above one of the deep gardens.

Delicately the boy removed his nose plugs. 'I wear these because of hay fever when I'm working in this room.' Then his face wrinkled in disgust. 'That smell. Ugh. It's something rotten. I'll go and see, shall I?'

Lar Proctor slithered off the bed. 'Wait a moment. Don't open that curtain until I'm decent.' He burrowed into his robe and drew it tightly round him. 'Now you can draw the curtain.'

The boy drew back the heavy drape and they both stepped out on to the veranda.

They found themselves looking into the face of a giant multicoloured pansy which puffed and fluttered.

'Why, it's beautiful,' said the boy and dropped down dead.

Lar Proctor looked at the swirling colours. Velvet purple, gash red, screaming blue, knife silver, smother brown . . . the colours turned and they twisted his spirit and drew it from him like yarn. Lar Proctor sagged with his empty mouth open. His body slumped over that of the boy.

* * *

The Diphilus had to be careful. There was much heat on Central and more than once it found itself burned as it rolled through ducts and squeezed itself along pressure pipes. At the heart of this planet, it knew, was its enemy – a blazing inferno of dazzling particles trapped within a magnetic net. That was the source of all Central's power and the Diphilus decided to keep well away from it.

It took up lodging in a cold store in which were hung the heavy bodies of creatures like tortoises, each with its bell-shaped shell still intact.

Once a man and a woman came to take meat. The Diphilus touched them and stole their electricity, and when their bodies were frozen it hung them up on the racks.

The Diphilus, with its boundless curiosity and sense of wonder, came to know Central in a way that the Hooded Parasol could not. Immersed for millennia in abstractions and the peculiar relationships between spiritual power and the life and death of stars, it took delight in discovering that it could turn lights on and off and make vacuum chutes work and doors open and close merely by playing with its potential. The shuttle it ignored, since symbol meshing was an old art; and while it was perhaps the greatest art, the Diphilus wanted to play. Simple circuits. The Diphilus was like a child with a train set.

One morning it started the lift doors working like castanets until the motors burned out. The Senior Proctor was trapped between floors for three hours. It opened the space hangars without warning and a whole maintenance crew, complete with the ships they were working on, was sucked out into the vacuum of space. Once it turned the central heating off in a dormitory sector and locked the windows open. On that night fish tanks froze to solid blocks.

Eventually it explored along the cables of the hidden bio-crystalline brains and there it discovered madness. It detected the shapes of thought of one of its own kind brought in from the far Norea. It felt the laughter of a brother it had never known.

Tampering with those delicate circuits was the Diphilus's undoing.

Beyond the everyday running of the Homeworld, the computers of Central were in disarray. People were beginning to panic. The scientists who controlled Central said that the artificial planet had developed an eccentric magnetic field. This, they said, explained the bizarre events. But panic bred panic and panic led to contradictions.

One night the Diphilus turned on all the lights and then switched them off seconds later. And then on again. From the shuttle platform above Central it looked as if the metal world was a gigantic light bulb switching on and off.

The fluctuations in potential were enormous. The computers tried to cope switching power from gardens to cold stores, to emergency services, to stabilizers, to factories, to living quarters. The generators in the heart of the planet went crazy, trying to balance surge and trough in the same instant.

The bio-crystalline computer, with only half its circuits functioning, thought it saw an easy economy and cut power to itself. Dominoes started to fall. Eventually the circuits which controlled the great magnetic net at the heart of the planet failed. At the same moment the generators went into high demand and a fireball started in the black centre of the plasma.

The destruction took nanoseconds.

The Parasol, dilating, shrivelled to smoke.

The Diphilus roared as it ignited.

A fire in the bleakness of space blossomed and spread.

It would blaze for centuries before it cooled to a glassy cinder.

Thus ended Central, and the rule of the Proctors, and one curious Diphilus.

50

ULTIMA THULE

Laurel made love in an artless and total way. The direct-
ness of her passion took Pawl's breath away. She received
him with a singleness of attention which liberated him to
be all the good things he could be.

He flowed over and she flowed with him, before and
after, and they lay together warm and panting like an
animal that has two hearts.

Lying there in that state in which secrets seem to belong
to another world, Pawl felt her creep into his mind. She
was a drowsy presence, a tumble of hair and warm lips,
and she made her home inside him.

Was it ever like this? thought Pawl, and found that he
could not remember. The past was sinking like an abandoned ship.

In the morning they unpacked clothes. Pawl could see a
growing quickness in Laurel's eyes as she held the bright
gowns against her and swayed with them. She tied a red
and green scarf in her hair, just as Laurel had when they
were together on Lotus-and-Arcadia.

They began to joke about the past, laughing at memories, but Pawl noticed that Laurel only talked about the
times when she had been with him. Rummaging among
Pawl's trunk she found the Beltane family emblem and
held it up.

'What's this? It's heavy.'

'Your family emblem.'

'Of course.'

They made love when the desire took them and in the afternoon Pawl built a garden.

Laurel dragged a chair from the main survival dome and sat close to Pawl while he dug. He could feel her eyes on him as he managed the lines of a fence and marked out where he would plant the vegetables.

She paid no attention to Odin, nor did she mention him, though she passed by him many times. It was as though she could not see him. When Pawl introduced him she nodded in a casual way, and that was all.

Pawl worked until the sweat poured off him, making rivers through the dirt on his skin. He delighted in feeling his muscles work and in showing off before his lady.

In the late afternoon she rose from her chair. 'Come on, Pawl. Let's swim. There's a pool over there.' And without waiting for reply she ran to the edge of the clearing and disappeared into the scraggly bush. Pawl ran after her. He remembered, when they were landing, seeing one of the round black pools close by.

Laurel worked her way easily through the bush while Pawl found the going difficult. Soon all he knew of her was the swish of leaves and the occasional breaking branch well ahead. Fear gripped him and he barged ahead like a wild pig butting under the branches, heedless of the scratches that opened up on his arms.

Suddenly the bush ended and opened on to a slope of grass which led down to the dark water. Laurel was at the lake edge wading out about to plunge.

'Wait for me.' Pawl stumbled down to the margin and Laurel, laughing, cupped water in her hands and splashed him.

'Come on, dive with me.'

Pawl looked at the dark rippleless water and knew that he could not.

'Come on.'

Pawl shook his head. 'I'll wait. Be careful. Don't go too far.'

Laurel laughed at this. 'I'm a born aquatic, remember.' She fanned her webbed hands. 'And besides, there's nothing on this world can do me harm. Not even Odin. Watch.'

She dived, and moments later broke the surface far out in the lake. She waved to him and then dived again.

Numb with unknown fears Pawl squatted down in the marshy grass at the lake's edge and watched. Laurel swam and dived and lunged from the surface and fell back, kicking the water to brown lather. Pawl watched to see other ripples on the smooth lake. He wondered at her. The black water menaced him but she cavorted without fear.

Eventually she swam back to him, darting through the water like an otter. She stood up ten yards from the shore where the water lapped just to her breasts. 'Come in, Pawl. Try it. Nothing will hurt you. Here, hold my hand.' She waded from the water with her arms held out. 'Come on.'

Uncertainly Pawl stood and then began to edge into the water. It was surprisingly warm and thicker than he had expected. He could not see his feet. Laurel's hand took his wrist in her firm grip. 'Come on. Nothing to be afraid of.'

Slowly he edged deeper until he could crouch down and the water came up to his chin. Laurel pushed him and he made a few pathetic moves with his arms until he felt something slide over his feet and along his belly, and he lost his balance threshing, and went under.

Death. That was what Pawl thought. *Death*. The blackness was total and squeezed into his nose and mouth and ears and through his skin. He gasped and tasted the bitterness . . . and then he was up and panting and Laurel was with him holding him with her arms round his waist so that he could not fall again. She helped him to the shore, and there he collapsed down spluttering, with the black water dribbling from his mouth.

'I'm sorry,' she said. 'I didn't know you were so afraid.' She rubbed her hands over his curved back and kissed his neck. He felt her breasts with their nipples firm press into his back.

'Laurel.'

'I am Laurel. Thank you for coming for me. Thank you for coming to my world.'

Ten minutes later he had overcome his panic and was able to laugh. They sat together by the lakeside in the late evening sun. Laurel fetched some small blue star-headed flowers and draped them over his arms. She plunged her hand into the dark water and brought it up, holding a small silver eel squirming in her palm. 'This is the only creature that lives here,' she said. 'It cleans the roots of the trees.' And then she let it go, lowering her hand into the water. The eel flipped over the web between her first and second finger and was gone. 'On this world everything belongs. Everything has its job. Me and you.' She stood up. 'We'll go back now.'

They took their time climbing back through the bush and gathered fruit and flowers. Pawl was surprised that he felt so relaxed inside himself. Though he did not understand what had happened, in that plunge he had accepted and been accepted by this world and he was now no longer a visitor, he was an inhabitant. He did notice, however, that the scratches on his arms had completely healed.

During their absence Odin had moved. He had shifted some yards further away from the domes in the direction of the silver tree. Patiently, but with painful slowness, he was inching up the slope towards where the nearest of the silver roots broke through the green soil.

'Shall I help you?' asked Pawl, speaking only with his mind. But he received no reply. The silence was like a wall. But beyond the wall, beyond his grasp, there was something like a fire burning.

'Leave him,' said Laurel. 'He will make peace on his own. Did you bring your book with you? I want you to read to me. Every moment is precious. There is so much I need to learn and unlearn."

That night the pain of Odin broke through.

Pawl was lying back, thinking about the events of the day, when he heard Odin's voice calling to him. It was the voice of a child and Pawl had no option but to get up and go to him. Laurel rose with him but Pawl hushed her and she lay back.

Outside the clearing was deep purple with Erix light. Odin had made it to the base of the tree and now stood raised up on the lips of his basal sucker. He was like a purple sheaf of wheat. All his tendrils were extended and stood out stiff from his body.

'Tonight I die. Sit close. There are things I must say.' Pawl settled.

'I have feared this moment, Pawl. I have been your friend, and I have been your greatest enemy. I killed Laurel.'

Then, in simple phrases, Odin described how he had captured Laurel's mind and drowned her. He explained how he had been the agent of the Inner Circle and how the great Tree on Sanctum had lent him vanity to enable him to achieve the deed. 'That vanity is now withdrawn and all I have left is the guilt. Guilt has killed me. I was a simple Gerbes, undistinguished among my race. I was taken for no fault of my own and made into the great deceiver. Forgiveness cannot help. There can be no forgiveness, only a withering of the spirit and awareness. Life is cruel, Pawl Paxwax, and the only dignity we have is in enduring.'

Pawl listened and then he asked one question. 'Why me?'

'Because you loved, and because your love was fierce and because you set your love above everything else. But that is not all the reason. It is a matter of spirit, Pawl. You have a fierce spirit. You know how it burns in you. The spirit burns beyond time and place. The Craint knew that and that is why they summoned you. That is why they honoured you in this life.' Odin sighed, like a wind passing over water and reeds. 'Ultimately there is only goodness, but that is hard to see. I try to keep my mind on goodness. That thing up there – ' some of Odin's flukes moved and directed their small purple mouths up towards Erix – 'it is nothing . . . But its nothing must be held at bay. It is the emptying of desire. This world holds it in check and – ' Odin's words suddenly became laboured – 'and we all do what we can. We offer our best. You, Pawl, offer your love.'

Pawl could think of nothing to say. There was nothing he wanted to say. He felt himself void of desire. Words seemed unreal.

Odin continued and his voice became slightly stronger. 'Now, Pawl. I have one last request. You humans honour such things, don't you? Help me through. I can see only dark and light. When I have gone, all that I am, my soul, my stone, will be in your hands. I give it to you willingly. Do with it what you will. It is ended.'

The flukes on Odin's hide stood out even more stiffly as though straining. Behind Pawl there was movement.

Laurel, her skin a mottle of black and purple, stepped close. She plunged her hand deep into the raised tendrils and squeezed.

Pawl rolled away on his back, his hands over his ears, as pain flooded through his mind. 'Live,' he screamed. 'Live.'

All the tendrils fell at once. The great sucker closed and opened and the small shape of Odin drooped and fell. Pawl felt the pain recede and in its place there came a great calm, a singing which grew until it became a high rushing wind . . .

. . . and the wind departed and there was silence.

Laurel's arms were round him. She rocked him like a baby.

Later she lifted him up and helped him inside.

High in the sky Erix moved on, its leaden light heavy on the green of Thule.

In the grey morning Pawl left his bed and went outside. A heavy dew had made everything damp. He walked up from the house to where the roots of the tree lifted from the earth. There he found a glossy stump. The remains of Odin were deliquescing. The small body was decaying to water and fibre. Visible already was Odin's stone. It was a misshapen but rounded lump of rock through which ran fine wrinkles, like the stone of a peach. He reached in and the stone came away from the jellied parts of Odin which still held it. It was remarkably heavy and Pawl had to use both hands to lift it.

Odin had carried this stone all his years. Round it had flowed all his life. Pawl held the stone and then listened to the silence, the awful silence. He was alone now. No, not alone, for Laurel was here. But alone in a private way.

Pawl sat down on the wet grass with the stone between his legs and wished he could cry. So much said. So much left unsaid. Poor Odin. Poor lovely, gentle creature. This stone was all that remained.

51

ON SABLE

Helium's fur had been dyed blue in honour of his age and the three-hundredth anniversary of his accession to the Mastership. He sat and looked at his reflection dismally. Helium hated birthdays and public celebrations of all kinds. His delight was in the more simple things of life, like his pipe, and so he dallied and was late for the main festivities.

Among other things, he missed a water dance in which the young Bogdanovich males courted the eligible Shell females. The dance was formal, which meant that hand-touching only was allowed. No slide-over high-jinks were permitted. They would come later when the older members of the Conspiracy retired and the young could have their head.

The dance took place in Clover Shell's new garden which was called Thalatta in honour of the dead planet. It was a *fun* garden. There was a kelp forest with quiet corners where warmer water gushed up and where a loving couple could find privacy. For the adventurous there were deep caves under the islands where mock spearfish and needlefins lay in wait. There was a wide lagoon with a mirror bottom where swimmers could admire their own grace.

What Laurel would have made of the garden is anyone's guess. But the Shell-Bogdanovich liked it and as far as they were concerned that was all that mattered.

The Thalatta garden was to be Helium and Clover's gift to the entire family and on this day Helium was to open it to the vast network of pipes and ditches which allowed aquatic life to thrive in this dry part of Sable.

Finally Helium arrived, ejected into the garden by a pressure chute. He could see that Clover was not pleased. Quickly he swam to the central island and slithered up on to a dais made of jade on which a cool fountain played. When Helium arrived the music stopped and the couples gathered in the water round the island. Helium stood up.

'Members of the Bogdanovich and Shell families, Clover and I bid you welcome. I am glad to see so many of you wearing blue today. That makes me feel less lonely in my age.' Applause greeted this but Helium held up his blunt hand and the applause died. 'But to you greens and reds I bid a special welcome for it is upon your strength and pride that the future of the Conspiracy depends.' This time Helium let the applause run its natural course. 'In a mere twenty years, Clover and I shall be choosing our successors and many of you will be contenders.' There were shouts and somersaults at this.

'Anyway, you haven't come here to hear me talk all day, so, without further ado, I declare this new garden open and may you all find happiness in it.'

Helium signalled, and engineers who had been waiting for over an hour threw the switches that opened the lock gates. Slowly the gates swung open and there was a rush of water into the artificial sea. It lifted the kelp and the bobbing swimmers. With the water came darting white eels.

Those who had plotted the downfall of the Shell-Bogdanovich Conspiracy had chosen well. At this stage of their development the elvers were little more than a jaw and a stomach. Though mature Link Worms were solitary creatures and could grow to a great length, as elvers they hunted in packs. When there was no more prey they devoured one another.

They fell upon the young Shell-Bogdanovich and where they swam the water became red. Bodies screamed and twitched before being dragged under. Those that made it to the side heaved themselves up on to the rocks with the eels hanging off them. The sea garden became a cauldron.

Clover clambered up to the jade dais and stood with Helium.

Neither could comprehend what was happening.

52

ULTIMA THULE

An unnatural sound broke over Thule. Pawl had become accustomed to the silence, broken only by the gentle susurration of the wind in the bush and the patter of rain. This growl came from elsewhere. Pawl rushed out of the survival dome and peered up at the milky sky. His view was limited. Most of the sky was dominated by the vast veiny canopy of the tree, and the walls of the clearing rose sheer.

But the thunder increased and then slowly a spaceship, small for the amount of noise it made, slid into view. It was only a few hundred feet above the top of the bush.

Pawl recognized a Dragon Class ship, of the kind much in vogue among the younger members of the Families on Lotus-and-Arcadia. This ship was equipped for duelling.

The ship halted in the air and the volume of noise increased until five gravity lines probed down to the earth and found purchase. The ship settled and the noise dropped away to a whisper. Cannon located at the lateral edges of the ship pivoted and fired at the ground. Fire plumed and a dense cloud of smoke lifted and swept round the underbelly of the ship and up into the pale sky. It was a pointless show of strength.

The ship settled on to its own charred earth just a few hundred feet from Pawl's clearing. A door irised open and a dark figure came to stand at its threshold.

'So there you are, Pawl Paxwax. I've found you at last. I've come to kill you.' It was Paris.

* * *

Laurel came to stand beside Pawl. 'My brother?' she said wonderingly. 'What brings him?'

Pawl shrugged. 'He says he's come to kill me. I think he means to fight.'

Any further talking was cut short by a call from the edge of the clearing. 'Stand clear, Pawl Paxwax.' Paris emerged, dark and stealthy. He seemed to have grown. In his hand he carried an automatic particle pistol such as Pawl had once worn. 'Stand away from that creature. What is it? Another of your dummies? Oh, yes, I've heard all about you, Pawl Paxwax.' Paris was close now.

'Why have you come here? What do you want with me? Turn round and go back to your ship. Leave us alone.'

'You killed my sister. You killed my father. Every disaster in my family can be traced to you. Now I am going to kill you.'

'Put down your gun, Paris.' It was Laurel speaking. 'You can't kill on this world.'

'Can't I?' Paris's tone was still confident but his hand shook. The sight of Laurel, her voice, her physical presence all undermined him. He licked his lips. 'It speaks like Laurel even. What kind of magic is this?'

'No magic. Go away.' Paris raised his arm. 'Will you kill me like this? Unarmed? Won't you even give me the chance to fight?' Pawl was challenging Paris. His training on Terpsichore was coming to his aid. In a straight contest of strength Paris would win. He was undoubtedly stronger than Pawl and faster too. But Pawl had studied more. All he needed was one advantage. And if he saw that . . .

But Paris was not fooled. 'No words, Master of Paxwax. I will kill you any way I can.' Quickly he brought his hand up and fired.

In that moment everything started to move slowly for Pawl.

He saw Paris's finger pull the trigger. He saw the

particle beam grow like a rod of silver towards him. He saw it touch his chest and spread like a breaking wave, sending him backwards. Incredibly he saw his flesh open as it received the charge and then close again like crumpled paper that is smoothed under a hand.

Laurel stepped forward and Paris fired at her, so that for a few moments she became incandescent and the grass burned round her.

Then she had Paris and she lifted him and shook him so that the gun dropped from his hand and the visor of his helmet slipped over his face. When she set him free he fell down and hugged the earth, unable to tell up from down for the moment.

He crawled away and, when he reached the edge of the clearing, stood up and set off for his ship.

Laurel laughed. 'Did you think you could be harmed, Pawl Paxwax? We are on Thule now. Remember? Things are different here. Here nothing dies before its time.'

About an hour later Paris came back to the clearing. He sat down on the grass a few yards from Laurel and Pawl. The boy showed through the husky young man. 'My ship won't budge. Everything's dead except the stabilizers, and they're running down.'

He looked across at Pawl quickly. 'It's not funny. I don't want to be stuck on this planet. I don't suppose your ship . . .' He pointed to Pawl's survival rocket, which was already starting to rust along its inner seams.

Pawl shook his head. 'It wouldn't have enough power to get you above the trees.'

Paris's face looked tragic. 'How long before supply ships come?'

'They don't.'

'But . . .'

Laurel crossed to him and crouched down by him and put her arms round him. Paris looked away from her nakedness. 'Go back to your ship, my brother Paris. You cannot stay here with us. Wait until morning. Then you will leave and never return. You have a life to live beyond here.'

Paris looked at Pawl. 'I hate you,' he said. 'I loved my sister more than you will ever know.' Laurel touched his face and brought it round. Pawl saw Paris's strong face soften as he looked at her. 'Go now,' she said.

Paris stood up. He was obviously confused. He wanted to say something but couldn't find or didn't have the words to match his feelings. Finally he turned and trudged away without a backward glance. He broke into the trees at the end of the clearing and was gone.

The next morning Pawl heard the roar of Paris's rockets. The shadow of his ship passed quickly over the clearing and its sound faded as it climbed.

Paris was gone. For him, too, his part in the story was ended.

53

ON AN

The Dragon Emperor Wong Lungli was in the Pavilion of Passing Pleasures. He had always paid close attention to his health and despite his age still managed to satisfy his favourite concubines, especially when the moons of An were in the right quarter and Tiger Bone Syrup was to hand. Now he lay back, indecent as a dog, with his legs open and the filtered sun on his thighs.

Close to him but not touching him lay Meng Shui-lin, as beautiful as a doll, with raven black hair and a mind that was as dangerous as a steel trap. While Meng retained her looks and suppleness of body no other concubine was her rival. Just now she was whispering endearments and planned to advance the name of her son for a senior military post.

While she spoke there came from outside the pavilion a sound as though someone had popped a paper bag filled with air. Such a noise was unheard of in the quiet precincts of Imperial An. Her eyebrows puckered, for the noise had distracted the Emperor from the fine tale of lasciviousness she was telling him.

Bang. Again. From a different quarter.

The emperor's hand with its ball of nails lifted and his lips moved. The Lady Meng snapped her fingers and servants, who were kneeling behind light curtains some distance from the bed, stood up and scurried to the wide door of the pavilion.

'Ai-ee,' they cried and pointed to the sky.

Bang.

Bang. Bang.

The Lady Meng wrapped a gown round her and hurried to the door. She had expected to see fireworks. She saw instead, hanging in the sky, dull black balls.

Bang. One of the black spheres appeared directly above her. It was lower than the rest. She watched it split and then open into two spheres.

Bang. Bang. Bang. Bang.

The sky was filling.

Bang. Bang . . .

Behind Lady Meng there was a whispering. She turned and found the Dragon Emperor walking towards her, supported at the elbow by a small fat servant.

Bang. Bang. Bang.

Most of the spheres had converted into the double ball configuration. Then, in one move, they split wide open and disgorged white ships, which dropped and then began to fly, spreading out across the wide flat Imperial city. The ships began to fire, cutting open the roofs of the temple and slicing through the wide city streets.

There was screaming in the distance beyond the walls of the Imperial City. Belatedly particle cannon began to stab upwards but the ships were everywhere, buzzing like white flies round offal. One of the white ships tore over the Pavilion of Passing Pleasures and screamed into a curve with all guns firing as it laid waste the yachts and barges on the inland sea.

Wong Lungli recognized the shape of the ship and knew that his attackers were the Hammer. He pushed his servants away. He pushed the Lady Meng away, instructing her to return to her home beyond the kitchens where all the concubines lived.

Then he hurried down the dragon path and out of the garden and into an avenue of cypress trees. Wong Lungli could run when he wanted to. Despite his years he had a

383

loping stride which carried him down the avenue and through a circular door and into a small courtyard.

As he entered the courtyard he heard a sudden drumming and wondered what that could be. No time to stop and look. At the end of the courtyard was a tall brass door. This led through secret passages to a retreat known only to the senior fathers of the Wong. Here were kept food and water and a secret subterranean Gate. It was a secret well kept, for it was widely believed that no Gate could operate within the confines of a planet. Once through the door Wong Lungli would be safe.

Round his neck on a silver chain was a key. He had worn it since he was a child. Now he needed that key. He cursed his fingernails for he could not hold the small sliver of metal. Outside the giant brass doors he sat down on the tiles and began to bite at his fingernails, trying to free his fingers.

While so engaged he heard the drumming again. Very close now. And he became aware of a shadow which stretched along the garden towards him.

He looked up quickly and then could not look away. Rising up above the tile-topped wall was a giant hammerhead with a great wrinkled boss in the middle and two widespread black eyes which focused on him. He heard the drumming again.

The Hammer (Trader it was) watched as Wong Lungli staggered to his feet and then backed away along the wall. He dropped the key. He came to an alcove and dived into it. It gave on to a narrow passage which ran alongside the building with the brass doors. Behind him he heard the crunch and crash of masonry as the Hammer breasted the wall and with all legs working heaved itself over the rubble. Its sting opened and snapped shut and arched high above its hammer-head.

The Dragon Emperor was really running for his life

now. When he emerged from the passage he found himself facing three open gates. One led to the Imperial harbour, and he could see other Hammer moving there among the smoke and flame. The second led back to the city, and a black pall of smoke hung there. There was no longer any firing from the ground. The final gate led up a winding path to a small pagoda on the top of an artificial hill.

He heard drumming again and ran towards the hill.

Age began to tell and he lost one of his slippers. He felt a fearful pounding in his head and did not know if it was the drumming of the creature that followed him or not. The path was uneven and he stumbled. When he climbed to his feet he heard a puffing behind him like a whale venting and a trill of drumming so close that it almost seemed to be over him.

He stole a glance behind and found himself staring straight into a tentacle-fringed orifice. The Hammer was waiting for him! He watched as its sting came down and butted him, urging him up the hill.

Wong Lungli had never been so close to such a creature. On the practice ranges during Wong Lungli's time on Terpsichore there was always the comfortable smell of plastic. But this creature stank of venom and blood. In white terror Wong Lungli staggered on up the hill, herded by the Hammer and helped by thrusts in the back.

At the pagoda he realized why he had been driven there. He could see his city. The cherry trees were on fire. Fine pagodas blazed and their tiles exploded like firecrackers. He saw a Hammer stalk one of his palace guards. It ran beside him and then dabbed down with its sting and nipped him in half. He saw the earth cave in under concentrated dab rays and knew that even the private Gate was destroyed. He saw the inland sea burn.

For the last of the Dragon Emperors there was only

one way out. He saw the Hammer and he saw his world. With all his might he hurled himself head first against the stone pillars of the pagoda in an attempt to dash his brains out. But his body held back and he botched the job and was still conscious through a red curtain of pain when the Hammer picked him up and threw him like a doll down the hill.

The Hammer were berserk and thorough. At the same moment they appeared over An they also arrived over the other Wong cities. Everywhere the pattern of destruction was the same. They smashed the Way Gates and laid waste the land. They gave no quarter, killing prisoners and functionaries alike. They stung till their venom sacs were dry and they sank on their knees in fatigue and ecstasy.

But An came in for special treatment. On that world they destroyed all life. They flattened all the buildings and ploughed them under, turning their stings to plough-shares. They dragged into light priceless works of art, some of which had endured all the revolutions since the time mankind first left Earth. They broke the fine blue pottery without a qualm. They tore the silks and the tapestries and the timeless paintings and buried them.

They left An a dead world and set about creating their own bloody empire.

The wheel had turned but one notch. It was not broken.

54

ON ULTIMA THULE

Pawl knew none of this.

Life on Thule settled, and although Pawl did little except look after his small garden and make love to Laurel, he found himself happy beyond his hopes. He felt fully alive in a way that he had only glimpsed in those moments when he had managed to trap life in words. Not that he wrote any more, or attempted to. Just being was sufficient. Once he had feared boredom. Now, with nothing to do and a lifetime to spend, boredom was the last thing on his mind. The days seemed too short.

Pawl became the slave of his love. He knew what was happening. Laurel was a drug. Love was a drug. Each day she grew in his mind, becoming closer to his ideal, and yet somehow she was always in front of him, leading.

Then one night, one strange night, when Erix made the walls of the dome flicker with deep purple shadows, Laurel held him fiercely. She offered herself to him in every way and there was an urgency about her love-making which upset him. She wanted more, something that he could not provide. She wanted to be touched and taken in a way that was beyond him.

'Hold me, Pawl. Hold me. Stop time. For me. For you. Stop time.'

'Laurel.'

'Isn't that what you tried to do when you wrote down words? Isn't that your art?'

'I don't know.'

'You told me once. Oh, hold me, I am so cold. Time is dragging me.'

Pawl did not know what to do and so he held his trembling woman close to him and whispered what words he could. Words from their past. She said nothing, but squirmed against him as though she would climb into his skin.

Towards morning she lay soft and relaxed in his arms. 'It is not enough, is it?' she murmured. 'Oh Pawl. I am sorry. I have tried to love you. Love me.'

'I do. I do.'

'But it is not enough to hold me.'

The next night she would not sleep with him. She spent the entire night in the clearing. Pawl sat sadly to one side. She seemed miles away. When Erix passed, she snarled. When a brief spatter of rain fell, she spread her arms and hands and tried to catch the rain and drink it.

She was no longer Laurel. It was Laurel's body, but something occupied it. A stranger peered from her eyes. When she kissed Pawl once her lips were hard and unyielding. Finally, tired and depressed, Pawl entered the dome and collapsed on to the bed. He remembered Odin's words, 'She is a seed.' But still he did not understand.

When he awoke he felt a weight by his side, and discovered that Laurel had placed Odin's stone there.

Of Laurel there was no sign.

She seemed to have run away.

Pawl called for her. He wandered round the great tree. He sat listening. He scrambled down to the lake and beat his way through the dense bush. And then finally night came and he made his way back to his camp and climbed into bed. In the morning he woke alone.

* * *

388

He hoed his garden. It was for recreation only. Pawl had discovered that he no longer needed to eat. Somehow he sustained himself by breathing and drinking.

While hoeing he had the sudden clear knowledge that Laurel was beyond the black-water lake. With that knowledge came an admonition that he should not go back to her yet.

But the knowledge of where she was released a great well of joy in him. She was safe and *there*, wherever *there* might be. And he hoed until his arms ached. That evening he tried to climb the silver tree to see if he could see the dark lake but the bark was too smooth and he slipped down.

The next morning Pawl was shaken awake. It was a dream shaking him. When he opened his eyes the shaking stopped and he stared at the grey domed roof. But it had been Laurel, or something like her, bending over him with rough hands. She was calling him to her.

Pawl shook the sleep from his head and walked out of the dome and into the misty clearing where dawn was still breaking and a fine rain was falling. He set out across the clearing and into the bush in the general direction of the lake. Pawl moved easily in the bush now, slipping under branches and round saplings.

He emerged from the bush, close to the lake but further round than he had ever explored. He crossed some soft sand and noticed that there was a set of footprints already there: shallow depressions filled with water.

He came to a river of dark water which sluiced over a shingle bar.

About two hundred yards up the river, on the opposite bank, stood Laurel. She stood very still and seemed taller.

Pawl waded across the shingle bank and ran towards

389

Laurel, calling her name. But he pulled up short before he reached her.

Laurel's legs were slightly spread and she was ankle deep in water. Her legs were thicker and veins stood out which ran from her knees right up her body to her neck. Her dappled colour had begun to fade to a uniform grey. Her arms had grown longer and the fingers with the webbing were stiff and reached down to her knees. They were growing towards the soil. Already there was a fusion taking place between her arms and the main part of her body. The neck was thicker too, and supported a head which was thinner and with the features drawn out. The eyes were closed and the nose was flattened and the mouth was open, as though waiting to drink the rain. Her hair was completely gone.

Pawl approached slowly. He spoke her name, but she did not move. He reached forward and with his fingers touched her face. It was as hard as hide that has been stretched in the sun.

He bent down and touched her feet. The toes were buried in the silt. They reminded him of something. Roots. That was it. They were like roots.

Laurel was turning into one of the trees.

Each day Pawl visited Laurel and each day he noticed changes. Laurel grew sturdier and more silver as she lost her humanness. Pawl realized as he sat and looked at her that although she had changed her form she was still Laurel. He thought he could feel love radiate from her and that made him peaceful.

For a while he wondered if he was destined to become a tree. But then he dismissed the thought. It was not in his nature. He was a maker, a doer.

He began to clear the space round Laurel so that she could grow more easily.

55

IN THE GALAXY

And what of the fate of the spaceways?

The order of the Families was destroyed and with it went the worst and the best of humanity. The chains of Way Gates, which had endured for so long that they seemed part of nature, were either smashed by alien war parties or 'died', for the sensitive cells of the bio-crystalline brains had little resistance when confronted by the logical illogic of the jovial Diphilus or the death-will of the Hammer.

The Gerbes settled on their world and were content to be forgotten.

The Hooded Parasol spread wherever they could and farmed native populations.

The Hammer fought among themselves and the Spider-ets rebuilt their workshops.

Drip by patient drip the great bowl of the galaxy filled.

Isolated, the planets and star systems which had once belonged to Great Families with splendid-sounding names, such as the Xerxes de la Tour Souvent or the Shell-Bogdanovich Conspiracy, went on their own ways.

Some communities died out. Many were destroyed by the aliens during what became known as the Great Purge. Others thrived.

Such a one was Mako.

Remember Mako?

Trade in the Rand Melon died overnight.

The Way Gate that had served that small planet so well suddenly stopped functioning. Its mirrors would not turn. Its Way Controller became slurred and silly and finally would not speak at all. There was no way to send the crop of Rand Melon off the planet.

The farmers of Mako reacted quickly. They dug up the plants and used the Rand Melon oils to give them power while they composted its leaves. There were limited stocks of food grain and livestock on the planet and these were gathered and protected during what proved to be a harsh winter.

There was starvation and cannibalism in outlying areas, that I can't hide from you. But the young and the strong and the most passionate survived.

In the spring, thin men ploughed the land and spread the seed. Thin women wove nets from the Rand Melon flax and these caught fish. And at harvest time everyone worked and everyone prayed.

The second winter was not so bad.

And during the third winter there was a surplus, just, of meat and grain.

With full stomachs, the people of Mako were able to look up to the stars again and the stars became objects of worship. Children were able to point and say, 'There's Clarissa's tears and there are the Proctor Fangs.' There was even a constellation called the Great Pawl in which there were two bright yellow stars. But the names meant very little. The past became mythology as the future preoccupied people's minds. And that is just the way it should be. However . . .

The Pocket remained the Pocket.

Deep inside Lumb, Pettet and Raleigh looked to where Erix and Thule turned round their small bright sun. There

392

was movement there. Slowly, and as mysteriously as they had come, the trio slipped back into the bright green gas of Emerald Lake. Within ten days they were gone.

It was as if they had never been.

BOOK THREE
Movement

The tree by the dark river is tall now, but in comparison with the other great trees it is only a sapling. Its canopy is just beginning to spread. In the dawn sunlight it is all grey and shining silver.

Climbing in its upper branches is a man. His face is ageless and without wrinkles, though he is very old. His skin has acquired a faint green luminescence and his eyes, still bright and yellow, stare into an inner distance rather like the blind, though he is not blind.

He clambers with the grace of a monkey and shinnies fearlessly up the smooth silver boughs. If he encounters moss he scrapes it away with his fingers, being careful not to mark the tree. He preens the tree and removes any dead white leaves.

Occasionally he looks down, hanging secure with one arm crooked in a fissure and one foot braced against the bark. He likes to remain many hundreds of feet high. He only ventures on the ground when he needs water or fruit. Strange things walk on the ground.

Once he met his father, stumping on thickset legs. The man with forked beard and long blond hair stopped and nodded and then marched on. He has met his mother too, several times, always as a young woman and laughing as though she hadn't a care in the world. His brothers have ambled past, and Pettet and Raleigh, and once Peron. Pawl knows them for what they are, seeds grown from his memory and passion, and is courteous, but he does not

397

let them take part of his life. Within minutes he can climb the tree and be lost in its upper branches.

He rarely meets the creatures that live in the other trees. Like him they shun encounters.

Pawl likes to stay high. He loves to curve his body through the matted fibres of the expanding canopy. If he looks down at all it is to confront his memories. And then he shakes himself and remembers, 'No regrets. Life is too short. So much to discover.'

Pawl has so much to do. The tree takes all his love.

It is a full-time job.

It will occupy him for the rest of his life.

THE END

The Ballad of
John Death Elliott

In which we are told the adventures of the alien ship called the Fare-Thee-Well *and of the anger of Captain Death and the destruction he brought to the prison called* Luxury.

Also revealed is the true history of the survivors from Luxury *and the manner in which they entered into that strange part of space called* Elliott's Pocket.

Now gather round while the fire burns bright
And a tale to you I'll tell
Of Captain Death and his sister Bett
And the ship called the *Fare-Thee-Well*.

Born together were Jack and Bett,
Like pisces on a plate.
They shared a mind. They thought as one.
She could finish a sentence he'd just begun,
'tis said she was there when the ship was won,
And certain she shared his fate.

Jack won the ship in a wager,
That's the story I heard tell.
On the turn of a knife he staked his life
To own the *Fare-Thee-Well*.

Sure the *Fare-Thee-Well* was no normal ship,
From an alien forge it came.
Quick as light it could turn and fight,
Pick straws from your teeth while you're setting to bite,
Then fade away like a shadow in the night,
And the Proctors feared its name.

Red as the scales of a Hammer,
Shaped like a mission bell,

Her holds were dark, her holds were wide,
An army if needs could there abide,
Fully equipped with arms beside.
Such was the *Fare-Thee-Well*.

Some say that Jack was a trader,
Dealing in corn and rice,
Hawking oils from the Pleiades
And sometimes sperm and spice.

If there were wars he ferried whores,
In peace he carried grain.
So the holds were tight and the price was right
You'd not hear Jack complain.

A happy time when laws were few, and life
Was fresh as a new picked peach.
And Jack's delight was to stretch his hand
Further than he could reach.

He visited worlds long since gone,
And swam in alien seas.
The whole of space was a wondrous box
To which Jack held the keys.

Full many a time the *Fare-Thee-Well*
Clashed with the Proctor fleet.
Caught on a lam their guns would slam,
They'd skirr and pitch and turn and ram,
Then burn with their rockets like a joint of ham
The pride of the Proctor fleet.

Each day word of their exploits
Was carried to far Central,
Where Pippin the First of the Proctors
Summoned his grim marshall.

He stroked his fangs as men of old
Stroked their proud moustache.
'I speak of Death and his sister Bett.
They mock our rule . . . call me Pipette.
So bring me their heads in a fine basket,

402

And burn their ship to ash,
I say. Burn their ship to ash.'

So a declaration was issued wide,
Proclaimed both near and far,
That any man who by action bold
Brought Death and his sister into the fold
Would spend his life mid silver and gold
As prince of his very own star.

Many men were tempted.
Many men met death.
Tangling with John Elliott
And his sister Elizabeth.

But one there was on the *Fare-Thee-Well*.
A friendlier man you'll never find,
And yet beneath his smiling face
There lurked a traitor's mind.

Lester John had fists of iron,
His eyes were merry and green.
But bonny face and clever tongue
May mask a mind that's mean.

Lester John had shoulders broad,
And stories he could tell,
Of early days in the wide space sea
Aboard the *Fare-Thee-Well*.

Under alien suns he'd fought by the side
Of Captain John Elliott.
But when he heard the Proctor lies
His friend he soon forgot.

He'd spent long nights of mirth and wine,
He'd kissed Jack's sister Bett.
But when he heard the Proctor lies
His love he did forget.

Feel no pity for traitors.
Consign them all to Hell.

They'll lie to your face: to love they'll pretend.
They'll say they give when they only lend,
Then turn their back when you need a friend.
'twas so on the *Fare-Thee-Well*.
And Lester John was the traitor's name
Aboard the *Fare-Thee-Well*.

Lester John drank beer one night,
Slapped Jack Death on the arm,
'Oh I will love your sister true
And never do her harm.'

Then he watched and waited and bided his time,
Stole the keys to Landship Three.
Took Bett from her bed with a gun at her head,
Broke open the door to the Landship shed,
The blast as he left should have wakened the dead,
And he took Bett to Luxury,
As a prisoner to Luxury.

Luxury. A planet of stone.
A place of grief and pain.
The hold where our ancestors
Were kept like beasts on a chain.

Seized by bullies with pass keys,
Whether at home or at school . . .
Name their crime! They stepped out of line.
Raised their hands and spoke their minds.
Danced to a tune that was not of the time.
And opposed the Proctor rule.

Slavery is a sickness,
By ignorance 'tis spread.
The ruler smiles like a crocodile
Over a lowered head.

The slave begets the warrior,
The warrior serves the king,
The king serves no one but himself,
Isn't that a funny thing.

Let history be your teacher,
And you who listen be brave.
Let no man be your master,
Let no man be your slave.

But back now to my story
Of the sufferings of Bett
And the vengeance wrought on Luxury
By Captain John Elliott.

The men who ruled over Luxury
Gathered at the landing port,
Gave a shout of surprise when they saw the prize
That Lester John had brought.

They thought of gold and girls and wine
As they gazed at Elizabeth.
'Sure, now that we have his sister,
We'll soon catch Captain Death.'

The prison was deep in a crater.
And down on the crater floor,
Leading to darkness and misery
Was a single iron door.

They took Bett under the surface,
Down to a small cold room,
And there they left her in darkness,
In the darkness of the tomb.

An iron bed on a white tiled floor
And round the sides a drain,
To carry away the filth and blood
Leaked by a body in pain.

'Hear me, John Death Elliott,
Hear me and feel accursed.
Your sister we hold in an iron net.
We keep her alive. We call her our pet.
If you beg on your knees you may see her yet.'
So said Pippin, the Proctor First.

Jack Death vowed that very day,
He vowed that self same morn,
He vowed by the face of his sister,
And he vowed by the yet unborn.
He vowed by the stars about him,
Adrift on that wide space-sea,
That not one guard would be left alive
On the planet called Luxury:
That by fire and knife
He would take the life
Of the rulers of Luxury.

Then Pippin the First of the Proctors
Offered amnesty so I heard tell
If Captain Death would come in peace
And surrender the *Fare-Thee-Well*.

But not a word said Captain Death
As secret plans made he,
To humble the fame of the Proctor name
And the rulers of Luxury.

The days slipped slowly past, poor Bett,
Her body began to waste.
Each day she withered like a flower
That in a book is pressed.

The days grew longer with the sun,
Grew shorter with the cold,
but no Captain Death came stalking
Like wolf into the fold.

Jack Death sped from star to star,
Came to the planet Fell,
And there shared food with the alien brood,
That had made the *Fare-Thee-Well*.

'Give me guns that can burn to dust
And parch an inland sea.
Give me guns that can crack like a nut
The planet called Luxury.
Give me of your strategy,

Weave any secret spell,
For I must win my sister back
Or die on the *Fare-Thee-Well*.
Yes, I will win my sister back
Or die on the *Fare-Thee-Well*.'

Alien builders tinkered and span
And the *Fare-Thee-Well* was remade.
She looked like an ancient freighter,
An innocent ship of trade.

But think of her like a scaly fist
Clothed in a silken glove.
See not a hawk with talons spread
But a gentle cooing dove.

And when the work was finished.
The *Fare-Thee-Well* rose free,
And set a hunter's course
For the planet called Luxury.

The sleepy guard shakes himself awake,
When he hears the radio din.
'May-day. May-day. Answer we pray,
We're a Pleiades freighter gone astray,
Adrift in space for many a day,
For pity's sake let us come in.'

Sure the *Fare-Thee-Well* looks innocent
As any Sunday school prize,
As a dew-decked apple picked at dawn,
As the smile in your grandmother's eyes.

And the laser cannon which probe her shape
Find nothing to cause a frown.
The satellite eyes turn their gaze away,
Resume their search in the Milky Way,
O the landing lights are bright and gay
In that fierce prison town.

See the ancient Pleiades freighter,
Glint in the rising sun.

Above the doomed city
The last day has begun.

The ghostly frighter slides through the sky,
Its jets like the claws of a beast.
Like a beast it growls as it comes around,
Like a beast it howls, and at the sound
Towers and villas come tumbling down.

Too late the cry goes out, 'Stand back.'
To late the cry, 'Retire.'
Too late the cannon take their aim.
John Elliott opens fire.

He burns the glittering satellites,
The defence of Luxury's skies.
Like Odysseus with Polypheme,
He puts out Luxury's eyes.

Liquid fire pours from the ports,
Spreads over the city in sheets.
Dab rays breach the city walls,
Smash the windows, burn the halls.
Hear O hear the masonry fall,
Down to the glowing streets.

The prison was deep in a crater,
With a high serrated rim,
And Captain Death was careful
That no fire fell therein.
Black as a scarab beetle,
Death to the prison came.
The *Fare-Thee-Well* dropped downwards,
Riding its bed of flame.

A mighty voice rang from its sides,
'Hear the words of Captain Death.
Open the gate of your prison keep.
Let Death within your prison peep,
For as ye have sown, so shall ye reap.
Now bring forth Elizabeth.'

They carried Bett to the surface
Wrapped in a prison sheet.
They lifted her up through the prison gate
And set her on her feet.

She stood and shook on swollen feet,
She stood like a girl with no soul.
She stared like the blind for they'd scrubbed her mind
As clean as a surgeon's bowl.

'Speak to me my sister.
Your eyes are the colour of lead.
Tell me how did they harm you?'
But never a word she said.

Death took her inside the *Fare-Thee-Well*,
Set every prisoner free,
And when they were safe in the ship's wide hold,
Death lifted from Luxury.

Many thousand captured souls
Were freed, so I heard tell.
With shaven heads and parchment skin
Sticks for bones, chapped and thin,
They were silent as death as they climbed within
The hold of the *Fare-Thee-Well*.

Names bring honour. Let me name a few.
A man called Pettet, a woman called Blue,
A Smith, a Lee, a child called Lyn,
A Minsk, a Raj and Haberjin.
Those I have missed be not offended.
Soonest begun is soonest ended.
The roots of every family tree
Trace back to the people of Luxury.
And those I mentioned at this time
Are only here to serve the rhyme.
Now since your gifts I hope to earn
To my story I'll return.

Above the hills of Luxury
An alien web Jack spun,

To trap the light of the night-time stars
And the heat of the noon-day sun.

The web glowed pale blue in the night,
Blazed silver in the day,
And focused all its energy
Into a single ray.

And on a word from Captain Death
The great web slowly turned.
The ray stabbed down and where it touched
The planet charred and burned.

It lingered over the crater
That cupped the prison home,
And the earth it frothed like water dropped
On to a burning stone.

It lingered over the city
Through all life there was dead,
And soon the planet's founding rock
Glowed a muddy red.

At last upon a misty morn
The sun let all men see
The ruin wrought by Captain Death
Upon proud Luxury.

An angry man, when anger cools,
May often feel regret.
And so it was on the *Fare-Thee-Well*
For Captain Jack Elliott.

He looked down where the planet turned,
Dark as the stone of a peach.
'Come all people with a will to survive.
Give thanks to the stars that we're still alive.
We'll find a place where we can thrive,
Far from the Proctor reach.'

Luxury will soon be cold,
Bereft of life, forlorn.

A monument to those who died,
A hope for those new born.

And life shall triumph over grief,
Wisdom over folly yet.
Hope will be an opening leaf,
Though we never will forget.'

Throw a log on the fire,
Warm your hands at the flame.
Hear how the people of Luxury
To the Pocket came.
Throw another log on the fire,
Hear the fate that befell
Captain Death and his sister Bett
And the brave ship *Fare-Thee-Well*.

Too long had the *Fare-Thee-Well* tarried,
For the vengeance of Captain Jack.
The Proctor fleet had gathered,
Came storming to attack.

The *Fare-Thee-Well* kicked through ninety degrees
Set a spiral and barrelled ahead.
Laid a par round a neutron star,
And to the Pocket sped.

The Pocket, a vast net in space,
A twist in the galaxy,
Which hid its dangers fathoms deep
Like reef in a calm calm sea.

A place where hairy comets wheeled
And Black Holes stripped the rind
From White Dwarfs and Giants Red
Caught in their gravity bind.

A fierce place, whose lines of force,
Could man-made ships destroy
As easy as a child can crush
A home-made paper toy.

Many ships to cross had tried,
Many ships now hung,
Turning in the solar wind,
Abandoned every one.
Some called the Pocket Eden,
Some called the Pocket Hell,
(Sure it proved sweet sanctuary
To those on the *Fare-Thee-Well*.)

Some said there was a pestilence,
A thing of mind not skin,
Infected hardy spacemen
Who tried to break therein.
And many were the warnings,
If into the Pocket you sped.
'First you'll feel your blood congeal,
Then joints'll ache like stretched on wheel,
Your skin'll burn and start to peel.'
That's what old spacemen said.
'If you dog the Pocket,
You'll hear within your head,
Like chant of souls in Purgatory,
The singing of the dead.'
Or so old spacemen said.

Think then of the *Fare-Thee-Well*
And the people from Luxury,
They were the first that ever burst
Into this strange space sea.

The *Fare-Thee-Well* set a burrowing course
For the hole in the Hurricane.
Behind her packed like baying hounds
The Proctor warships came.

Fortune smiled on the *Fare-Thee-Well*
Through the Hurricane span like a blade,
A moon from Mabel dragged her through
And the gallant ship was saved.

Fortune smiled on the *Fare-Thee-Well*
As she dived through Mabel's rings,

Then rode the wake of the Cherry Brake
In shadow avoided the Eye of the Snake
And burst into light over Emerald Lake,
The place where the Siren sings,
Where moons of Jet and Amethyst
Shine in red and amber skies.
O rare the beauty of that place,
Like fabled caves of Paradise.

And the people out from Luxury
At the ship's wide window stand,
And gaze as did the Israelites
Upon their promised land.

Pity the ships of the Proctor fleet
When to the Pocket they came.
Many dived, but few survived
The cut of the Hurricane.

Three ships foundered on Mabel
Whose mood had changed once more.
She caught them in her gravity trap
Like whales upon the shore.

One ship cleared the Cherry Brake
But the Snake it could not pass.
Straight ahead the Eye blinked red
And fused the ship to glass.

The people aboard the *Fare-Thee-Well*
Saw that ship as it froze,
Saw it brighten like a new trimmed lamp,
Saw it whiten like a Winter rose.

It is still out there. You can see it still.
Like something a craftsman made,
Fashioned from strands of silver thread
And plates of pale green jade.

Through an open dome you can climb aboard
And a body will welcome you.
With egg-white eyes and bleachen hair,

413

She crouches like a girl at prayer,
She was crouching thus when the Snake's bright glare
Stopped both ship and crew.

The stars shine dimly through the walls
Like lights 'neath a wide dark lake.
The long dead captain sits with his hand
Tight on the gravity brake.

About him his crew are like silver toys,
Like figures carved from ice,
Caught as they laughed, as they moved, as they spoke,
Caught by the turn of the dice.

And what were they thinking, that fatal crew,
That girl on her knees by the dome?
Was she kneeling to gather something she'd dropped
Or praying for safe journey home?

Then one by one the Landships rose,
From the *Fare-Thee-Well* cut free,
And ferried to their new-found homes
The people of Luxury.

It was then that Lumb became a home,
And Ra and Dis and Set,
And we became a people, one
Of Elliott's Pocket.

We lived by shadow of mountain stone,
We lived by water's grace,
And one by one and silently
Love joined us with this place.

The workshops on the *Fare-Thee-Well*
Helped us make a start.
And though Captain Death was generous,
No man could read his heart.

A leash-held dog that smells the dawn
Will soon begin to fret,

And bite its chain and pace and pull.
So with John Elliott.

One day he closed the great ship's doors,
Spoke with his sister Bett.
He'd heard a voice that called his name
From the deep Pocket.

He'd heard a siren voice that sang
Like the call of the turning tide,
And to that siren voice he ran,
Like lover to his bride.

Poor Bett, that girl like the walking dead,
Poor Bett robbed of her mind,
Who never cried or laughed or spoke,
Poor Bett he left behind.

She never cried or laughed or spoke
As Jack Death kissed her head.
'Till I return, my sister dear.'
But never a word she said.

She never laughed or cried or spoke
Save once she raised her head,
And rubbed the place that Jack had kissed.
'Ah, now I see he's dead.'
And that same hour saw Bett decline.
Her arms lay stiff at her side.
Her pale lips moved though no sound came
And gently so she died.

And what became of Captain Jack
And the proud ship *Fare-Thee-Well*?
That's a secret the Pocket keeps,
The truth no man can tell.

There are tales of a ghostly freighter,
Will come like a shooting star,
Blazing bright with Elmo's light,
Deadly as arrow that flies in the night,

Ready to serve and ready to fight
If danger comes from afar.

We of the Pocket remember
And once every year must tell,
The tale of Death and his sister Bett
And the proud ship *Fare-Thee-Well*.